Cucumber QUEST 3

The Melody Kingdom

Gigi D.G.

:01

First Second

New York

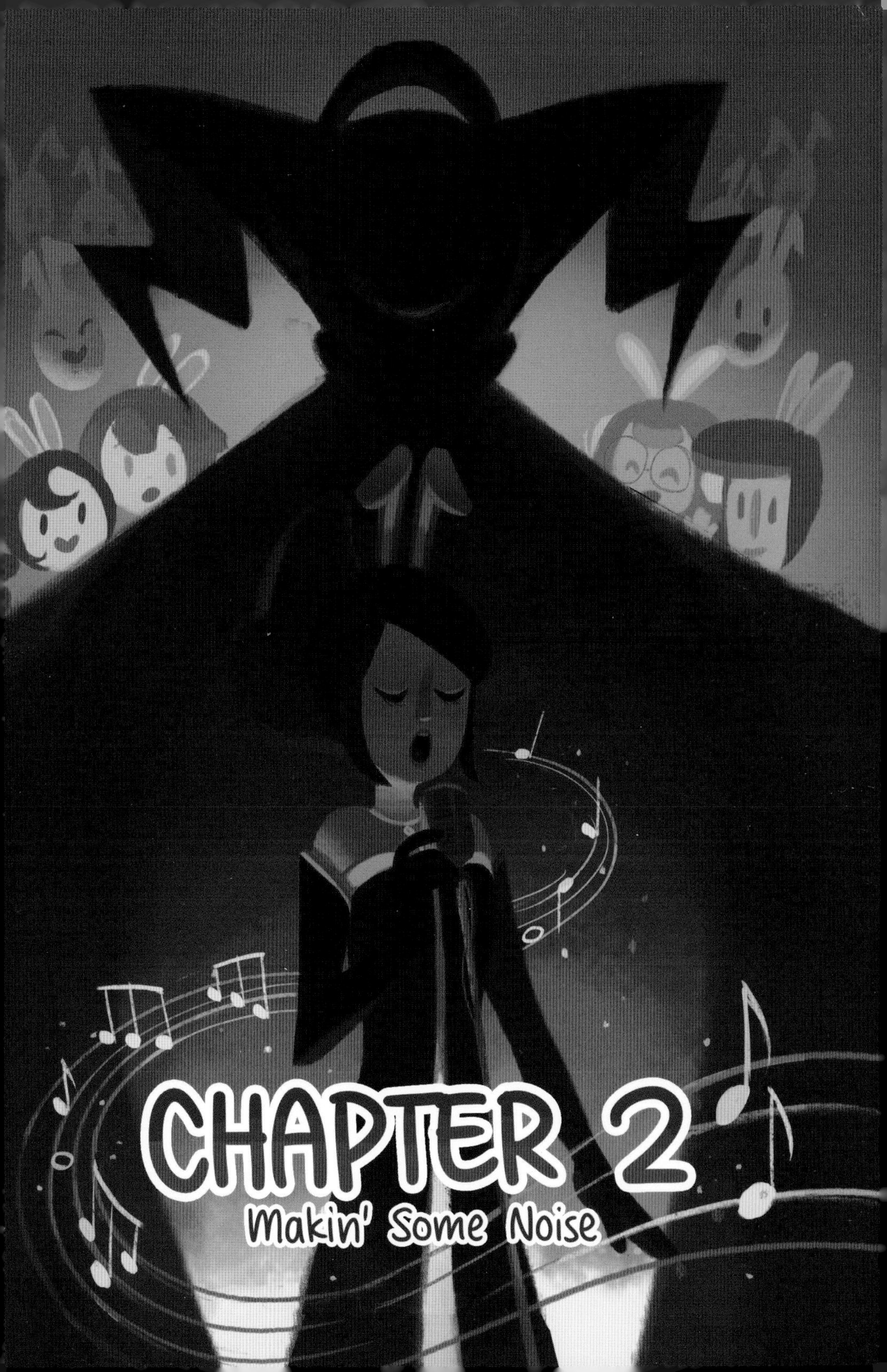
CHAPTER 2
Makin' Some Noise

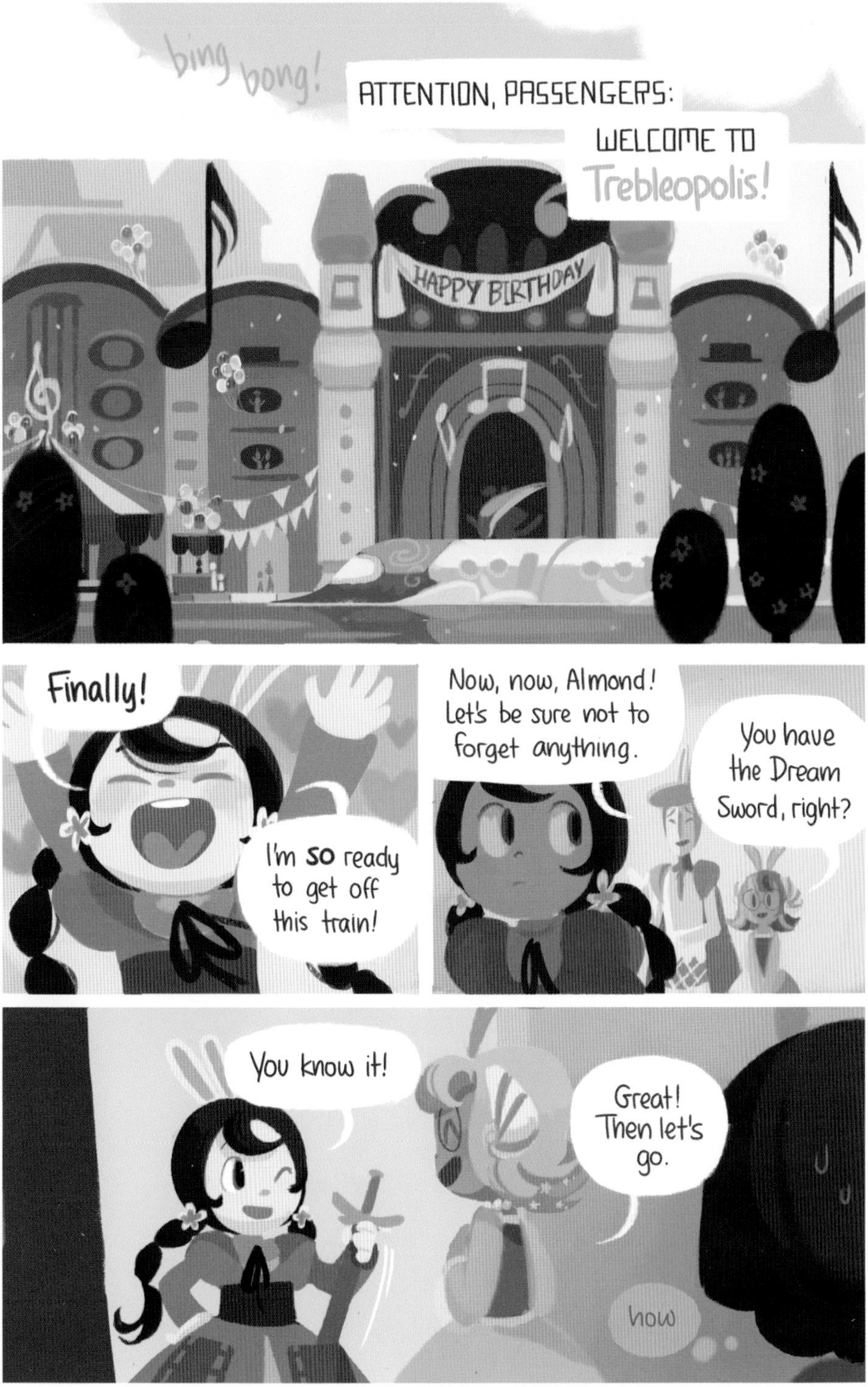
bing bong!
ATTENTION, PASSENGERS:
WELCOME TO Trebleopolis!
HAPPY BIRTHDAY
Finally!
I'm SO ready to get off this train!
Now, now, Almond! Let's be sure not to forget anything.
You have the Dream Sword, right?
You know it!
Great! Then let's go.
how

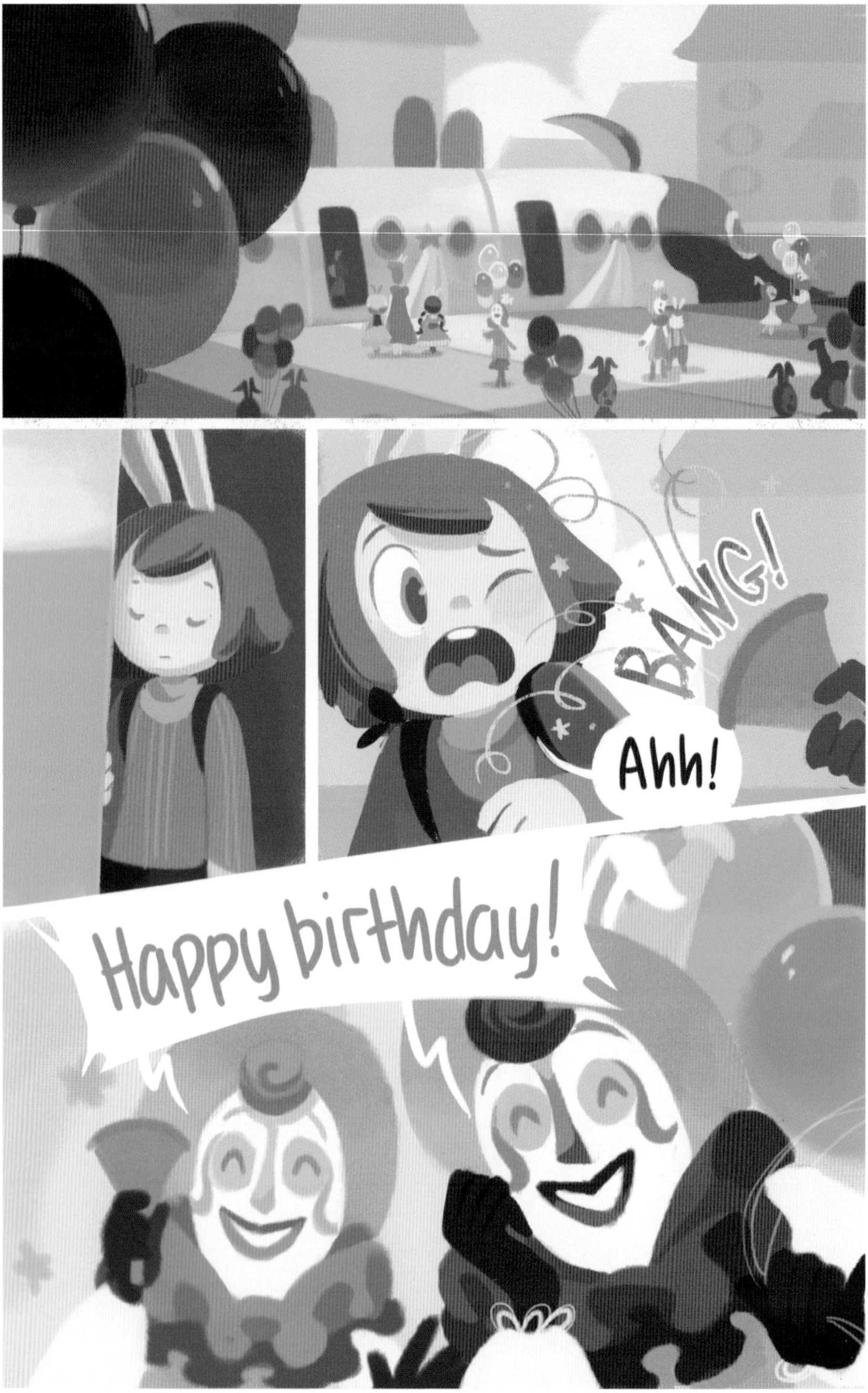
BANG!
Ahh!
Happy birthday!

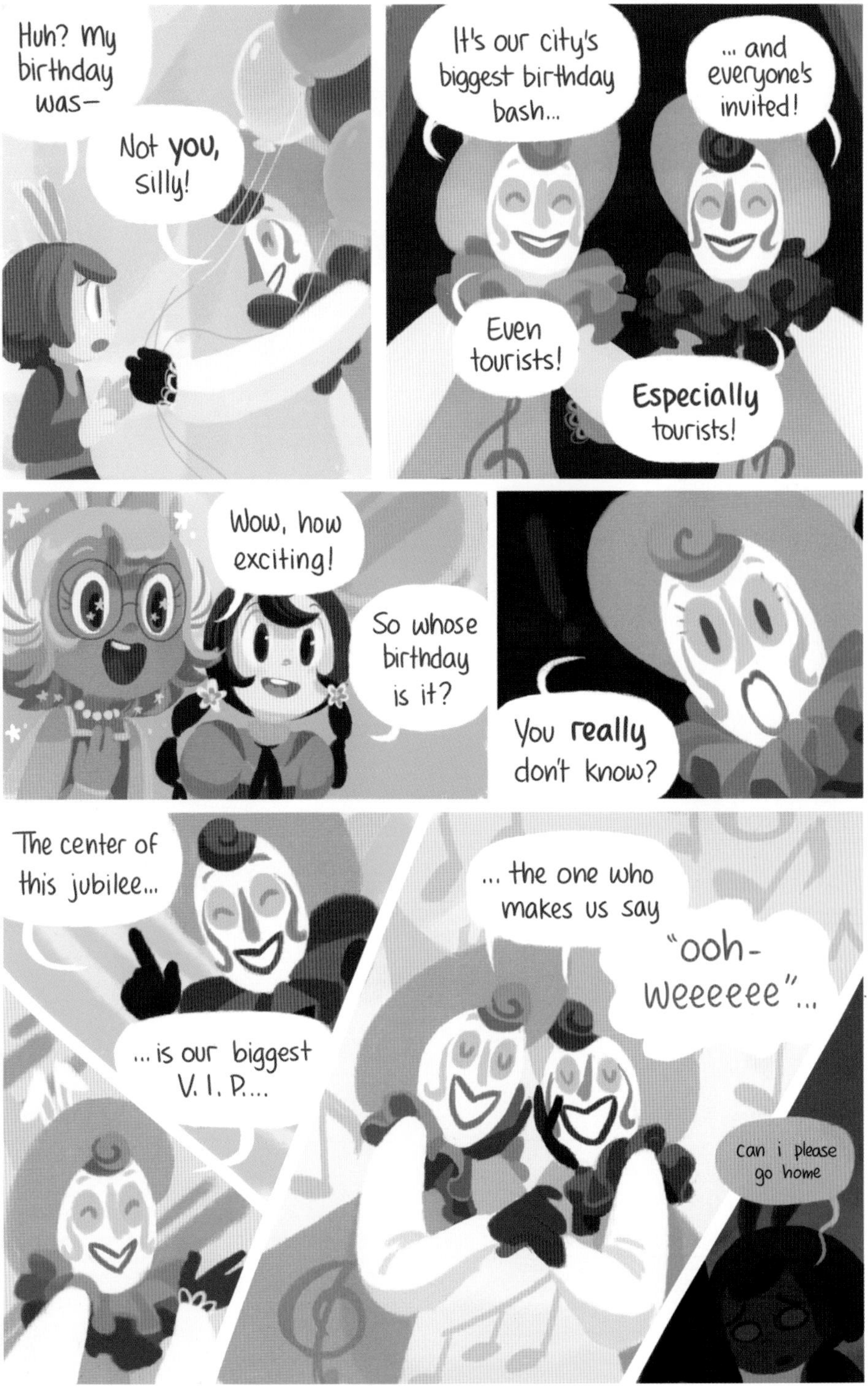
Huh? My birthday was—
Not **you**, silly!
It's our city's biggest birthday bash...
... and everyone's invited!
Even tourists!
Especially tourists!
Wow, how exciting!
So whose birthday is it?
You **really** don't know?
The center of this jubilee...
... is our biggest V. I. P....
... the one who makes us say "ooh-weeeeee"...
can i please go home

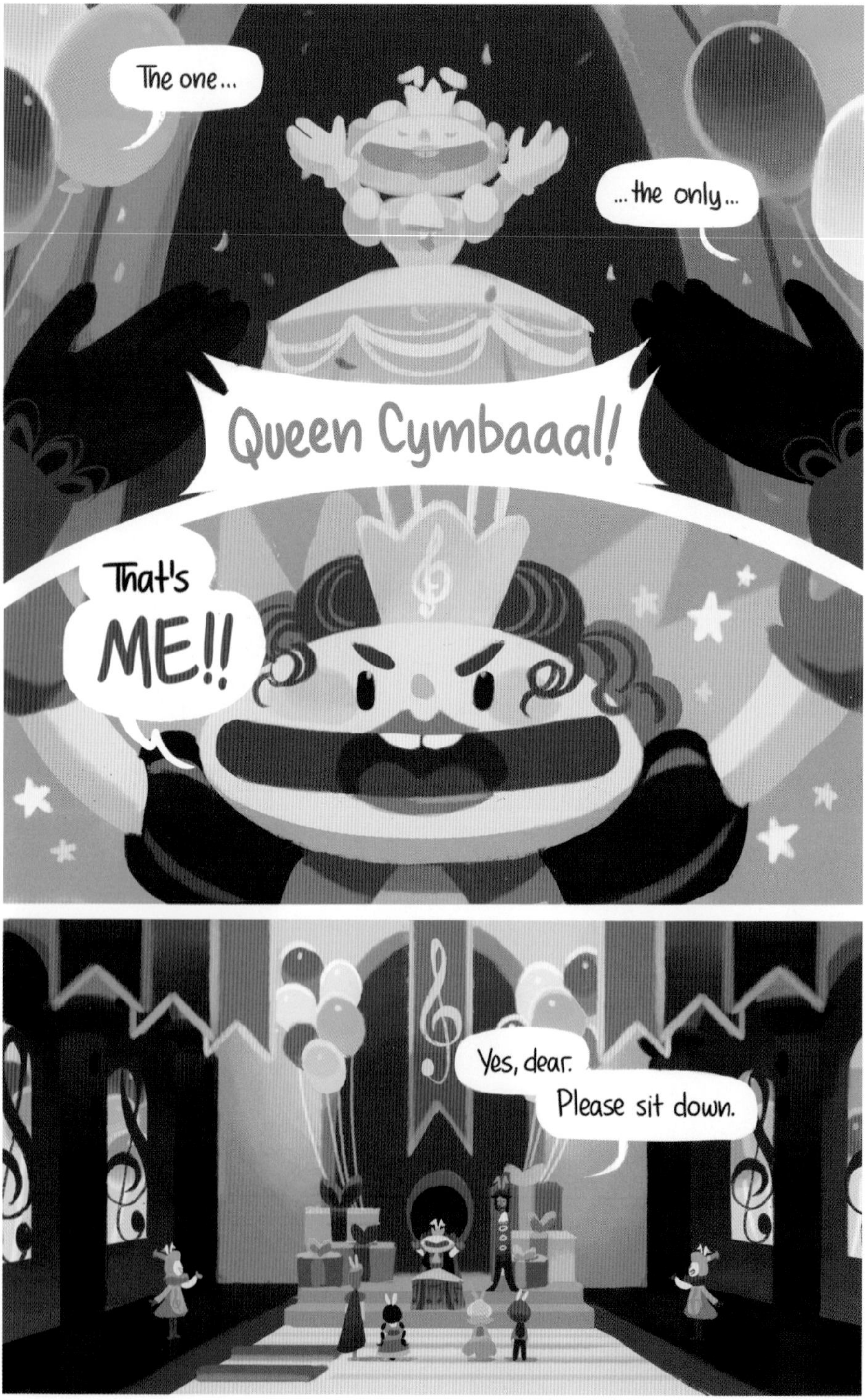
The one...
...the only...
Queen Cymbaaal!
That's ME!!
Yes, dear.
Please sit down.

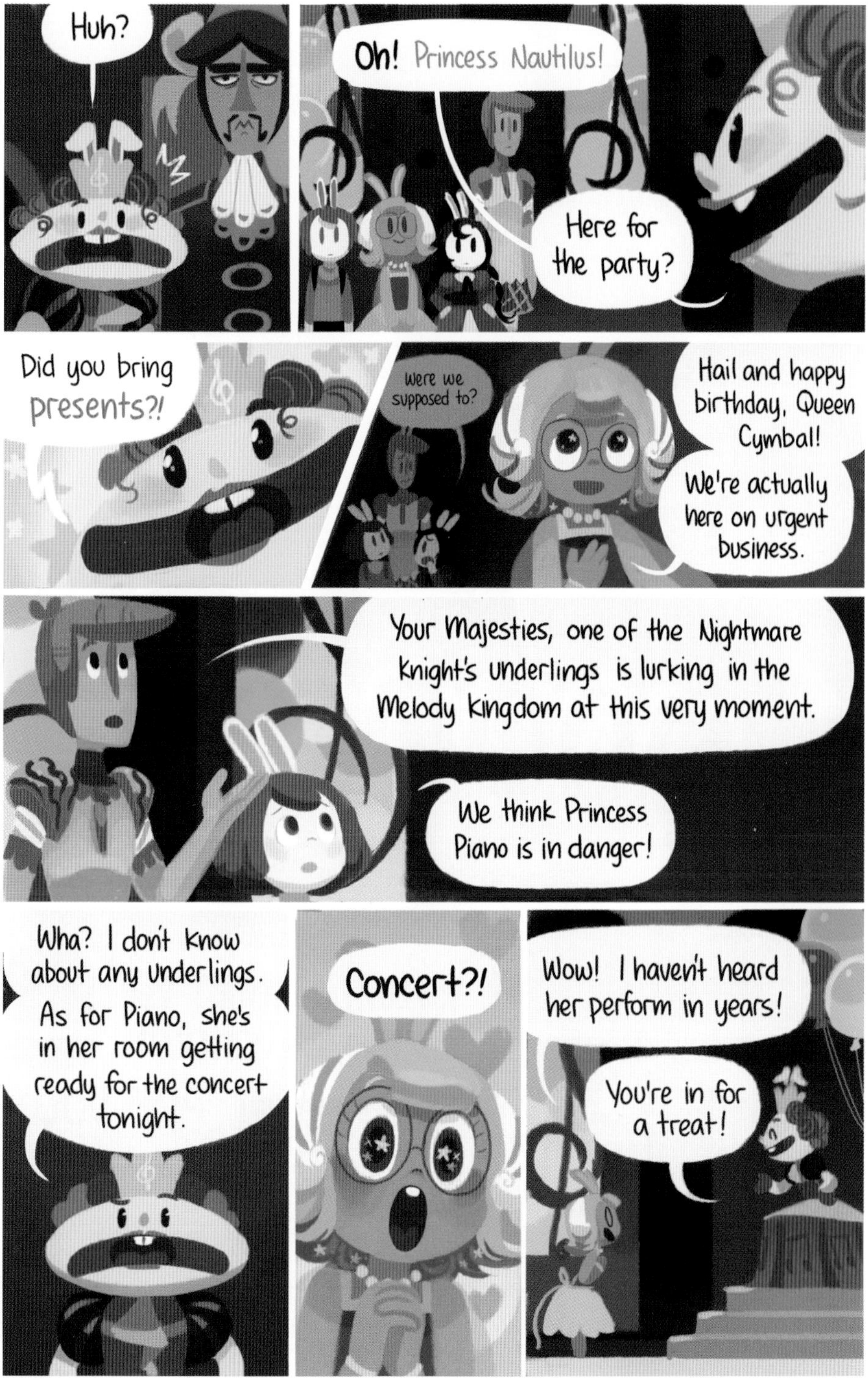
Huh?
Oh! Princess Nautilus!
Here for the party?
Did you bring presents?!
Were we supposed to?
Hail and happy birthday, Queen Cymbal!
We're actually here on urgent business.
Your Majesties, one of the Nightmare Knight's underlings is lurking in the Melody kingdom at this very moment.
We think Princess Piano is in danger!
Wha? I don't know about any underlings.
As for Piano, she's in her room getting ready for the concert tonight.
Concert?!
Wow! I haven't heard her perform in years!
You're in for a treat!

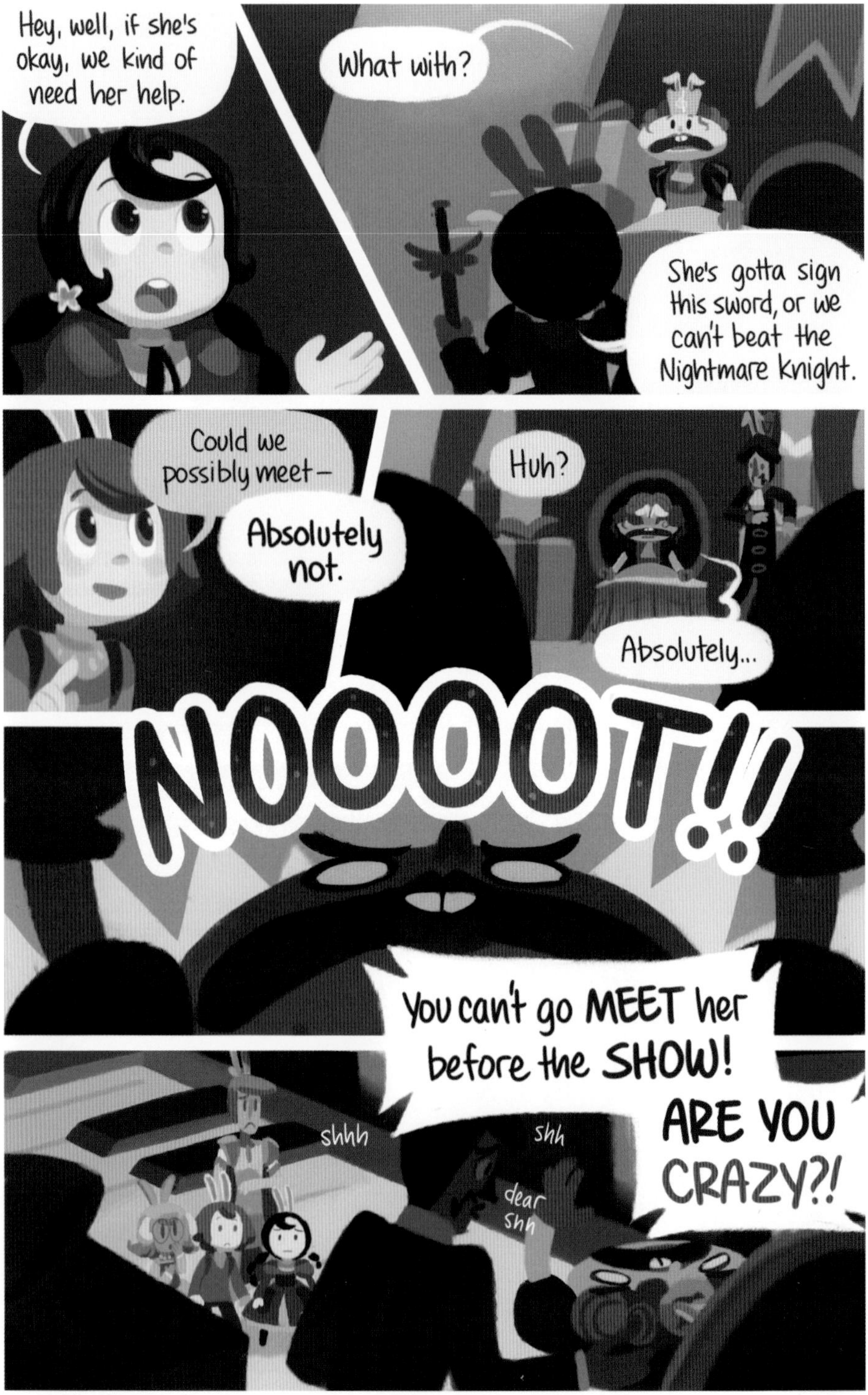
Hey, well, if she's okay, we kind of need her help.
What with?
She's gotta sign this sword, or we can't beat the Nightmare knight.
Could we possibly meet—
Huh?
Absolutely not.
Absolutely...
NOOOOT!!
You can't go MEET her before the SHOW!
ARE YOU CRAZY?!
shhh
shh
dear shh

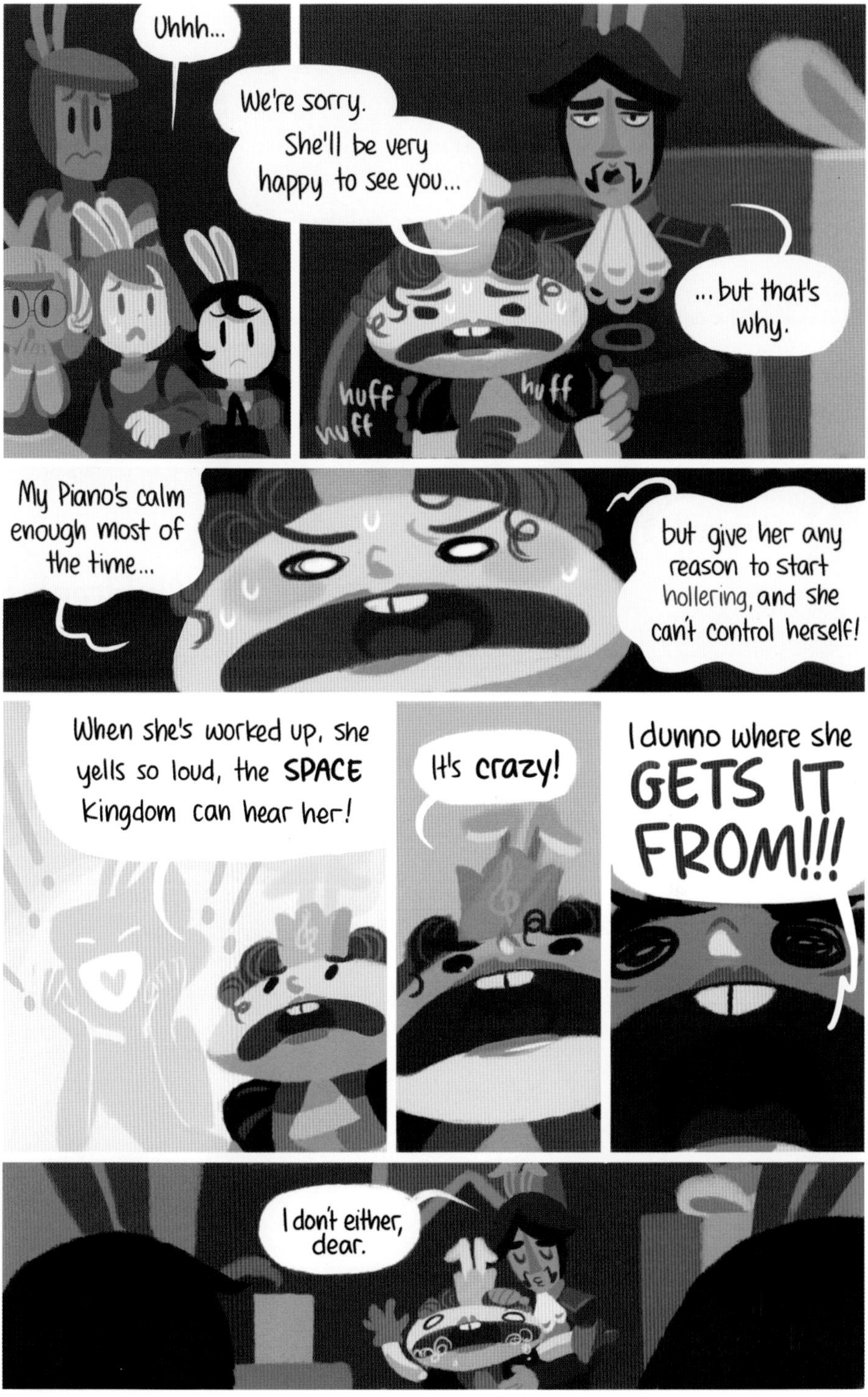
Uhhh...
We're sorry.
She'll be very happy to see you...
huff huff
huff
...but that's why.
My Piano's calm enough most of the time...
but give her any reason to start hollering, and she can't control herself!
When she's worked up, she yells so loud, the SPACE Kingdom can hear her!
It's crazy!
I dunno where she GETS IT FROM!!!
I don't either, dear.

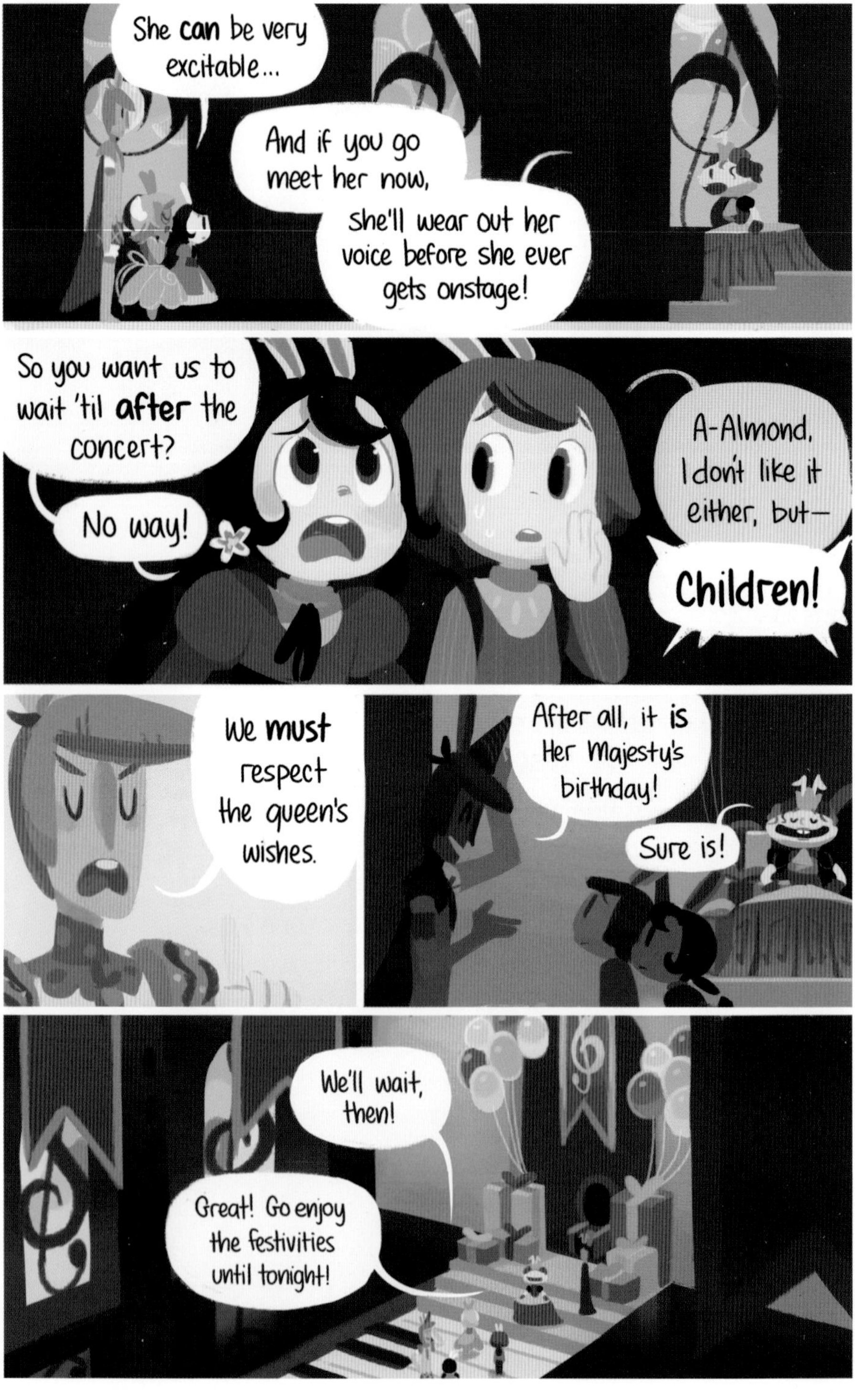
She **can** be very excitable...
And if you go meet her now,
she'll wear out her voice before she ever gets onstage!
So you want us to wait 'til **after** the concert?
No way!
A-Almond, I don't like it either, but—
Children!
We **must** respect the queen's wishes.
After all, it **is** Her Majesty's birthday!
Sure is!
We'll wait, then!
Great! Go enjoy the festivities until tonight!

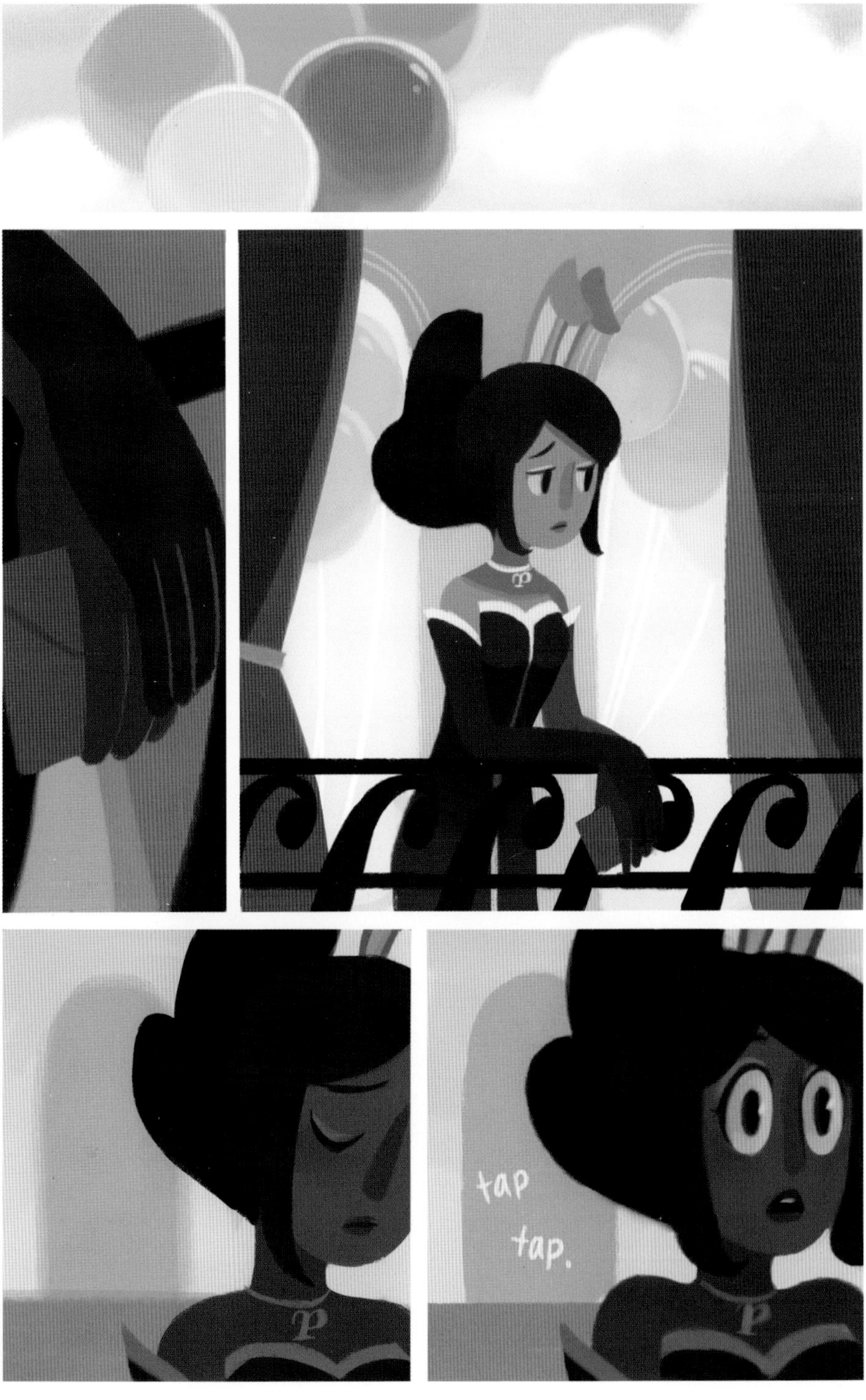
tap
tap.

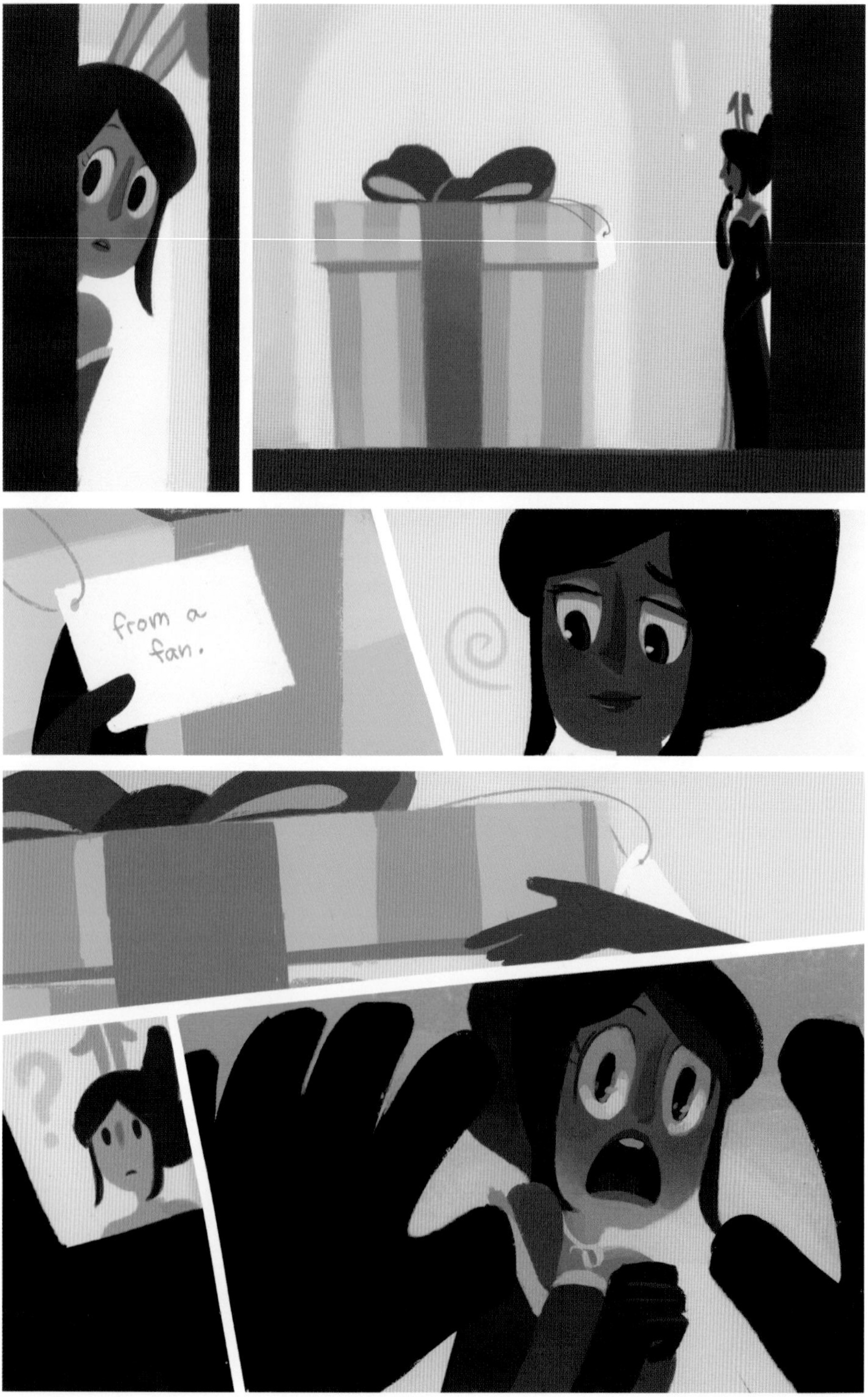
from a fan.

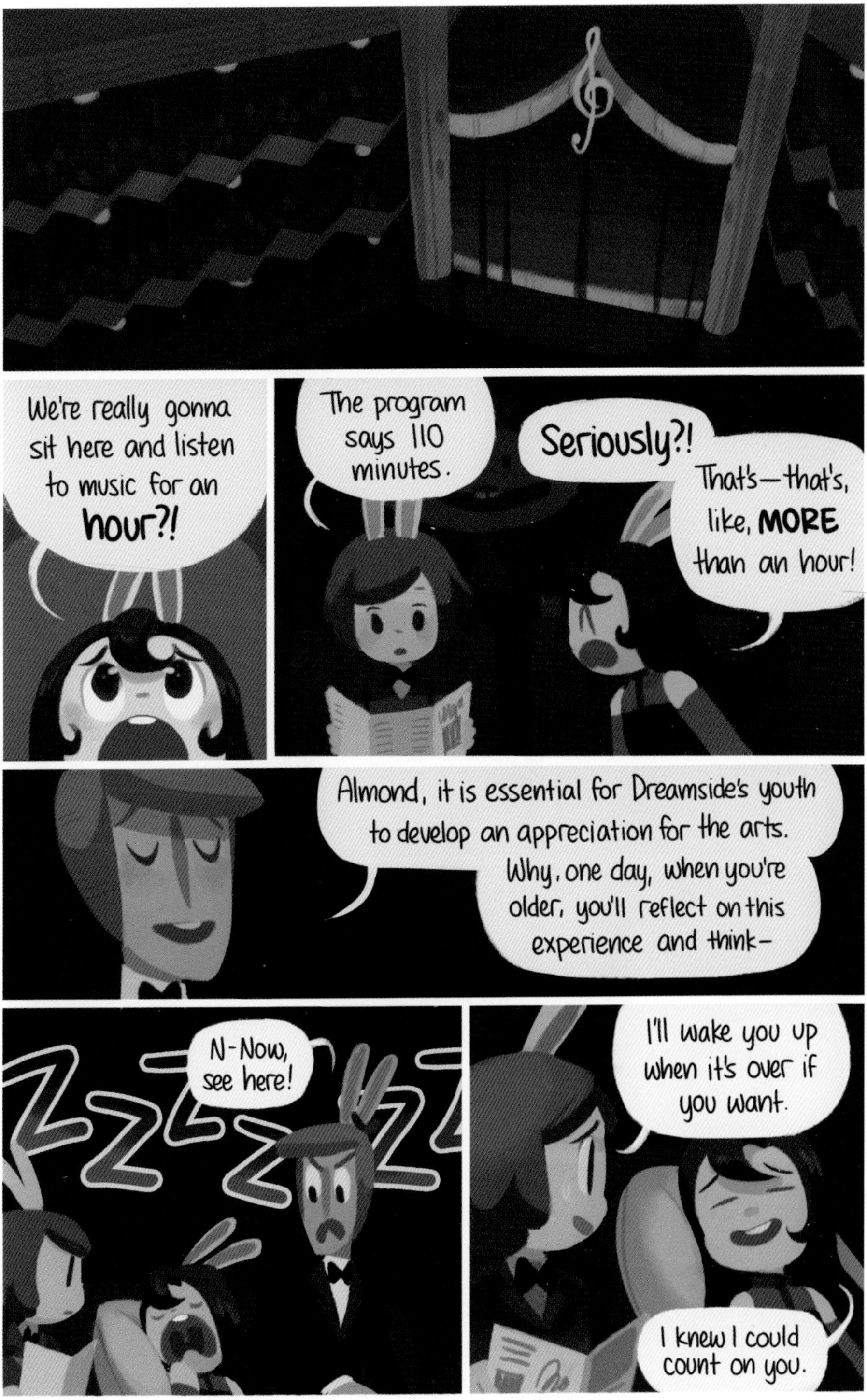
We're really gonna sit here and listen to music for an **hour?!**
The program says 110 minutes.
Seriously?!
That's—that's, like, **MORE** than an hour!
Almond, it is essential for Dreamside's youth to develop an appreciation for the arts.
Why, one day, when you're older, you'll reflect on this experience and think—
N-Now, see here!
I'll wake you up when it's over if you want.
I knew I could count on you.

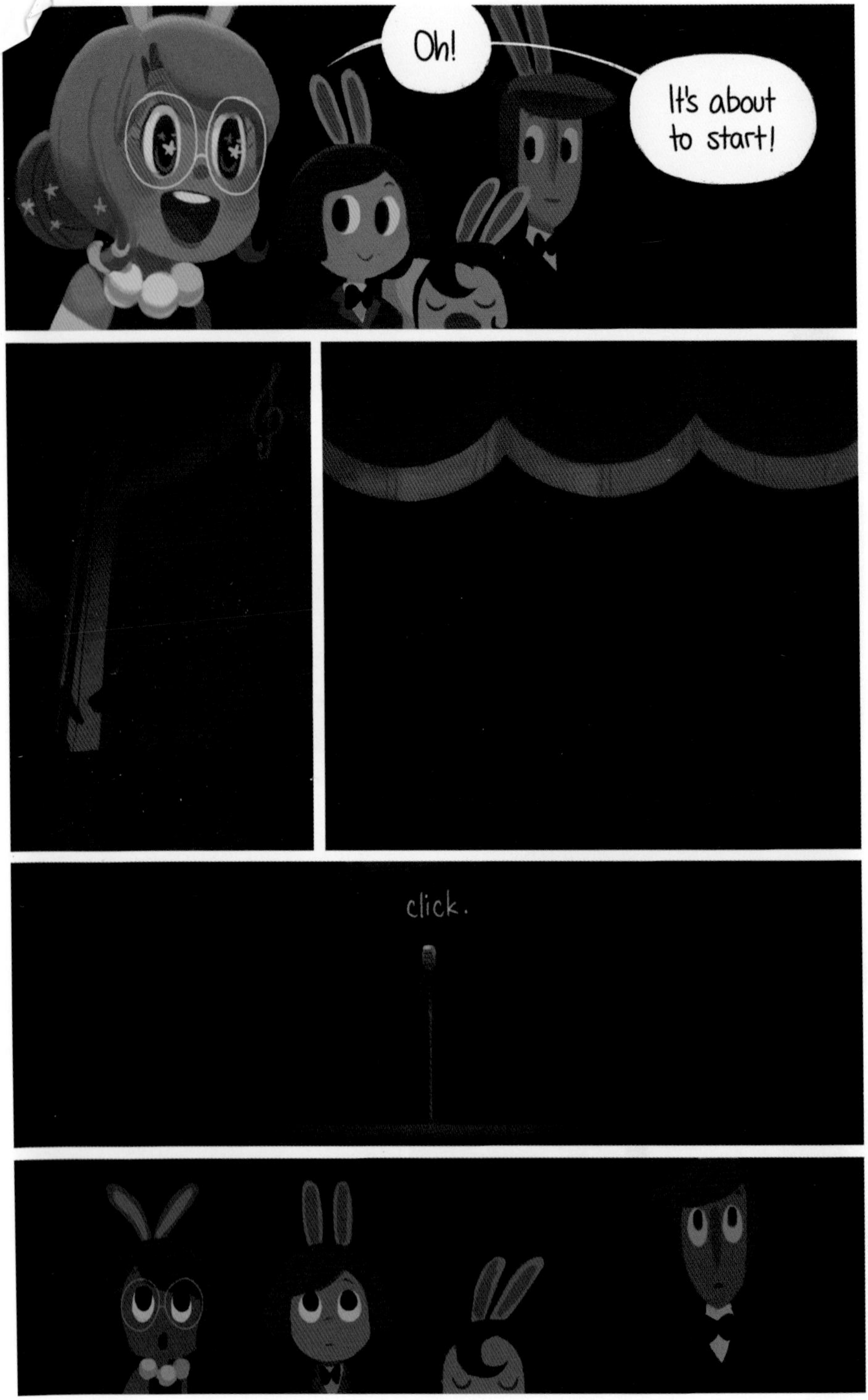
Oh!
It's about to start!
click.

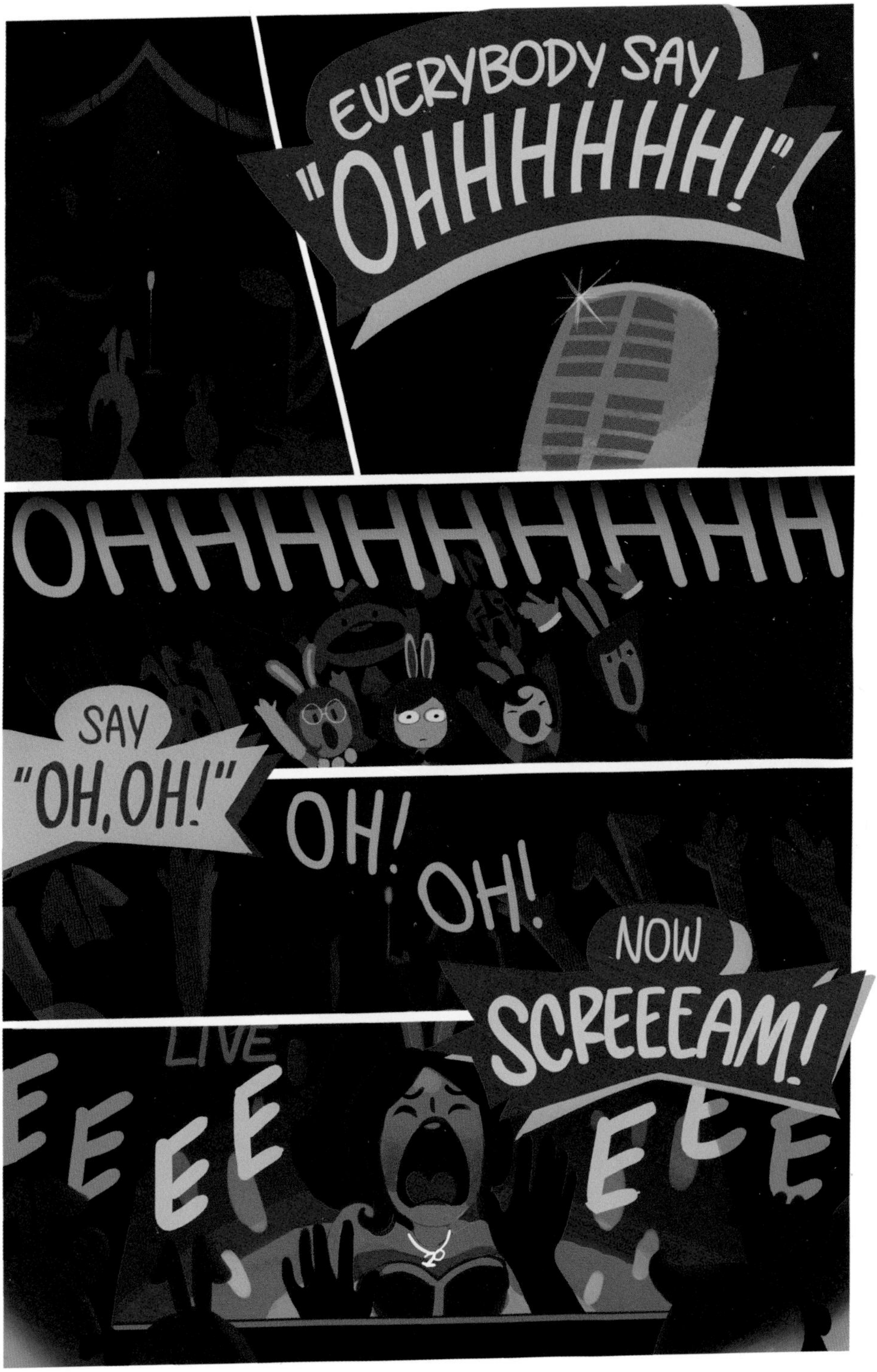
EVERYBODY SAY
"OHHHHHH!"
OHHHHHHHHHHH
SAY
"OH, OH!"
OH!
OH!
NOW
SCREEEAM!
LIVE
EEEE
EEEE

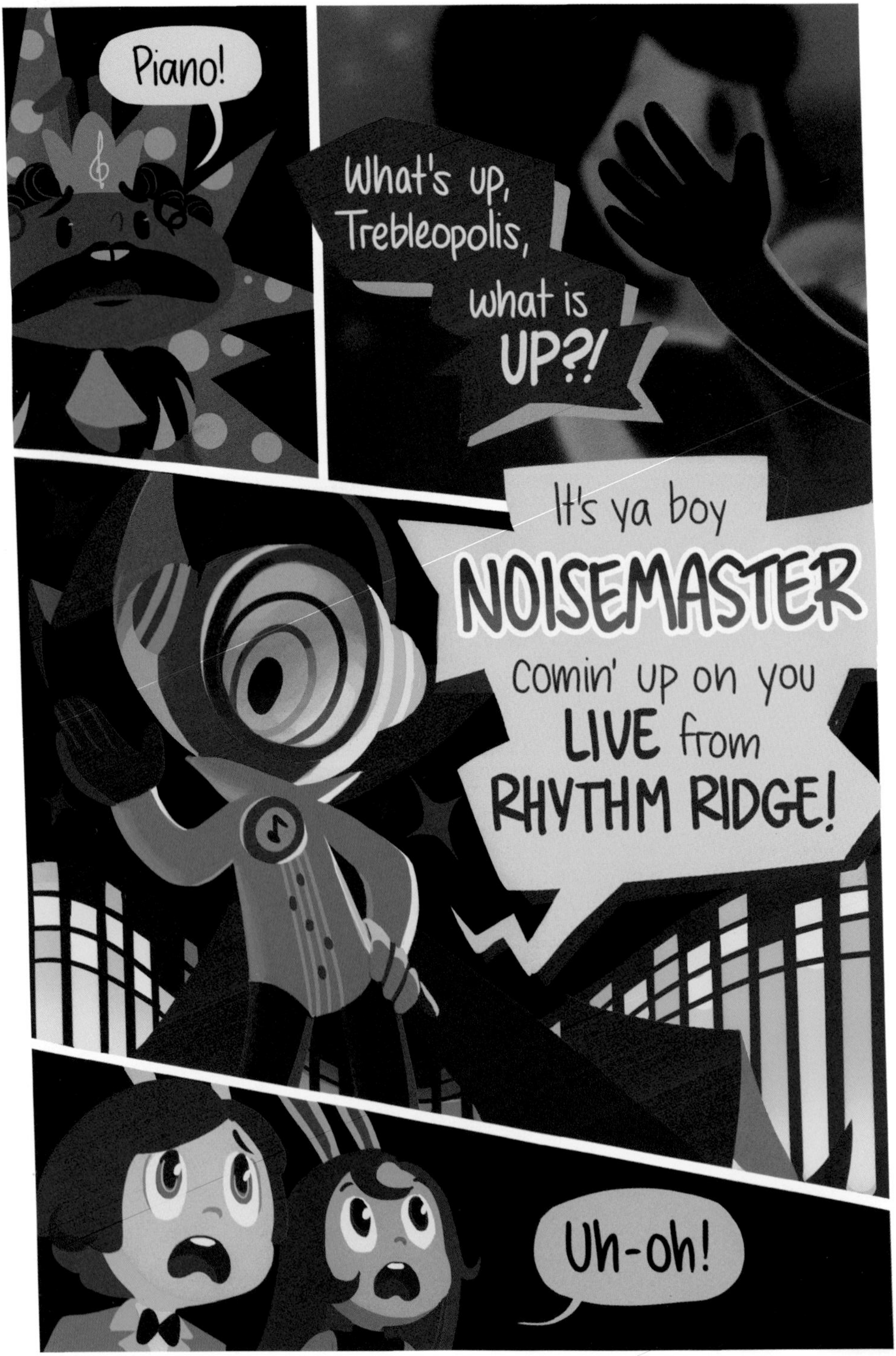
Piano!
What's up, Trebleopolis, what is UP?!
It's ya boy NOISEMASTER comin' up on you LIVE from RHYTHM RIDGE!
Uh-oh!

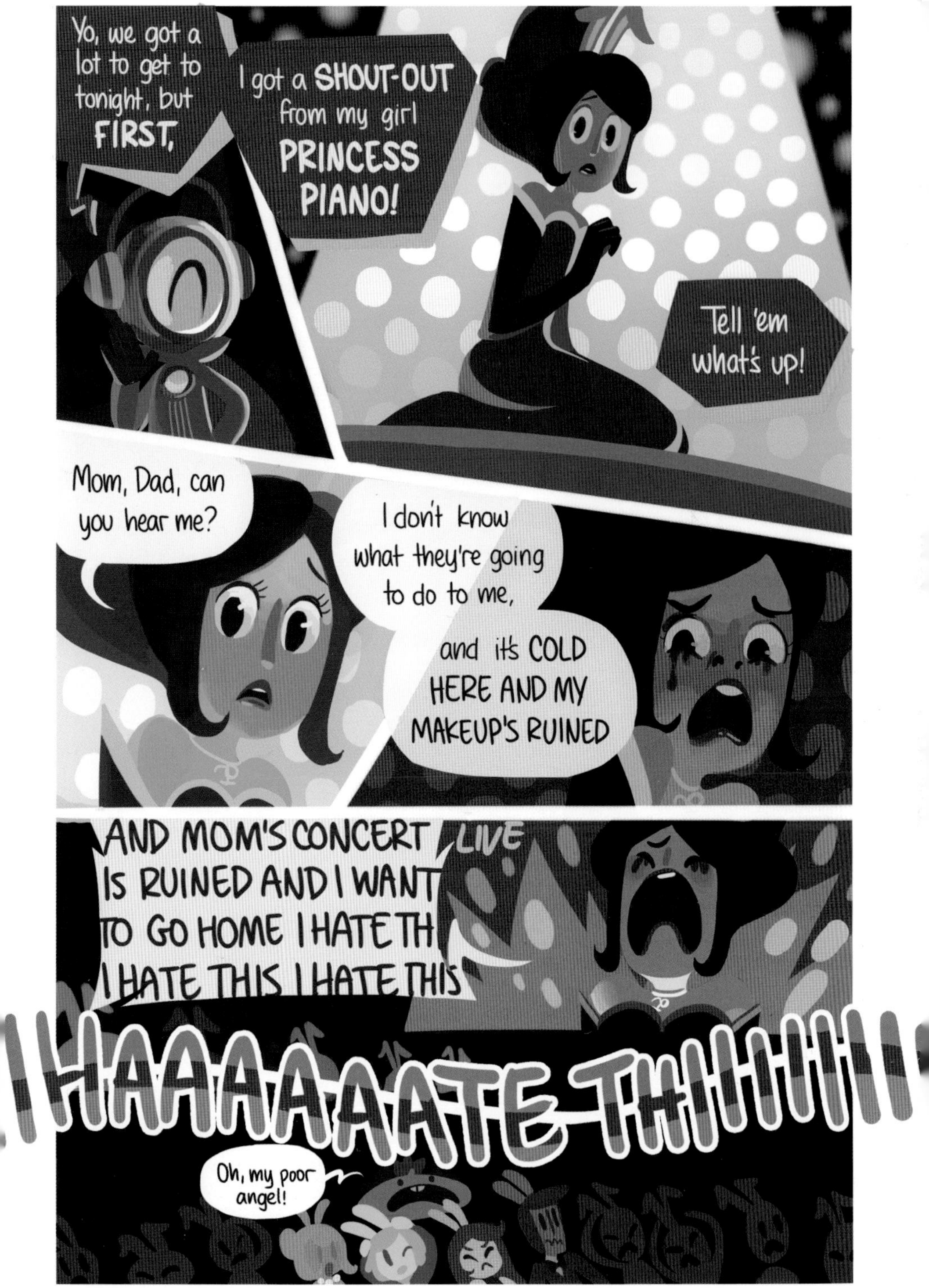

Yo, we got a lot to get to tonight, but FIRST,
I got a SHOUT-OUT from my girl PRINCESS PIANO!
Tell 'em what's up!
Mom, Dad, can you hear me?
I don't know what they're going to do to me,
and it's COLD HERE AND MY MAKEUP'S RUINED
AND MOM'S CONCERT IS RUINED AND I WANT TO GO HOME I HATE TH I HATE THIS I HATE THIS
LIVE
I HAAAAAAATE THIIIIIII
Oh, my poor angel!

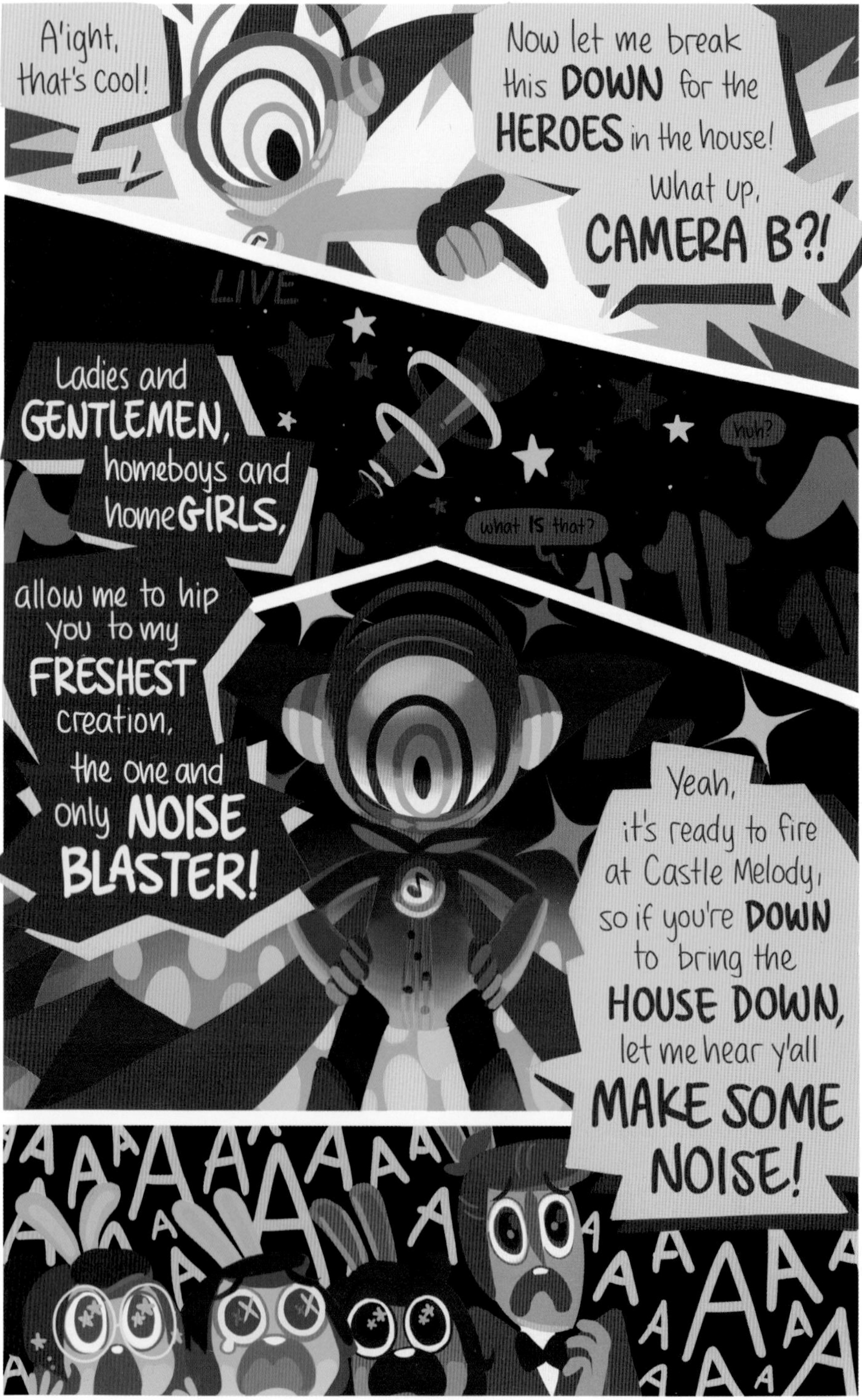
A'ight, that's cool!
Now let me break this DOWN for the HEROES in the house!
What up, CAMERA B?!
LIVE
Ladies and GENTLEMEN, homeboys and homeGIRLS,
huh?
what IS that?
allow me to hip you to my FRESHEST creation, the one and only NOISE BLASTER!
Yeah, it's ready to fire at Castle Melody, so if you're DOWN to bring the HOUSE DOWN, let me hear y'all MAKE SOME NOISE!
AAAAAAAA

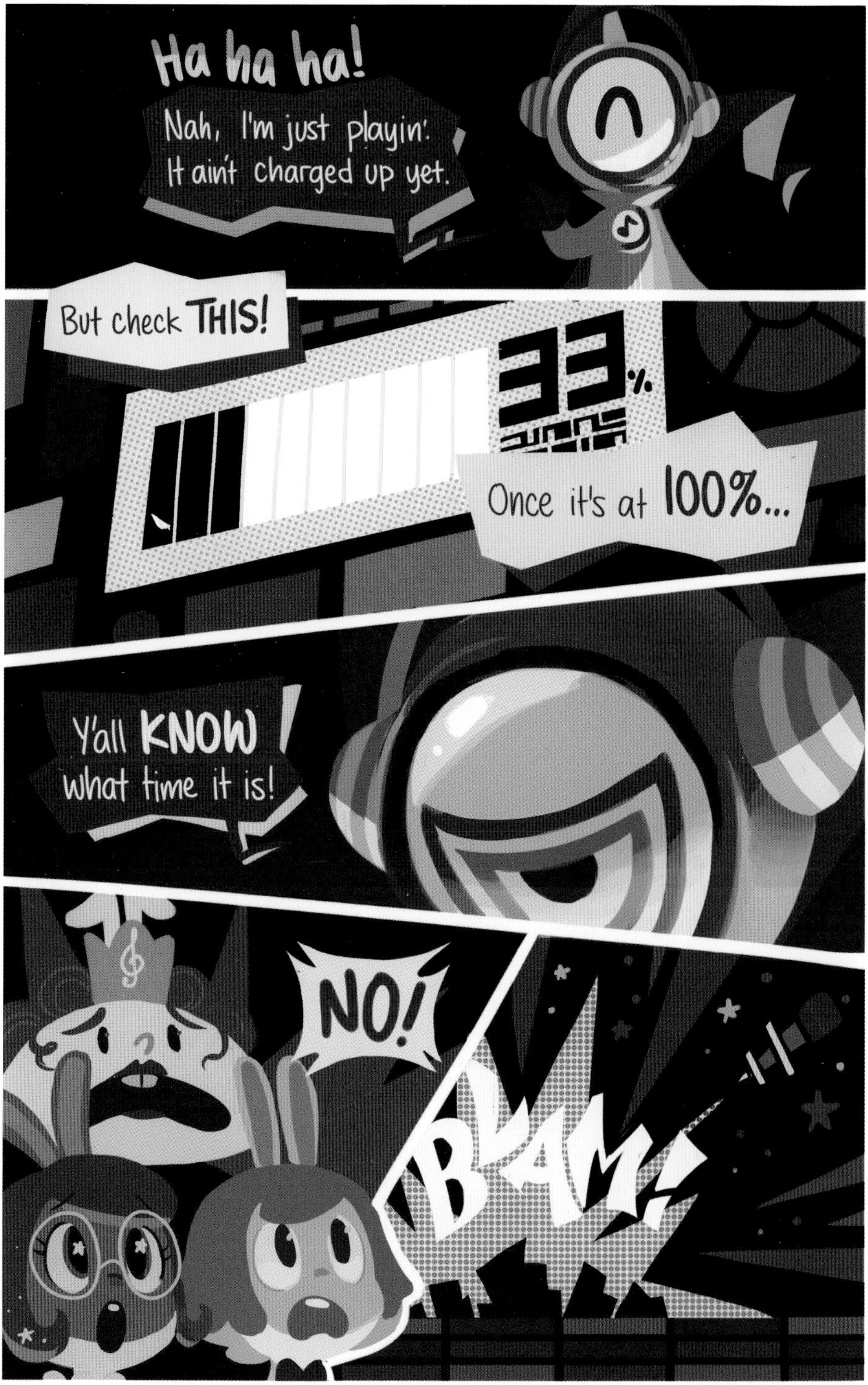

Ha ha ha!
Nah, I'm just playin'. It ain't charged up yet.
But check THIS!
33%
Once it's at 100%...
Y'all KNOW what time it is!
NO!
BLAM!

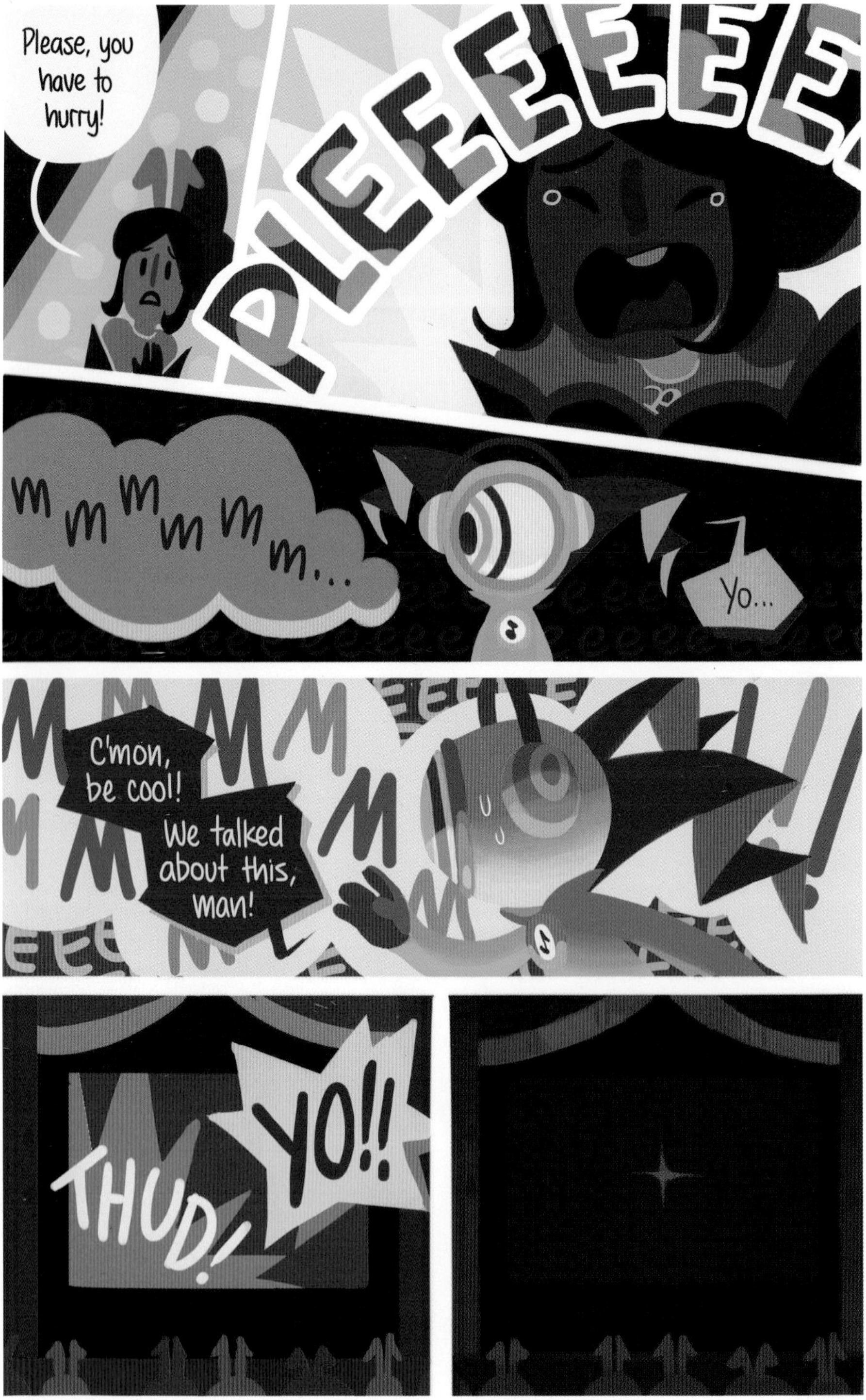

Please, you have to hurry!
PLEEEEEE
mmmmmmm...
Yo...
C'mon, be cool!
We talked about this, man!
THUD!
YO!!

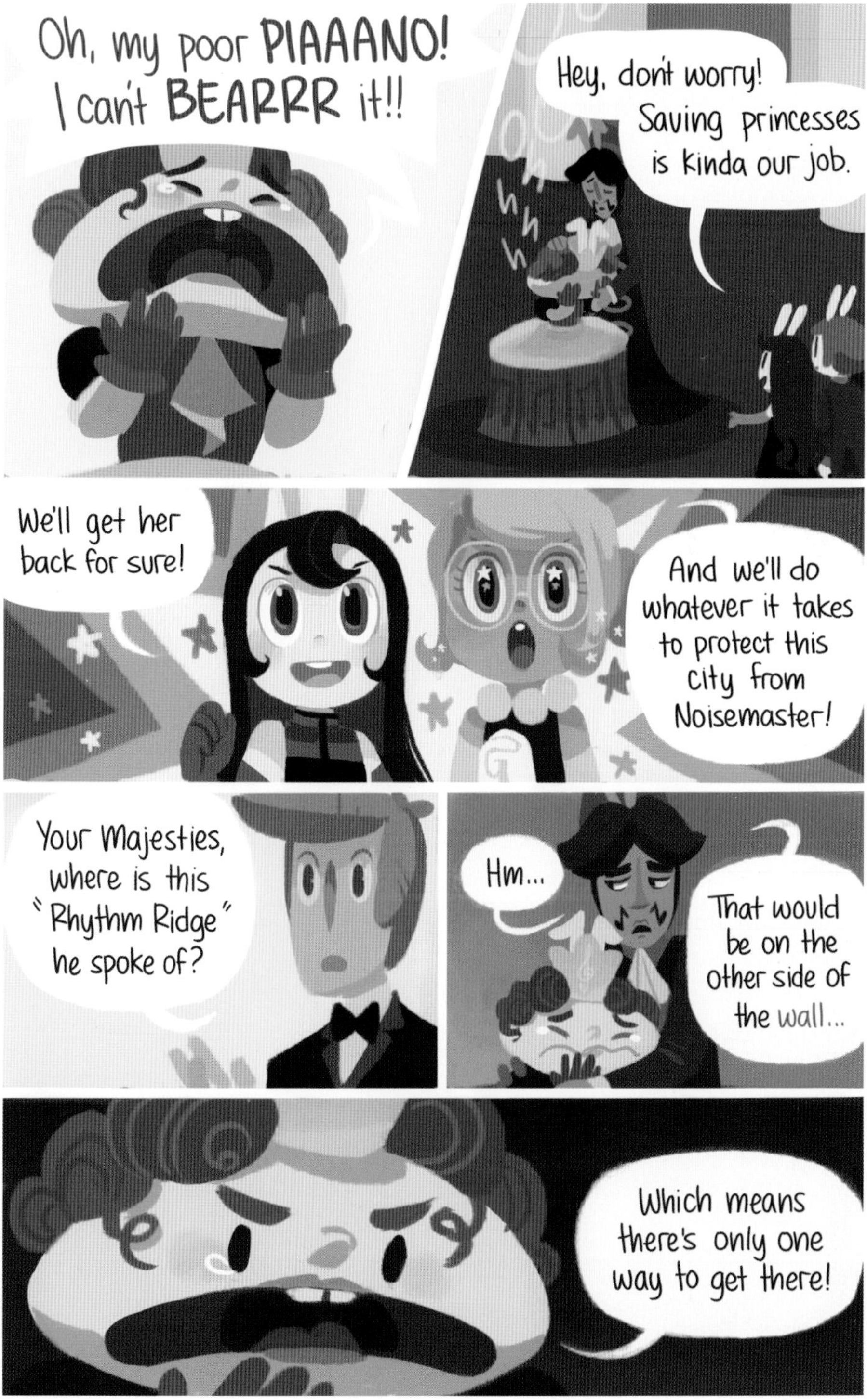
Oh, my poor PIAAANO! I can't BEARRR it!!
Hey, don't worry! Saving princesses is kinda our job.
We'll get her back for sure!
And we'll do whatever it takes to protect this city from Noisemaster!
Your Majesties, where is this "Rhythm Ridge" he spoke of?
Hm...
That would be on the other side of the wall...
Which means there's only one way to get there!

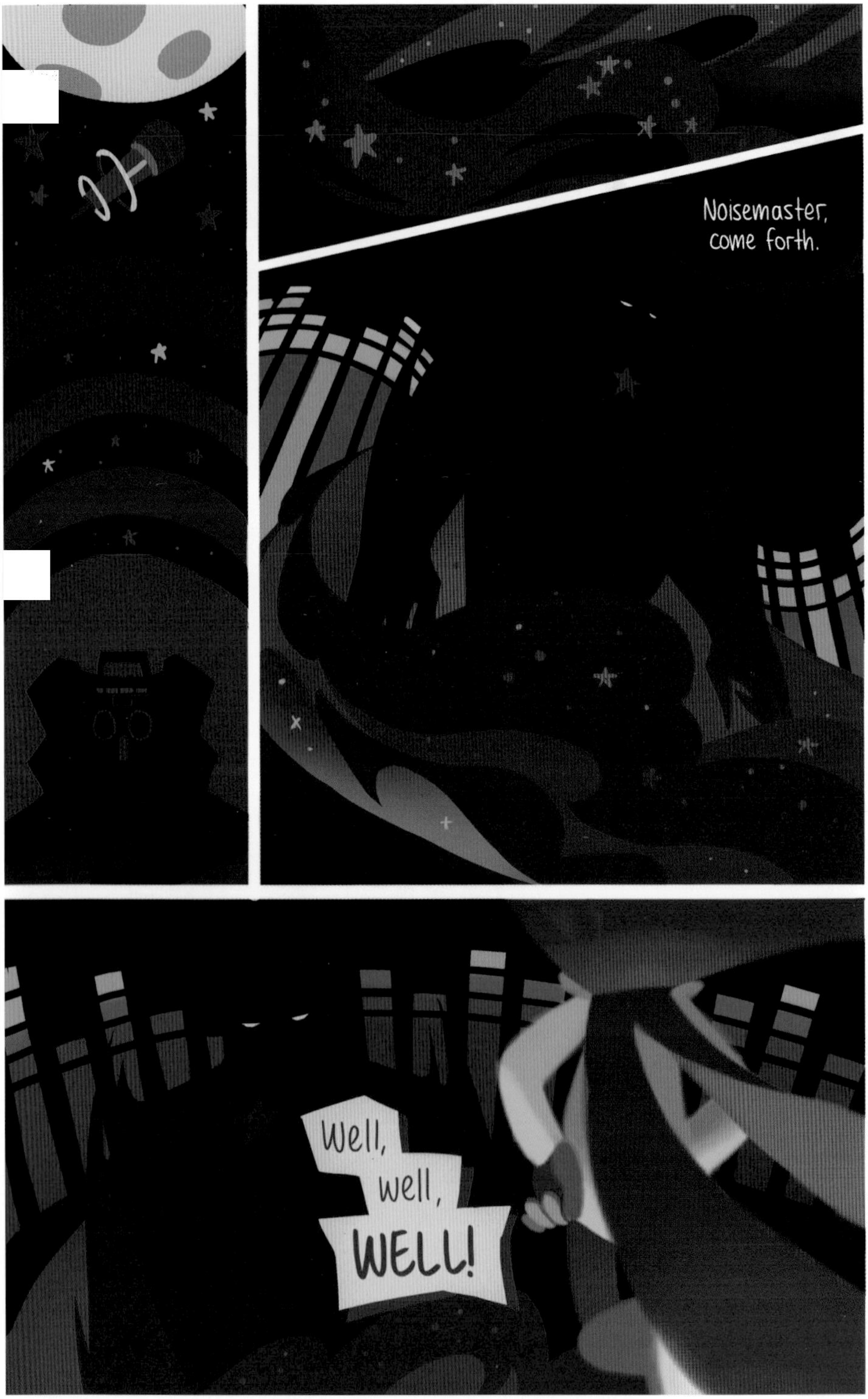
Noisemaster, come forth.
Well, well, WELL!

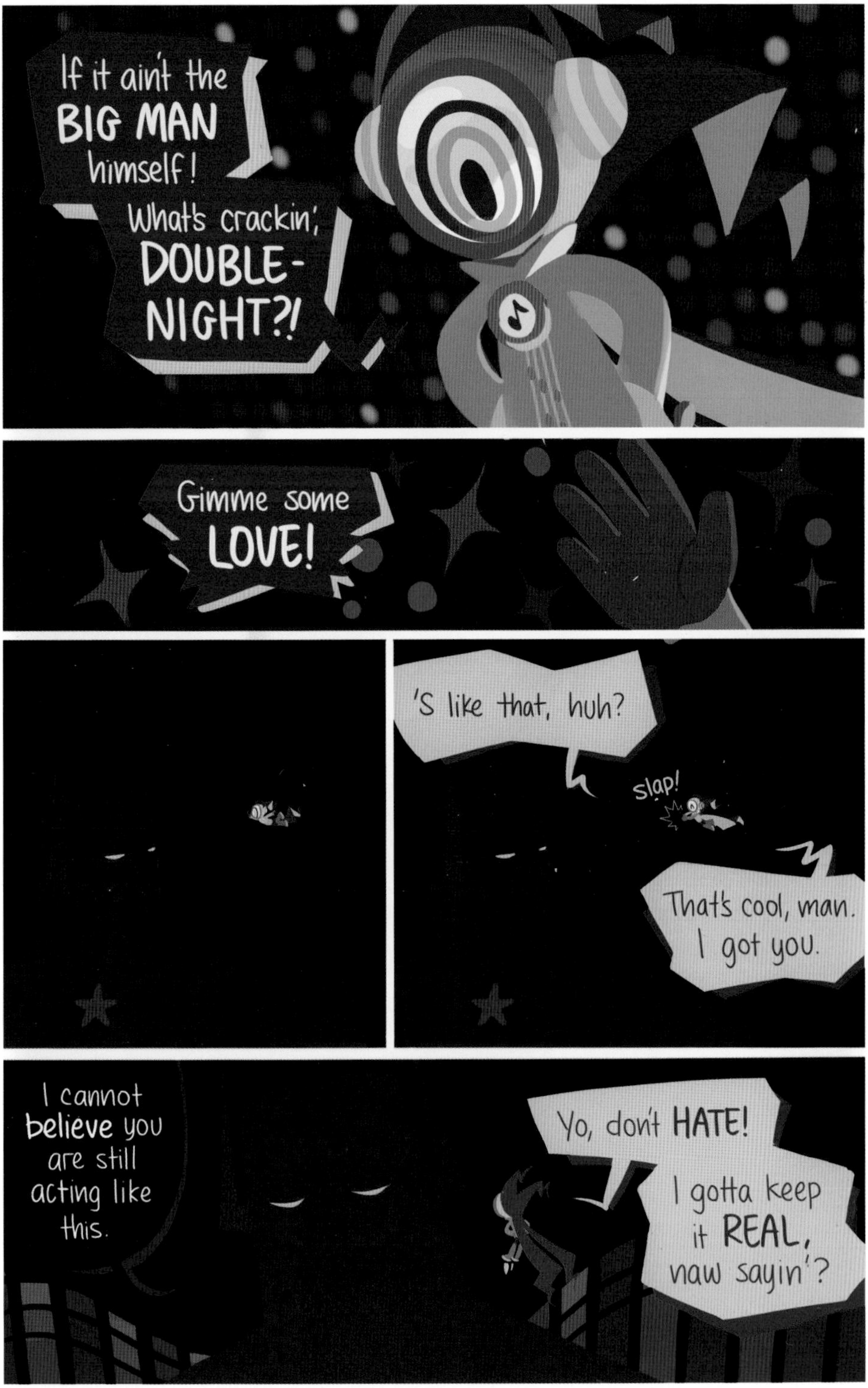
If it ain't the BIG MAN himself!
What's crackin', DOUBLE-NIGHT?!
Gimme some LOVE!
'S like that, huh?
slap!
That's cool, man. I got you.
I cannot believe you are still acting like this.
Yo, don't HATE!
I gotta keep it REAL, naw sayin'?

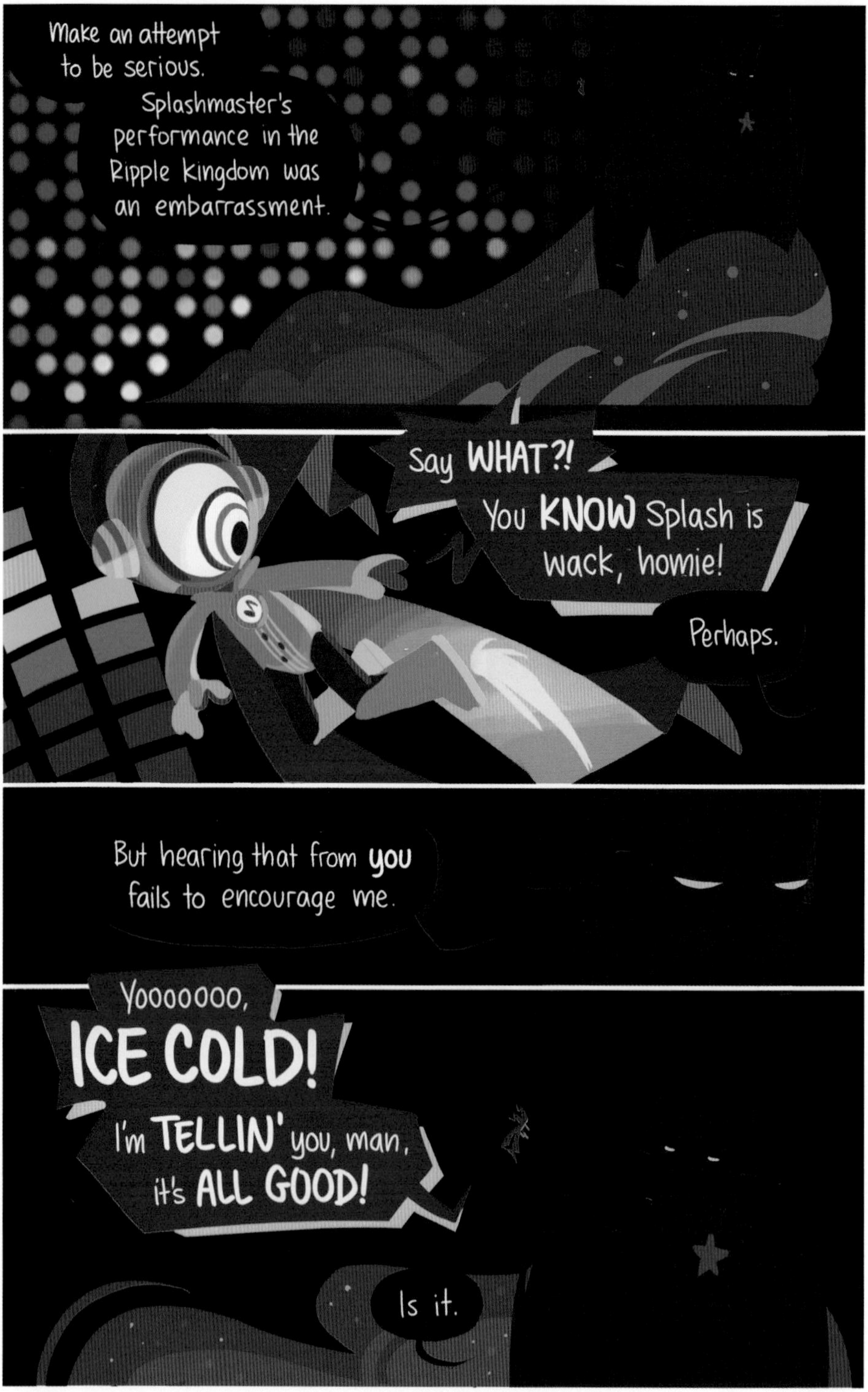
Make an attempt to be serious.
Splashmaster's performance in the Ripple Kingdom was an embarrassment.
Say WHAT?!
You KNOW Splash is wack, homie!
Perhaps.
But hearing that from you fails to encourage me.
Yooooooo,
ICE COLD!
I'm TELLIN' you, man, it's ALL GOOD!
Is it.

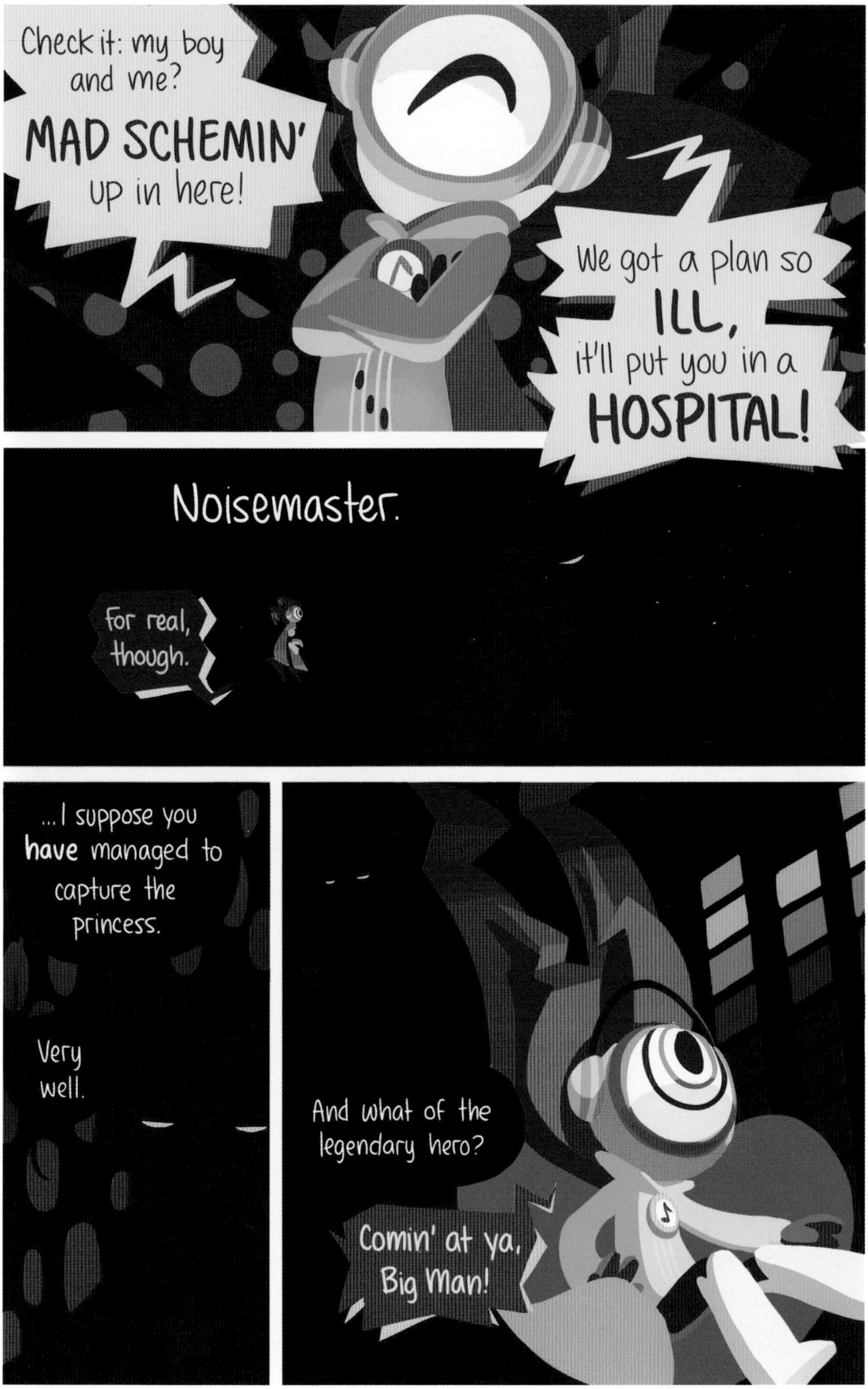
Check it: my boy and me? MAD SCHEMIN' up in here!
We got a plan so ILL, it'll put you in a HOSPITAL!
Noisemaster.
For real, though.
...I suppose you have managed to capture the princess.
Very well.
And what of the legendary hero?
Comin' at ya, Big Man!

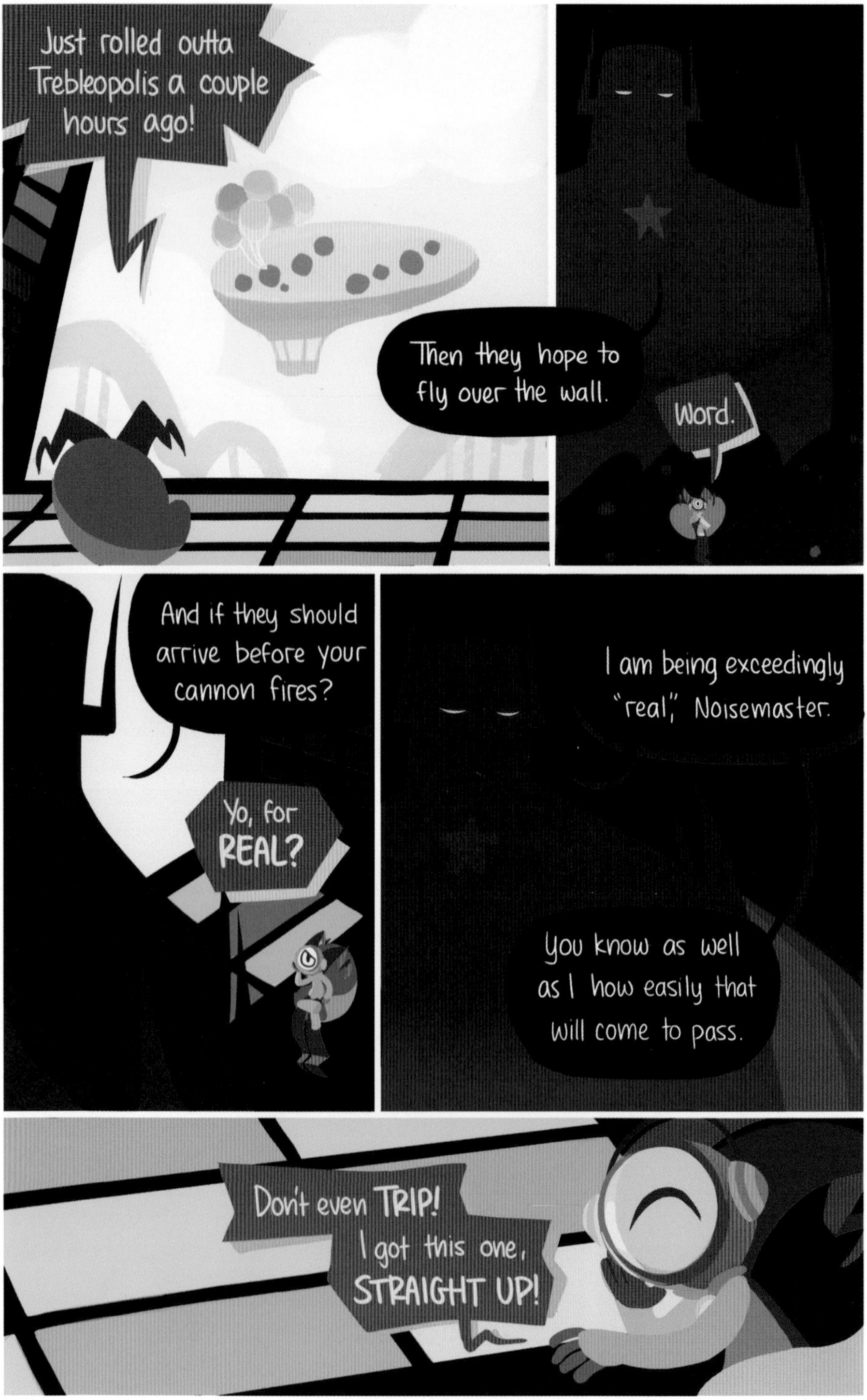
Just rolled outta Trebleopolis a couple hours ago!
Then they hope to fly over the wall.
Word.
And if they should arrive before your cannon fires?
Yo, for REAL?
I am being exceedingly "real," Noisemaster.
You know as well as I how easily that will come to pass.
Don't even TRIP! I got this one, STRAIGHT UP!

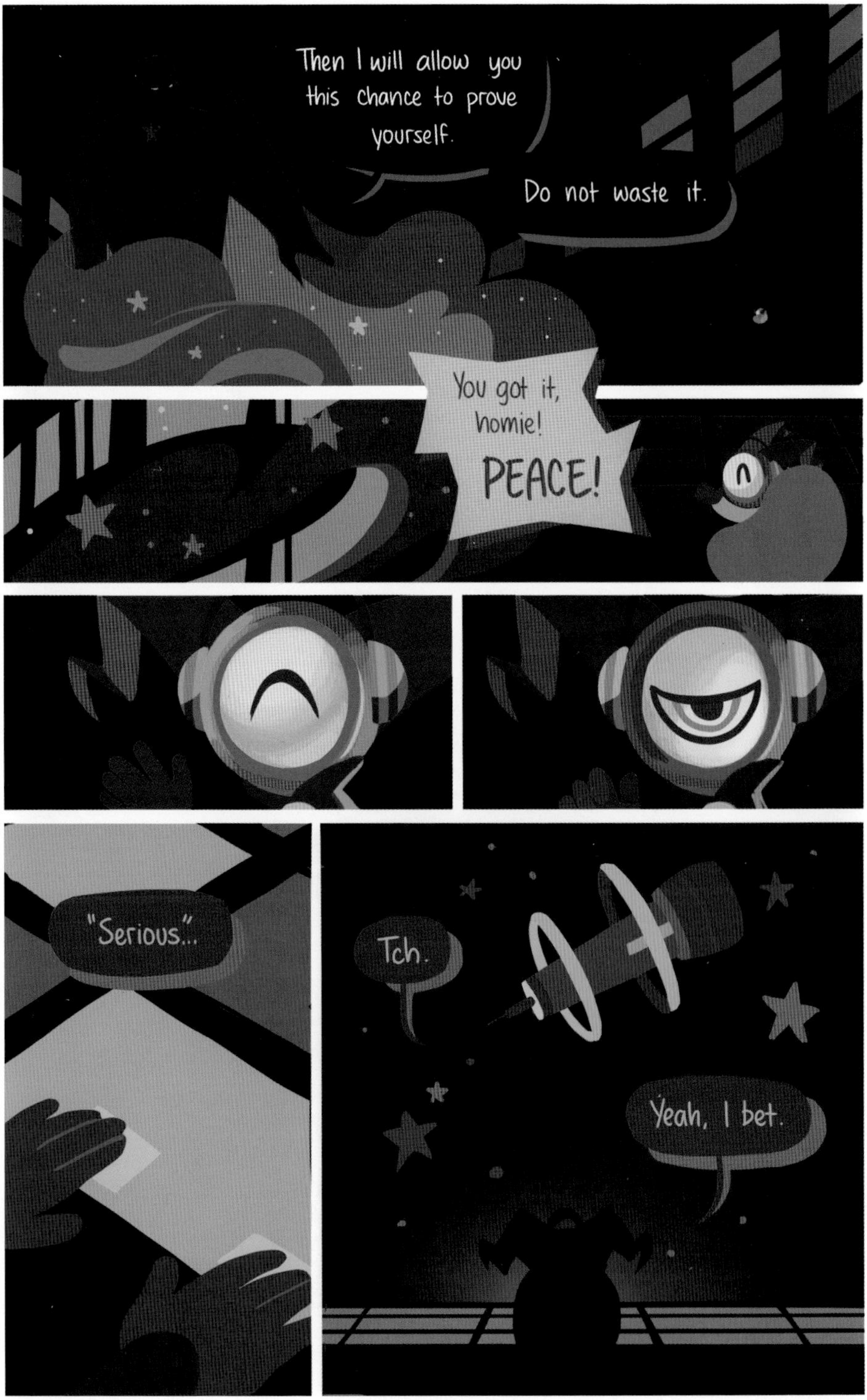
Then I will allow you this chance to prove yourself.
Do not waste it.
You got it, homie! PEACE!
"Serious."...
Tch.
Yeah, I bet.

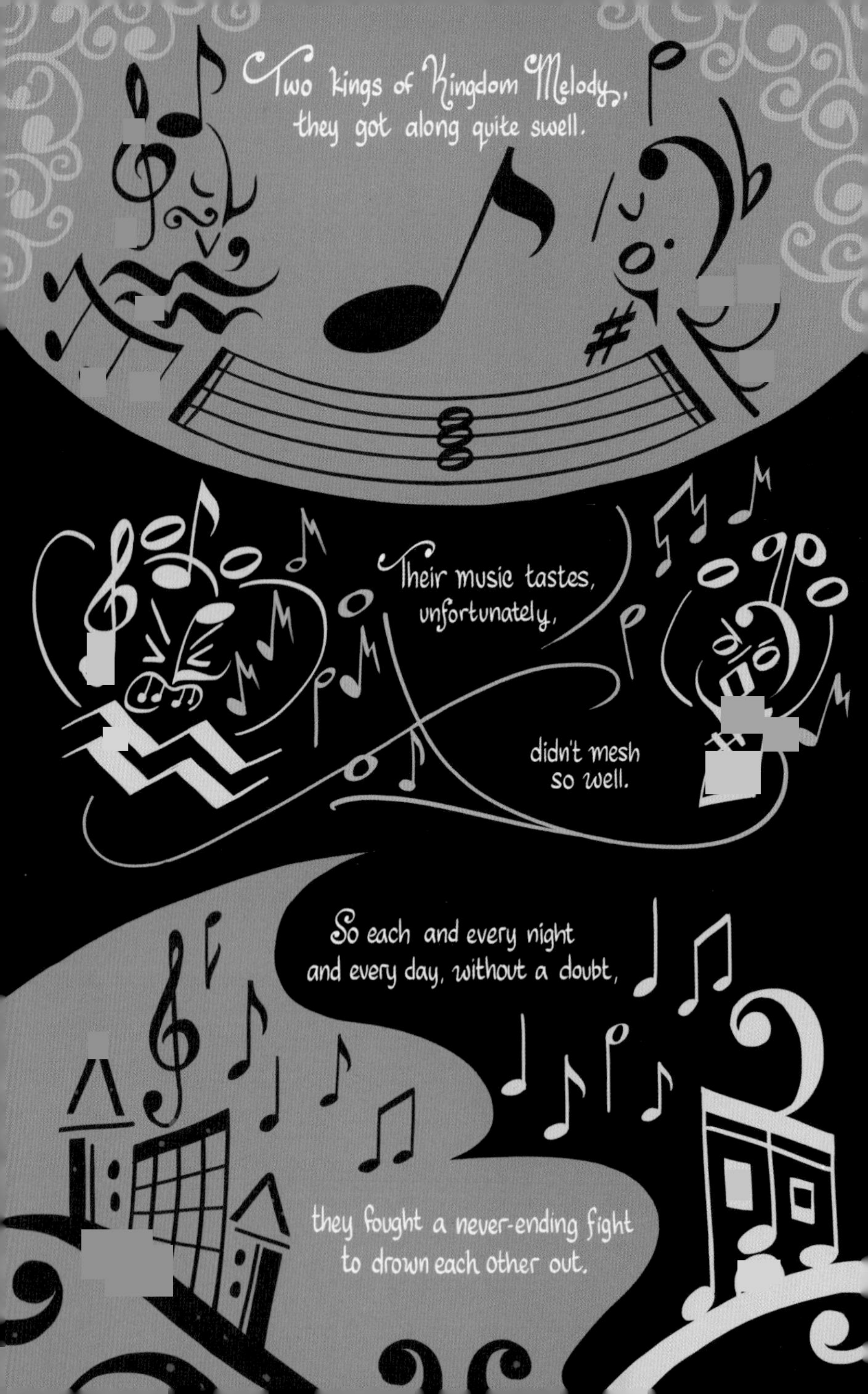
Two kings of Kingdom Melody,
they got along quite swell.
Their music tastes,
unfortunately,
didn't mesh
so well.
So each and every night
and every day, without a doubt,
they fought a never-ending fight
to drown each other out.

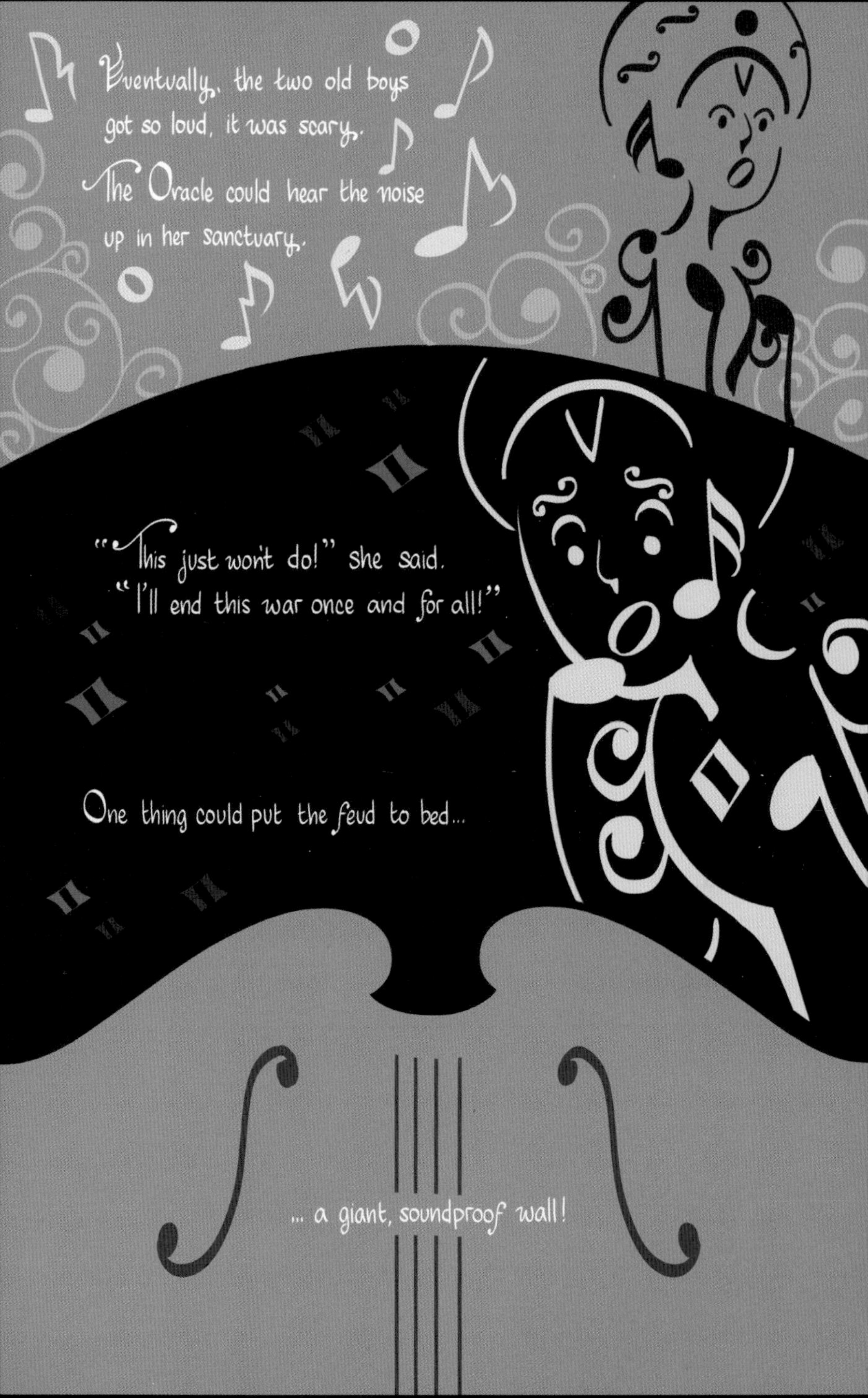
Eventually, the two old boys
got so loud, it was scary.
The Oracle could hear the noise
up in her sanctuary.
"This just won't do!" she said.
"I'll end this war once and for all!"
One thing could put the feud to bed...
... a giant, soundproof wall!

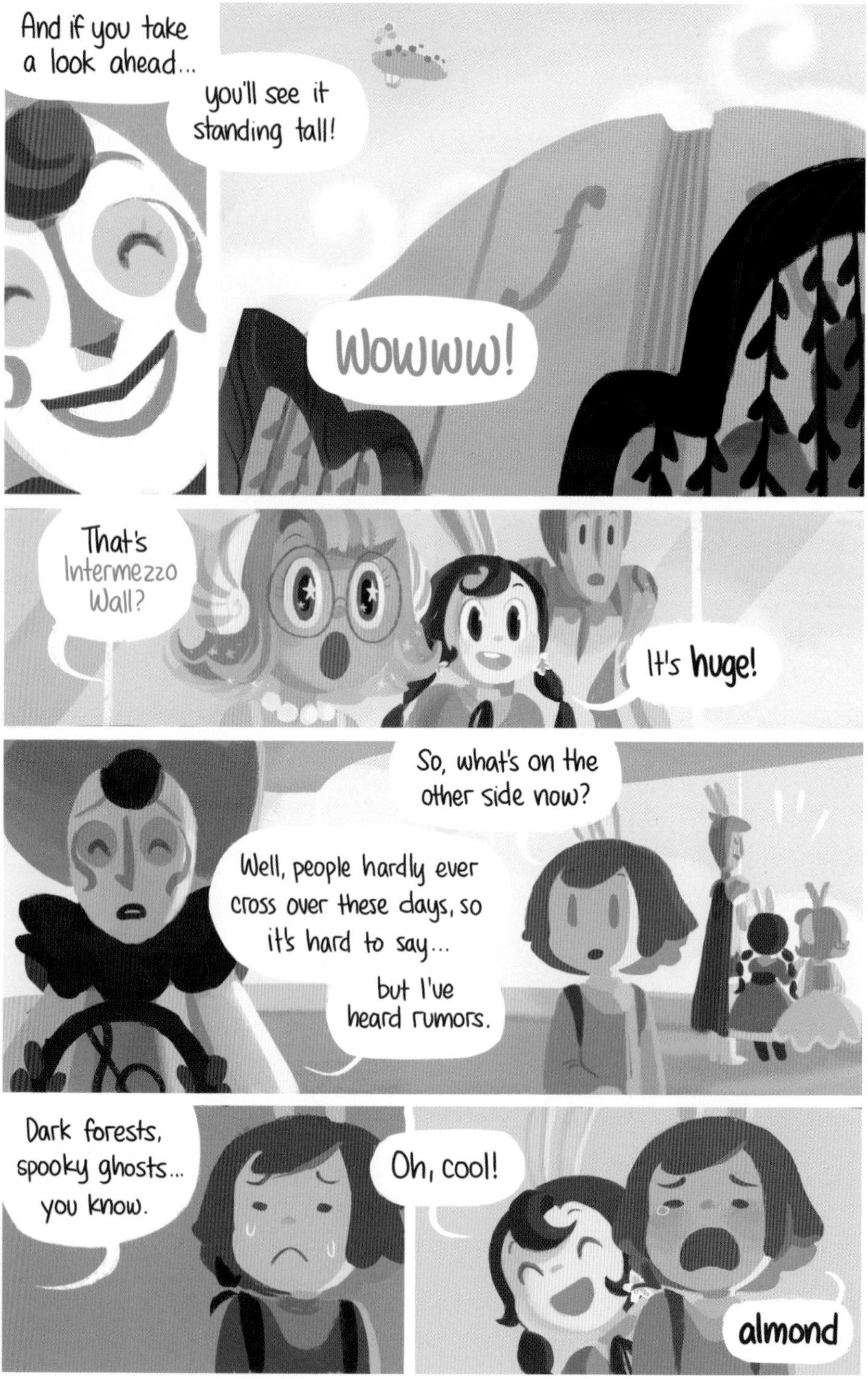
And if you take a look ahead...
you'll see it standing tall!
WOWWW!
That's Intermezzo Wall?
It's huge!
So, what's on the other side now?
Well, people hardly ever cross over these days, so it's hard to say...
but I've heard rumors.
Dark forests, spooky ghosts... you know.
Oh, cool!
almond

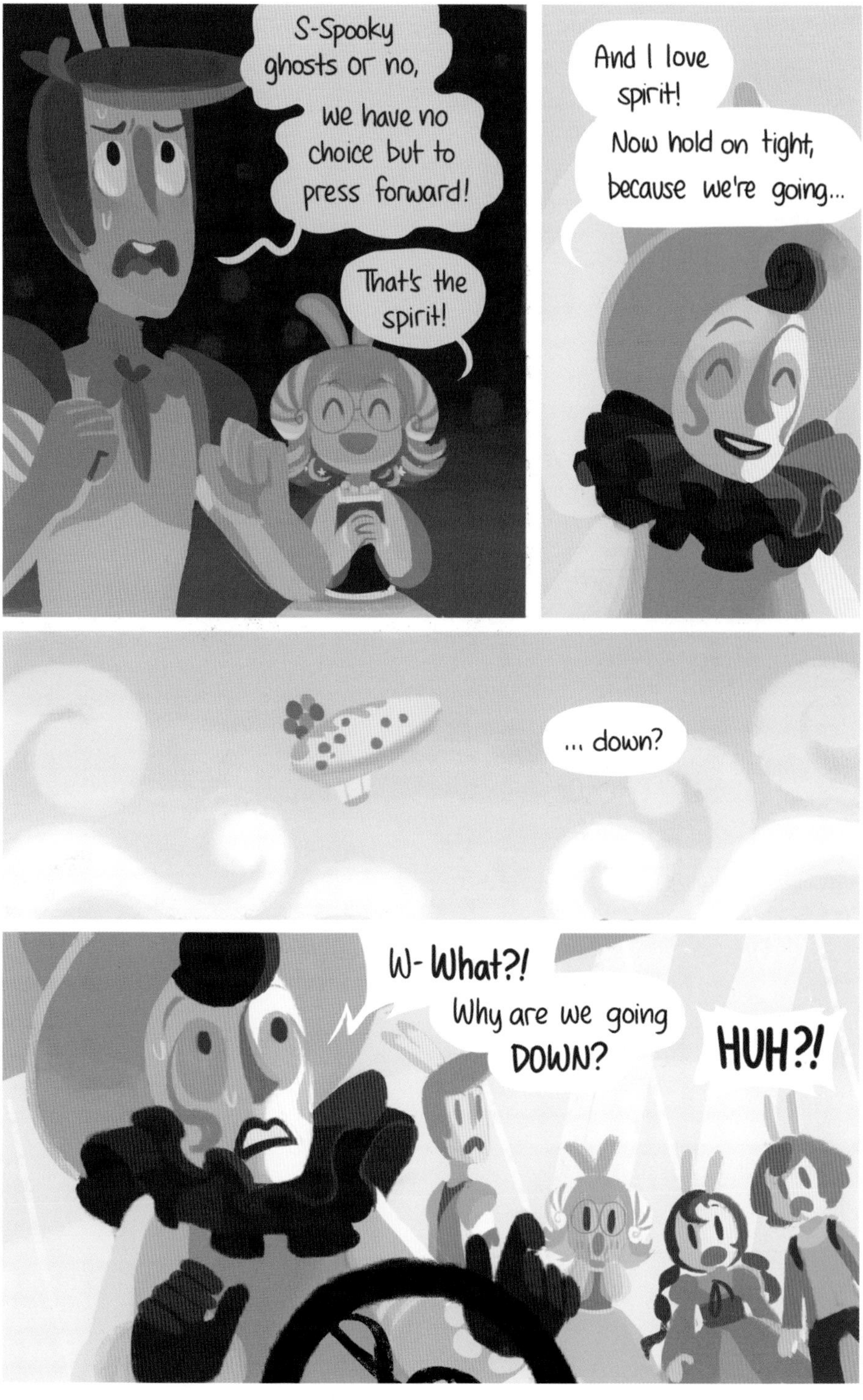
S-Spooky ghosts or no,
we have no choice but to press forward!
That's the spirit!
And I love spirit!
Now hold on tight, because we're going...
... down?
W- What?!
Why are we going DOWN?
HUH?!

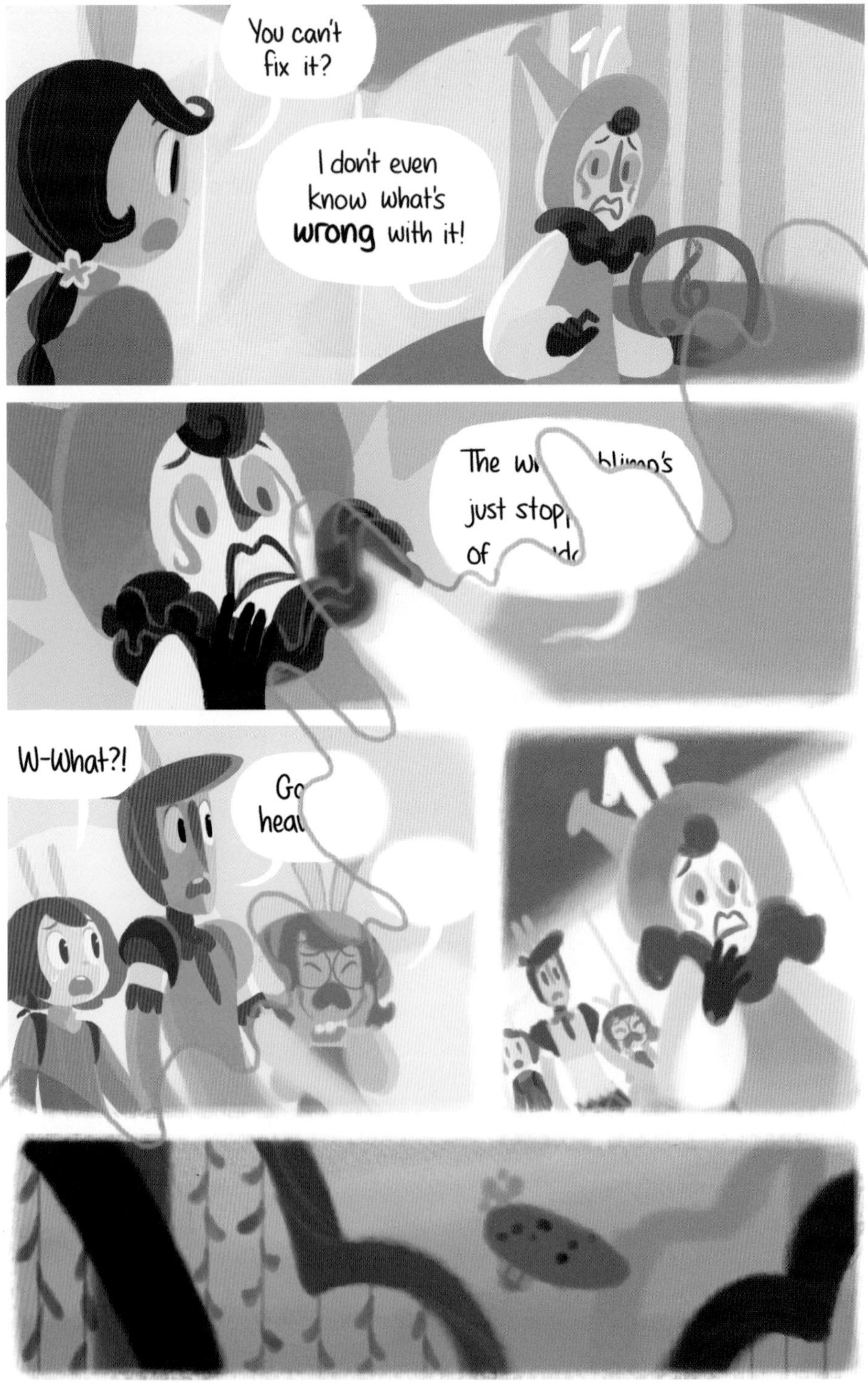
You can't fix it?
I don't even know what's **wrong** with it!
The
just
of
W-What?!

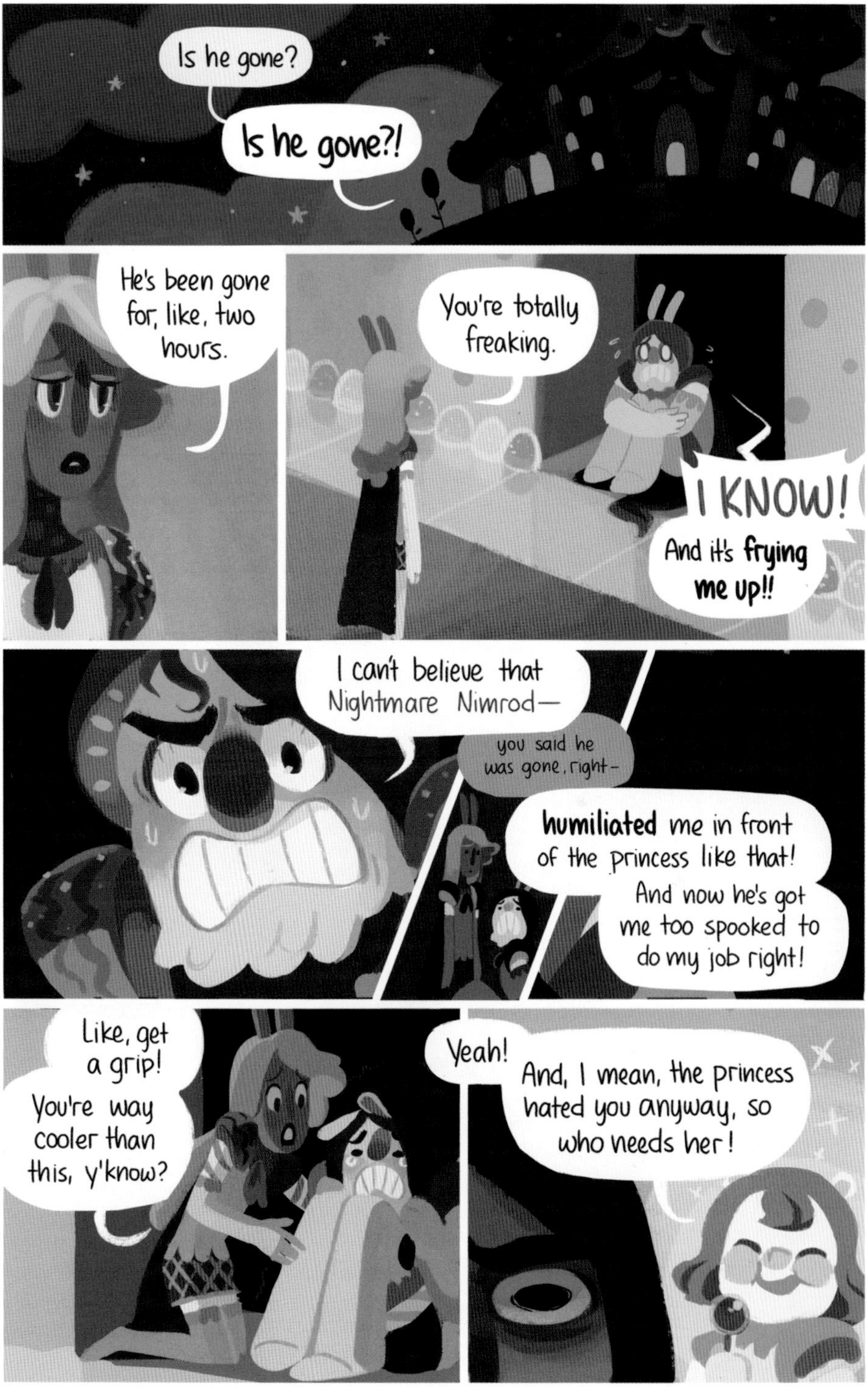

Is he gone?
Is he gone?!
He's been gone for, like, two hours.
You're totally freaking.
I KNOW!
And it's frying me up!!
I can't believe that Nightmare Nimrod—
you said he was gone, right—
humiliated me in front of the princess like that!
And now he's got me too spooked to do my job right!
Like, get a grip!
You're way cooler than this, y'know?
Yeah!
And, I mean, the princess hated you anyway, so who needs her!

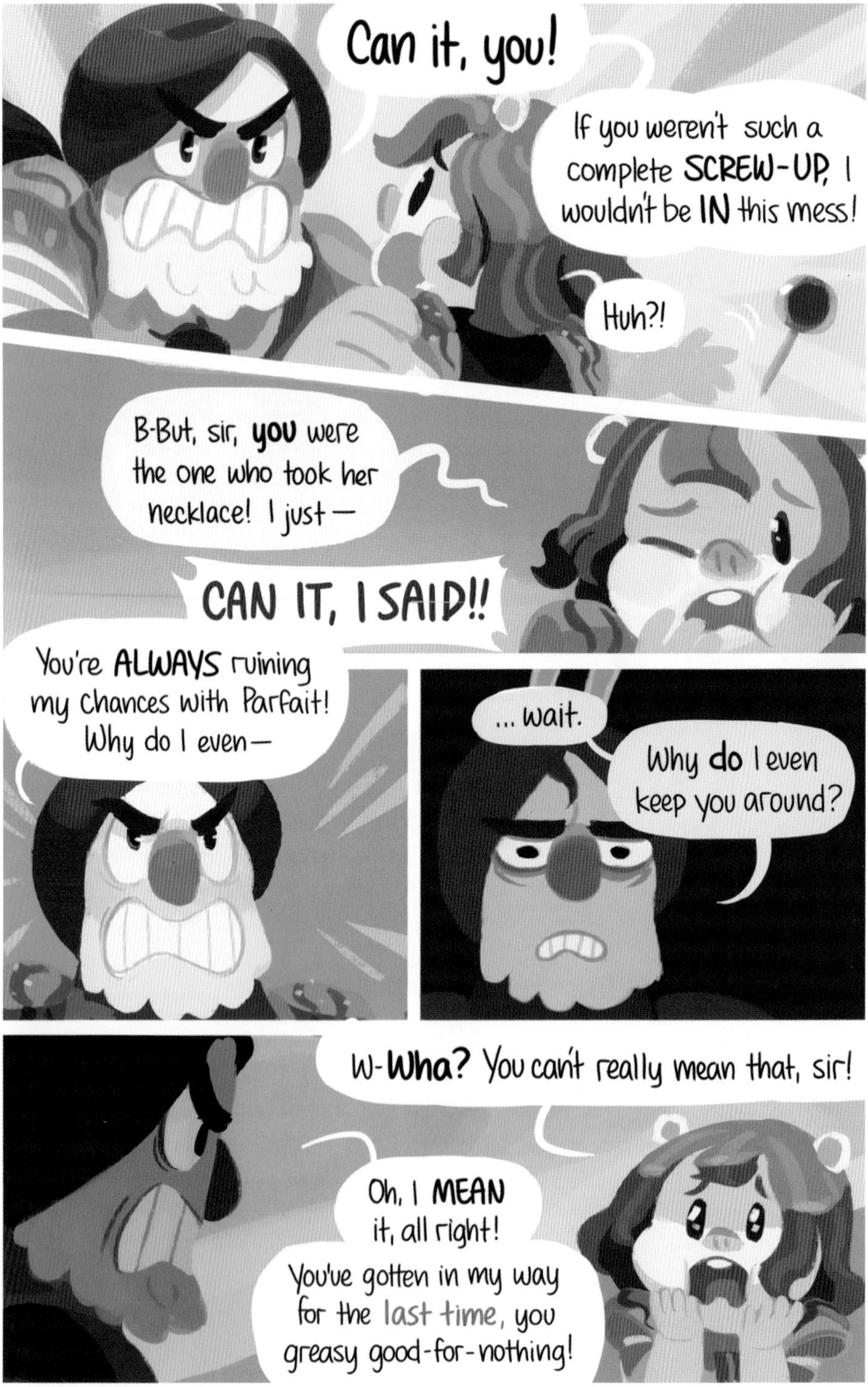
Can it, you!
If you weren't such a complete SCREW-UP, I wouldn't be IN this mess!
Huh?!
B-But, sir, YOU were the one who took her necklace! I just—
CAN IT, I SAID!!
You're ALWAYS ruining my chances with Parfait! Why do I even—
... wait.
Why do I even keep you around?
W-Wha? You can't really mean that, sir!
Oh, I MEAN it, all right! You've gotten in my way for the last time, you greasy good-for-nothing!

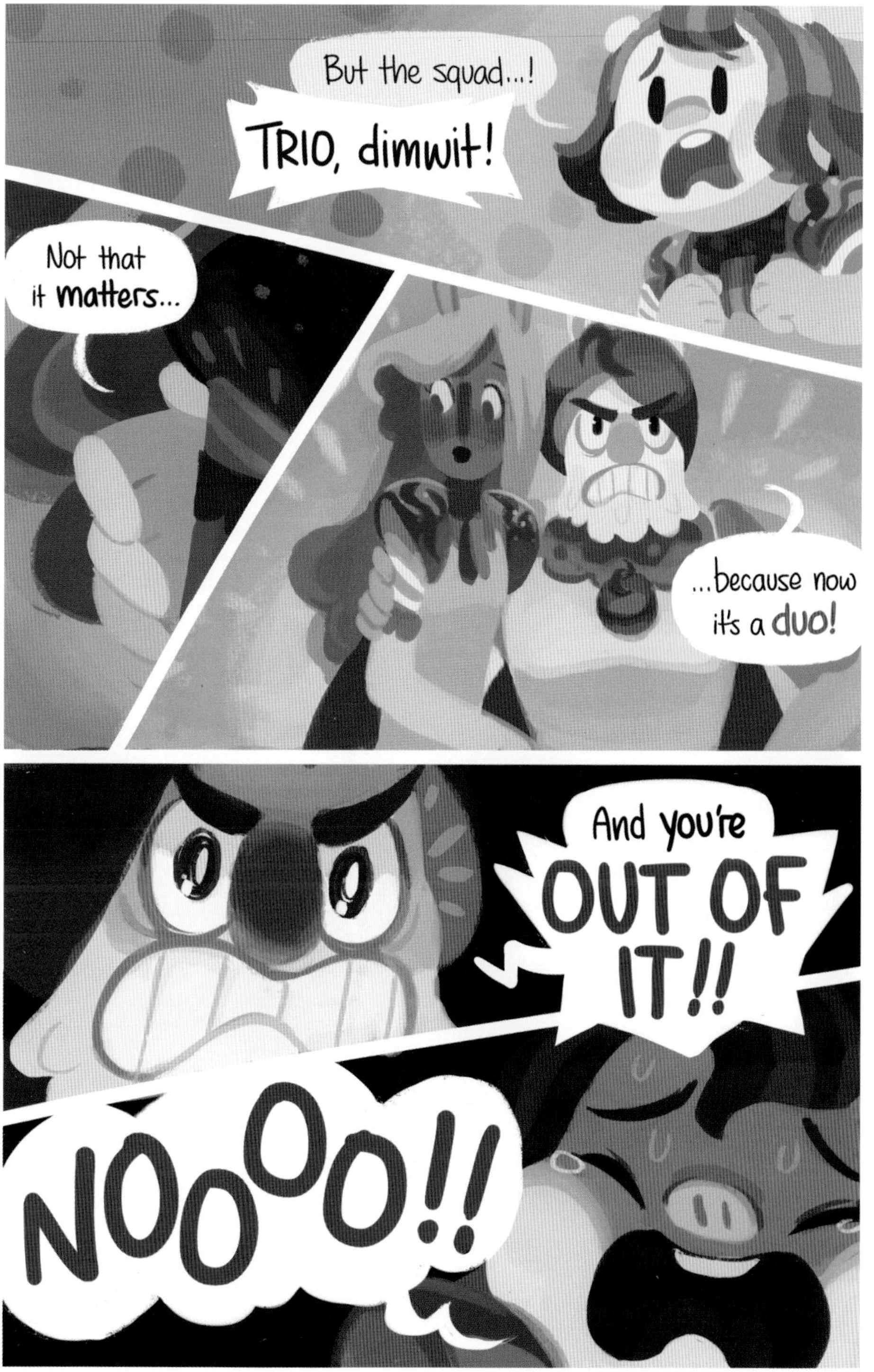
But the squad...!
TRIO, dimwit!
Not that it matters...
...because now it's a duo!
And you're OUT OF IT!!
NOOOOO!!

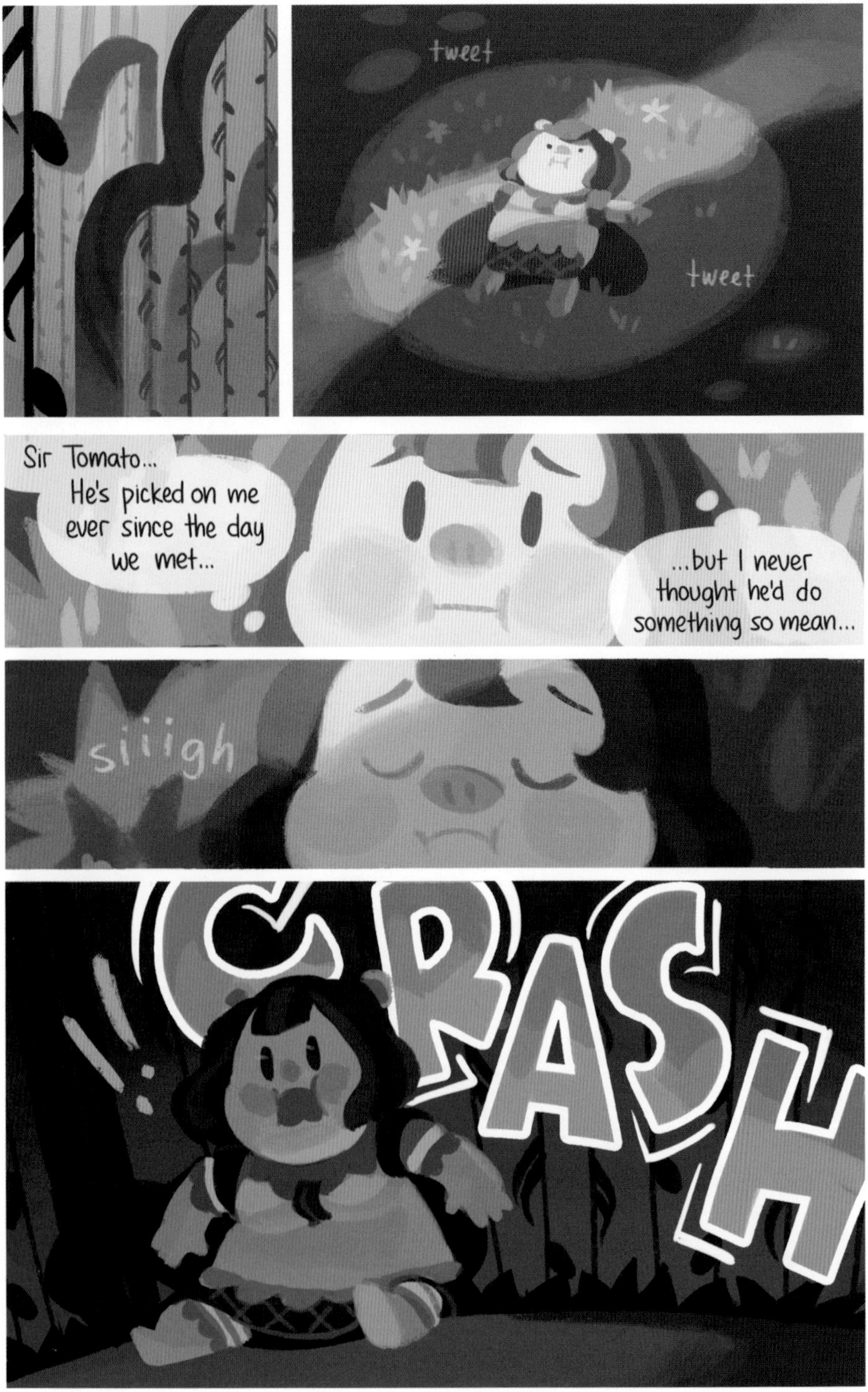
tweet
tweet
Sir Tomato... He's picked on me ever since the day we met...
...but I never thought he'd do something so mean...
siiigh
CRASH

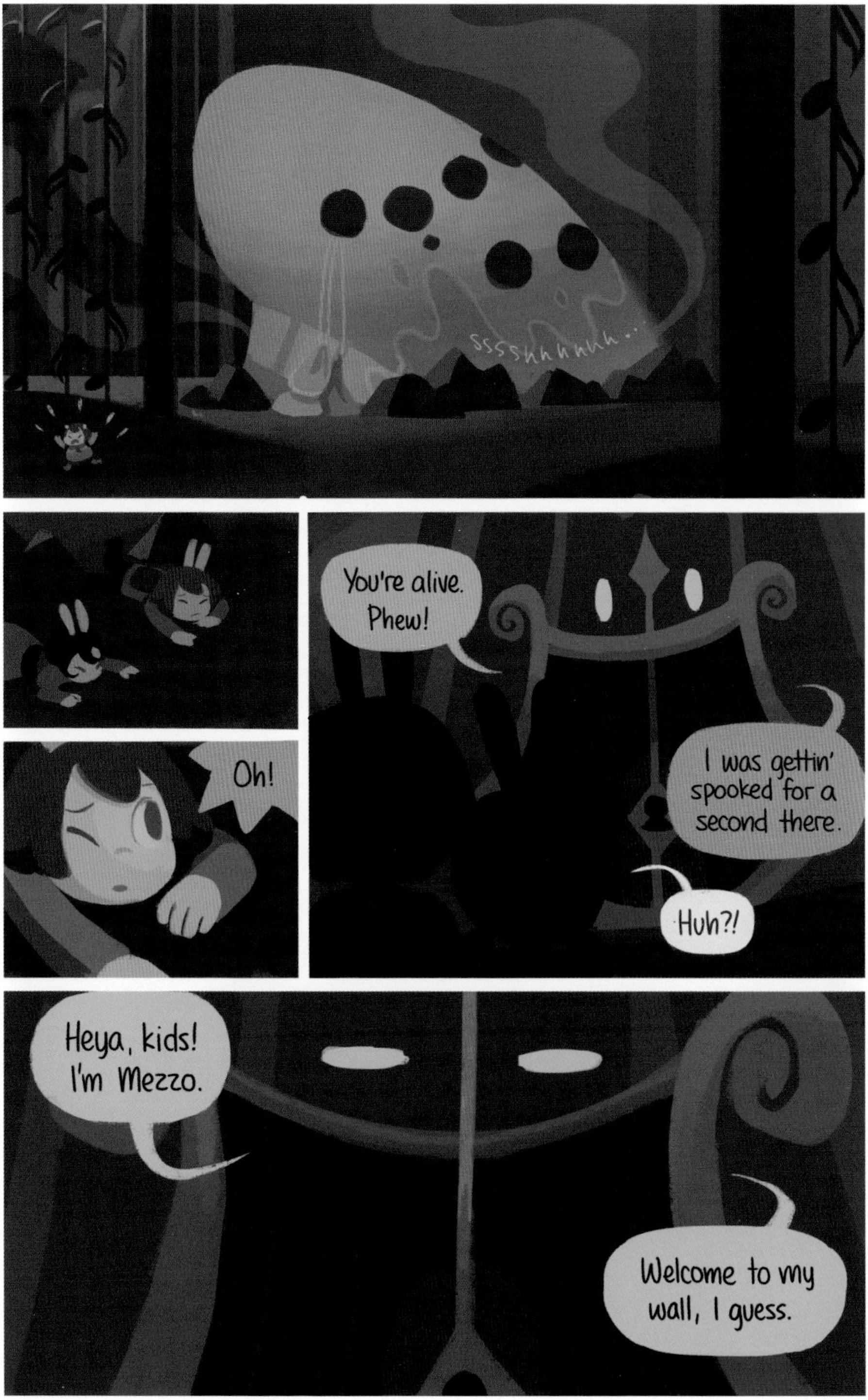

SSSShhhhhh..
You're alive. Phew!
I was gettin' spooked for a second there.
Oh!
Huh?!
Heya, kids! I'm Mezzo.
Welcome to my wall, I guess.

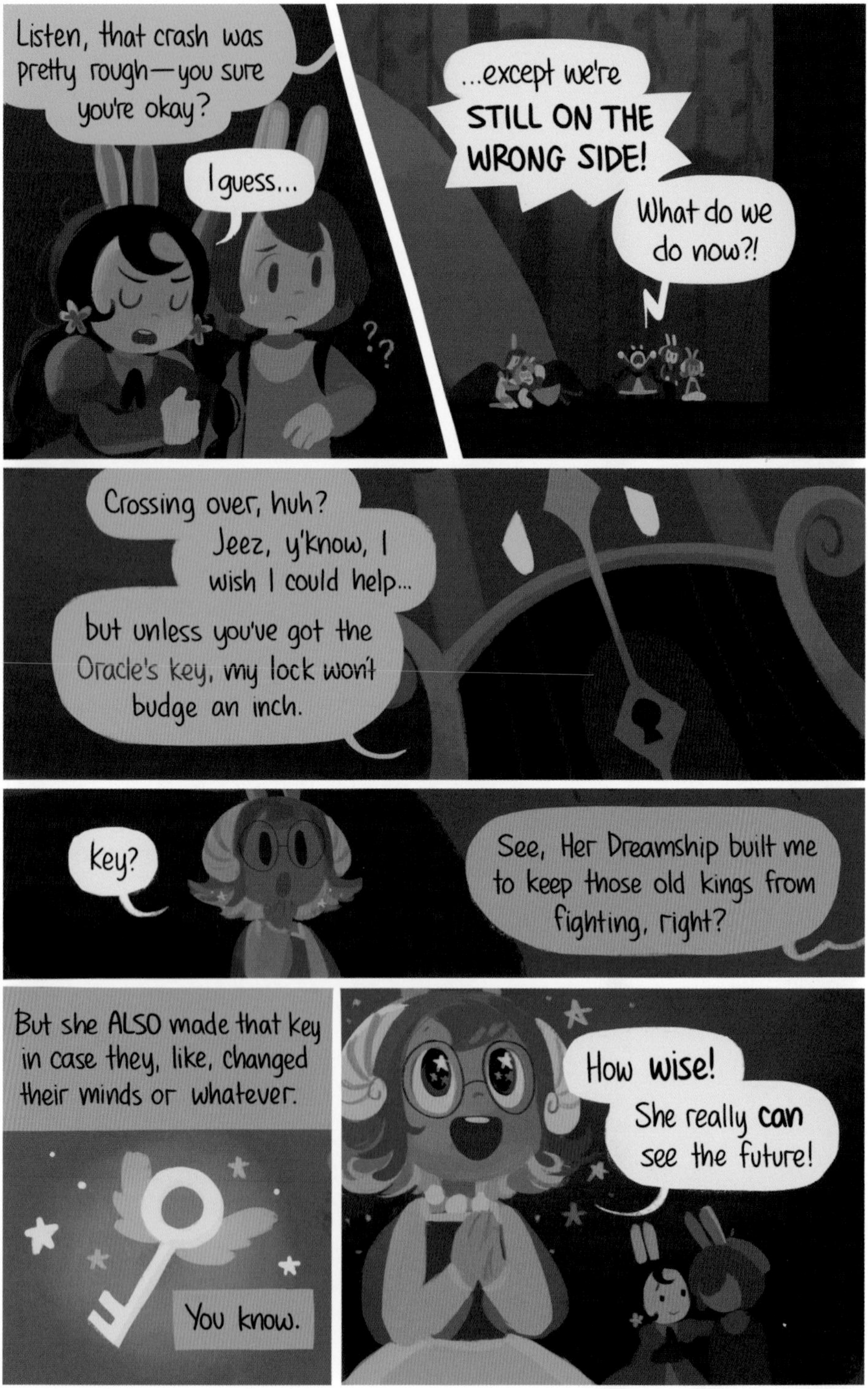
Listen, that crash was pretty rough—you sure you're okay?
I guess...
...except we're STILL ON THE WRONG SIDE!
What do we do now?!
Crossing over, huh?
Jeez, y'know, I wish I could help...
but unless you've got the Oracle's key, my lock won't budge an inch.
Key?
See, Her Dreamship built me to keep those old kings from fighting, right?
But she ALSO made that key in case they, like, changed their minds or whatever.
You know.
How **wise**!
She really **can** see the future!

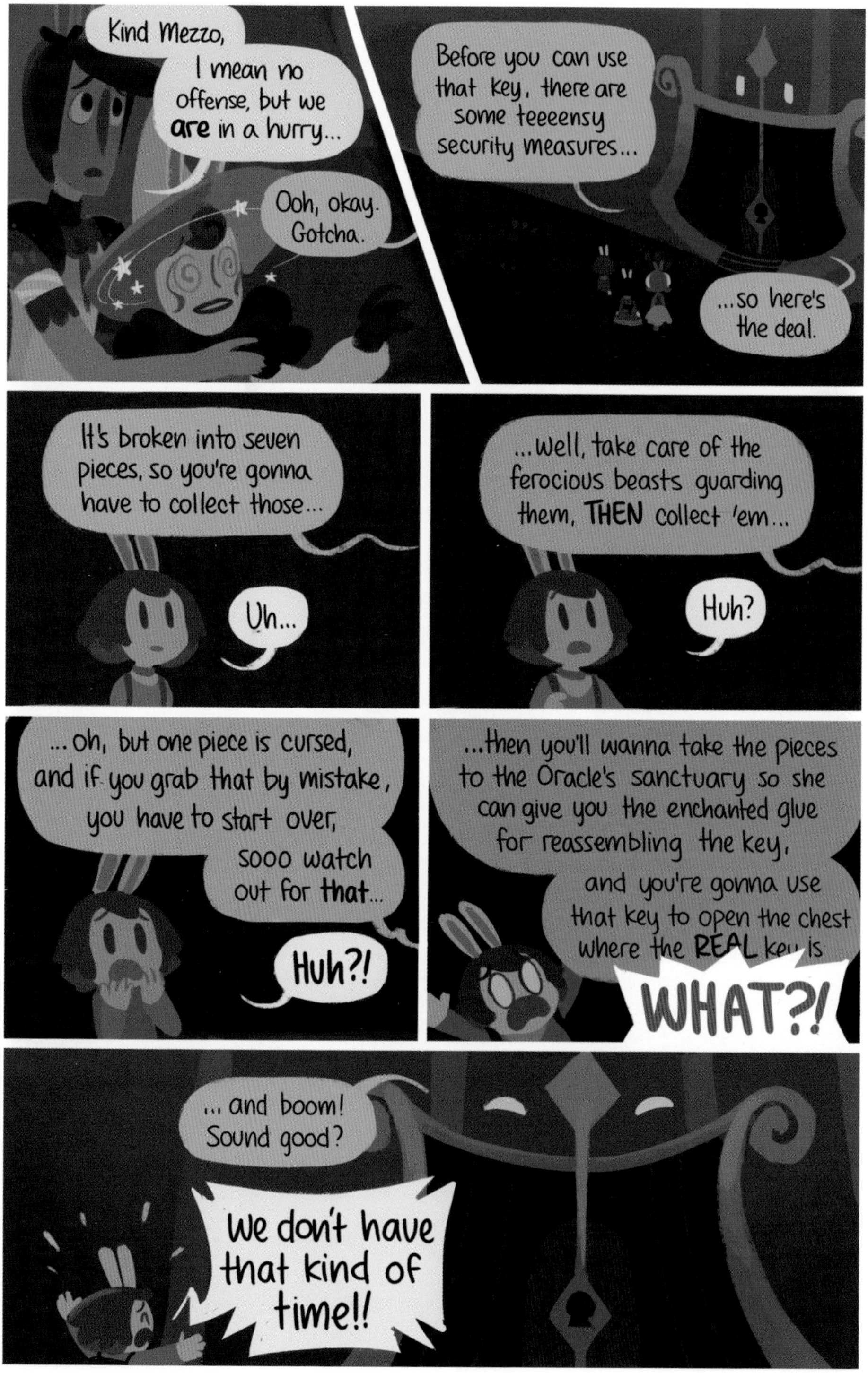
Kind Mezzo,
I mean no offense, but we **are** in a hurry...
Ooh, okay. Gotcha.
Before you can use that key, there are some teeeensy security measures...
...so here's the deal.
It's broken into seven pieces, so you're gonna have to collect those...
Uh...
...well, take care of the ferocious beasts guarding them, **THEN** collect 'em...
Huh?
...oh, but one piece is cursed, and if you grab that by mistake, you have to start over,
sooo watch out for **that**...
Huh?!
...then you'll wanna take the pieces to the Oracle's sanctuary so she can give you the enchanted glue for reassembling the key,
and you're gonna use that key to open the chest where the **REAL** key is
WHAT?!
...and boom! Sound good?
We don't have that kind of time!!

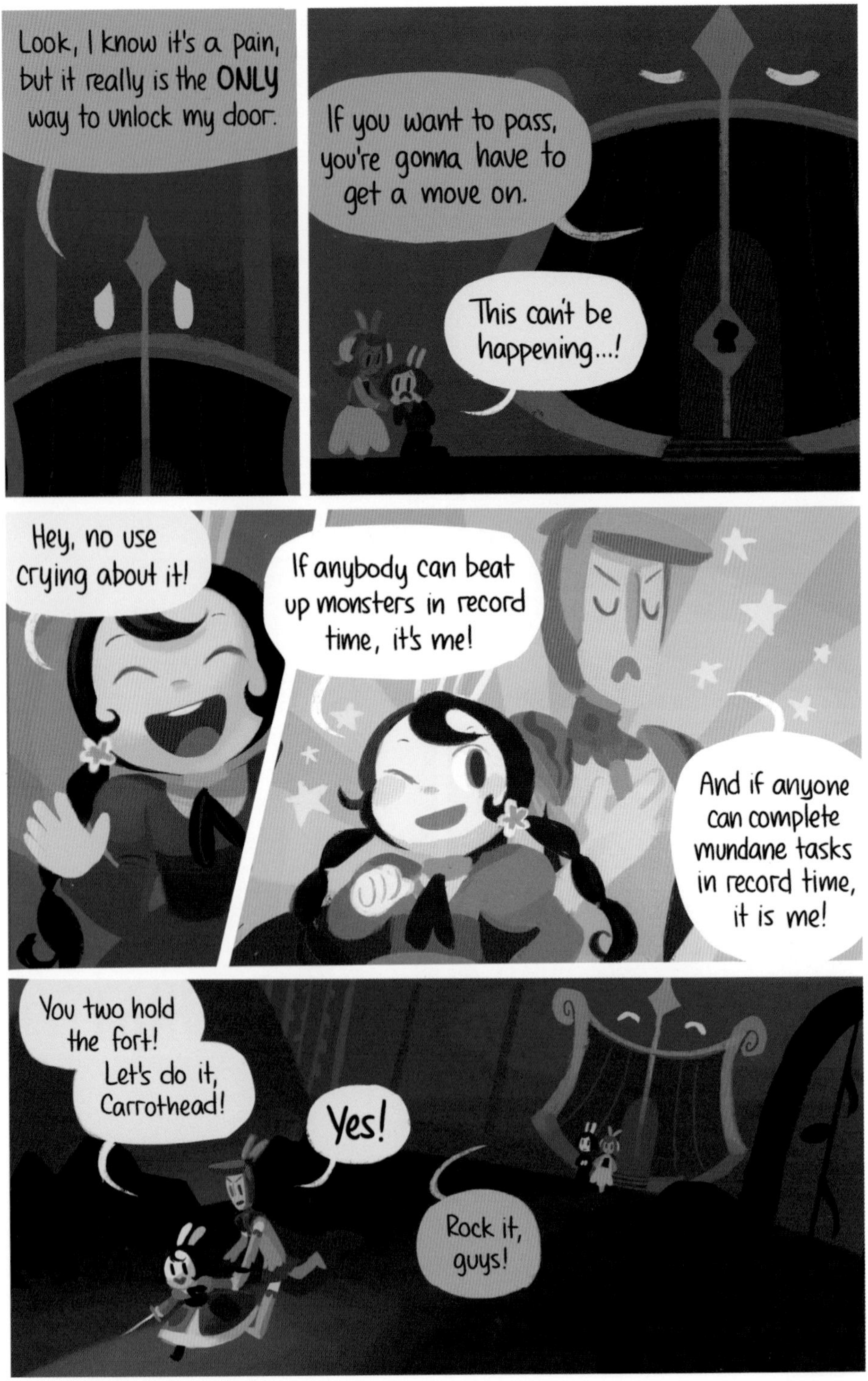
Look, I know it's a pain, but it really is the ONLY way to unlock my door.
If you want to pass, you're gonna have to get a move on.
This can't be happening...!
Hey, no use crying about it!
If anybody can beat up monsters in record time, it's me!
And if anyone can complete mundane tasks in record time, it is me!
You two hold the fort!
Let's do it, Carrothead!
Yes!
Rock it, guys!

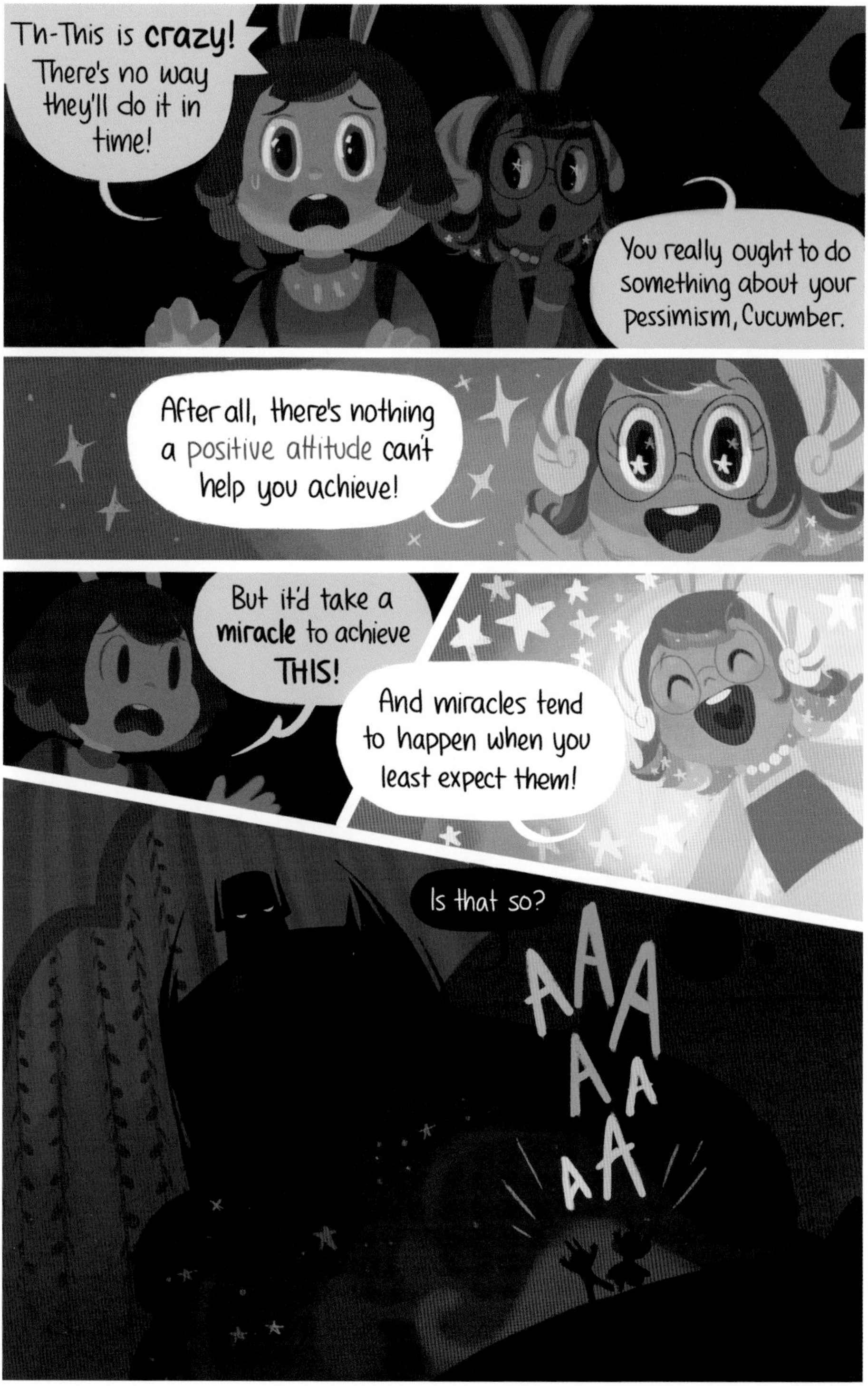
Th-This is crazy! There's no way they'll do it in time!
You really ought to do something about your pessimism, Cucumber.
After all, there's nothing a positive attitude can't help you achieve!
But it'd take a miracle to achieve THIS!
And miracles tend to happen when you least expect them!
Is that so?
AAAAAAAA

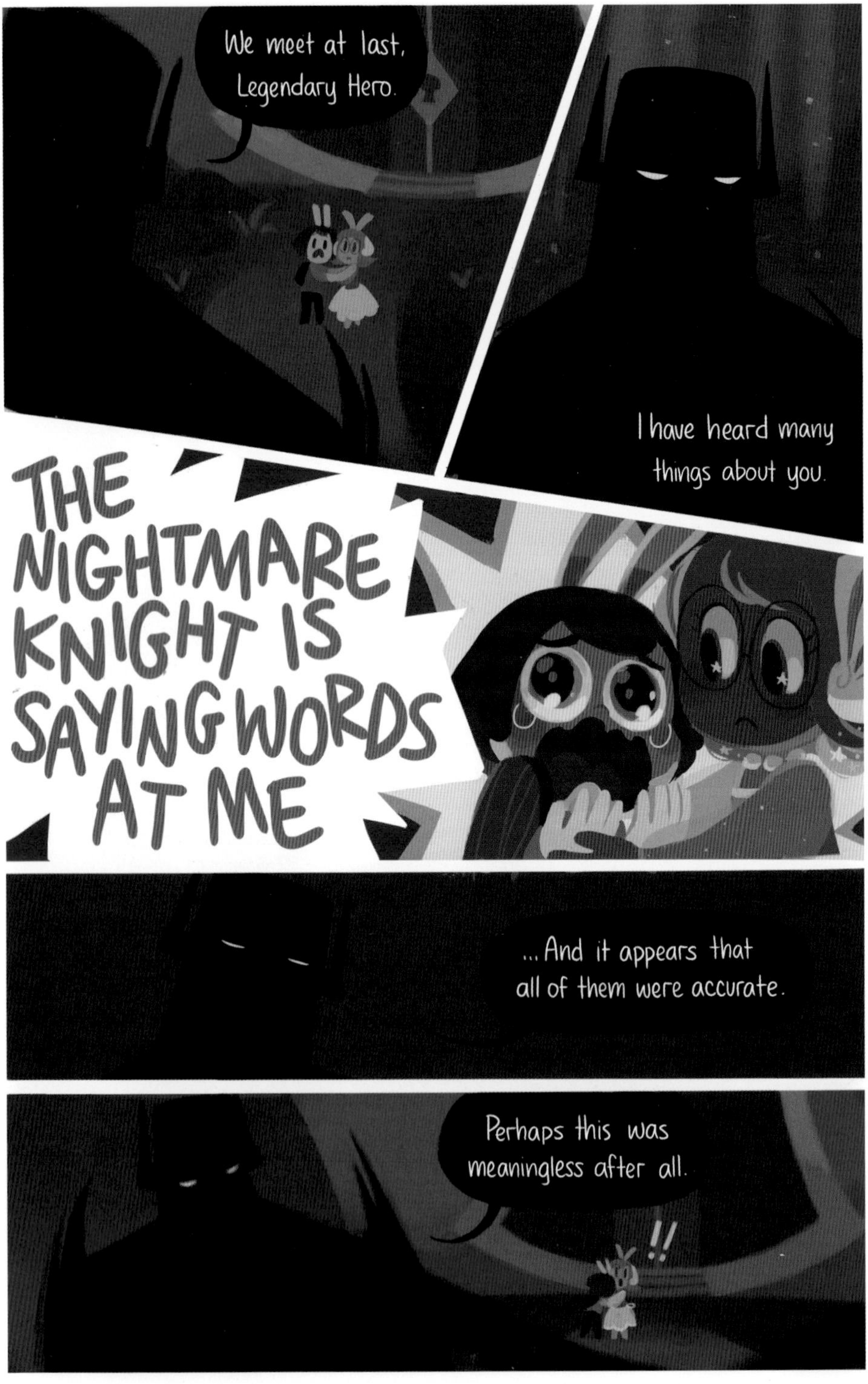
We meet at last, Legendary Hero.
I have heard many things about you.
THE NIGHTMARE KNIGHT IS SAYING WORDS AT ME
...And it appears that all of them were accurate.
Perhaps this was meaningless after all.
!!

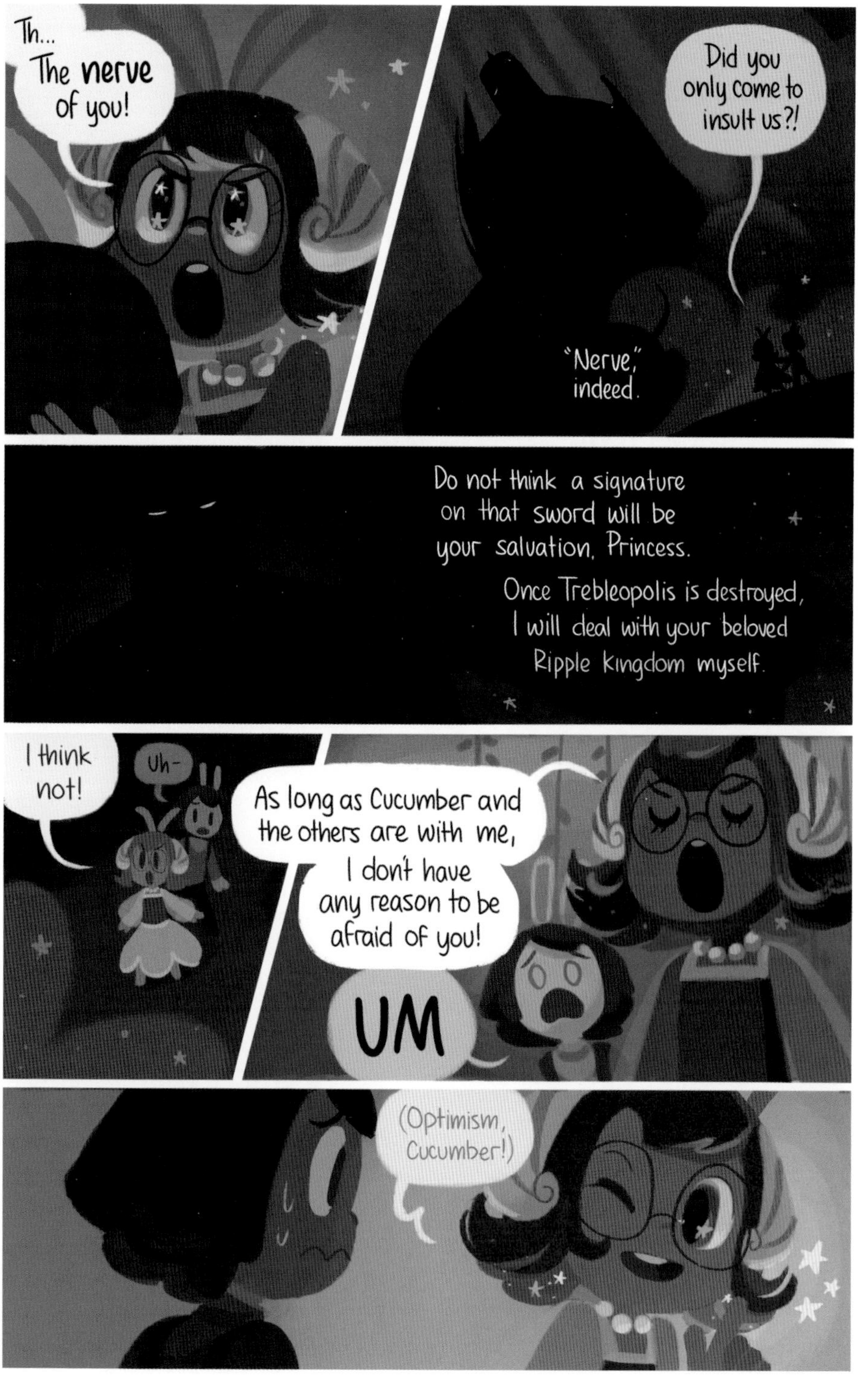
Th...
The nerve of you!
Did you only come to insult us?!
"Nerve," indeed.
Do not think a signature on that sword will be your salvation, Princess.
Once Trebleopolis is destroyed, I will deal with your beloved Ripple kingdom myself.
I think not!
Uh-
As long as Cucumber and the others are with me, I don't have any reason to be afraid of you!
UM
(Optimism, Cucumber!)

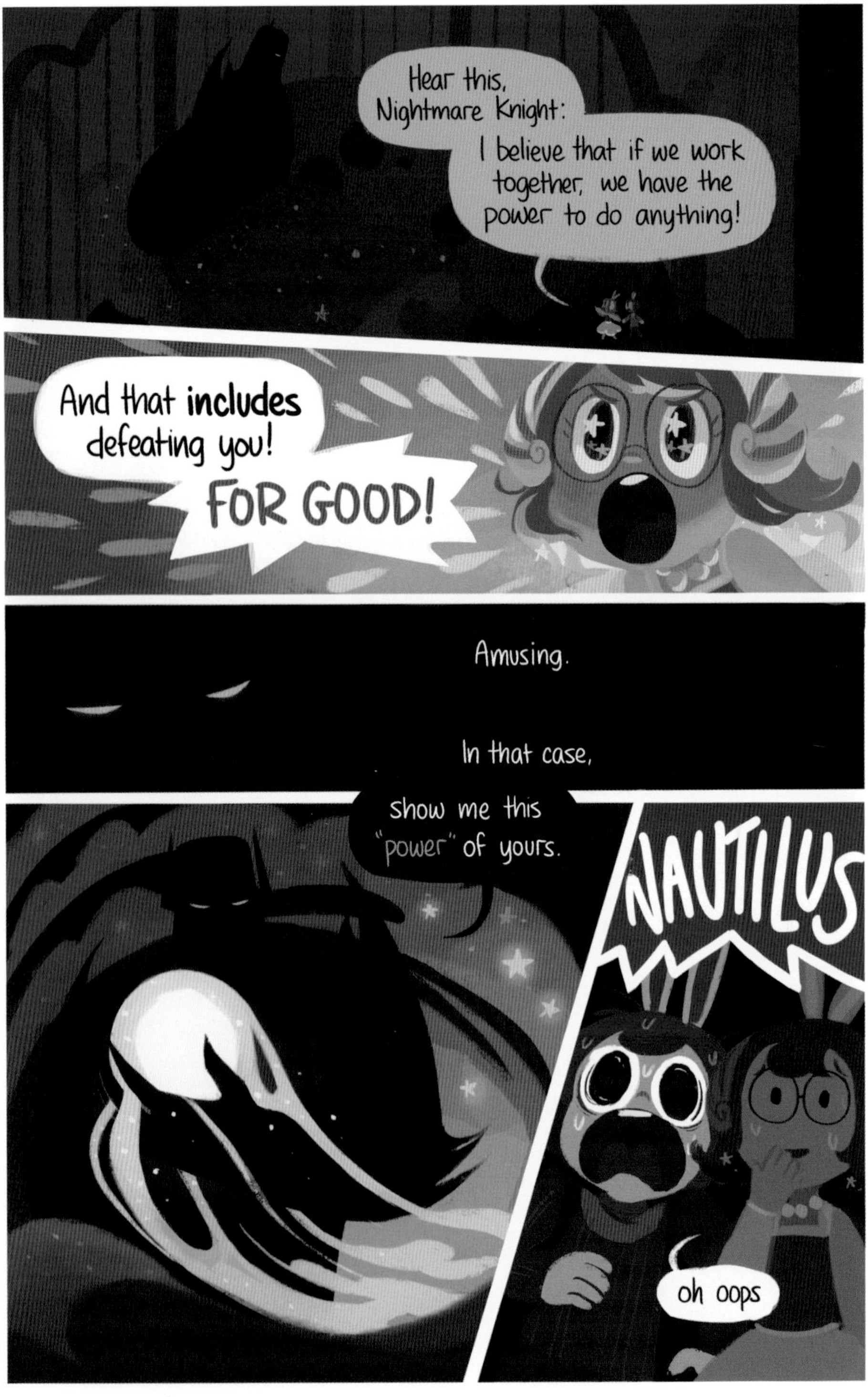
Hear this, Nightmare Knight:
I believe that if we work together, we have the power to do anything!
And that includes defeating you!
FOR GOOD!
Amusing.
In that case,
show me this "power" of yours.
NAUTILUS
oh oops

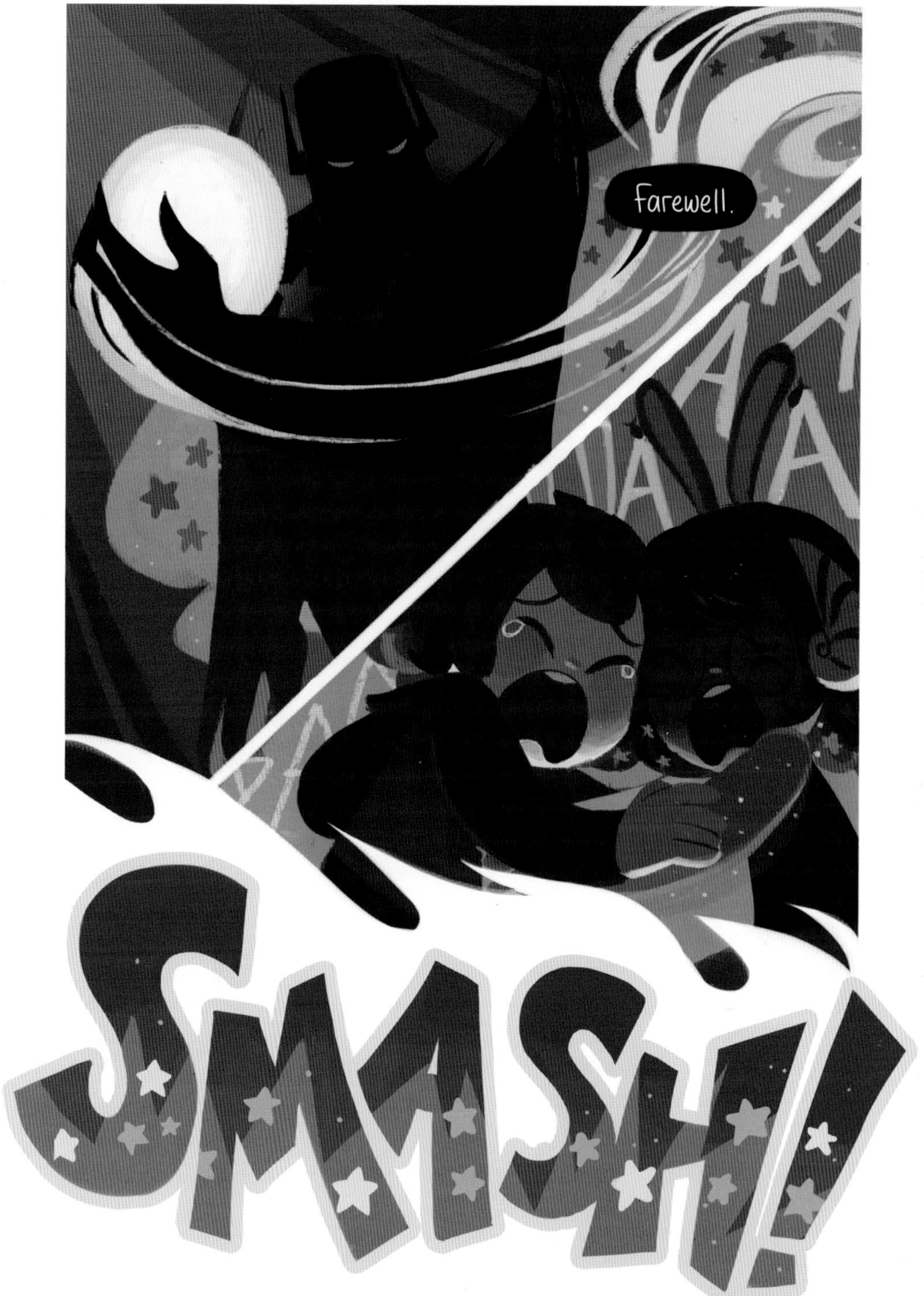
Farewell.
SMASH!

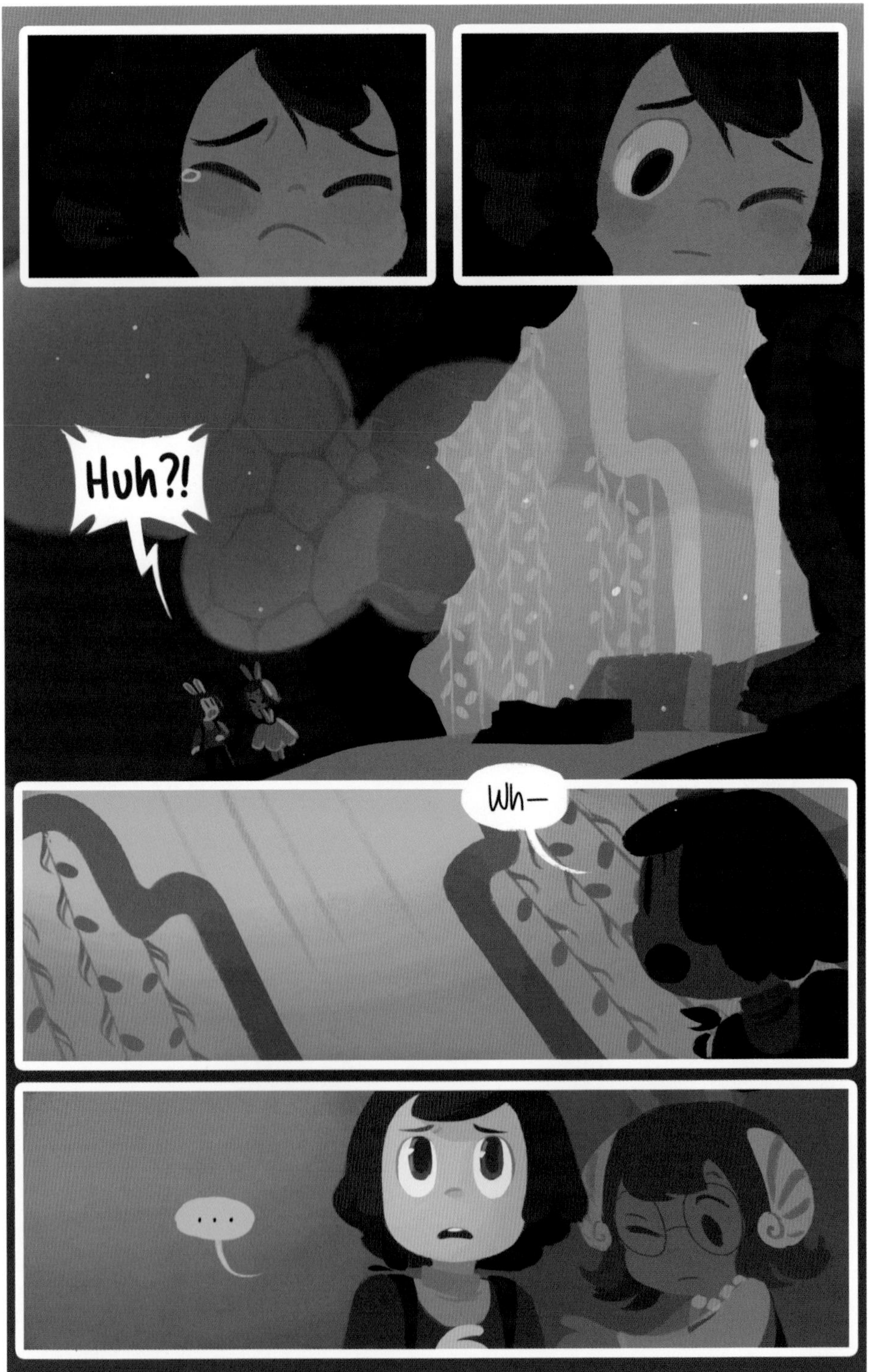
Huh?!
Wh—
. . .

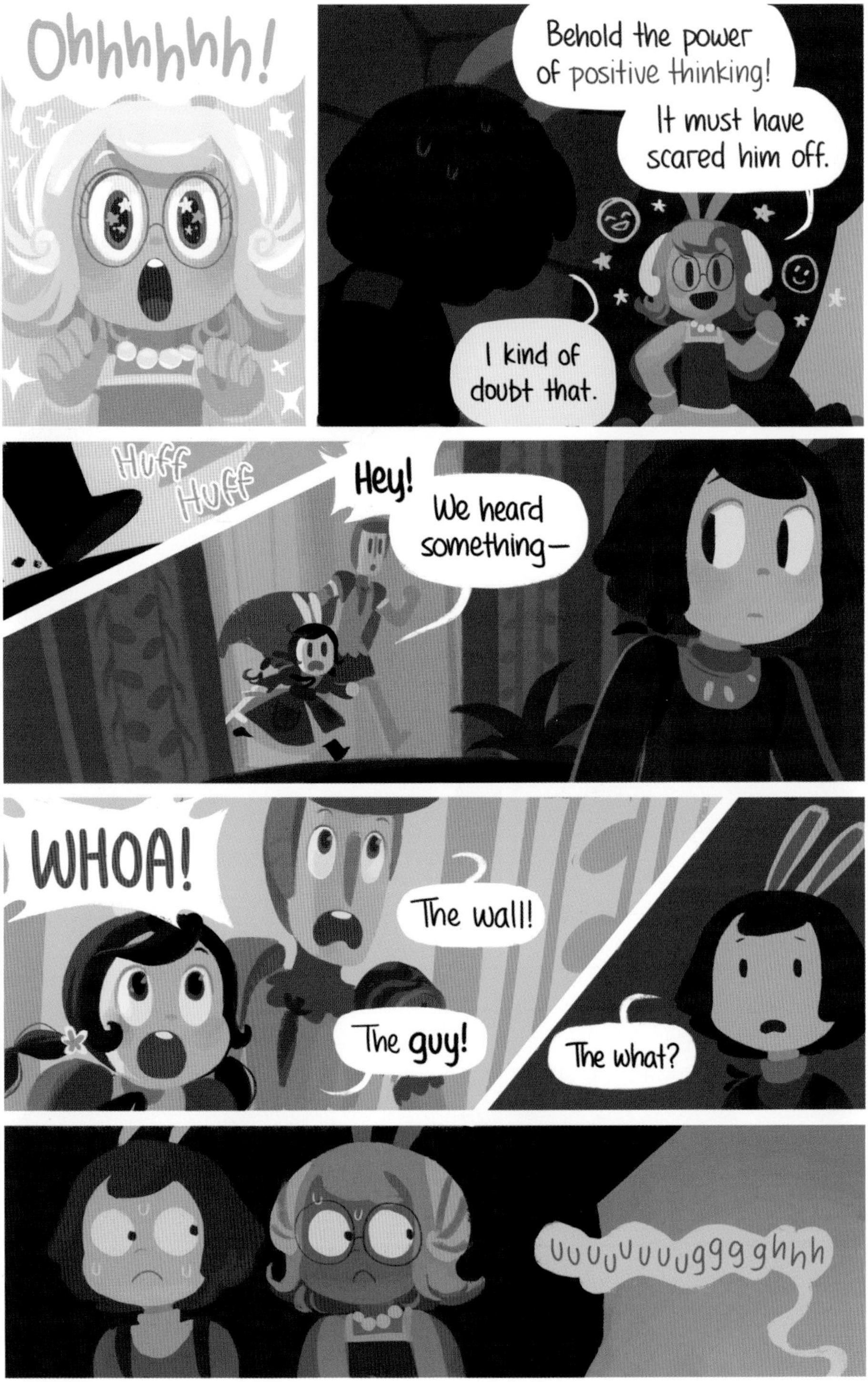
Ohhhhhh!
Behold the power of positive thinking!
It must have scared him off.
I kind of doubt that.
Huff Huff
Hey!
We heard something—
WHOA!
The wall!
The guy!
The what?
UUUUUUUggghhh

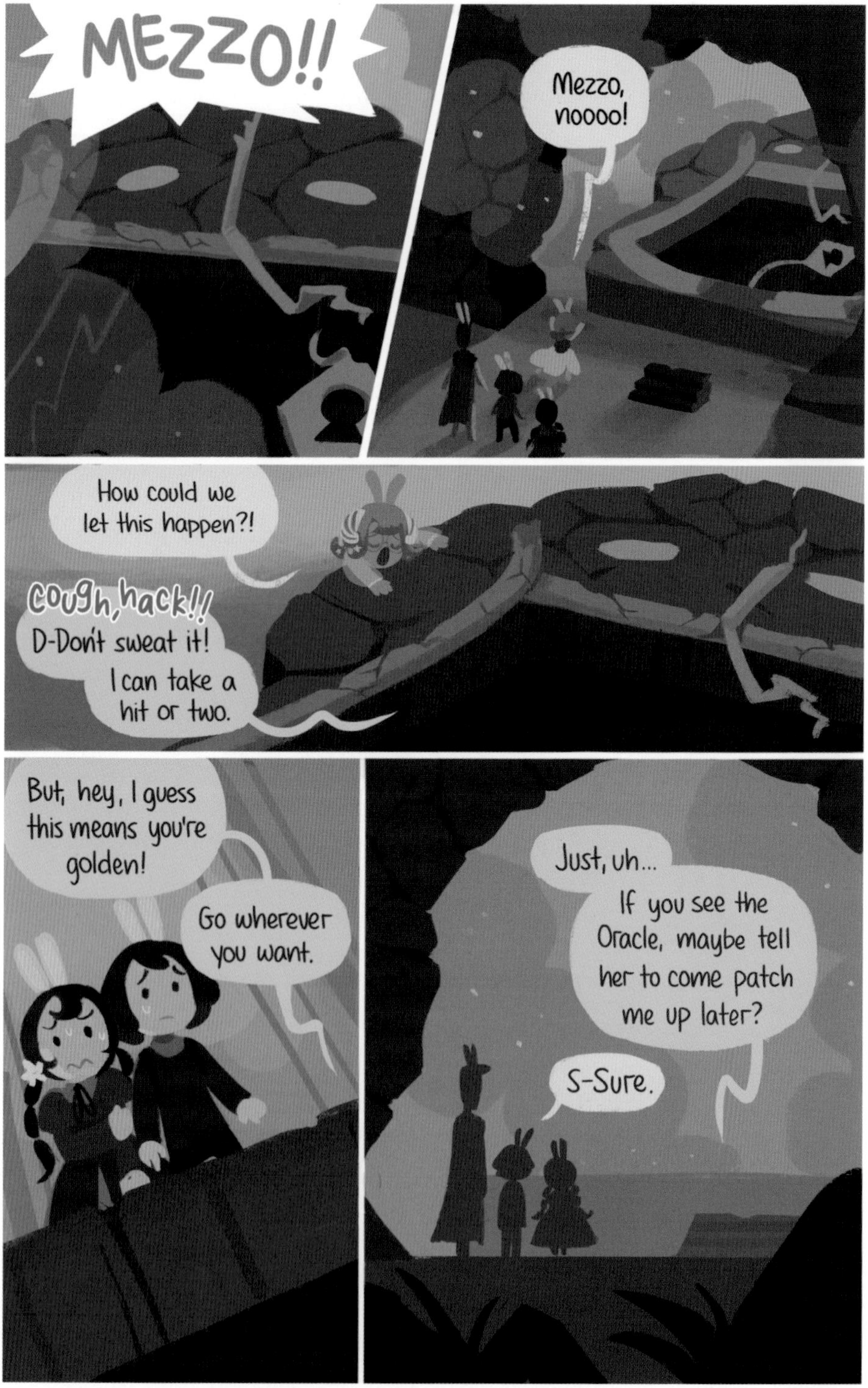
MEZZO!!
Mezzo, noooo!
How could we let this happen?!
cough, hack!!
D-Don't sweat it!
I can take a hit or two.
But, hey, I guess this means you're golden!
Go wherever you want.
Just, uh...
If you see the Oracle, maybe tell her to come patch me up later?
S-Sure.

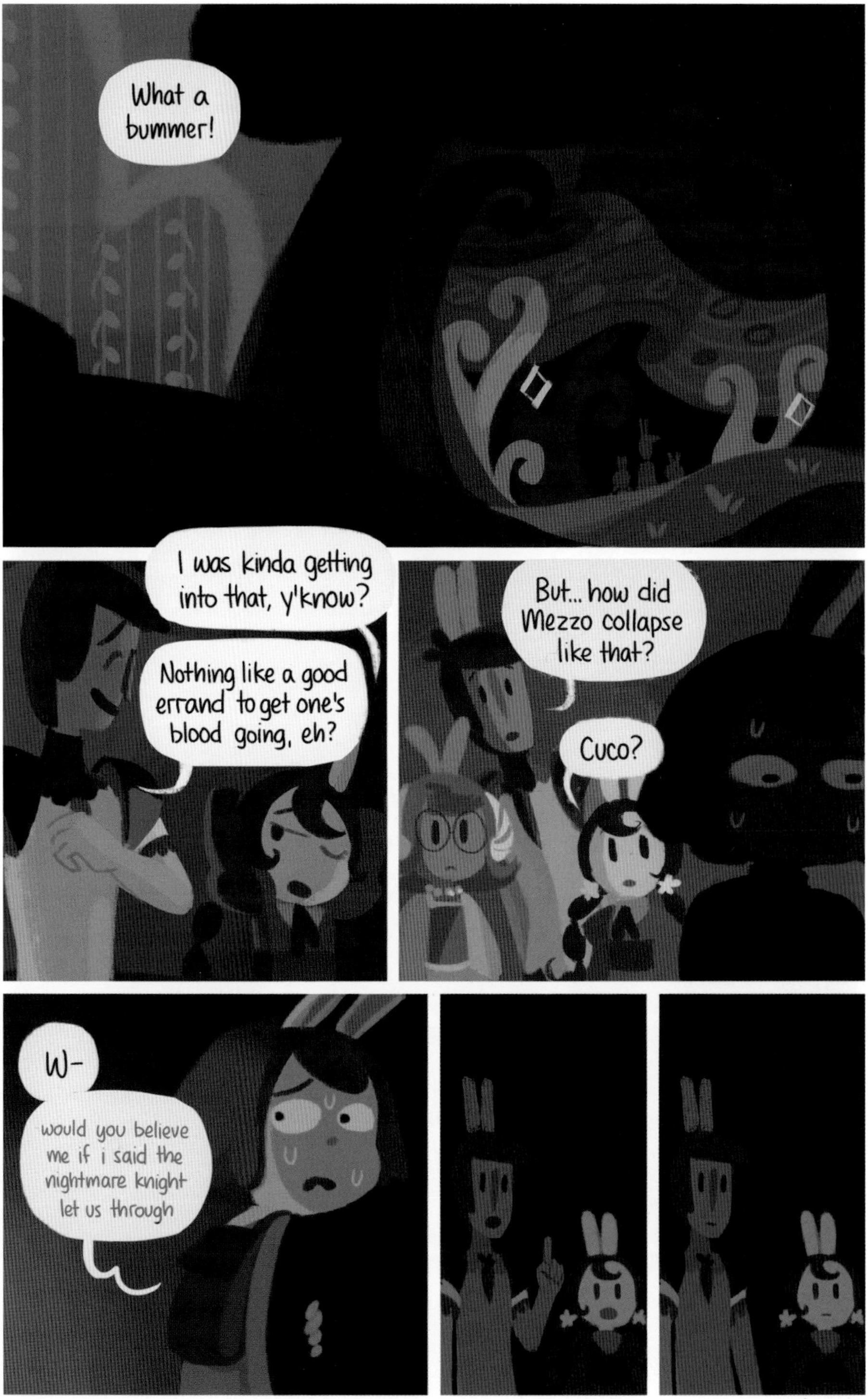
What a bummer!
I was kinda getting into that, y'know?
Nothing like a good errand to get one's blood going, eh?
But... how did Mezzo collapse like that?
Cuco?
W-
would you believe me if i said the nightmare knight let us through

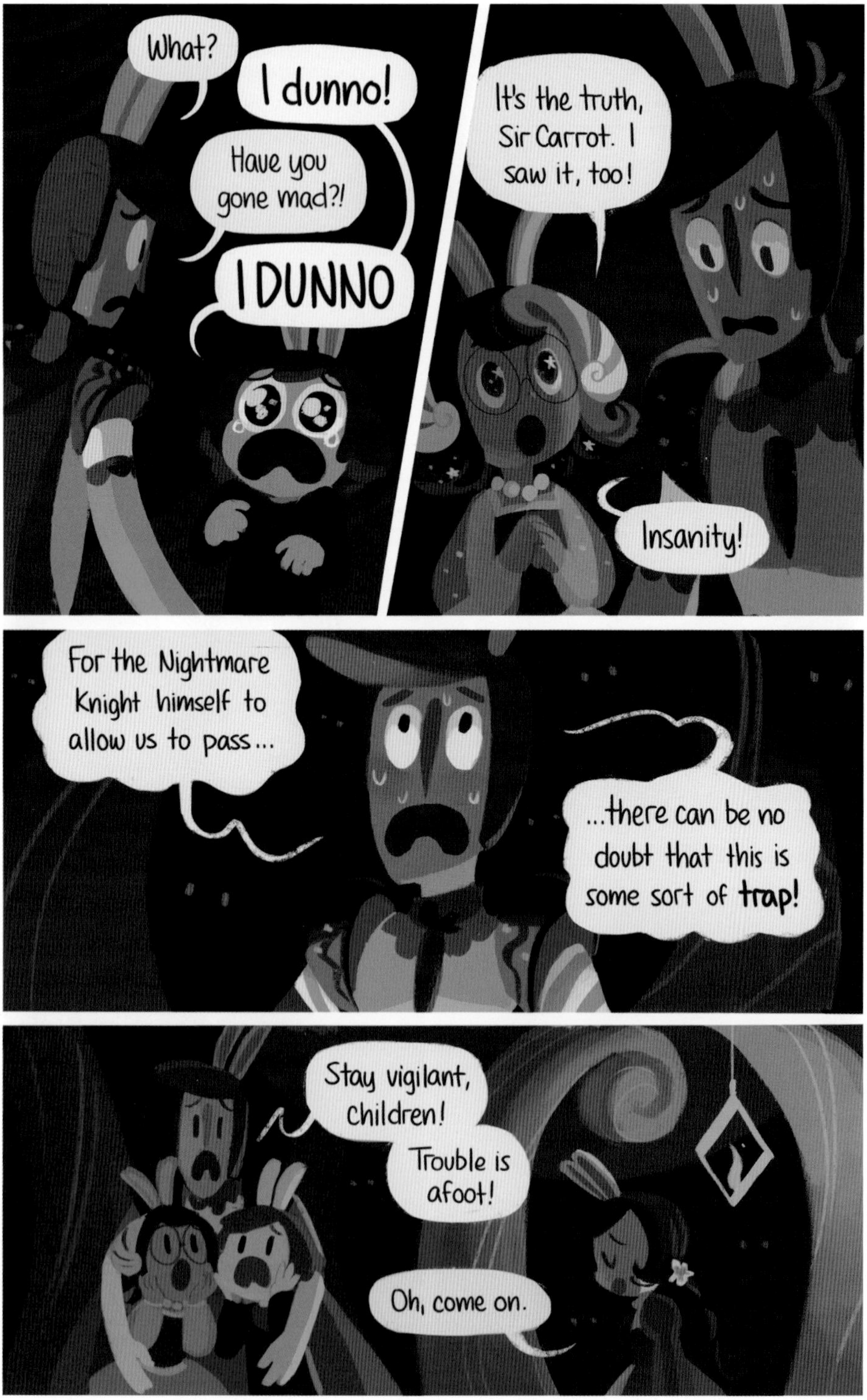
What?
I dunno!
Have you gone mad?!
I DUNNO
It's the truth, Sir Carrot. I saw it, too!
Insanity!
For the Nightmare Knight himself to allow us to pass...
...there can be no doubt that this is some sort of **trap!**
Stay vigilant, children!
Trouble is afoot!
Oh, come on.

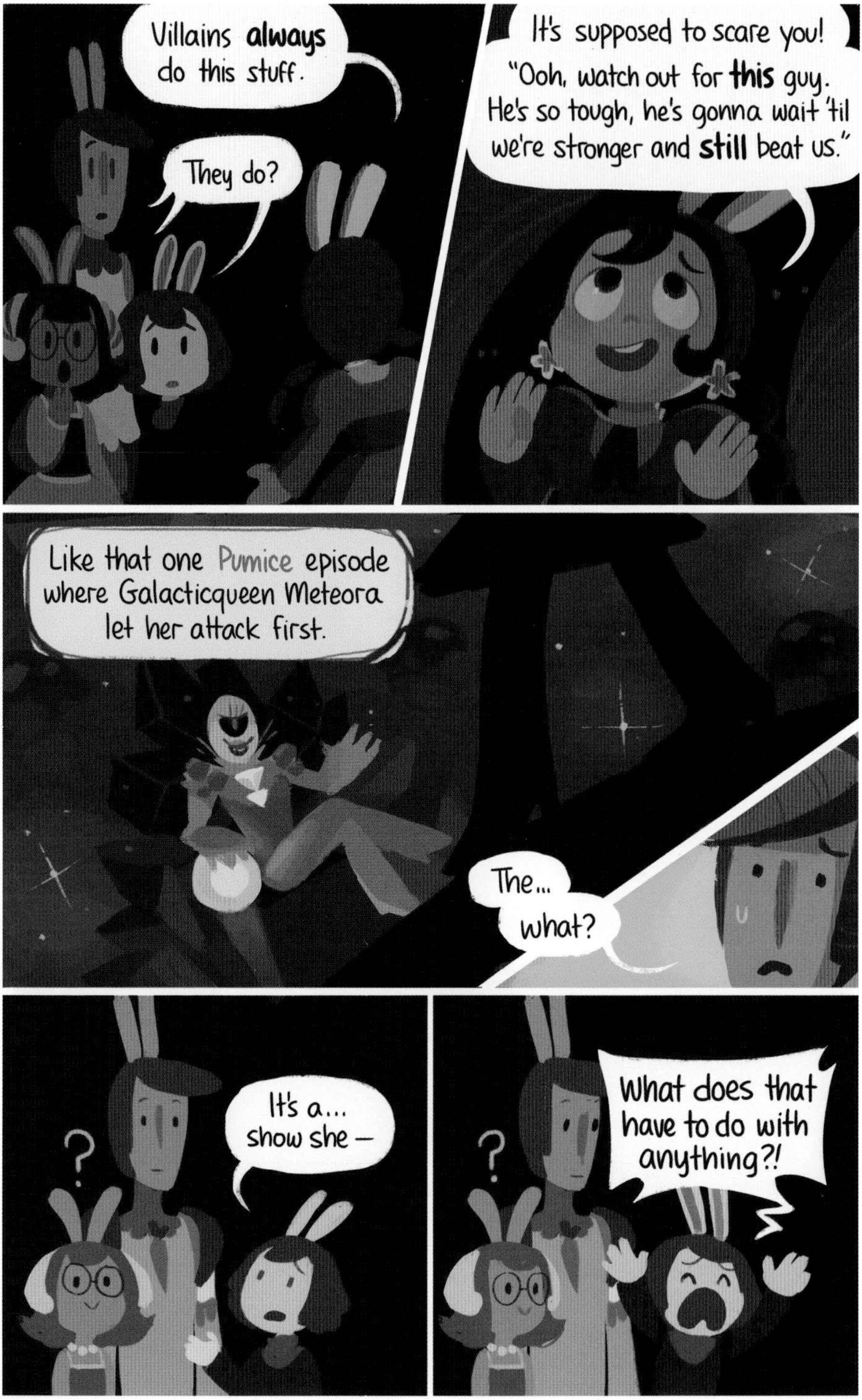

Villains **always** do this stuff.
They do?
It's supposed to scare you!
"Ooh, watch out for **this** guy. He's so tough, he's gonna wait 'til we're stronger and **still** beat us."
Like that one Pumice episode where Galacticqueen Meteora let her attack first.
The... what?
?
It's a... show she—
?
What does that have to do with anything?!

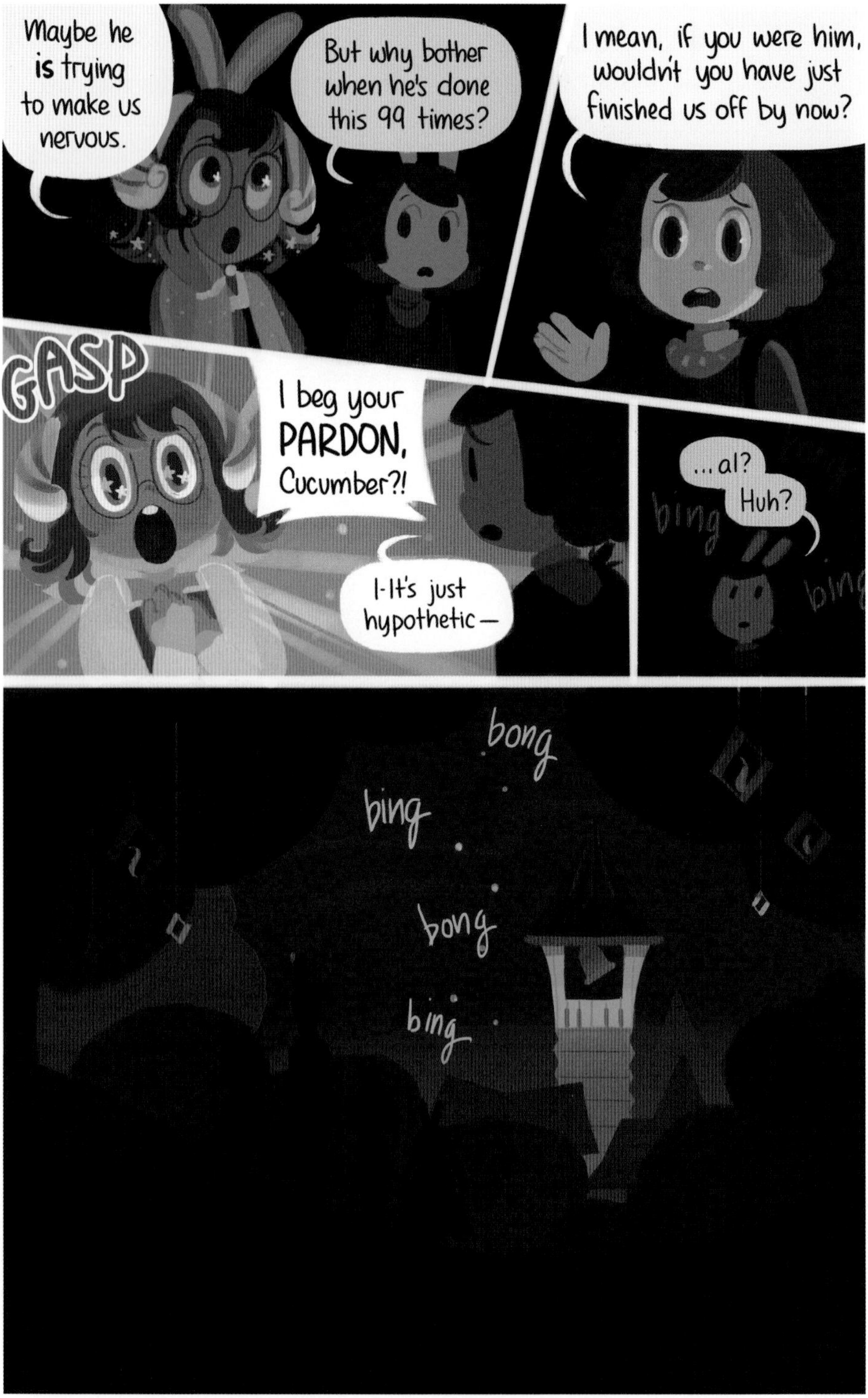

Maybe he **is** trying to make us nervous.
But why bother when he's done this 99 times?
I mean, if you were him, wouldn't you have just finished us off by now?
GASP
I beg your PARDON, Cucumber?!
I-It's just hypothetic—
bing
...al? Huh?
bing
bong
bing
bong
bing

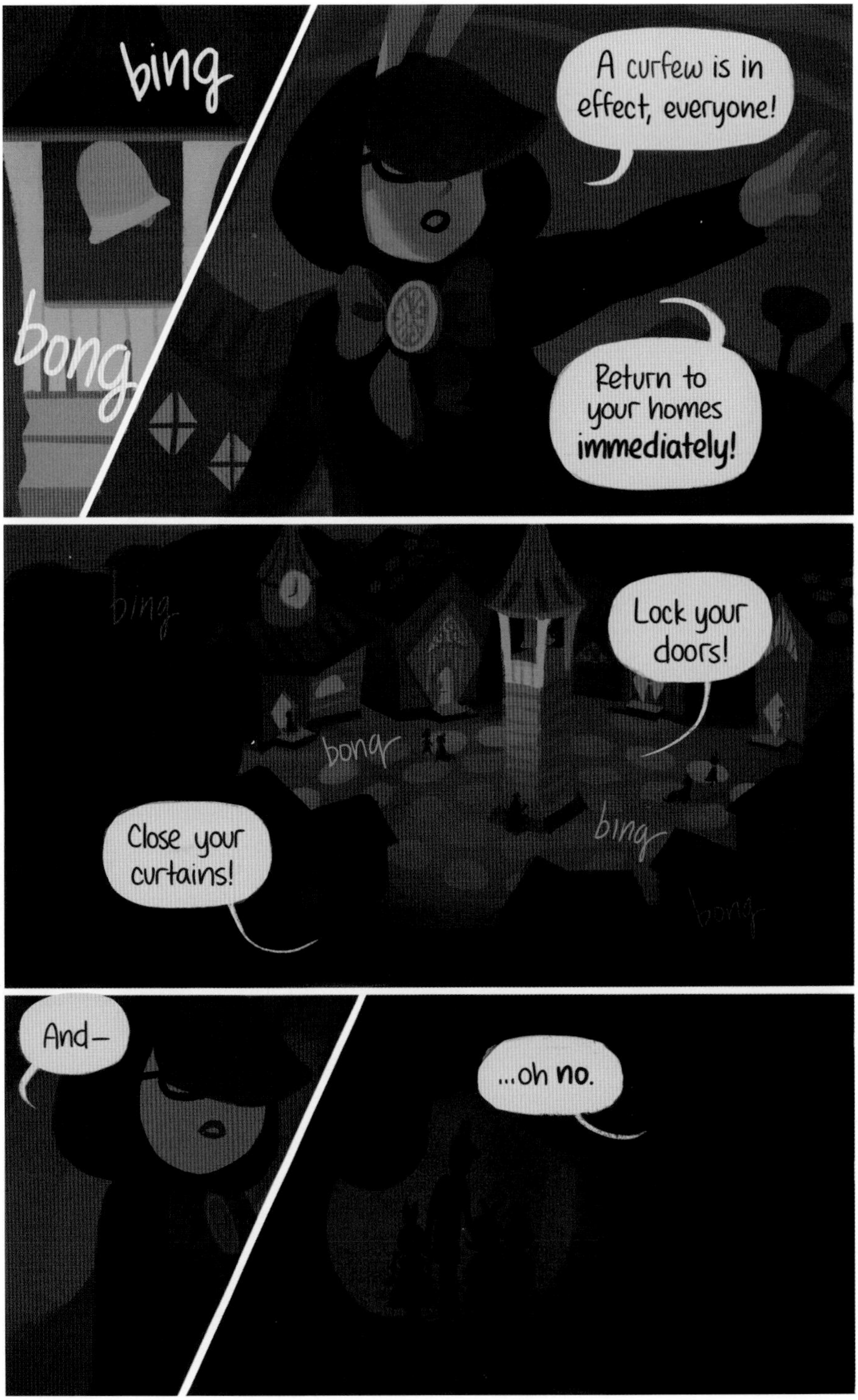
bing
bong
A curfew is in effect, everyone!
Return to your homes immediately!
bing
bong
Lock your doors!
bing
bong
Close your curtains!
And–
...oh no.

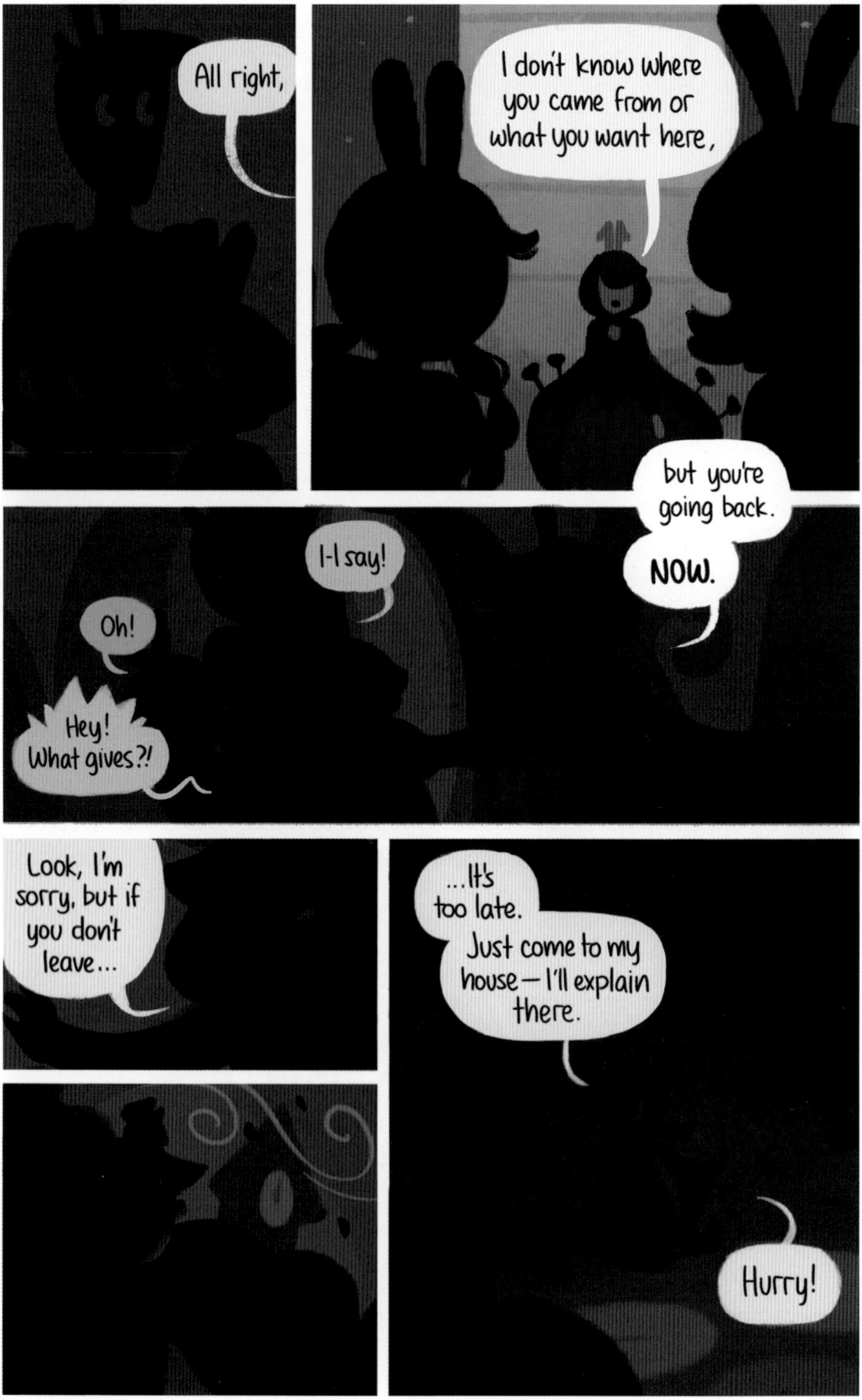
All right,
I don't know where you came from or what you want here,
but you're going back.
NOW.
I-I say!
Oh!
Hey! What gives?!
Look, I'm sorry, but if you don't leave...
...It's too late.
Just come to my house—I'll explain there.
Hurry!

Creeeeak

Do you all know where you are?

Now.

Er... not precisely.

Is Rhythm Ridge nearby? Because that's where we—

It'll have to wait.

This is Organetto, and I'm Lute, the mayor.

We've got a problem on our hands, and until it's dealt with, I can't let you out after curfew.

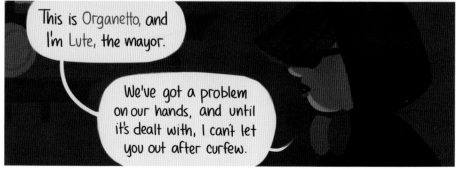

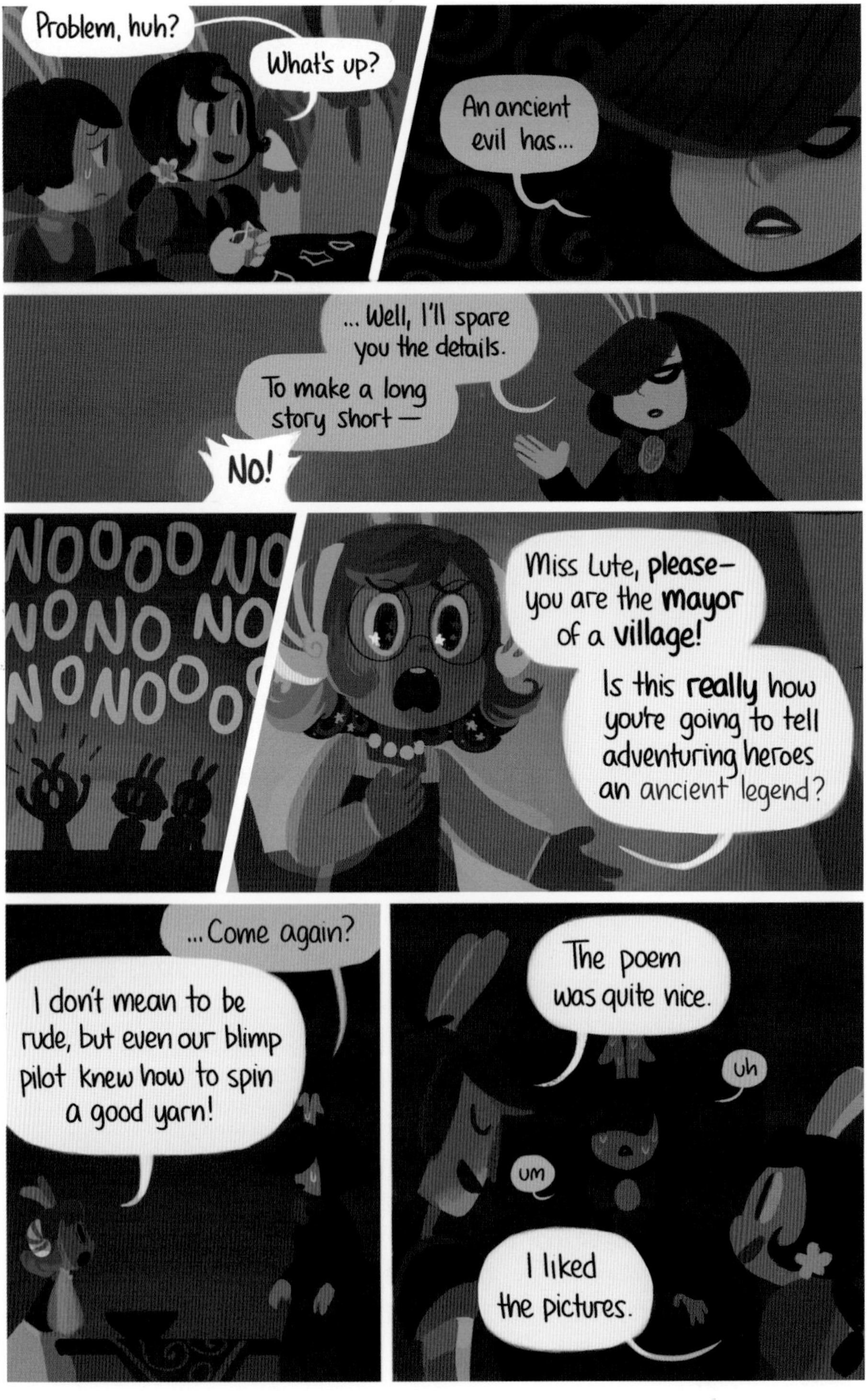
Problem, huh?
What's up?
An ancient evil has...
...Well, I'll spare you the details.
To make a long story short—
No!
NOOOO NO NONO NO NONOOOO
Miss Lute, **please**— you are the **mayor** of a **village**!
Is this **really** how you're going to tell adventuring heroes an ancient legend?
...Come again?
I don't mean to be rude, but even our blimp pilot knew how to spin a good yarn!
The poem was quite nice.
uh
um
I liked the pictures.

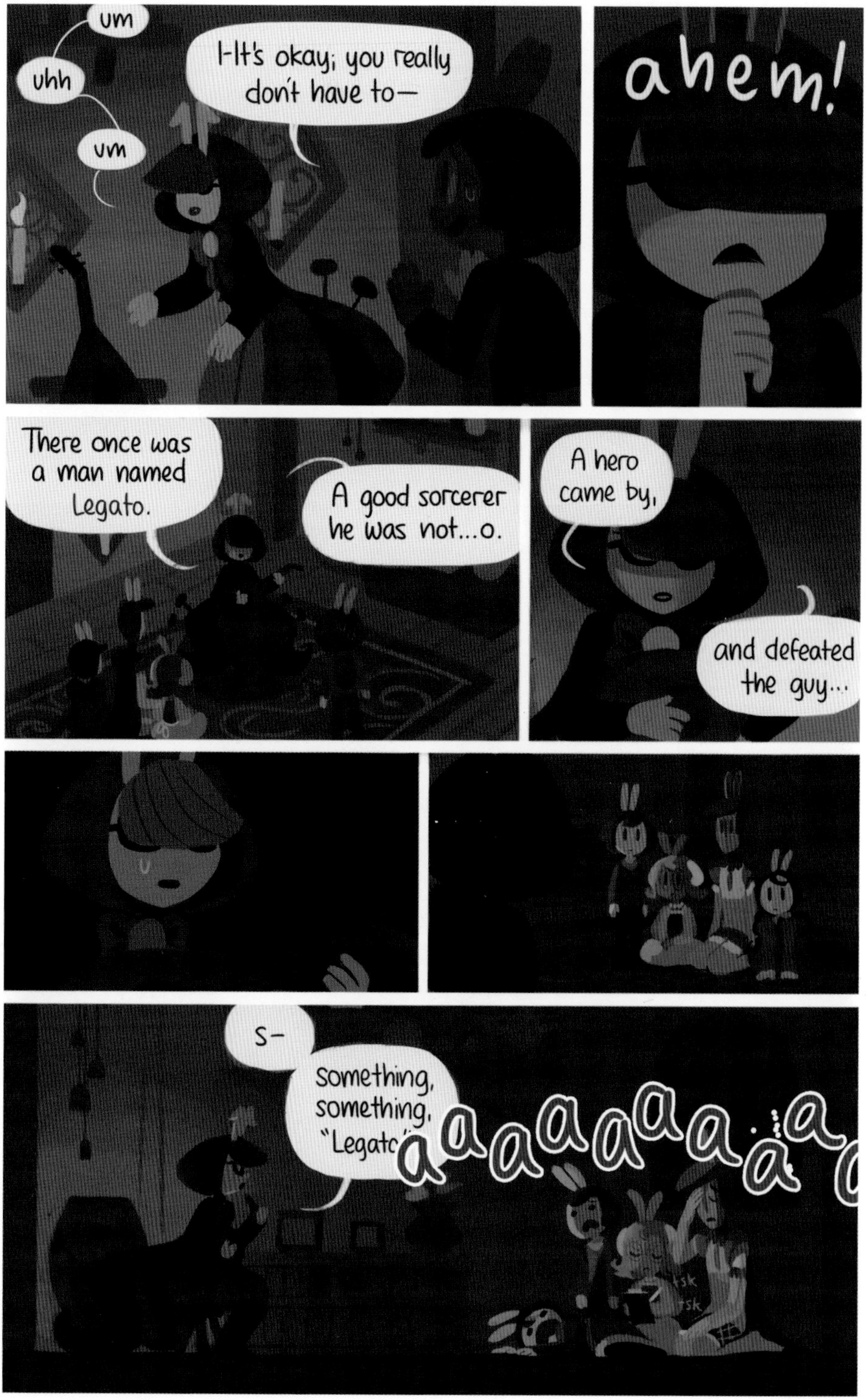
um
uhh
um
I-It's okay; you really don't have to—
ahem!
There once was a man named Legato.
A good sorcerer he was not...o.
A hero came by,
and defeated the guy...
S-
something, something, "Legato"
aaaaaaaaa...a
tsk
tsk

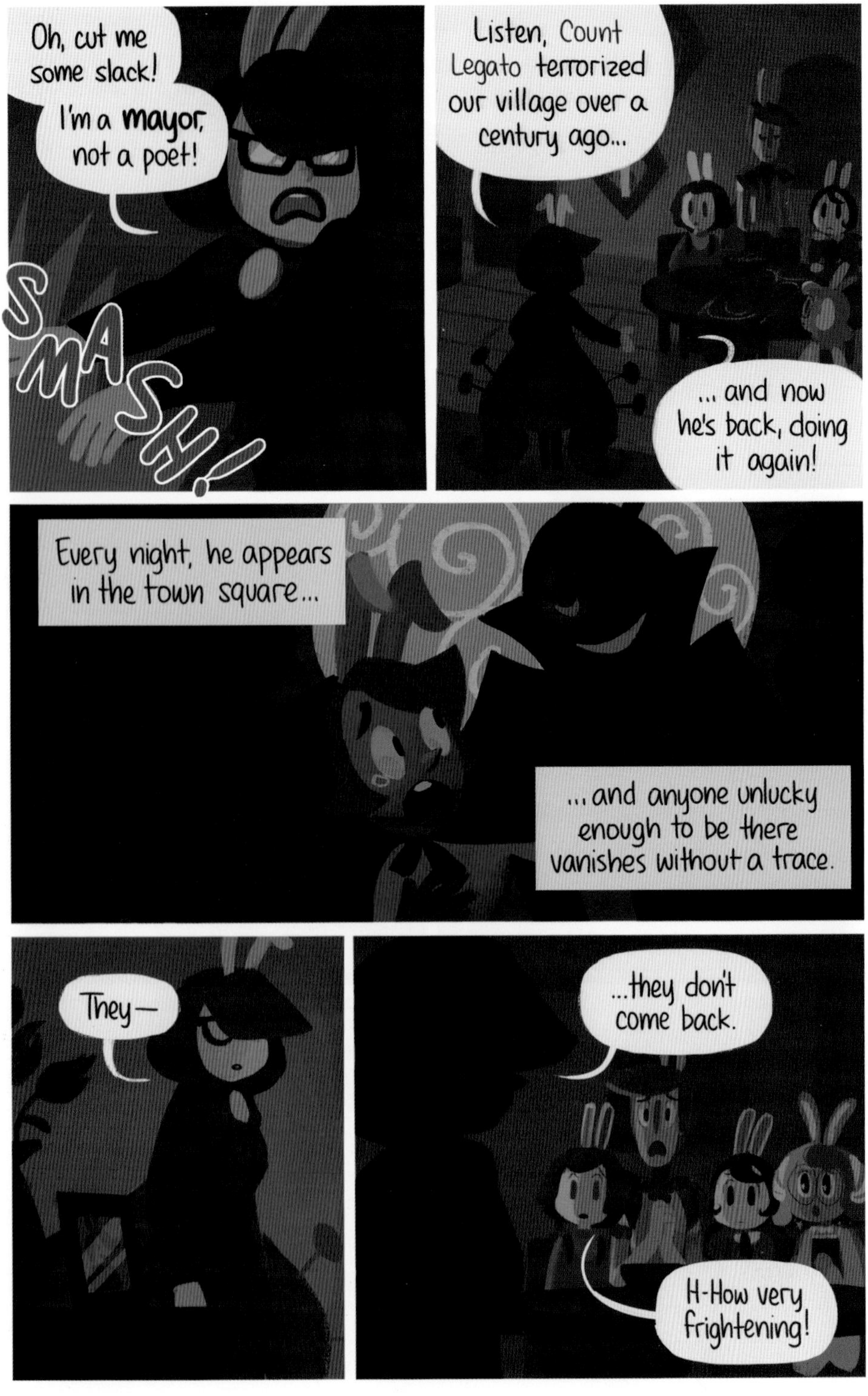
Oh, cut me some slack!
I'm a **mayor**, not a poet!
SMASH!
Listen, Count Legato terrorized our village over a century ago...
... and now he's back, doing it again!
Every night, he appears in the town square...
...and anyone unlucky enough to be there vanishes without a trace.
They—
...they don't come back.
H-How very frightening!

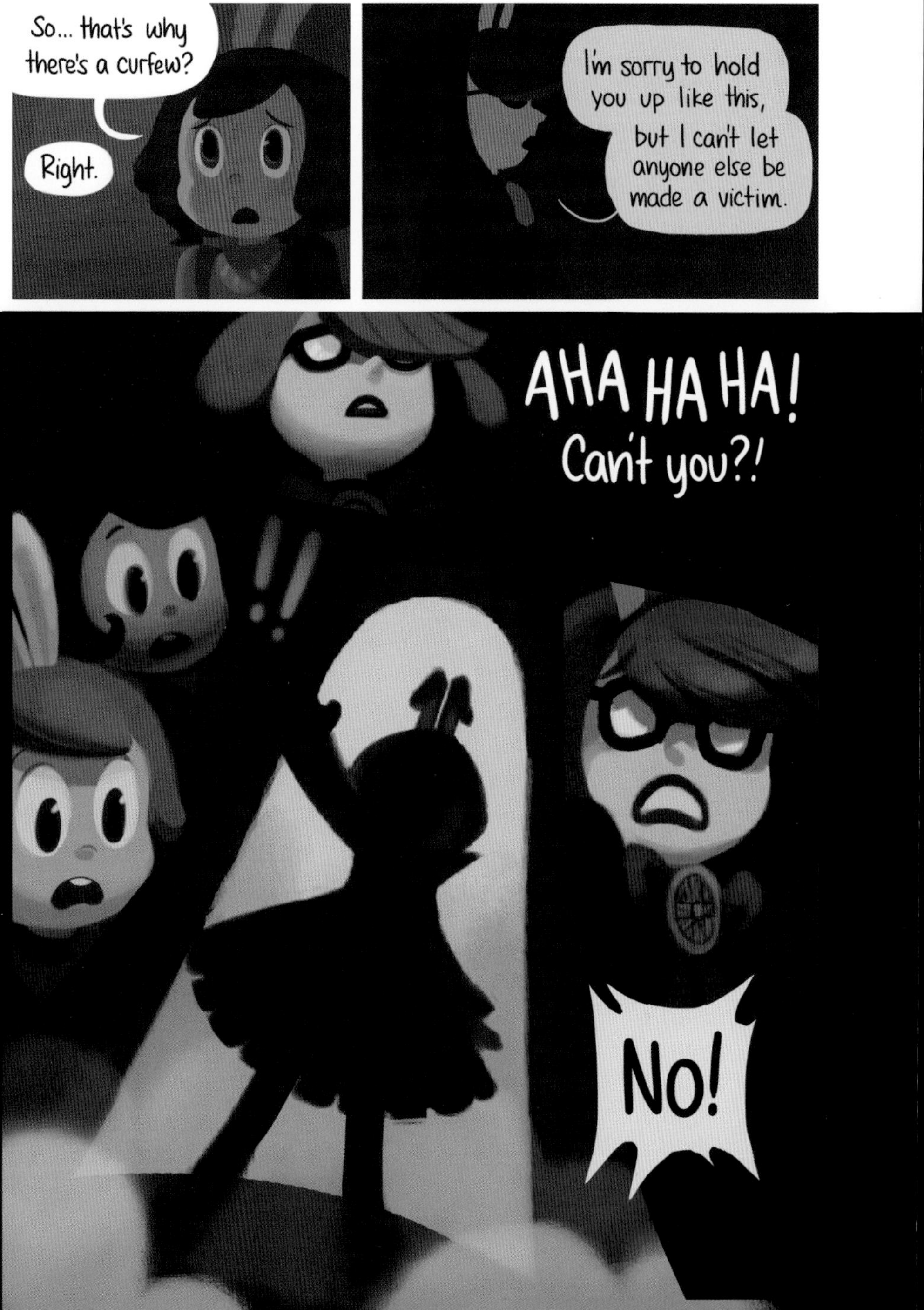
So... that's why there's a curfew?
Right.
I'm sorry to hold you up like this,
but I can't let anyone else be made a victim.
AHA HA HA!
Can't you?!
!!
No!

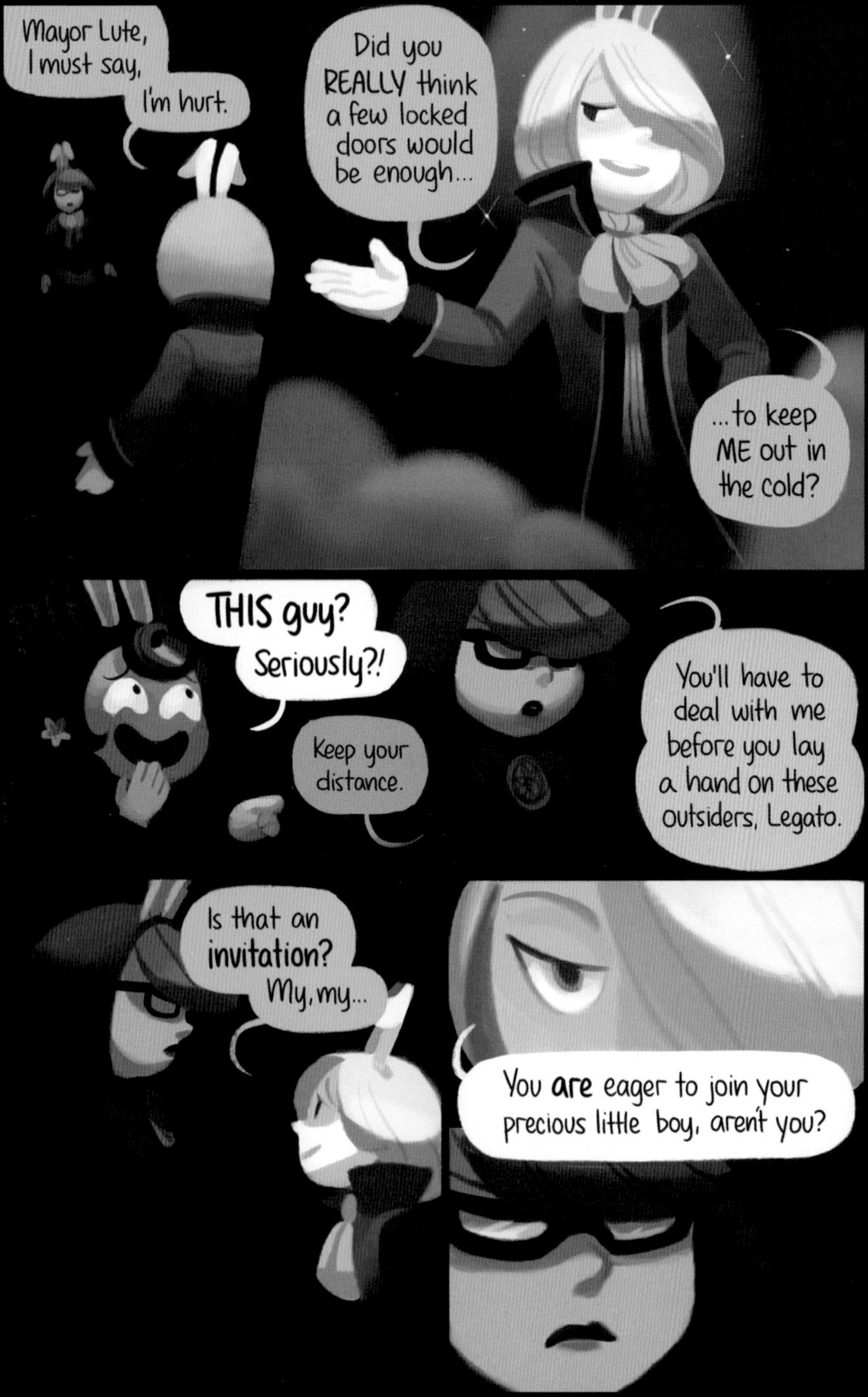
Mayor Lute, I must say, I'm hurt.
Did you REALLY think a few locked doors would be enough...
...to keep ME out in the cold?
THIS guy? Seriously?!
Keep your distance.
You'll have to deal with me before you lay a hand on these outsiders, Legato.
Is that an invitation? My, my...
You **are** eager to join your precious little boy, aren't you?

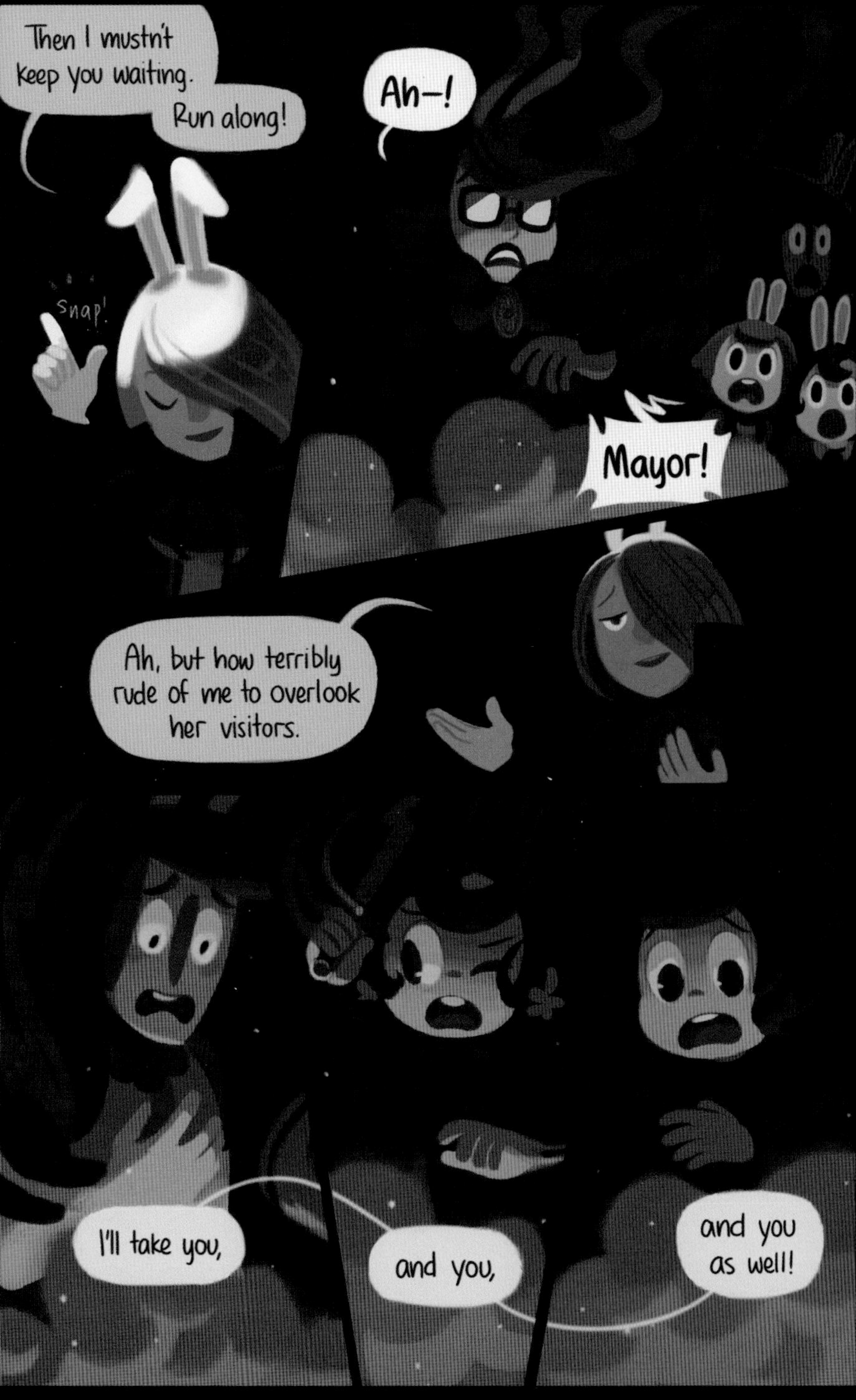
Then I mustn't keep you waiting.
Run along!
Snap!
Ah-!
Mayor!
Ah, but how terribly rude of me to overlook her visitors.
I'll take you,
and you,
and you as well!

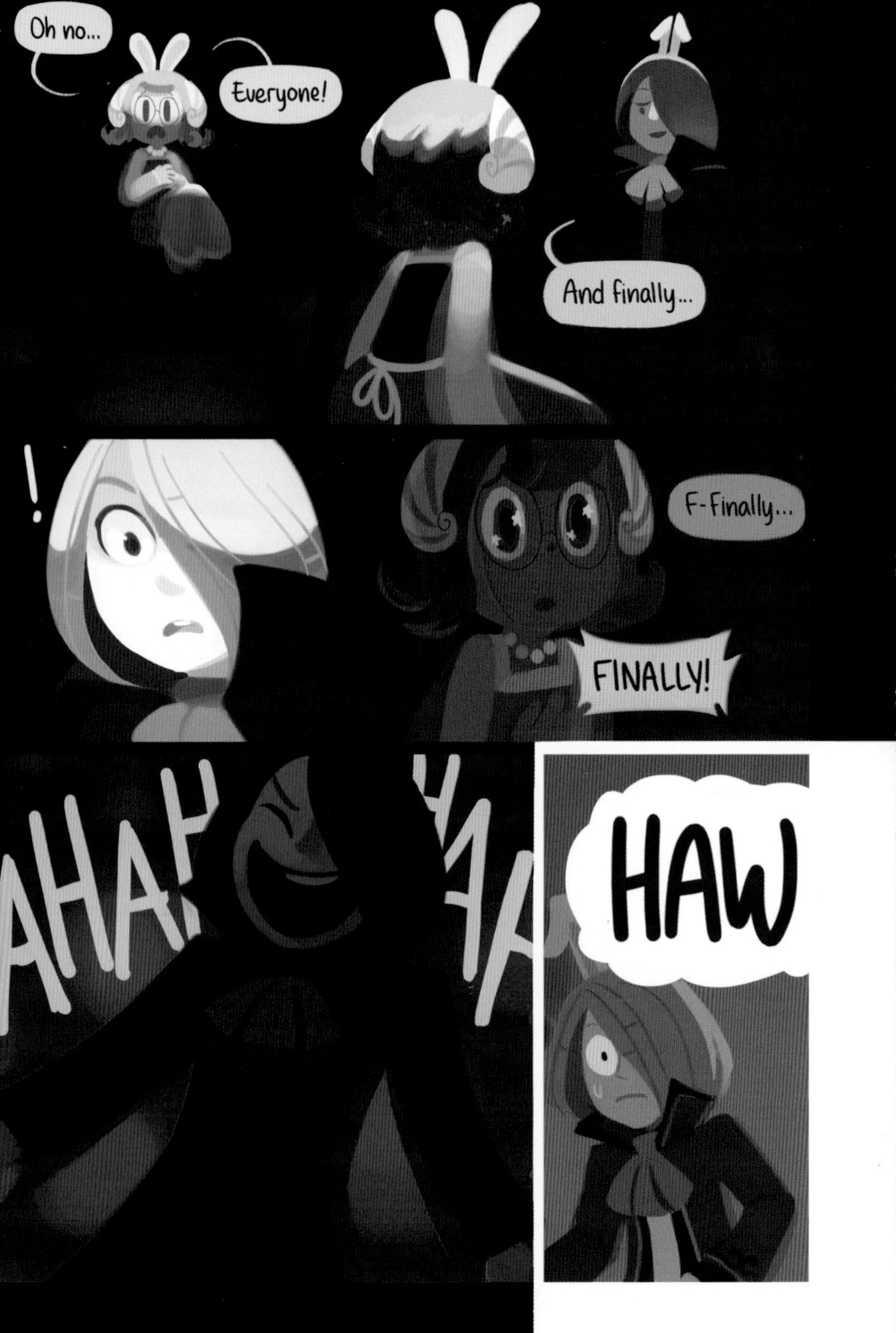
Oh no...
Everyone!
And finally...
!
F-Finally...
FINALLY!
AHAHAHA
HAW

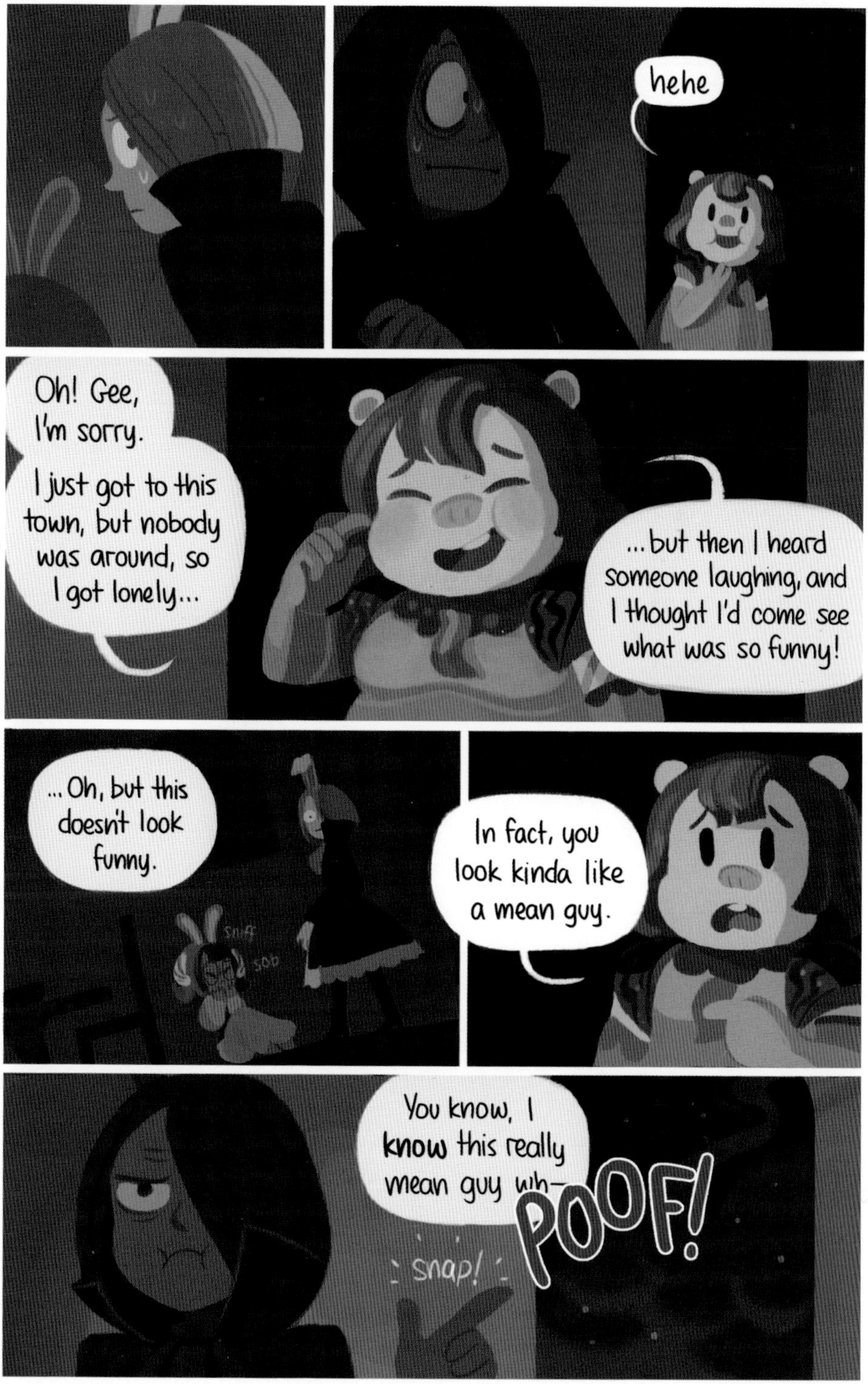
hehe
Oh! Gee, I'm sorry.
I just got to this town, but nobody was around, so I got lonely...
...but then I heard someone laughing, and I thought I'd come see what was so funny!
...Oh, but this doesn't look funny.
sniff
sob
In fact, you look kinda like a mean guy.
You know, I **know** this really mean guy wh—
snap!
POOF!

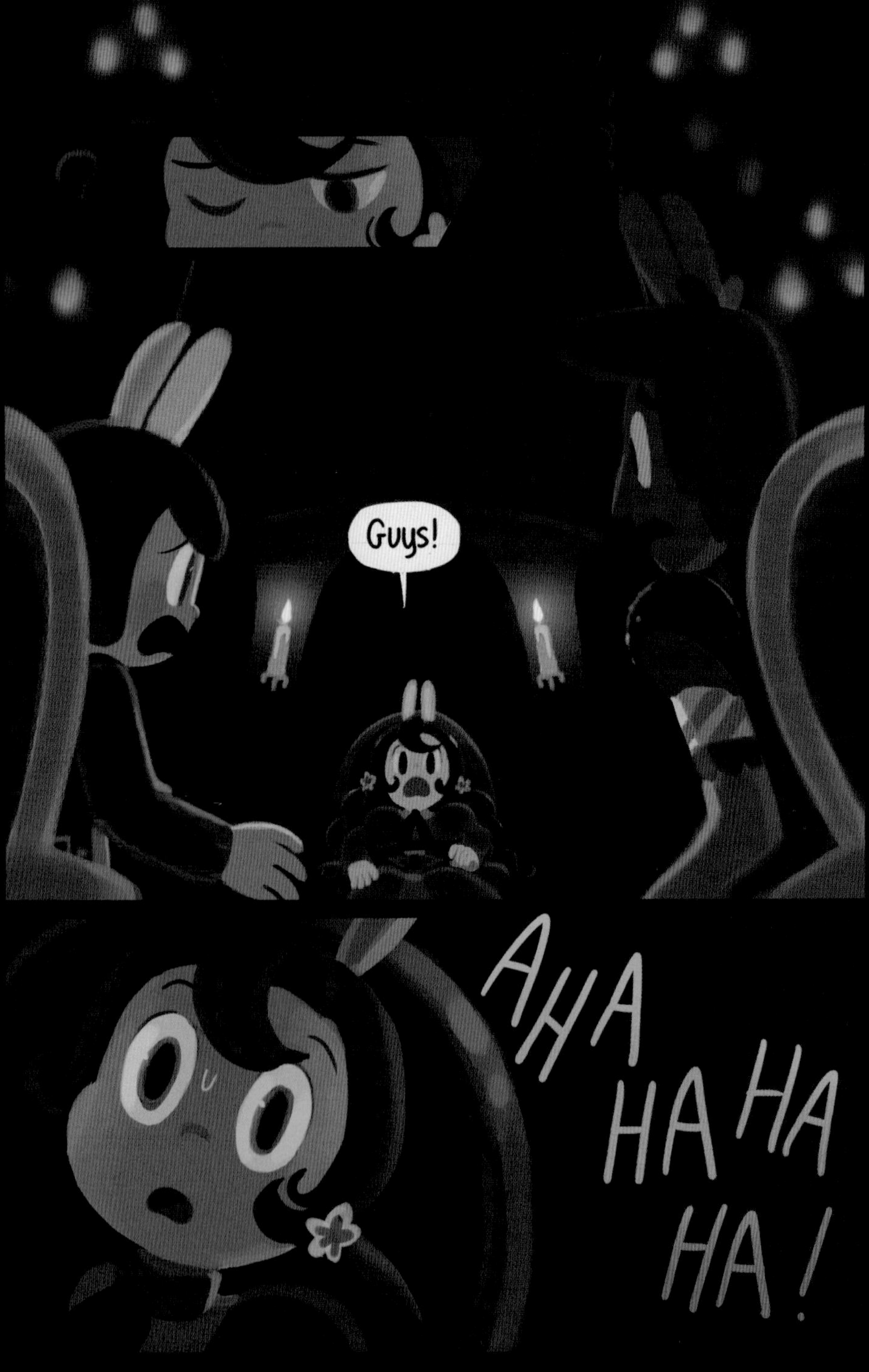
Guys!
AHA HA HA HA HA!

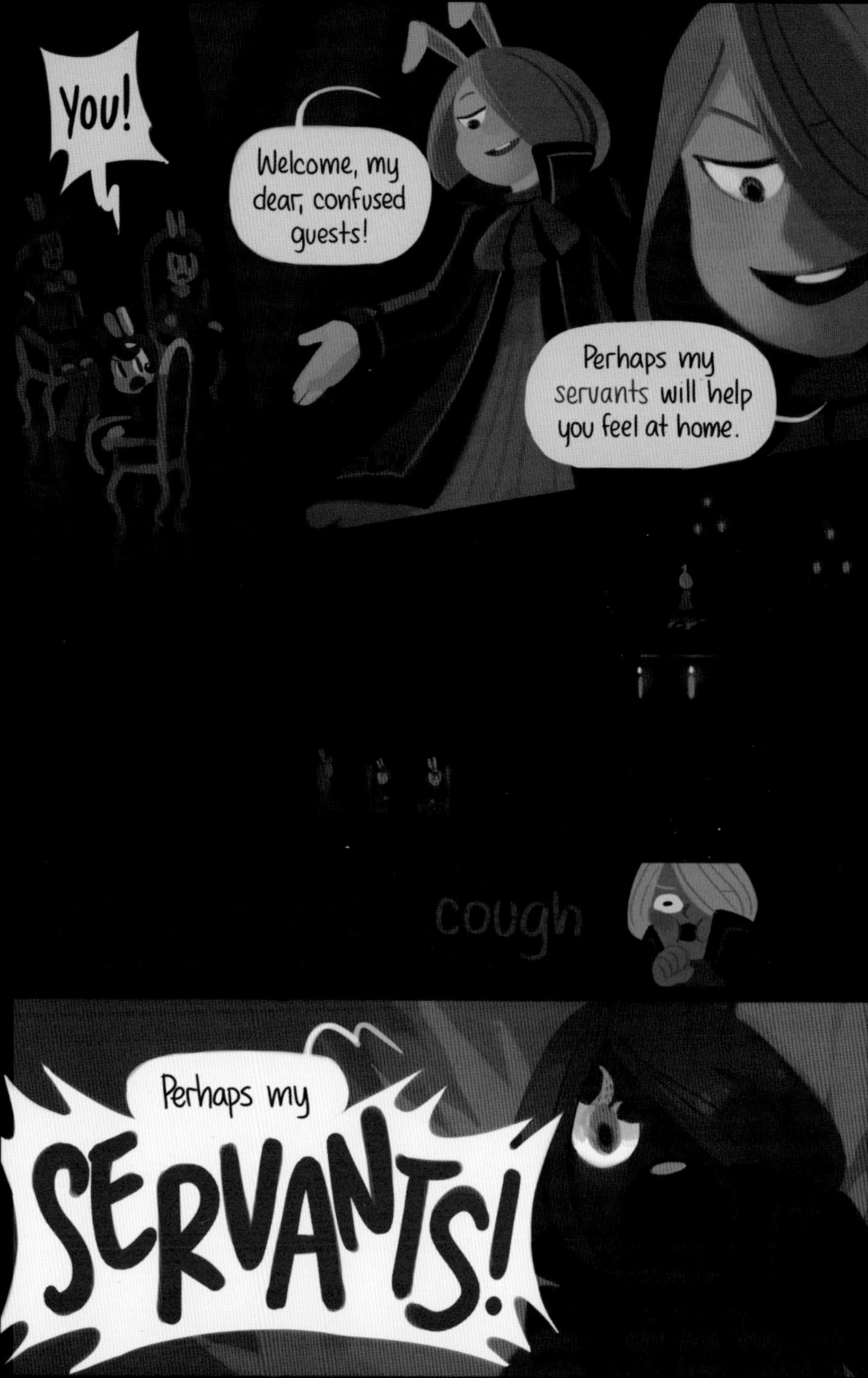
YOU!
Welcome, my dear, confused guests!
Perhaps my servants will help you feel at home.
cough
Perhaps my
SERVANTS!

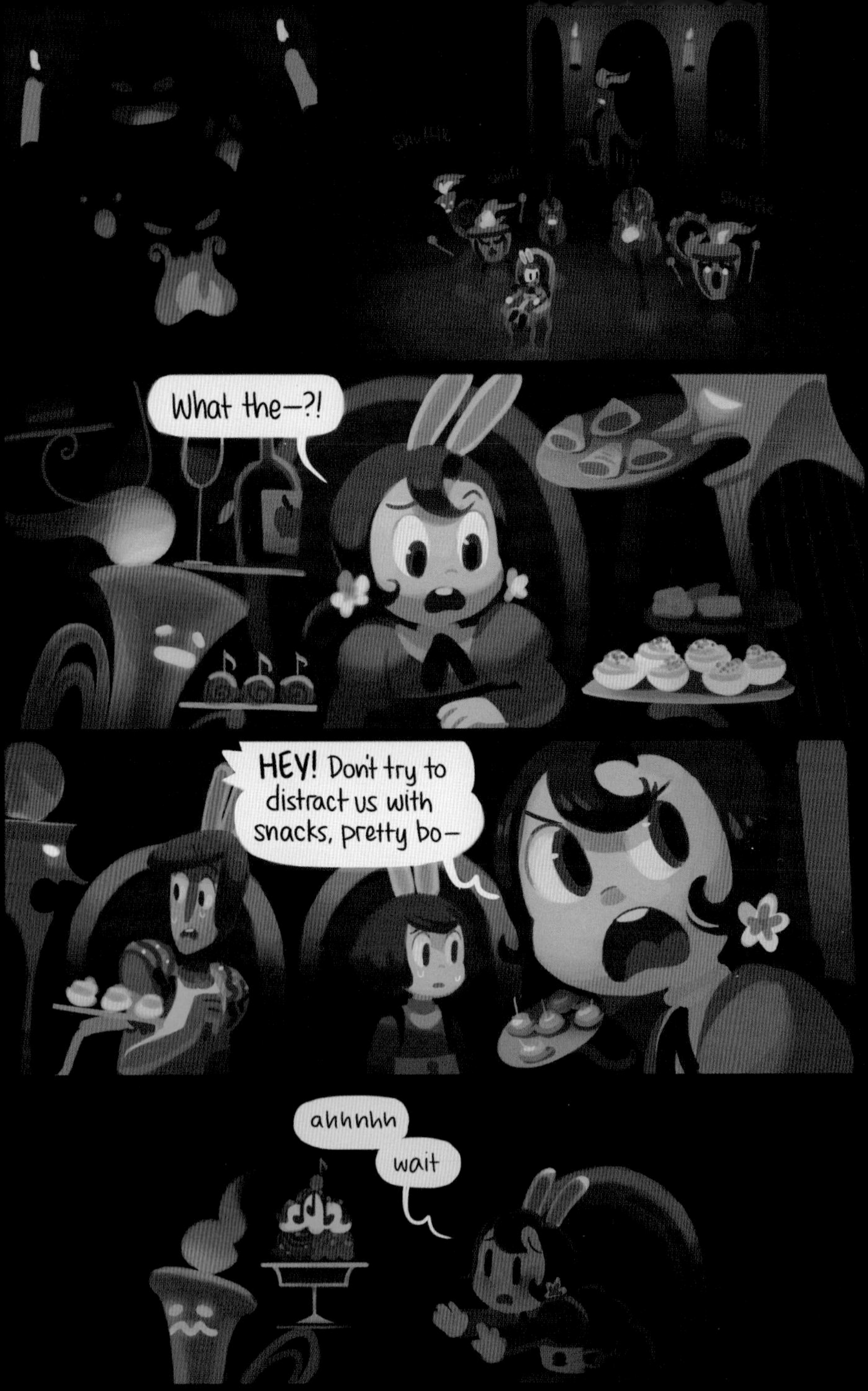
What the—?!
HEY! Don't try to distract us with snacks, pretty bo—
ahhhhh
wait

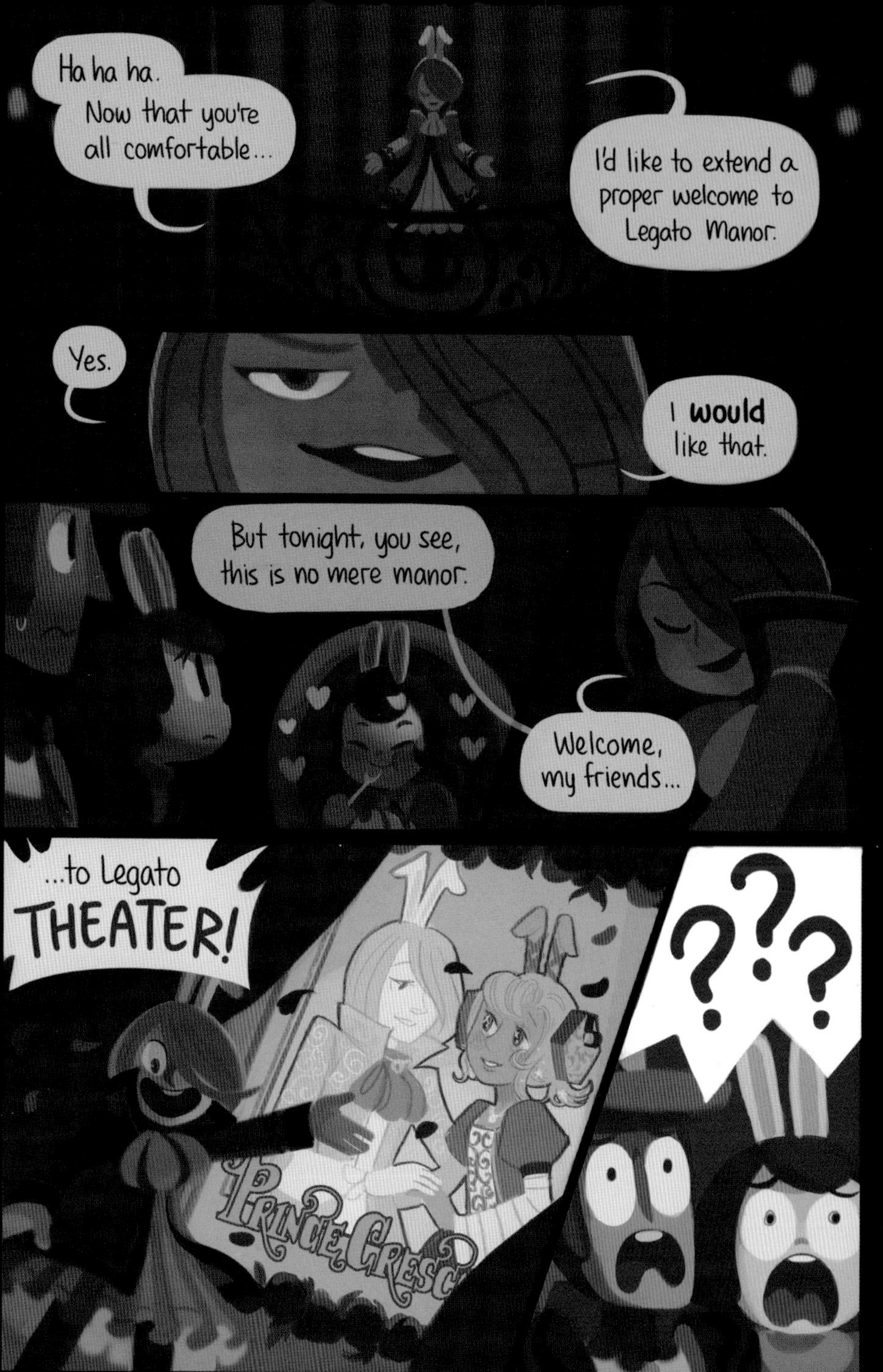
Ha ha ha. Now that you're all comfortable...
I'd like to extend a proper welcome to Legato Manor.
Yes.
I **would** like that.
But tonight, you see, this is no mere manor.
Welcome, my friends...
...to Legato THEATER!
???
PRINCE CRESC

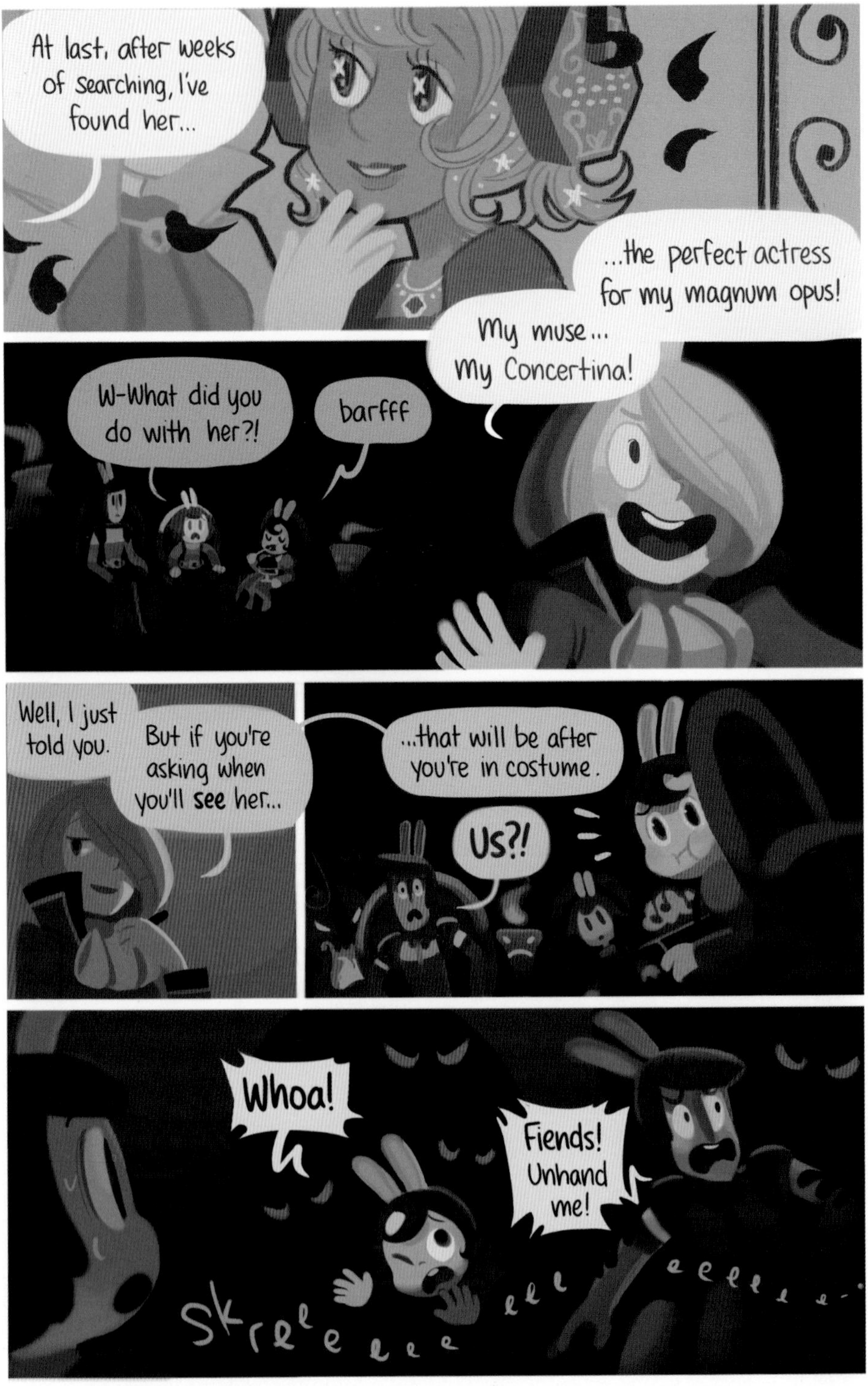

At last, after weeks of searching, I've found her...
...the perfect actress for my magnum opus!
My muse... My Concertina!
W-What did you do with her?!
barfff
Well, I just told you.
But if you're asking when you'll **see** her...
...that will be after you're in costume.
Us?!
Whoa!
Fiends! Unhand me!
Skreeeeeeeeeeeeeeee...

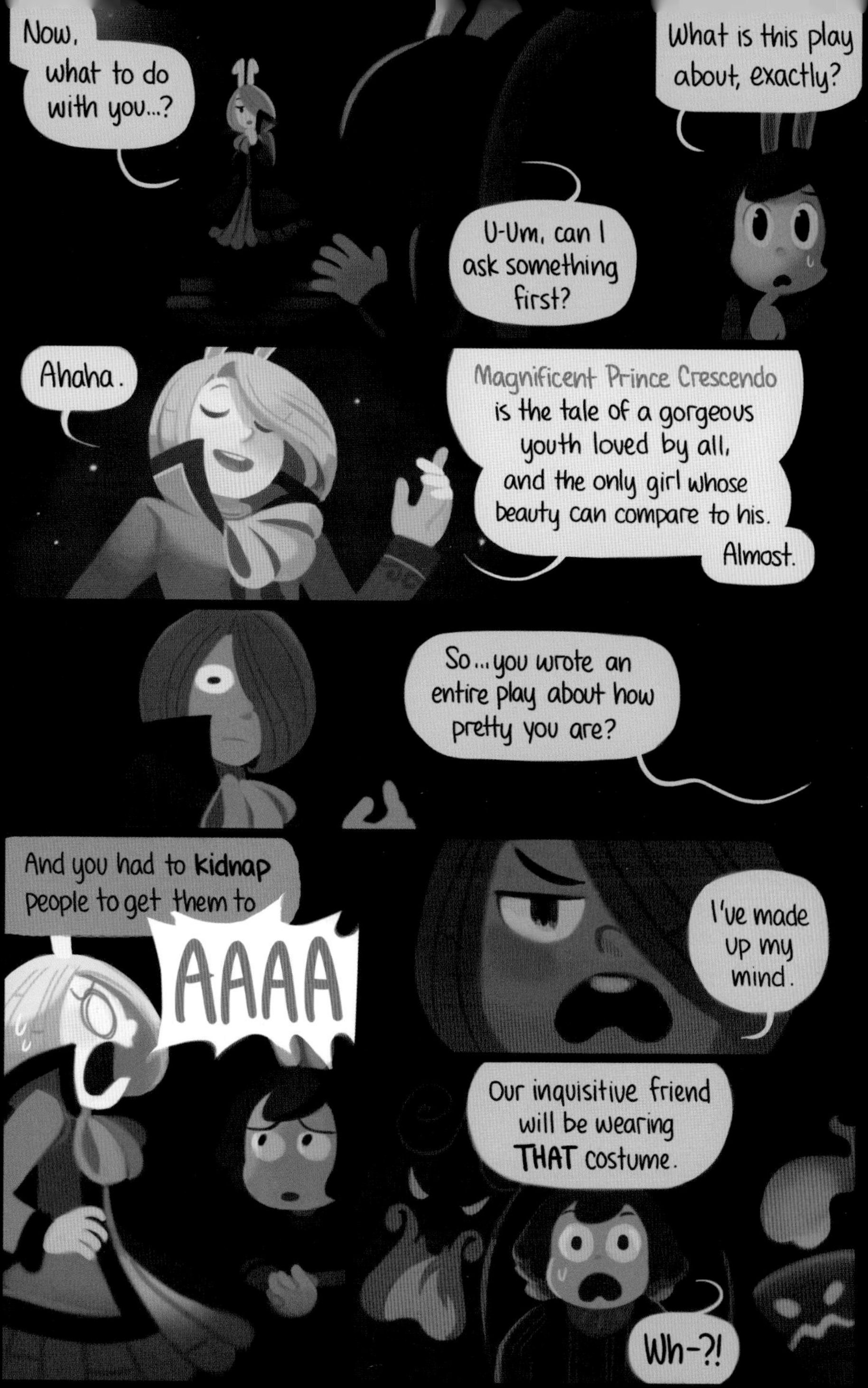
Now, what to do with you...?
What is this play about, exactly?
U-Um, can I ask something first?
Ahaha.
Magnificent Prince Crescendo is the tale of a gorgeous youth loved by all, and the only girl whose beauty can compare to his.
Almost.
So...you wrote an entire play about how pretty you are?
And you had to **kidnap** people to get them to
AAAA
I've made up my mind.
Our inquisitive friend will be wearing **THAT** costume.
Wh-?!

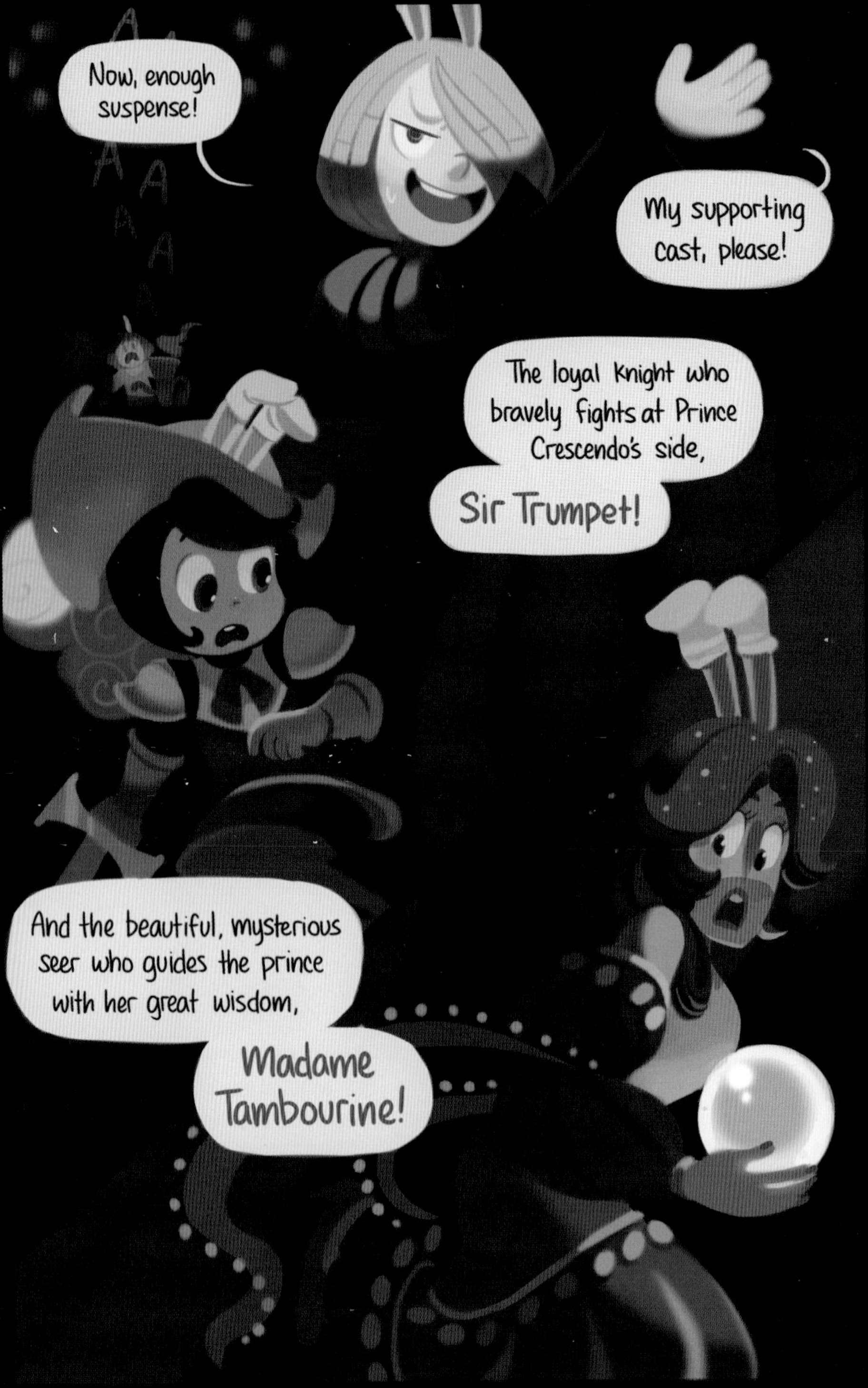
Now, enough suspense!
My supporting cast, please!
The loyal knight who bravely fights at Prince Crescendo's side,
Sir Trumpet!
And the beautiful, mysterious seer who guides the prince with her great wisdom,
Madame Tambourine!

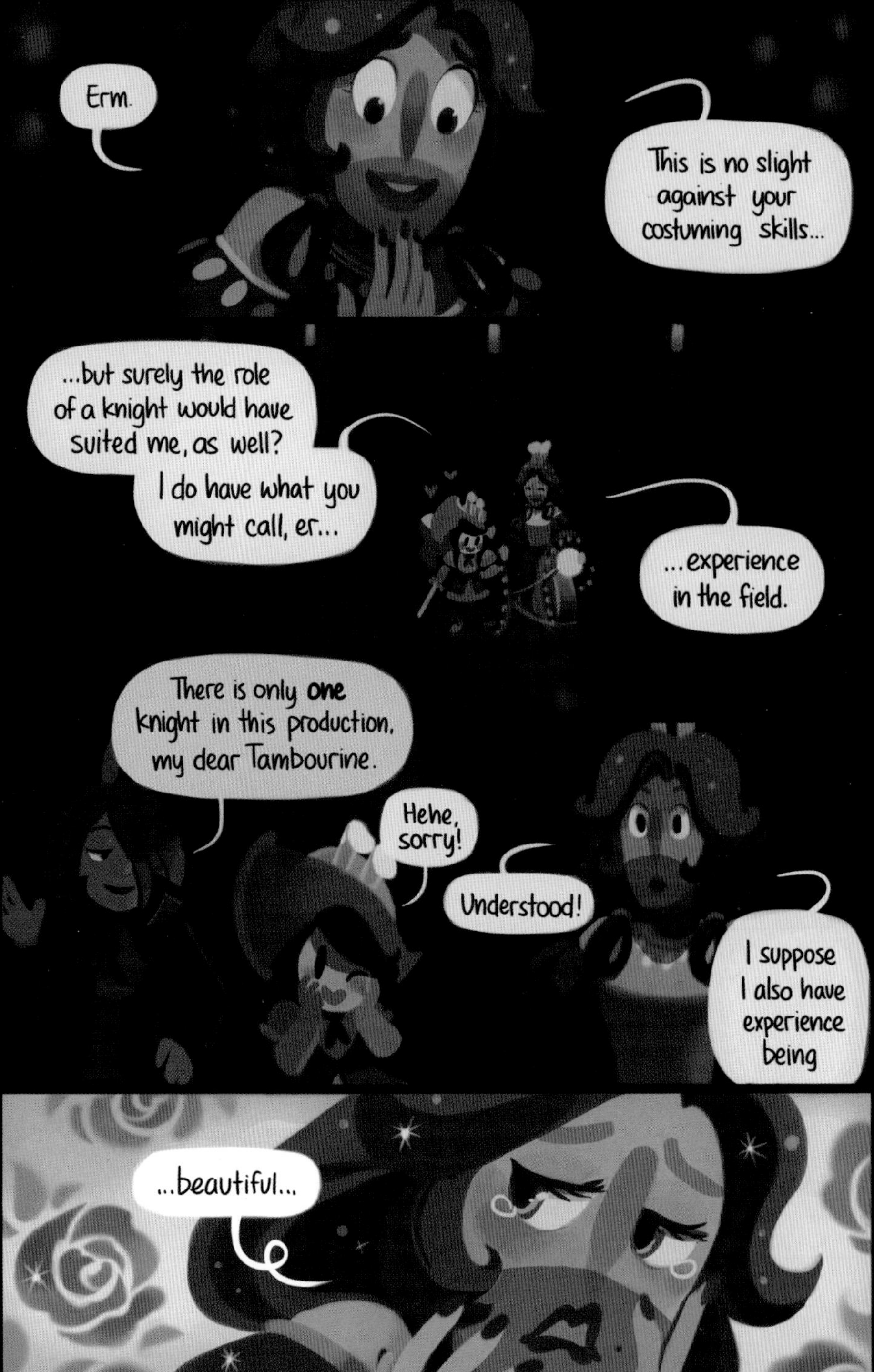

Erm.
This is no slight against your costuming skills...
...but surely the role of a knight would have suited me, as well?
I do have what you might call, er...
...experience in the field.
There is only **one** knight in this production, my dear Tambourine.
Hehe, sorry!
Understood!
I suppose I also have experience being
...beautiful...

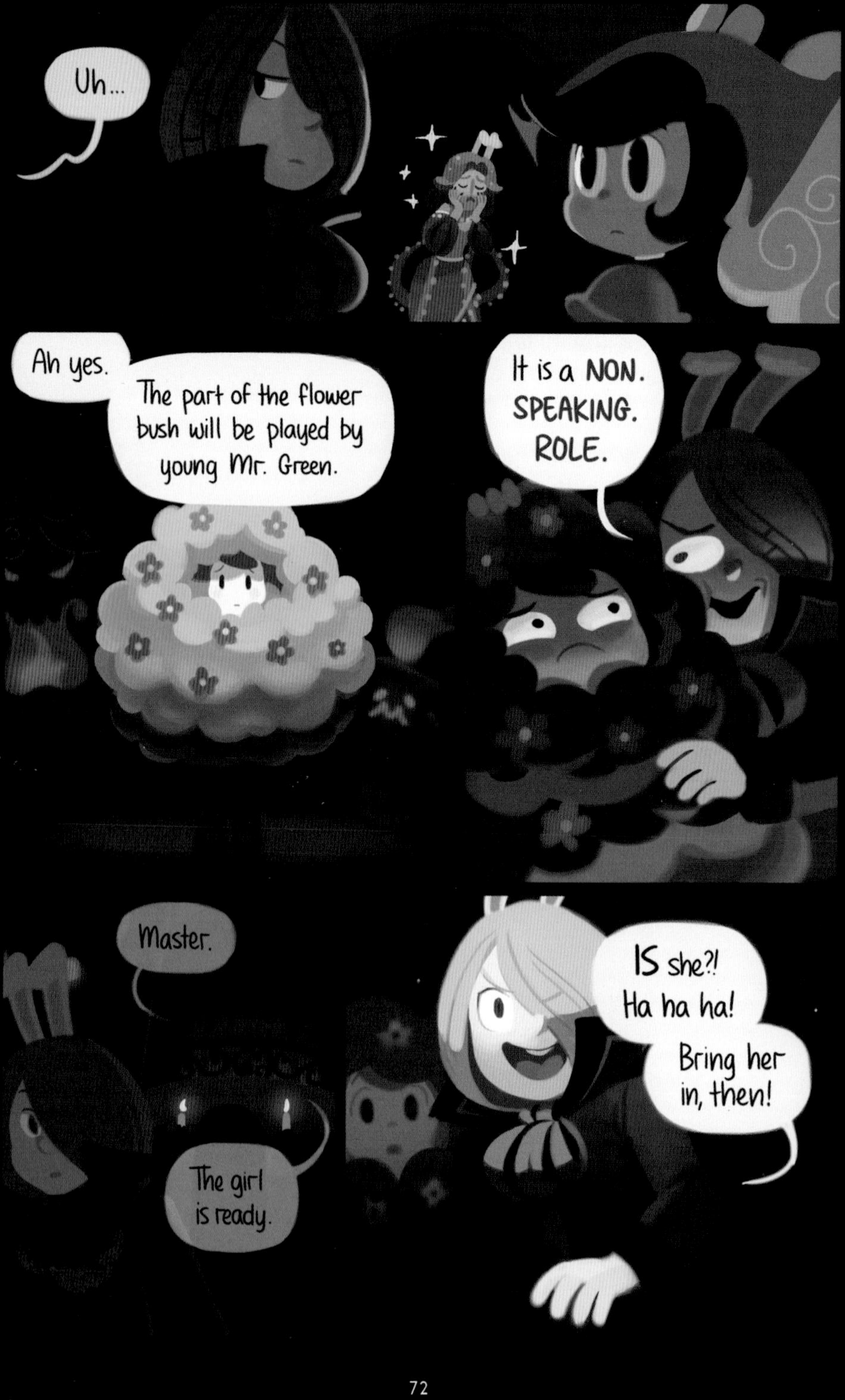
Uh...
Ah yes.
The part of the flower bush will be played by young Mr. Green.
It is a NON. SPEAKING. ROLE.
Master.
The girl is ready.
IS she?! Ha ha ha!
Bring her in, then!

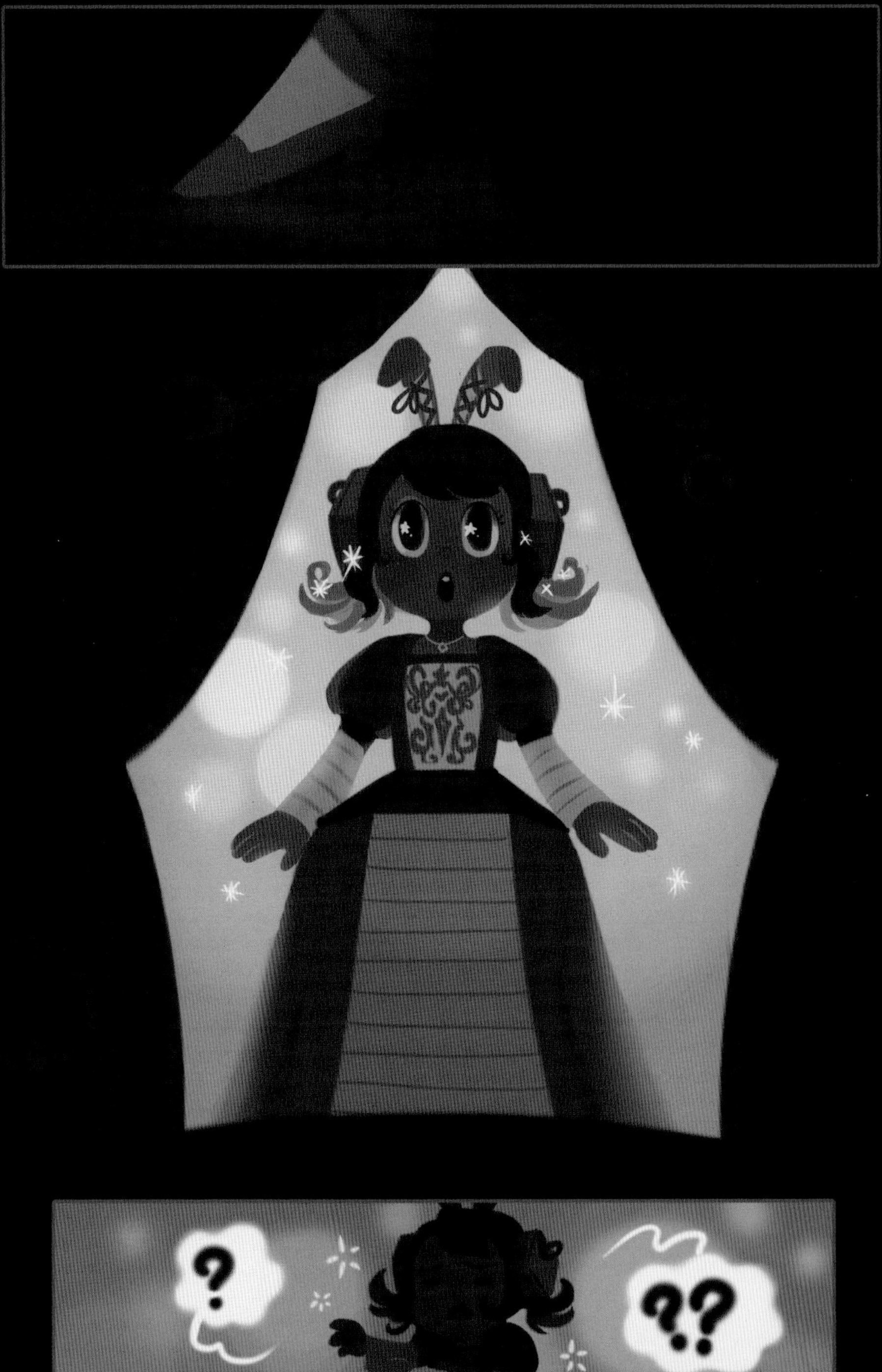
?
??

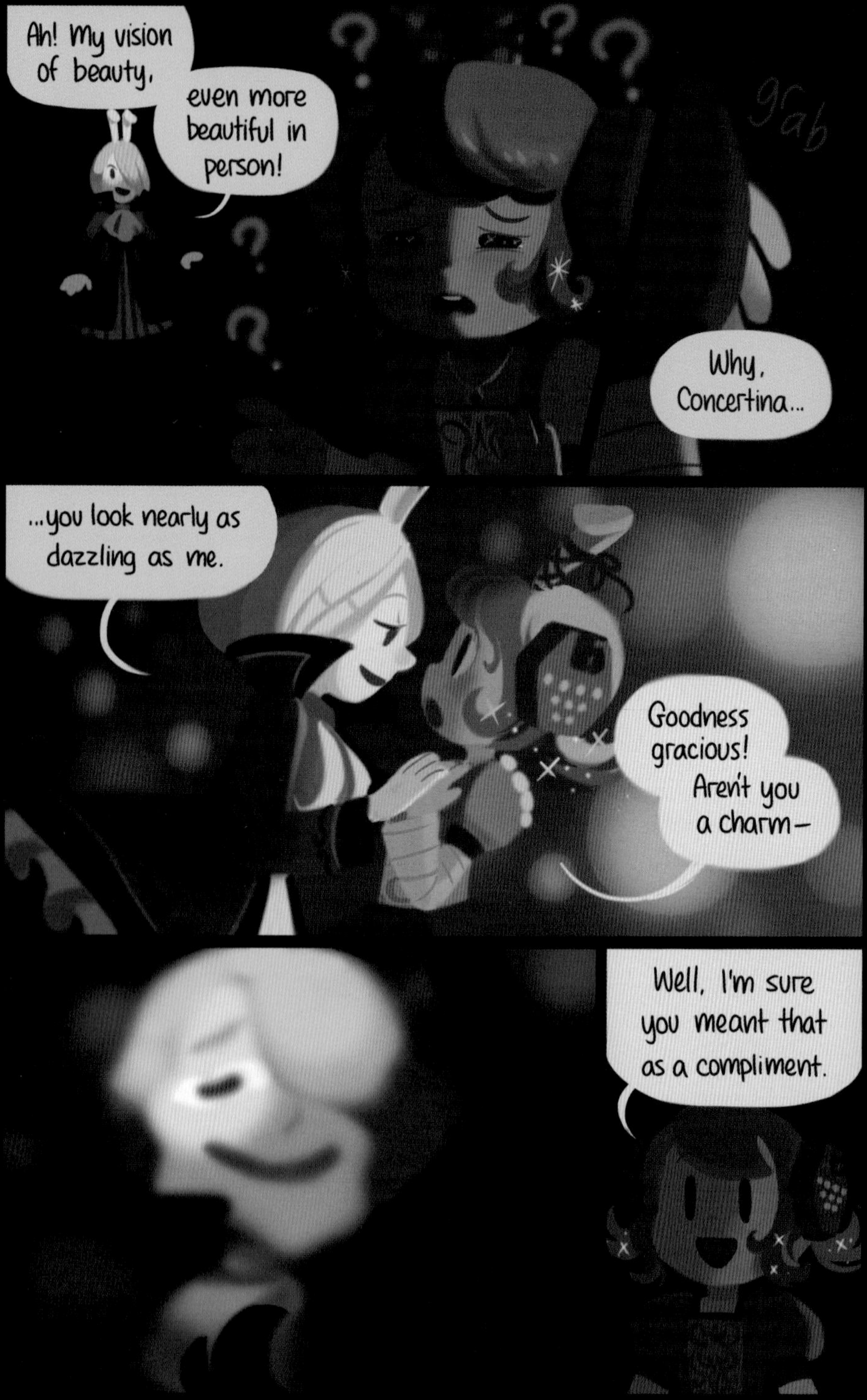
Ah! My vision of beauty,
even more beautiful in person!
grab
Why, Concertina...
...you look nearly as dazzling as me.
Goodness gracious! Aren't you a charm–
Well, I'm sure you meant that as a compliment.

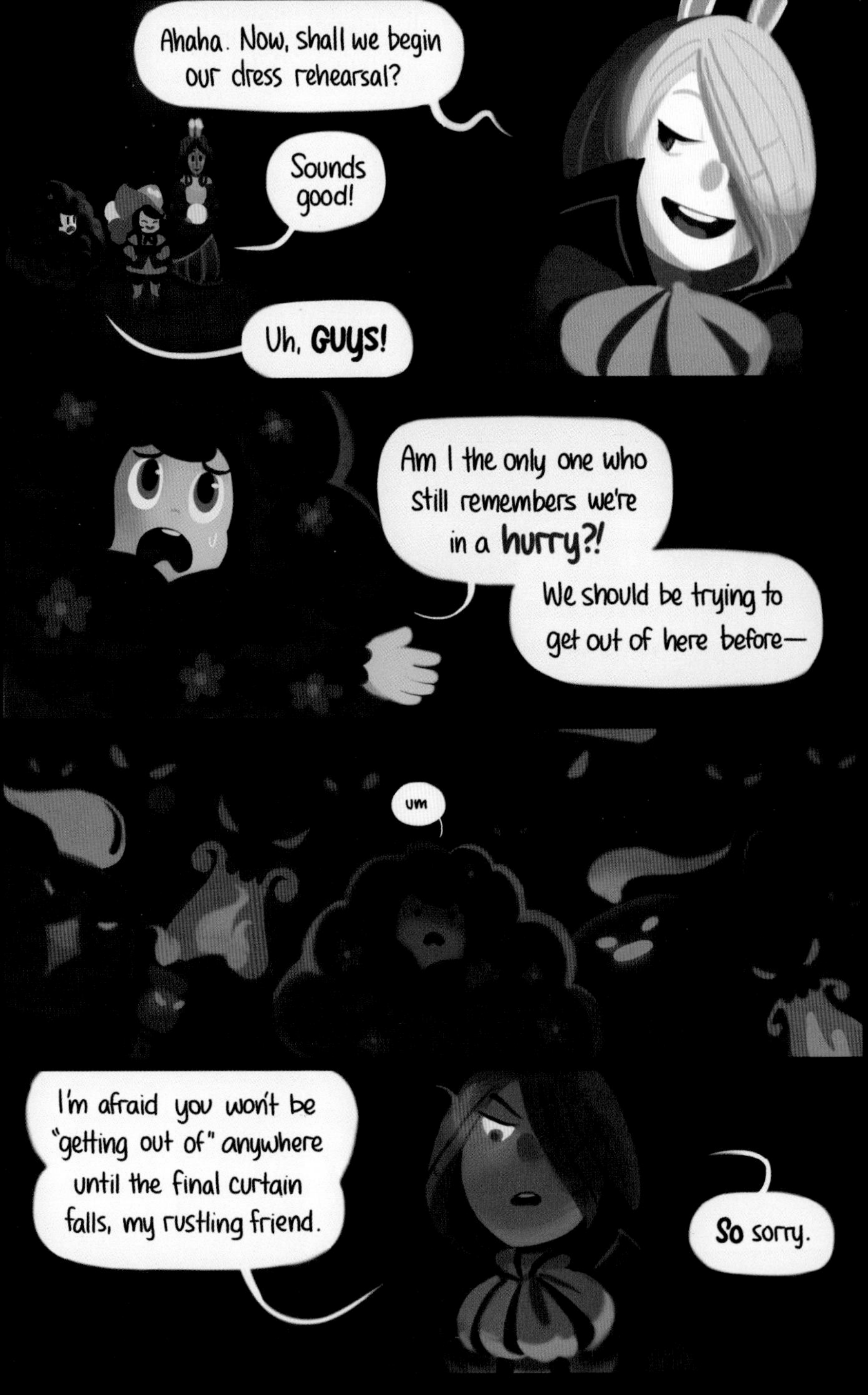

Ahaha. Now, shall we begin our dress rehearsal?
Sounds good!
Uh, GUYS!
Am I the only one who still remembers we're in a hurry?!
We should be trying to get out of here before—
um
I'm afraid you won't be "getting out of" anywhere until the final curtain falls, my rustling friend.
So sorry.

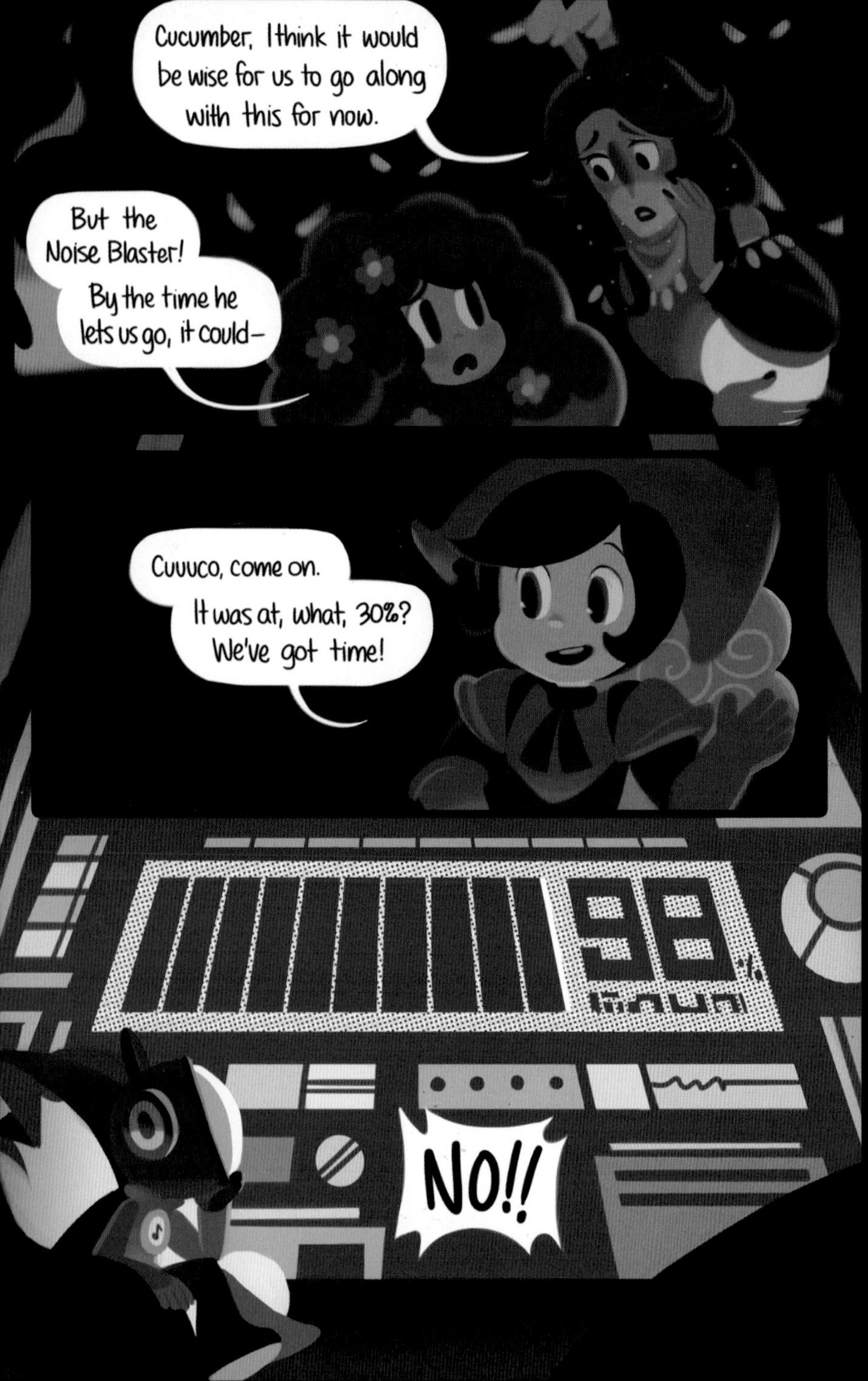
Cucumber, I think it would be wise for us to go along with this for now.
But the Noise Blaster!
By the time he lets us go, it could-
Cuuuco, come on.
It was at, what, 30%? We've got time!
98%
NO!!

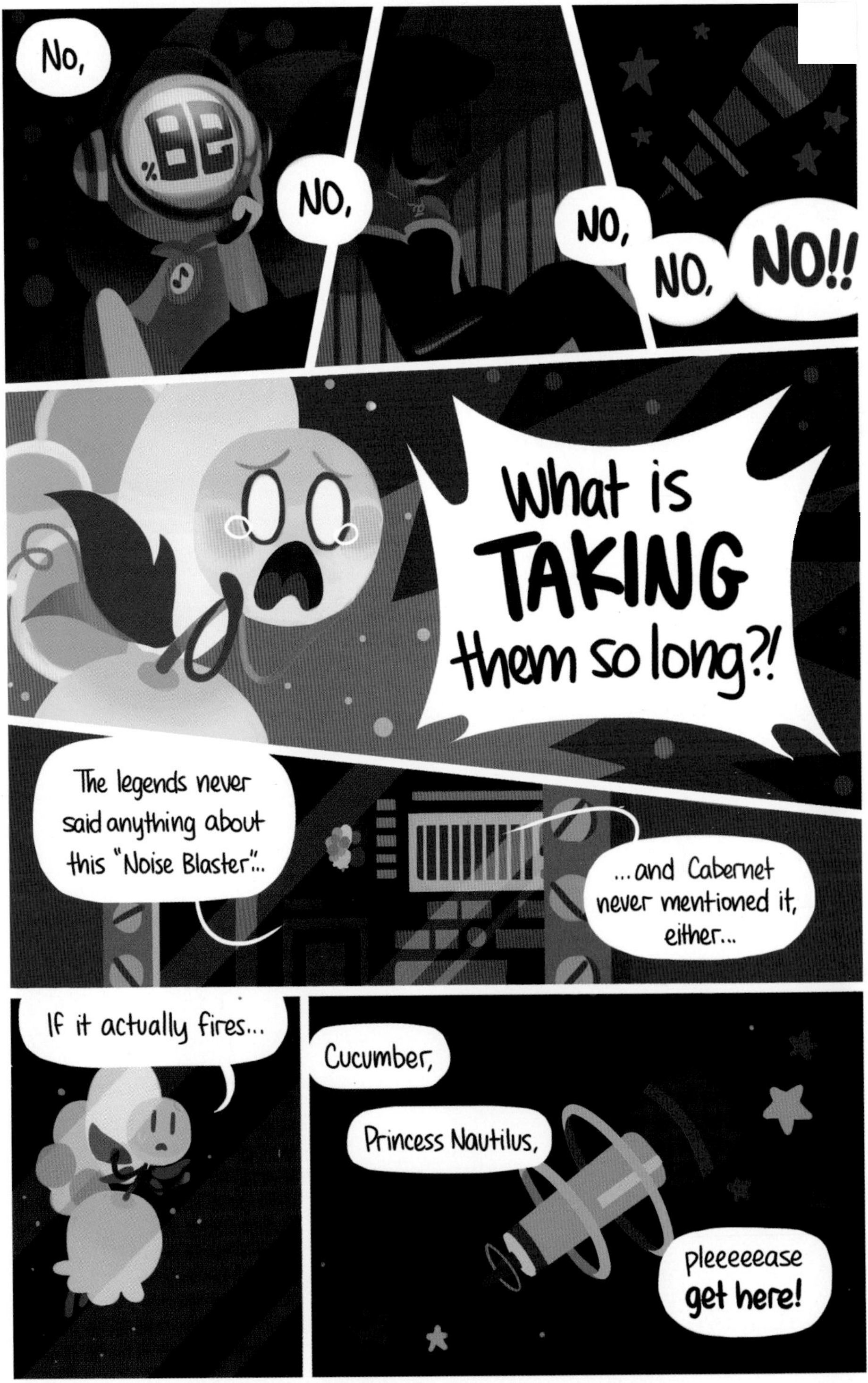
No,
NO,
NO,
NO,
NO!!
What is TAKING them so long?!
The legends never said anything about this "Noise Blaster"...
...and Cabernet never mentioned it, either...
If it actually fires...
Cucumber,
Princess Nautilus,
pleeeeease get here!

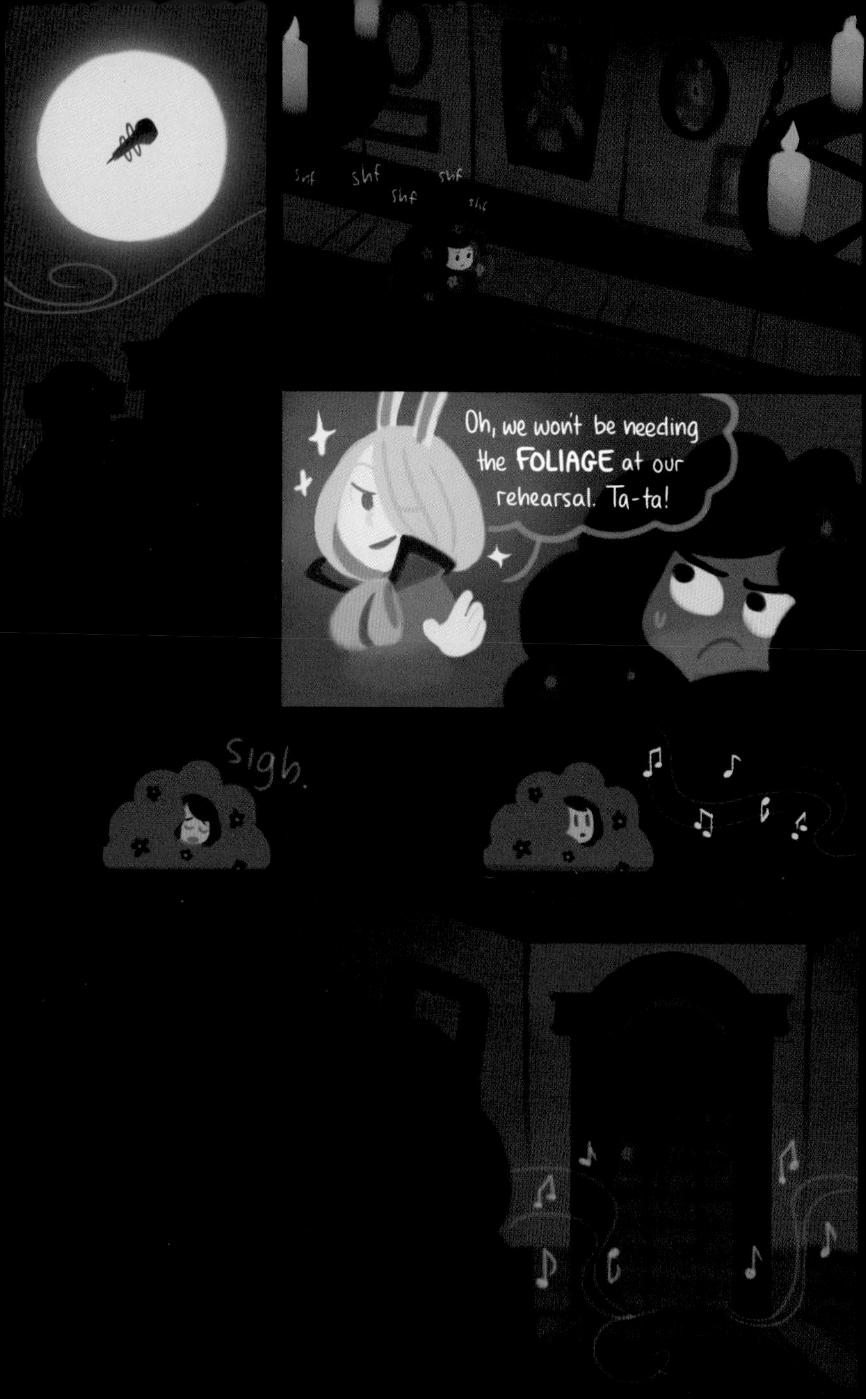
shf shf shf
shf
shf
Oh, we won't be needing the **FOLIAGE** at our rehearsal. Ta-ta!
Sigh.

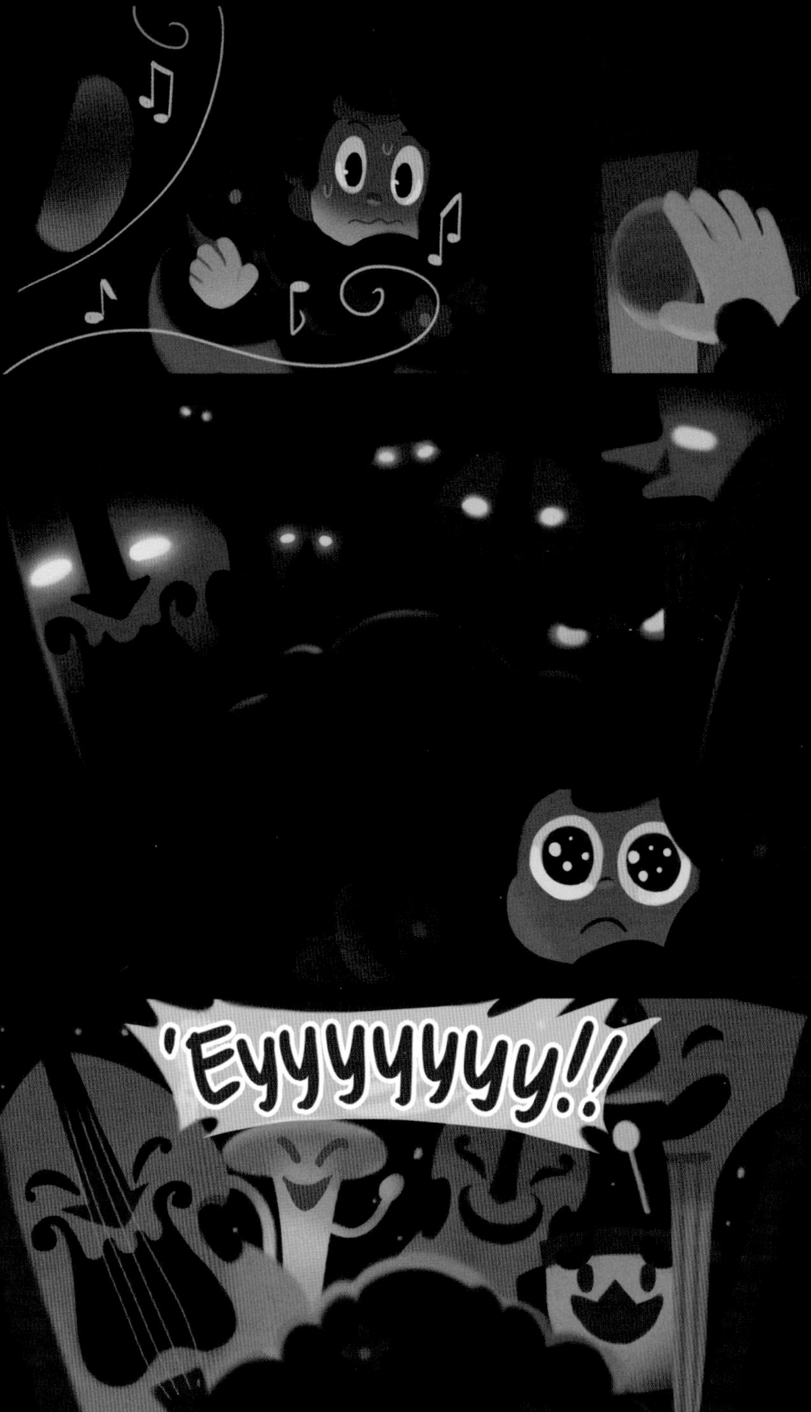
'Eyyyyyyy!!

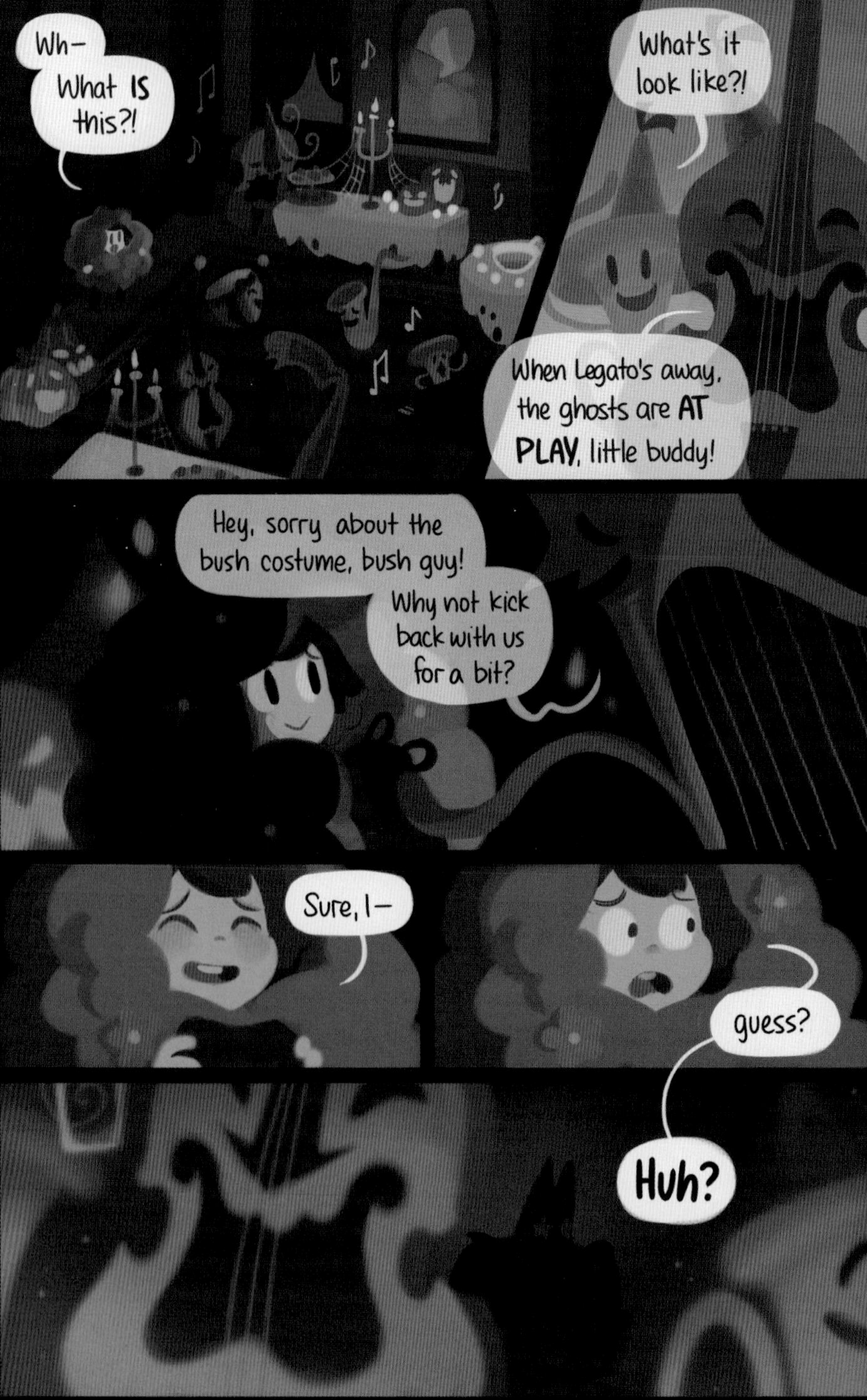
Wh-
What IS this?!
What's it look like?!
When Legato's away, the ghosts are AT PLAY, little buddy!
Hey, sorry about the bush costume, bush guy!
Why not kick back with us for a bit?
Sure, I-
guess?
Huh?

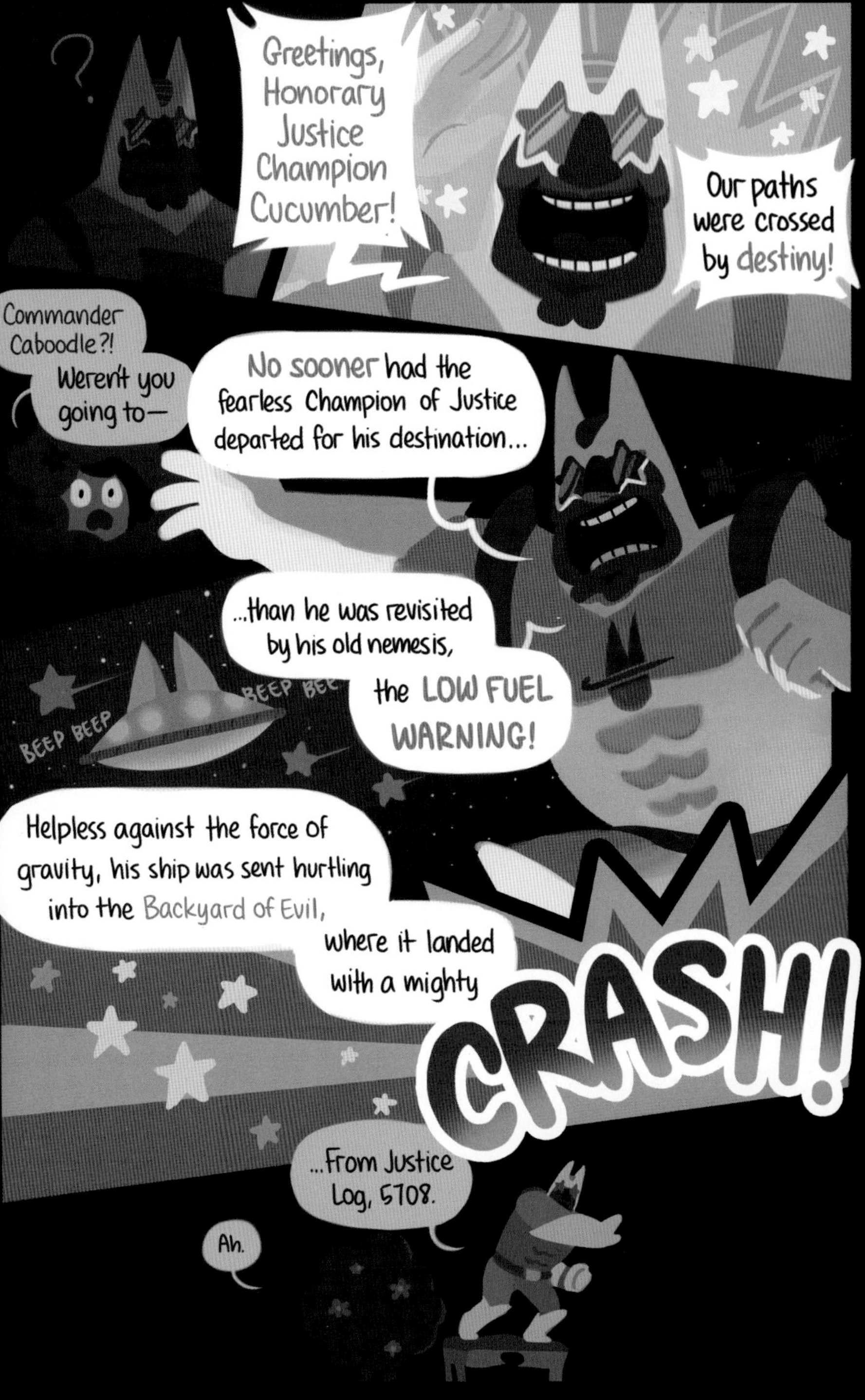
Greetings, Honorary Justice Champion Cucumber!
Our paths were crossed by destiny!
Commander Caboodle?!
Weren't you going to—
No sooner had the fearless Champion of Justice departed for his destination...
...than he was revisited by his old nemesis,
the LOW FUEL WARNING!
BEEP BEEP
BEEP BEE
Helpless against the force of gravity, his ship was sent hurtling into the Backyard of Evil,
where it landed with a mighty
CRASH!
...From Justice Log, 5708.
Ah.

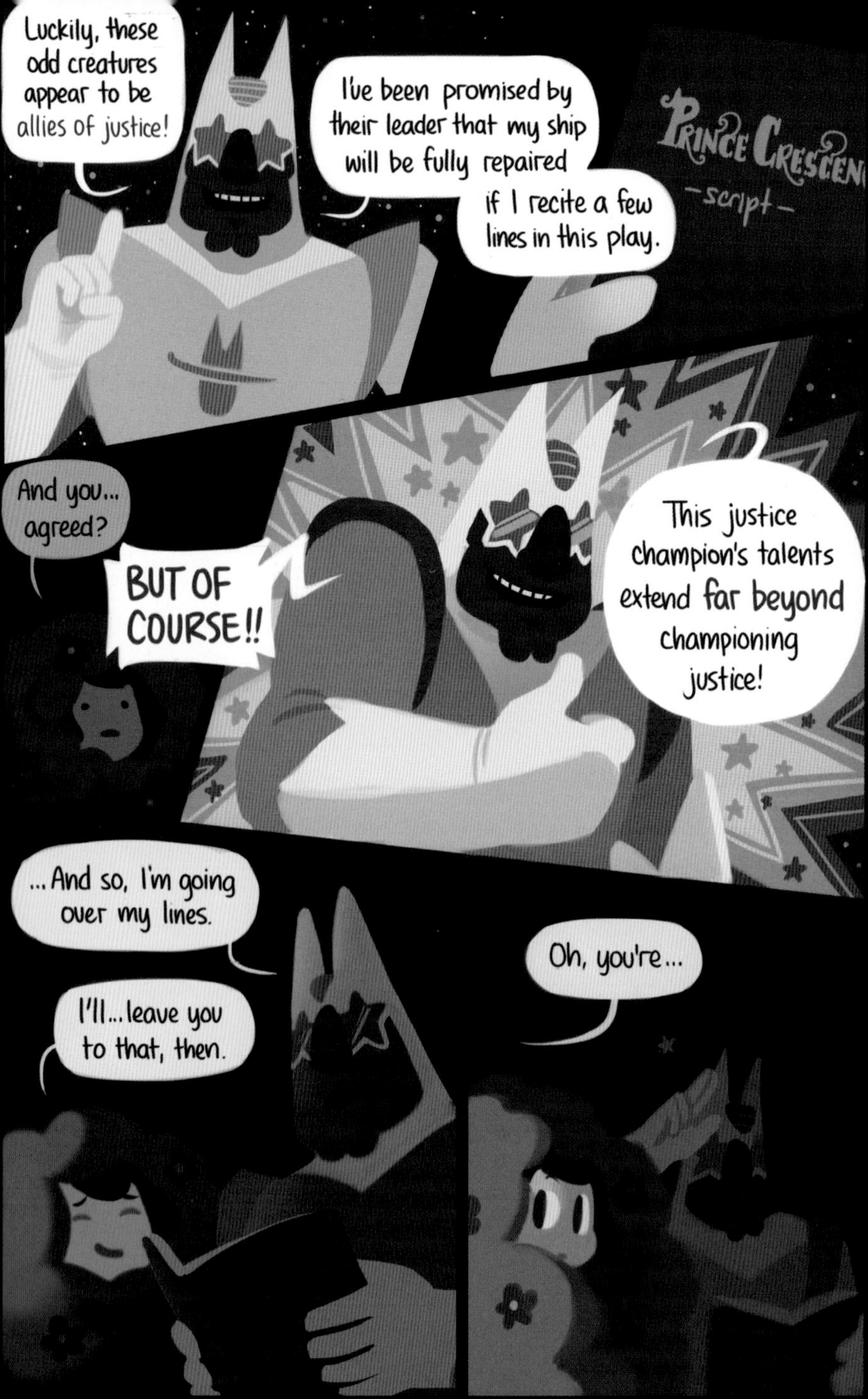
Luckily, these odd creatures appear to be allies of justice!
I've been promised by their leader that my ship will be fully repaired
if I recite a few lines in this play.
PRINCE CRESCEN
-script-
And you... agreed?
BUT OF COURSE!!
This justice champion's talents extend far beyond championing justice!
...And so, I'm going over my lines.
I'll...leave you to that, then.
Oh, you're...

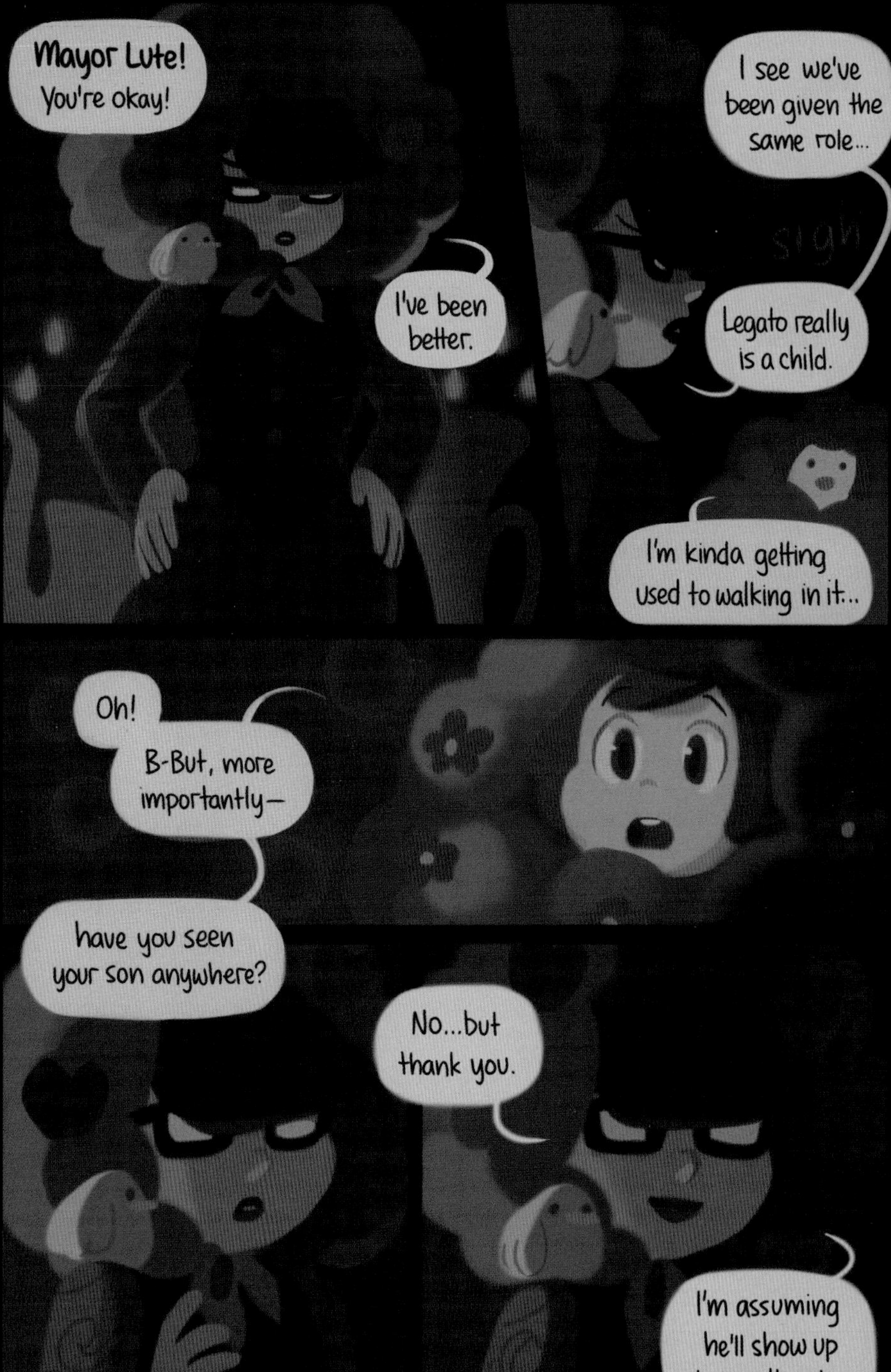
Mayor Lute! You're okay!
I've been better.
I see we've been given the same role...
sigh
Legato really is a child.
I'm kinda getting used to walking in it...
Oh!
B-But, more importantly—
have you seen your son anywhere?
No...but thank you.
I'm assuming he'll show up during the play.

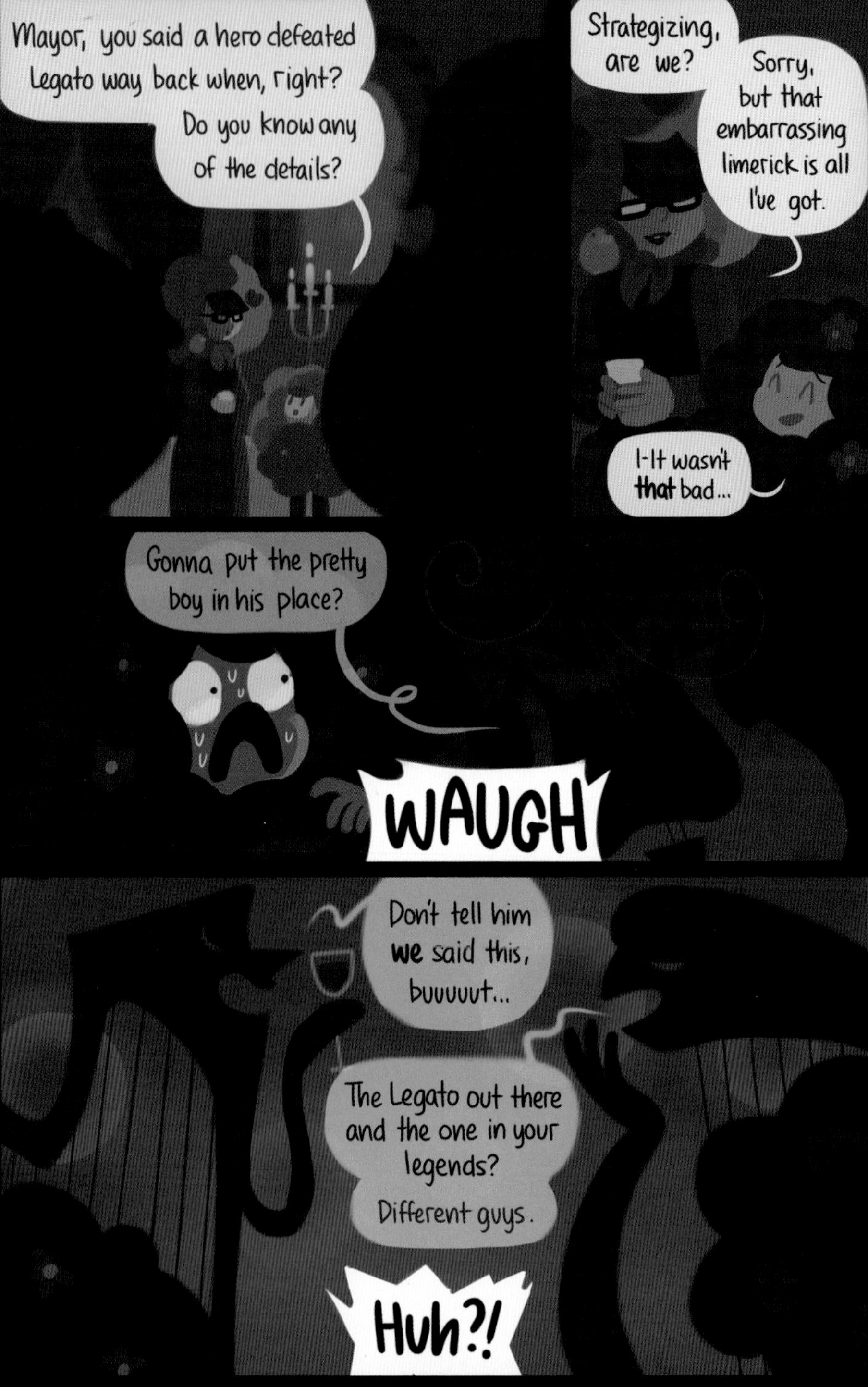
Mayor, you said a hero defeated Legato way back when, right?
Do you know any of the details?
Strategizing, are we?
Sorry, but that embarrassing limerick is all I've got.
I-It wasn't **that** bad...
Gonna put the pretty boy in his place?
WAUGH
Don't tell him **we** said this, buuuuut...
The Legato out there and the one in your legends?
Different guys.
Huh?!

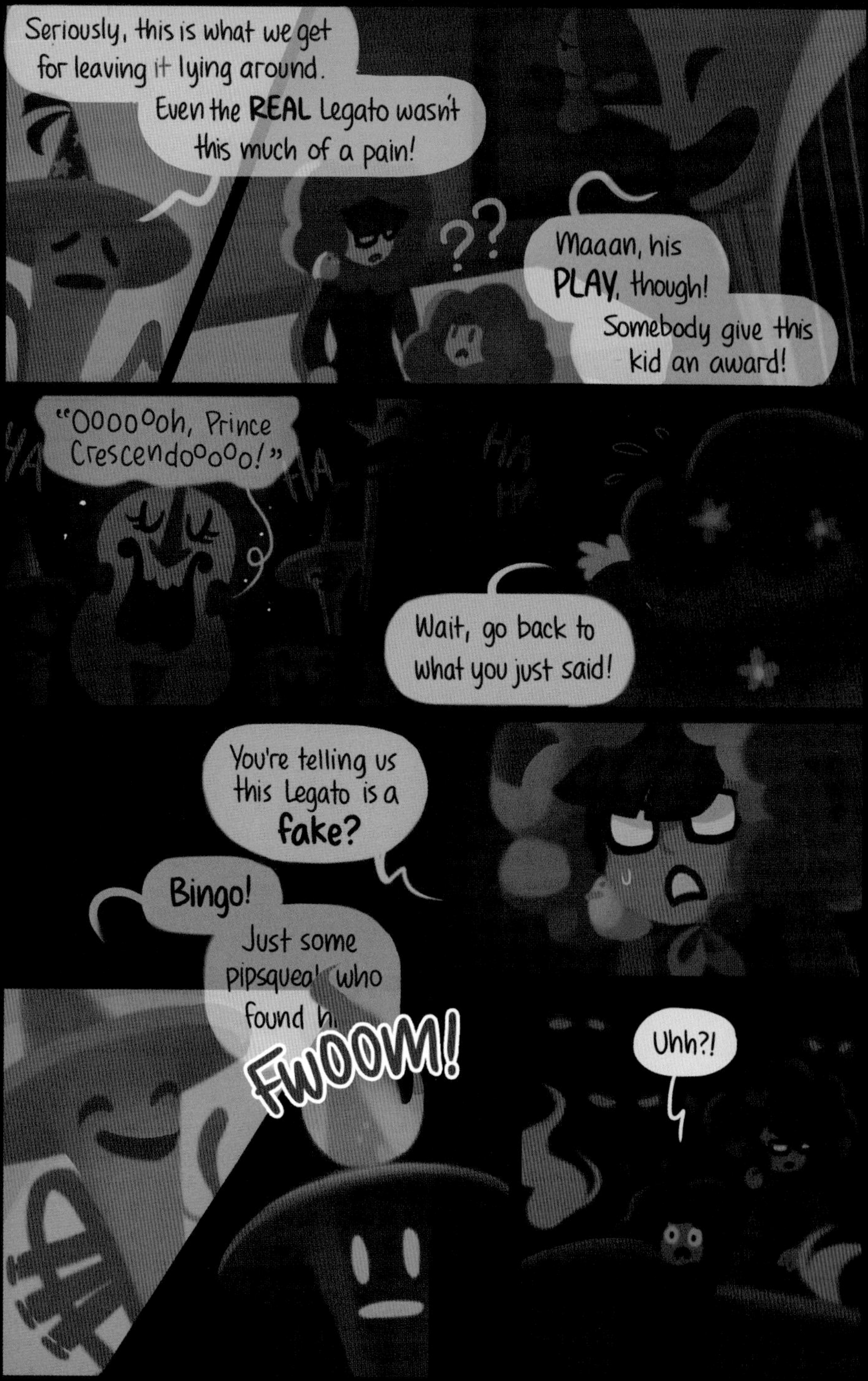
Seriously, this is what we get for leaving it lying around.
Even the REAL Legato wasn't this much of a pain!
??
Maaan, his PLAY, though!
Somebody give this kid an award!
"Ooooooh, Prince Crescendooooo!"
HA HA
HA HA
Wait, go back to what you just said!
You're telling us this Legato is a fake?
Bingo!
Just some pipsqueak who found h
FWOOM!
Uhh?!

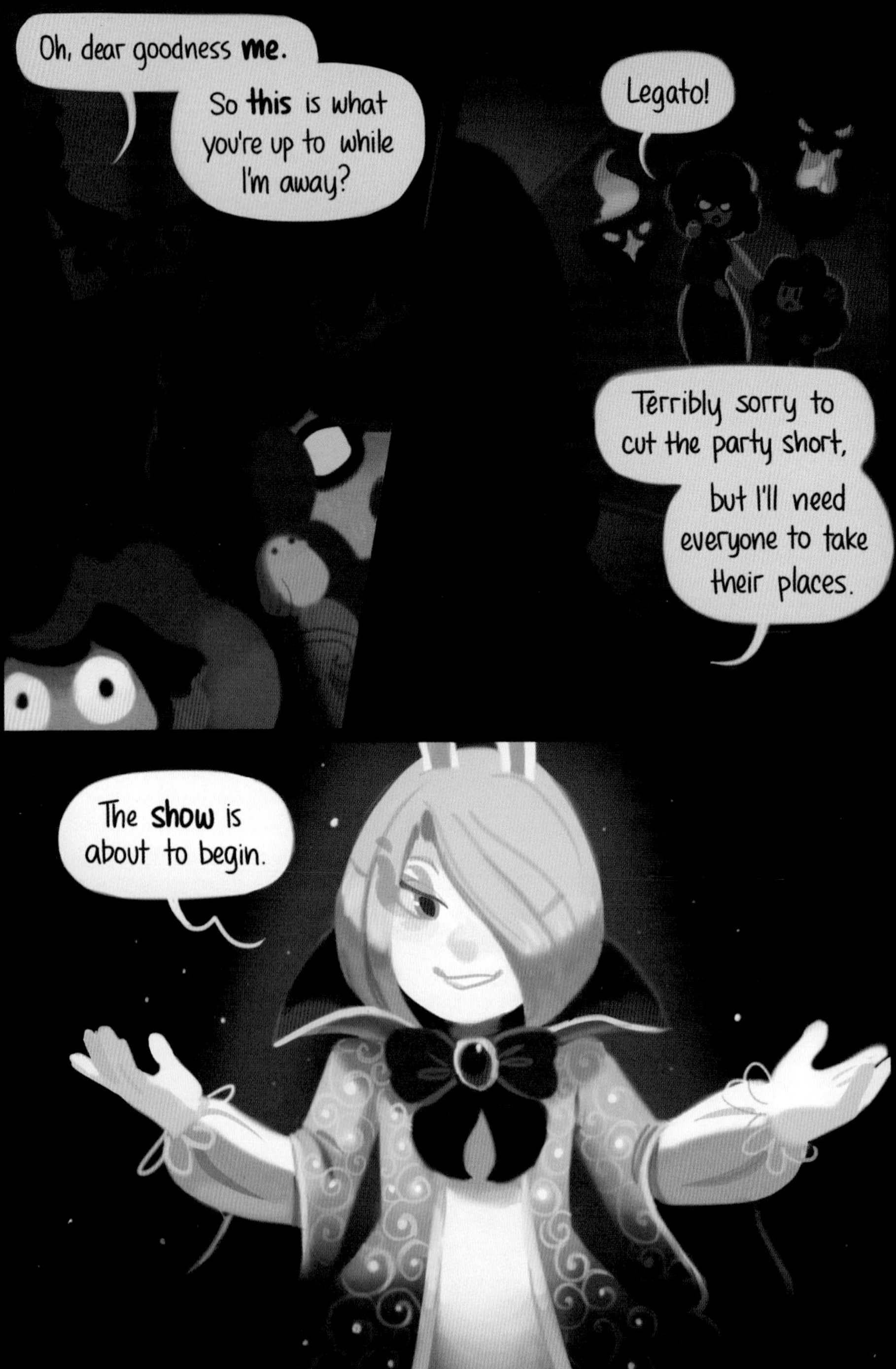
Oh, dear goodness **me**.
So **this** is what you're up to while I'm away?
Legato!
Terribly sorry to cut the party short,
but I'll need everyone to take their places.
The **show** is about to begin.

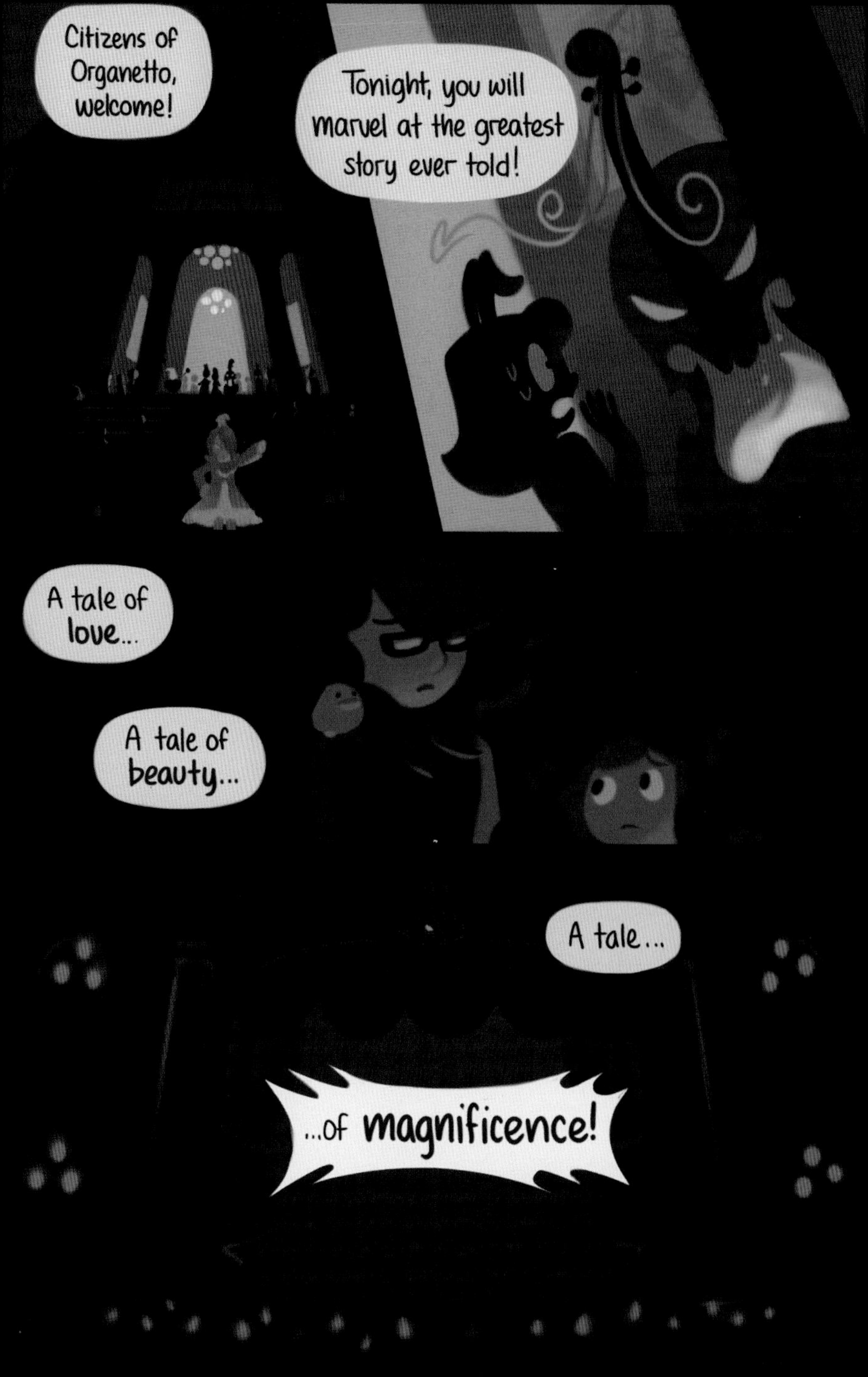
Citizens of Organetto, welcome!
Tonight, you will marvel at the greatest story ever told!
A tale of love...
A tale of beauty...
A tale...
...of magnificence!

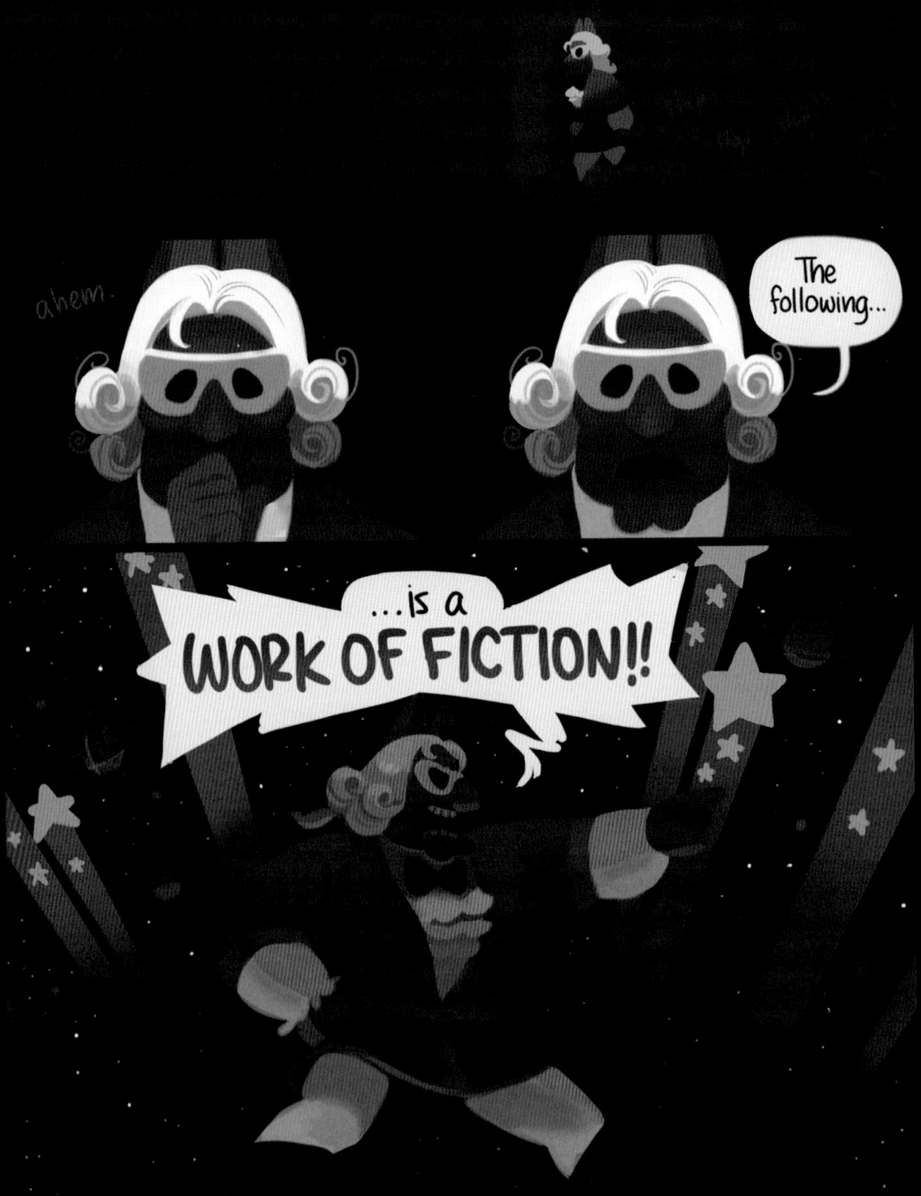
ahem.
The following...
...is a
WORK OF FICTION!!

THE CHARACTERS ARE FICTIONAL!
THE EVENTS ARE FICTIONAL!

But the laughter you will share...
The tears you will shed...
Ha ha haaa.
THOSE ARE REAL!!

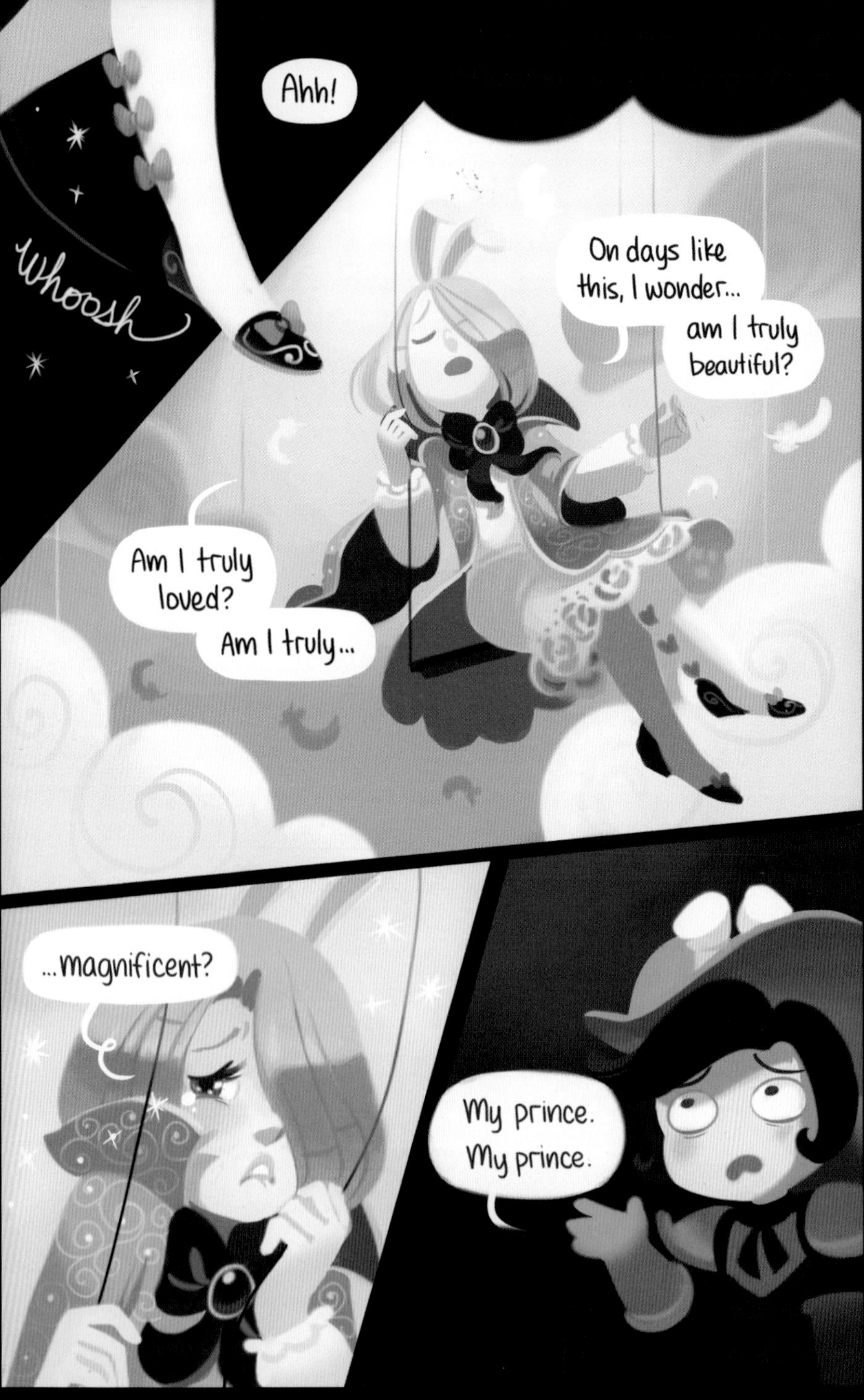
Ahh!
Whoosh
On days like this, I wonder...
am I truly beautiful?
Am I truly loved?
Am I truly...
...magnificent?
My prince. My prince.

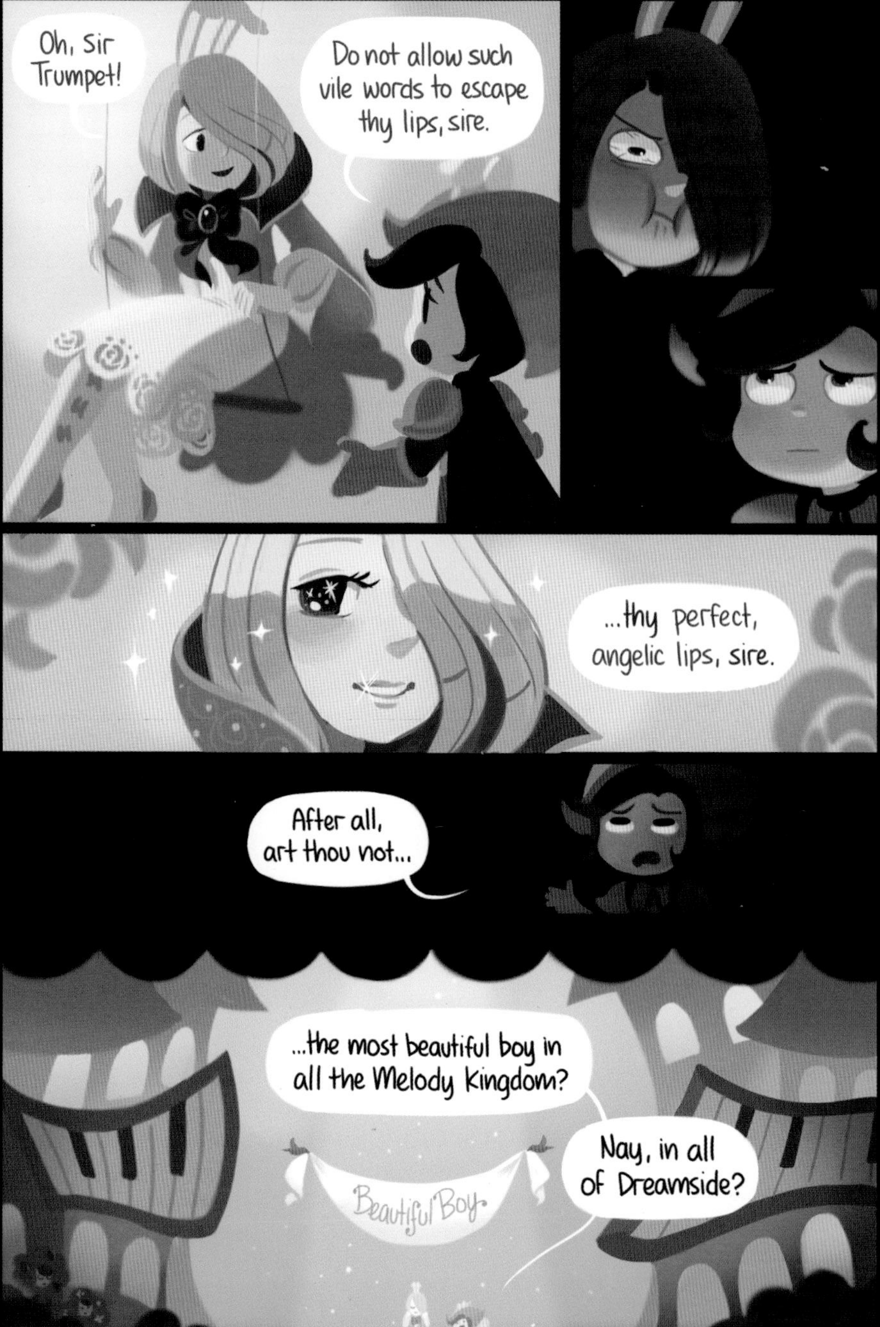
Oh, sir Trumpet!
Do not allow such vile words to escape thy lips, sire.
...thy perfect, angelic lips, sire.
After all, art thou not...
...the most beautiful boy in all the Melody Kingdom?
Nay, in all of Dreamside?
Beautiful Boy

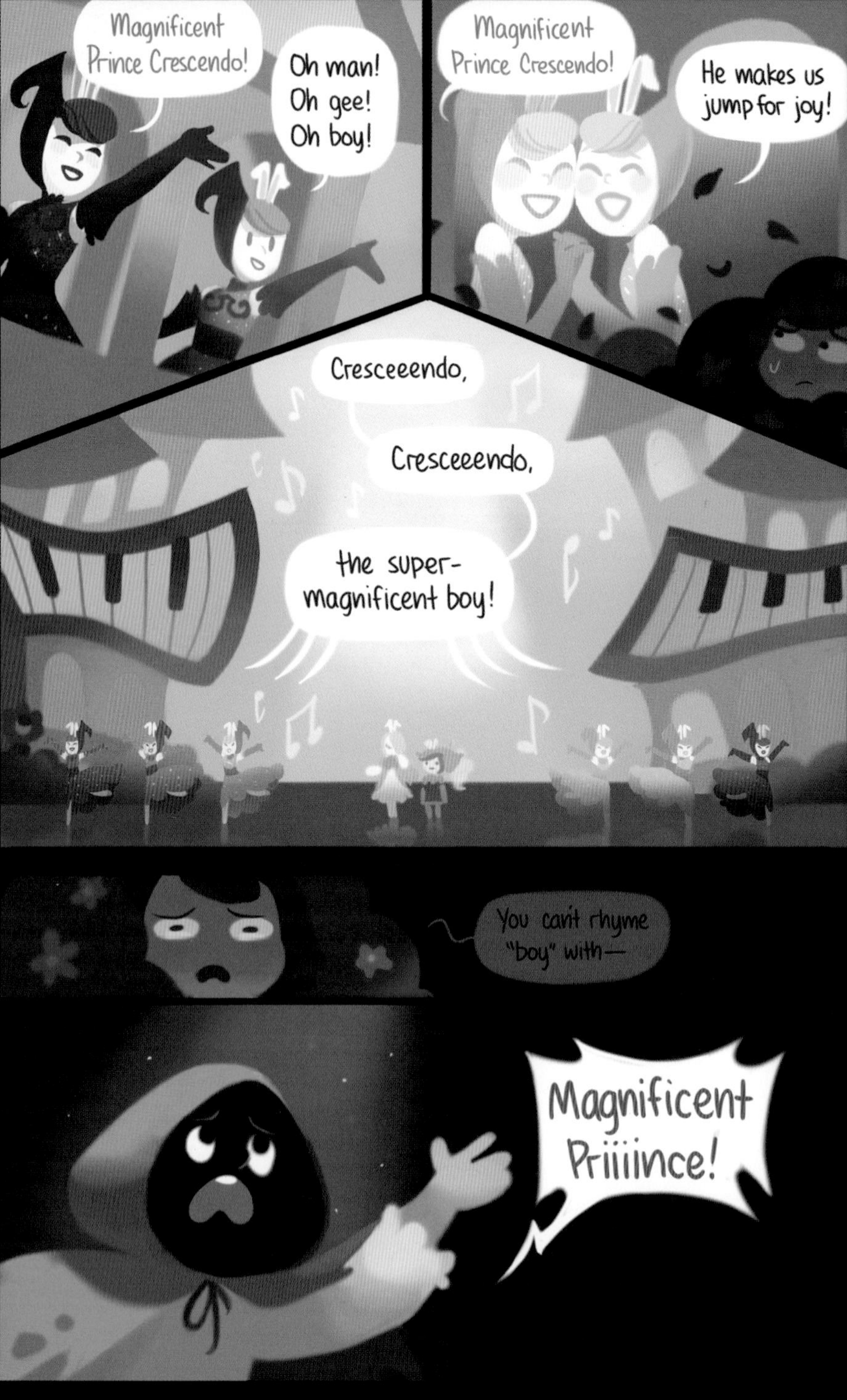
Magnificent Prince Crescendo!
Oh man! Oh gee! Oh boy!
Magnificent Prince Crescendo!
He makes us jump for joy!
Cresceeendo,
Cresceeendo,
the super-magnificent boy!
You can't rhyme "boy" with—
Magnificent Priiiince!

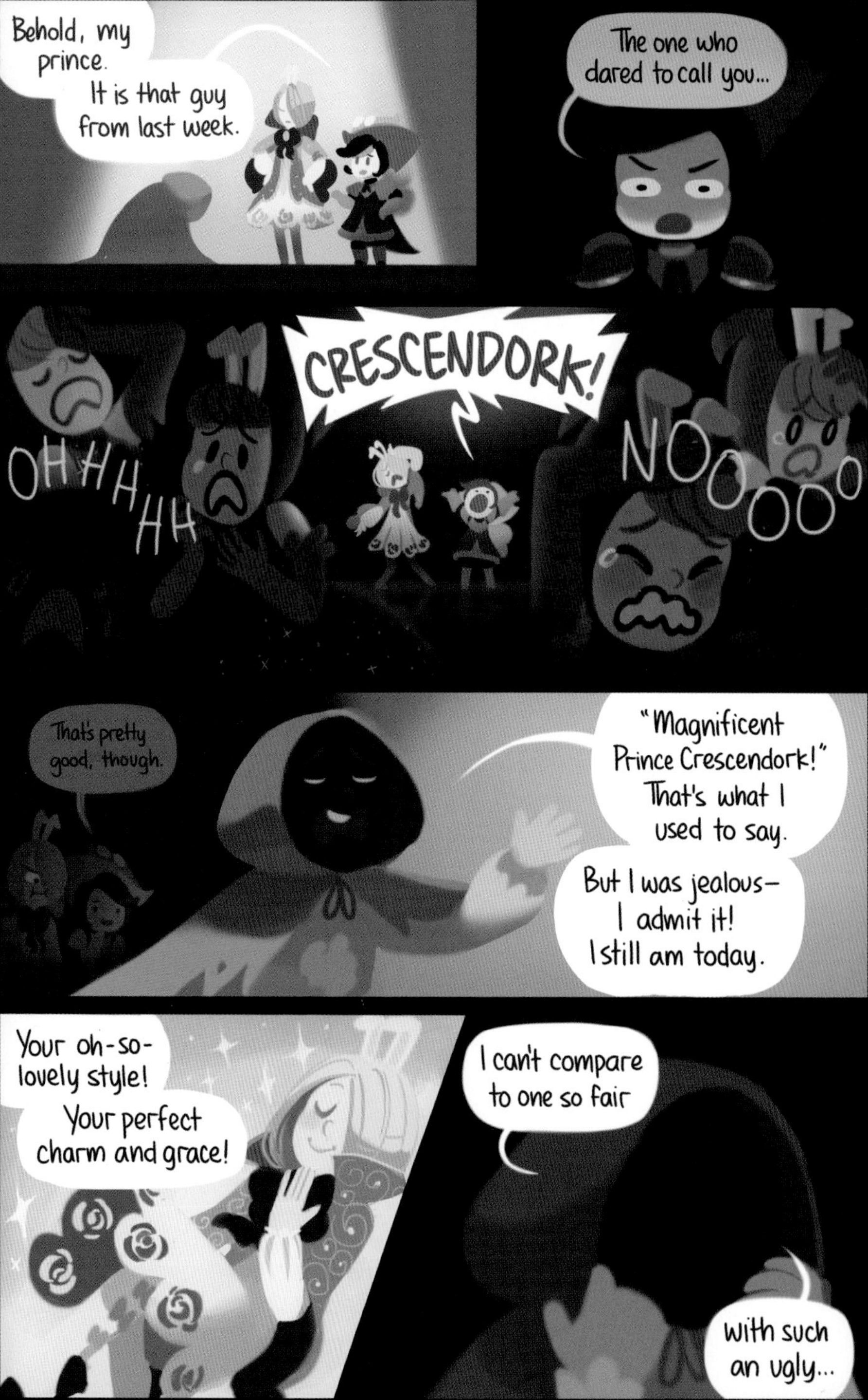

Behold, my prince.
It is that guy from last week.
The one who dared to call you...
CRESCENDORK!
OHHHHHH
NOOOOOOO
That's pretty good, though.
"Magnificent Prince Crescendork!" That's what I used to say.
But I was jealous— I admit it! I still am today.
Your oh-so-lovely style!
Your perfect charm and grace!
I can't compare to one so fair
with such an ugly...

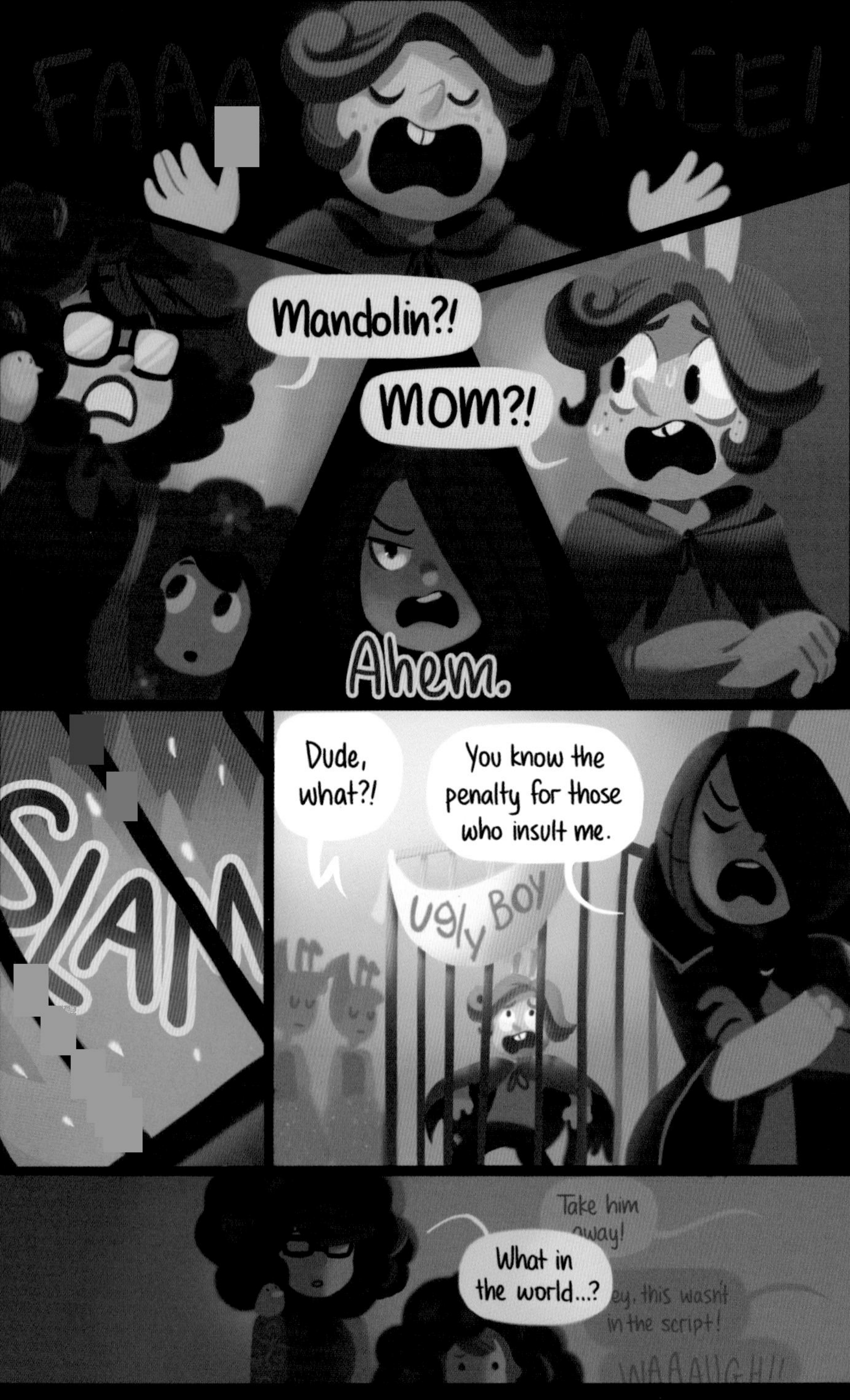
FAAA
AACE!
Mandolin?!
MOM?!
Ahem.
SLAM
Dude, what?!
You know the penalty for those who insult me.
Ugly BOY
Take him away!
What in the world...?
ey, this wasn't in the script!
WAAAUGH!!

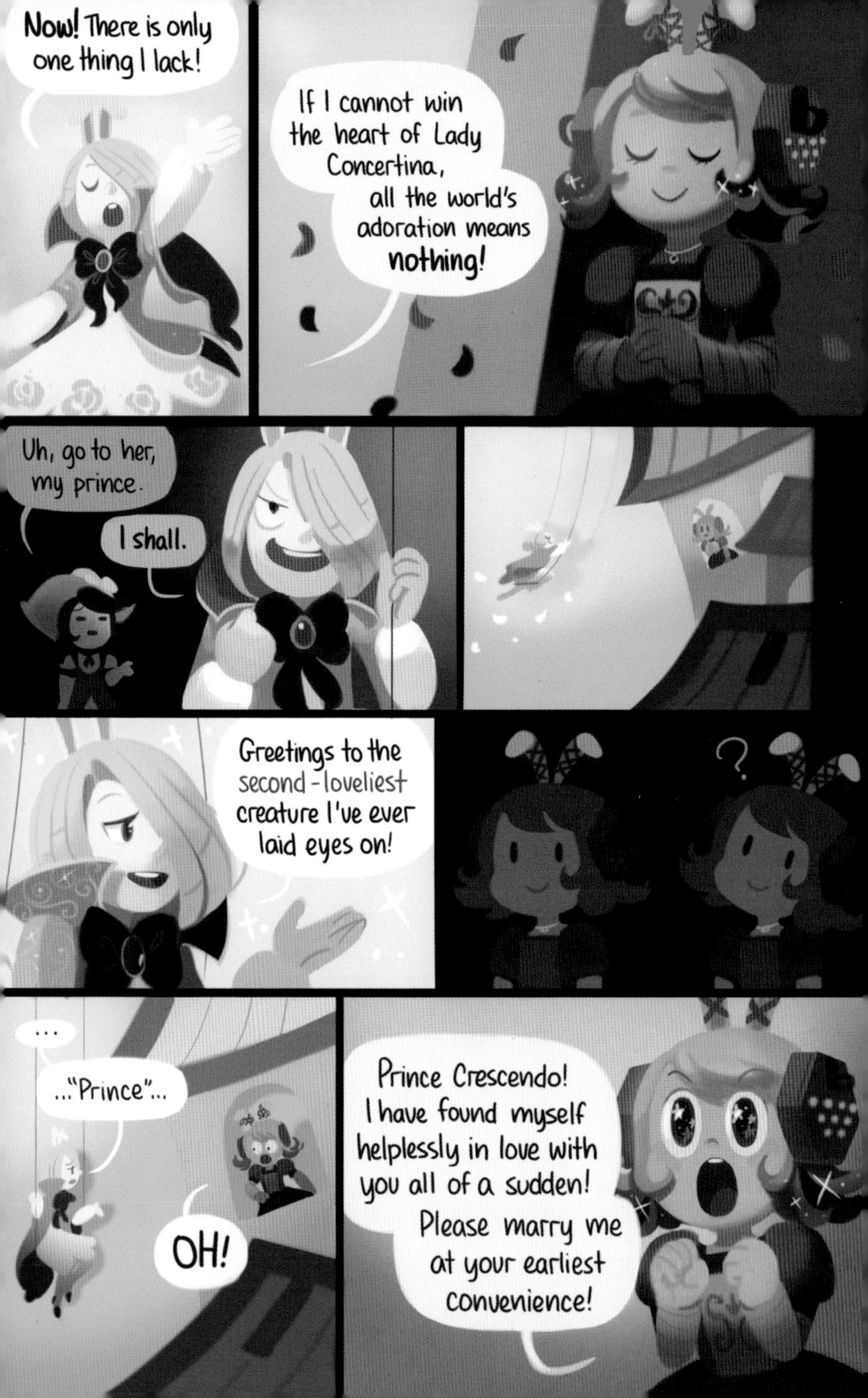
Now! There is only one thing I lack!
If I cannot win the heart of Lady Concertina, all the world's adoration means **nothing**!
Uh, go to her, my prince.
I shall.
Greetings to the second-loveliest creature I've ever laid eyes on!
?
...
..."Prince"...
OH!
Prince Crescendo! I have found myself helplessly in love with you all of a sudden!
Please marry me at your earliest convenience!

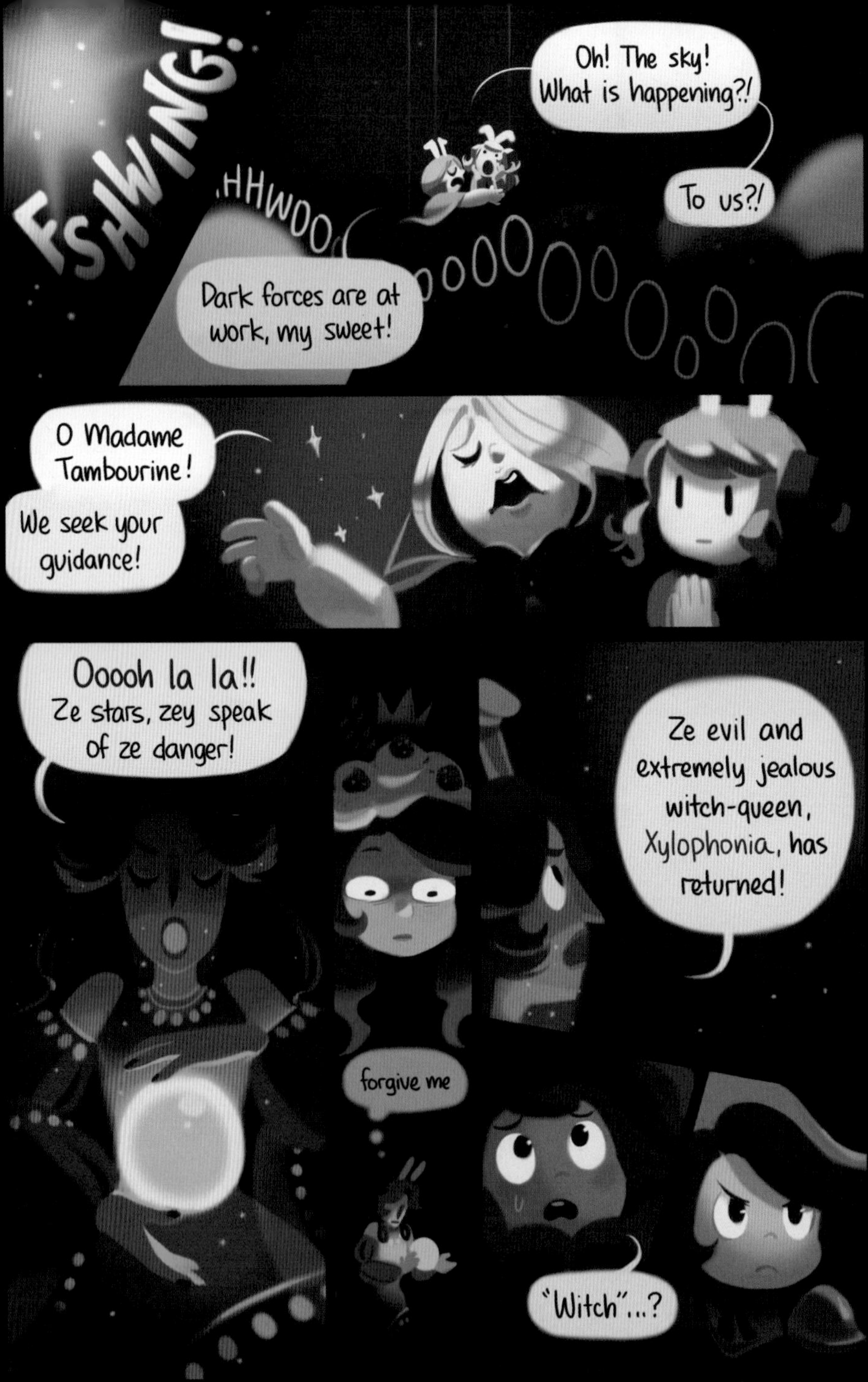
FSHWING!
Oh! The sky! What is happening?!
To us?!
HHWOOOOOOOOOOOO
Dark forces are at work, my sweet!
O Madame Tambourine!
We seek your guidance!
Ooooh la la!! Ze stars, zey speak of ze danger!
Ze evil and extremely jealous witch-queen, Xylophonia, has returned!
forgive me
"Witch"...?

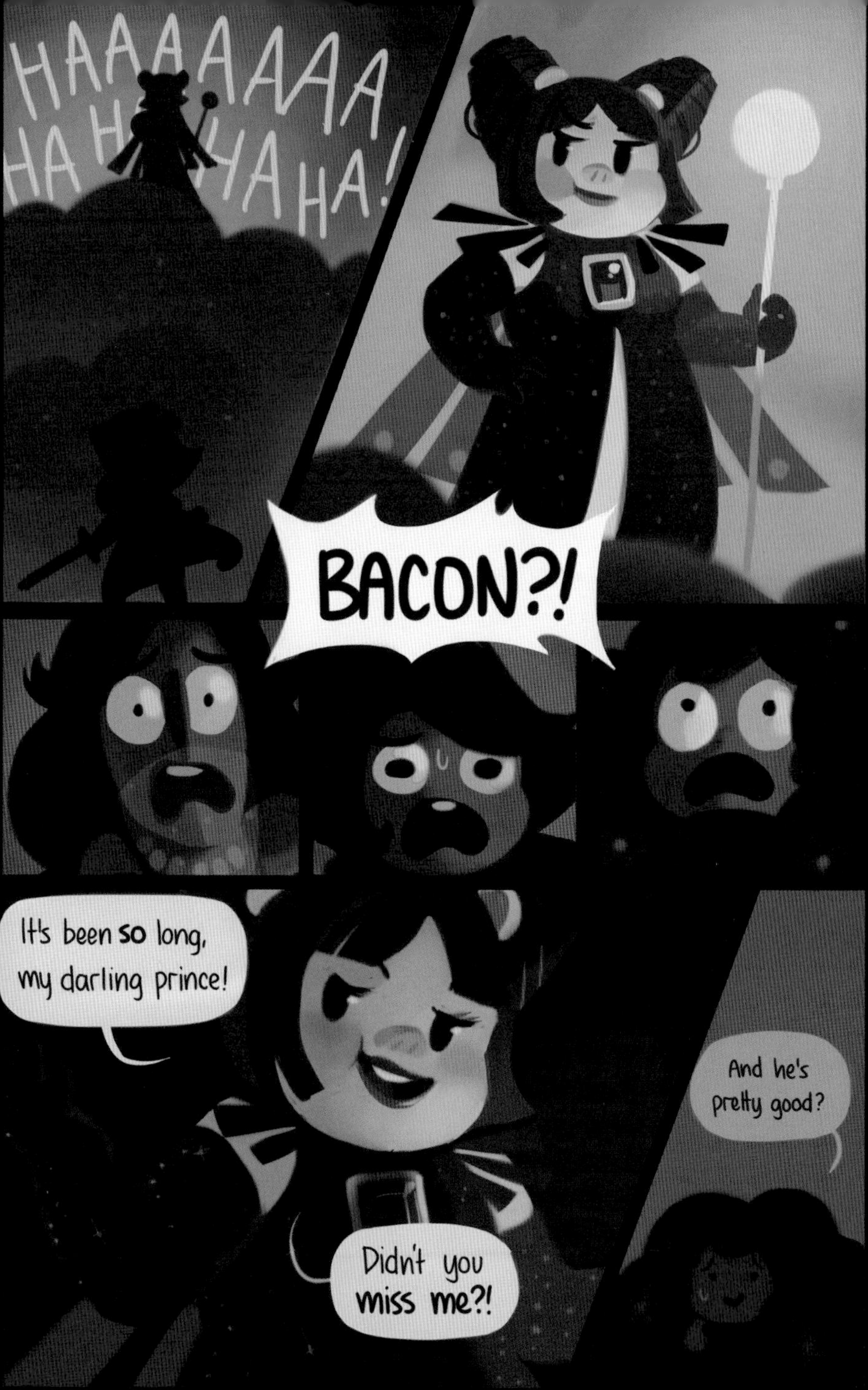
HAAAAAAA HA HA HA HA!
BACON?!
It's been so long, my darling prince!
Didn't you miss me?!
And he's pretty good?

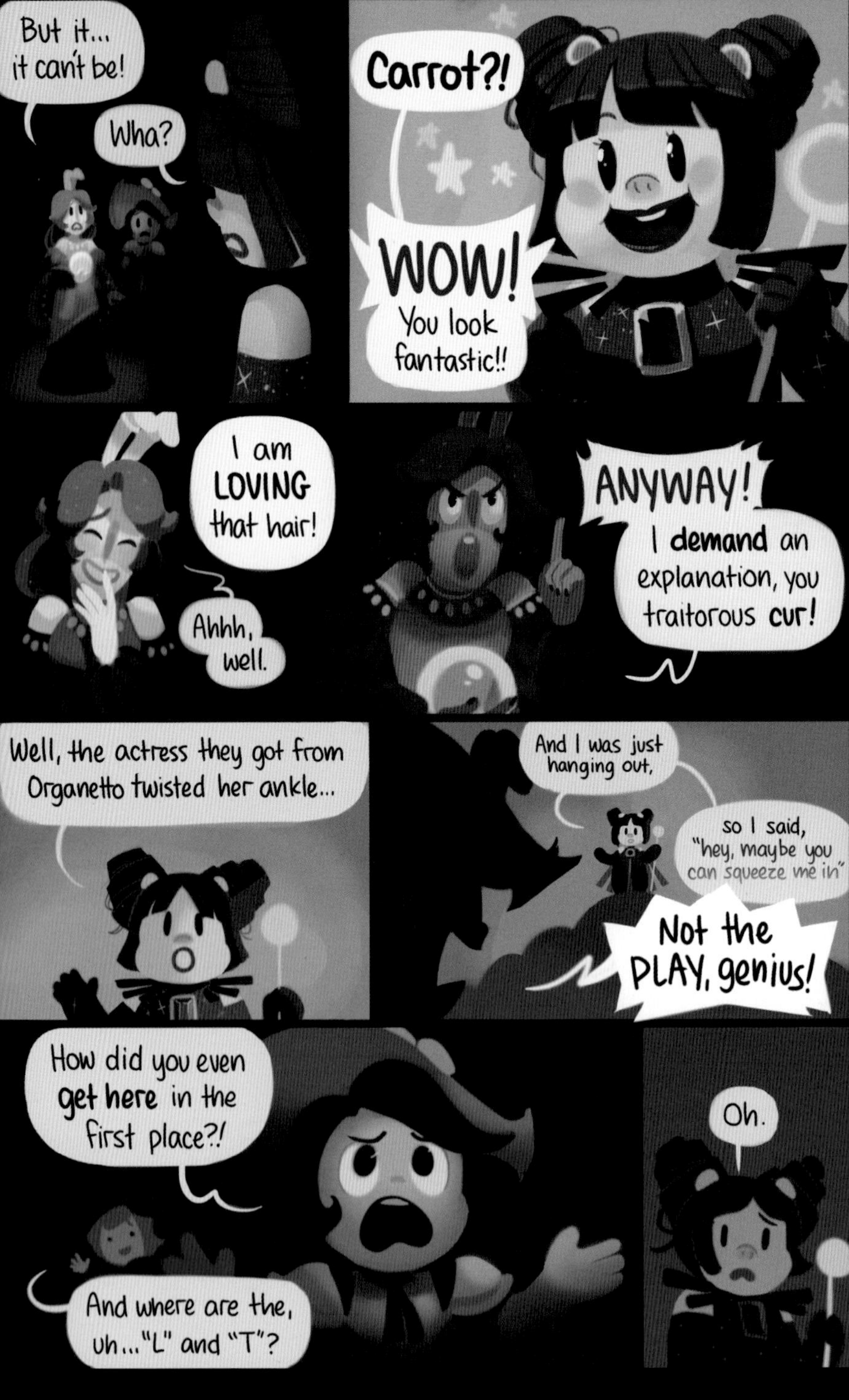

But it...
it can't be!
Wha?
Carrot?!
WOW!
You look fantastic!!
I am LOVING that hair!
Ahhh, well.
ANYWAY!
I demand an explanation, you traitorous cur!
Well, the actress they got from Organetto twisted her ankle...
And I was just hanging out,
so I said, "hey, maybe you can squeeze me in"
Not the PLAY, genius!
How did you even get here in the first place?!
And where are the, uh..."L" and "T"?
Oh.

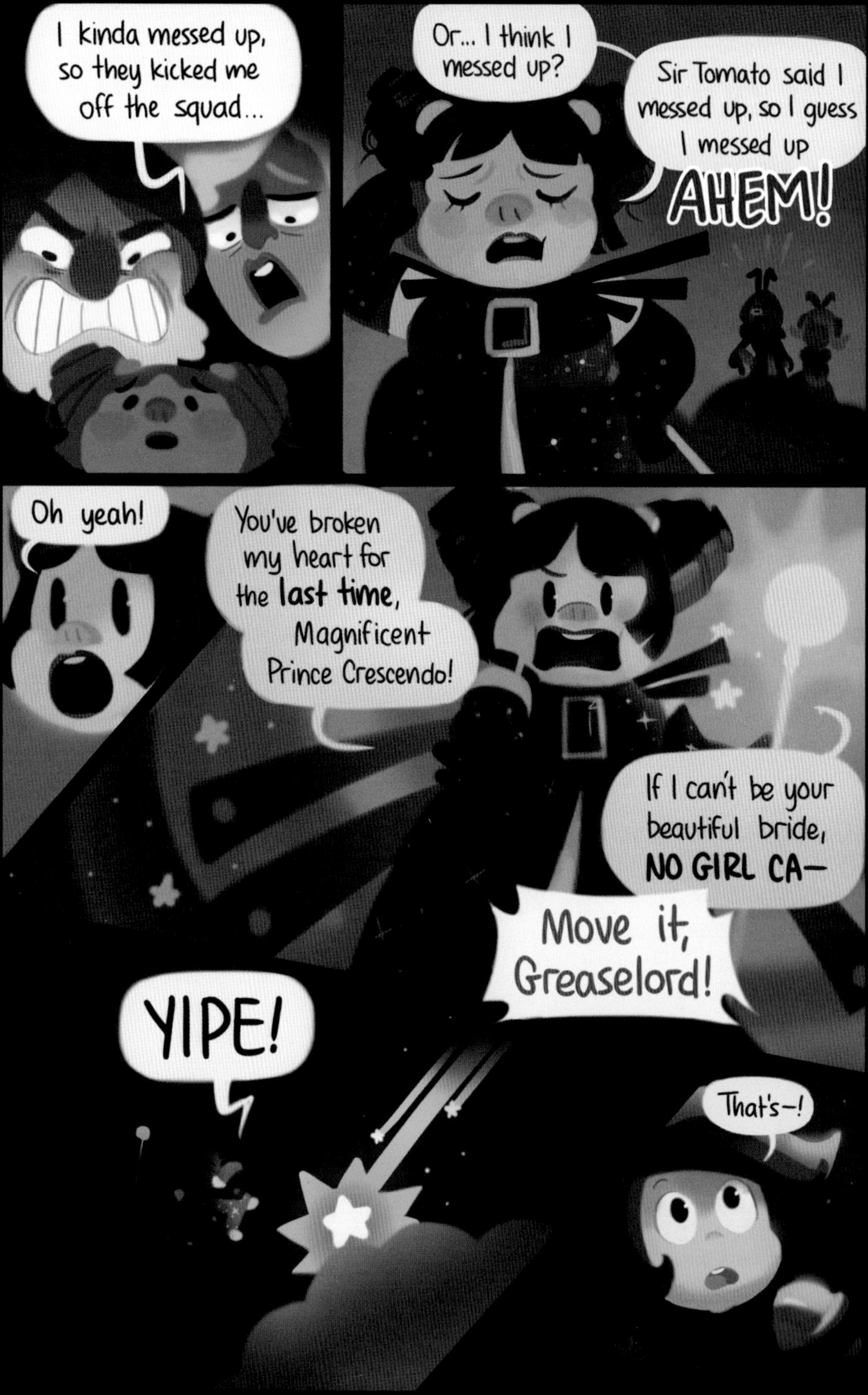
I kinda messed up, so they kicked me off the squad...
Or... I think I messed up?
Sir Tomato said I messed up, so I guess I messed up
AHEM!
Oh yeah!
You've broken my heart for the **last time**, Magnificent Prince Crescendo!
If I can't be your beautiful bride, **NO GIRL CA—**
Move it, Greaselord!
YIPE!
That's—!

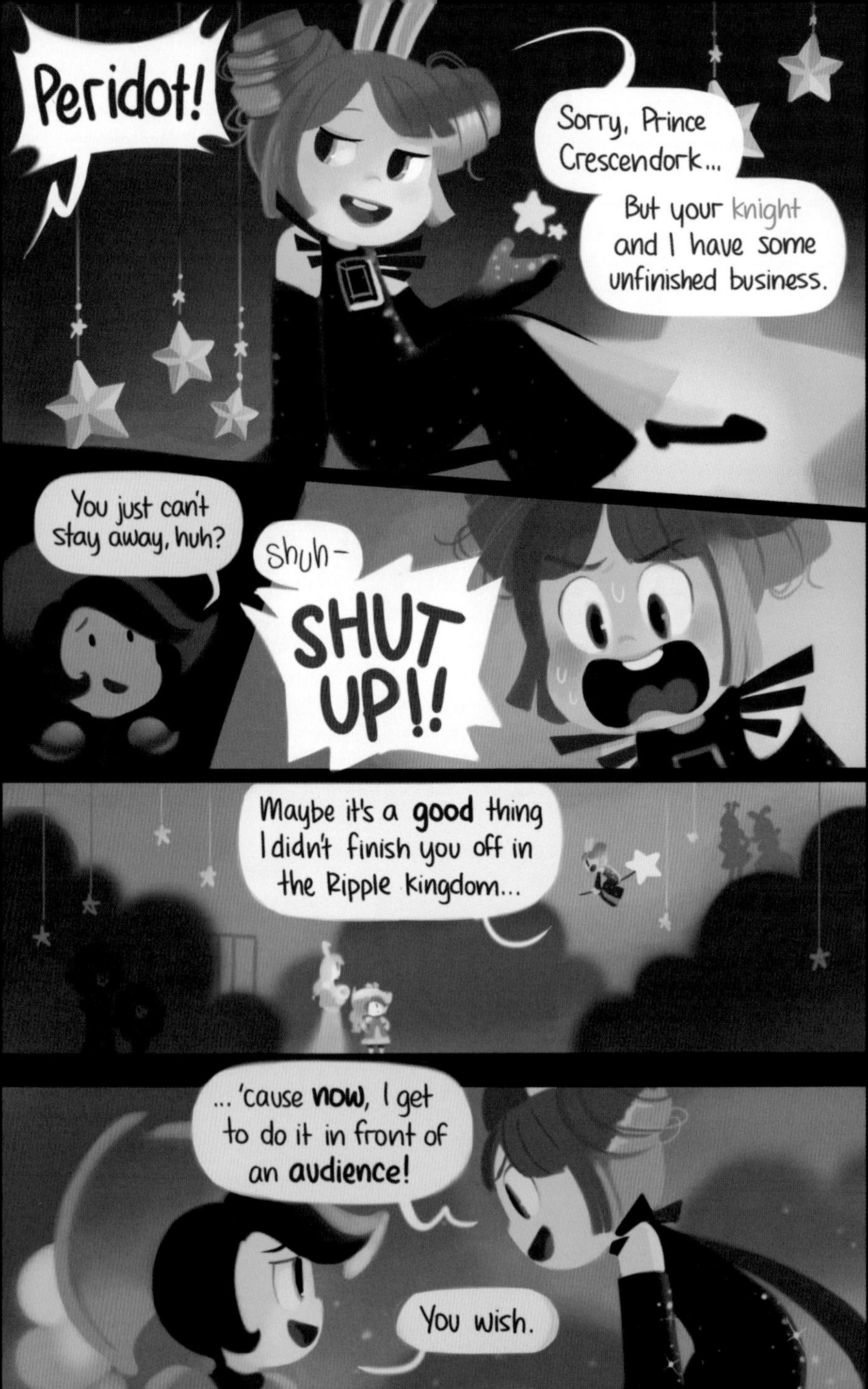
Peridot!
Sorry, Prince Crescendork...
But your knight and I have some unfinished business.
You just can't stay away, huh?
Shuh-
SHUT UP!!
Maybe it's a **good** thing I didn't finish you off in the Ripple Kingdom...
...'cause **now**, I get to do it in front of an **audience**!
You wish.

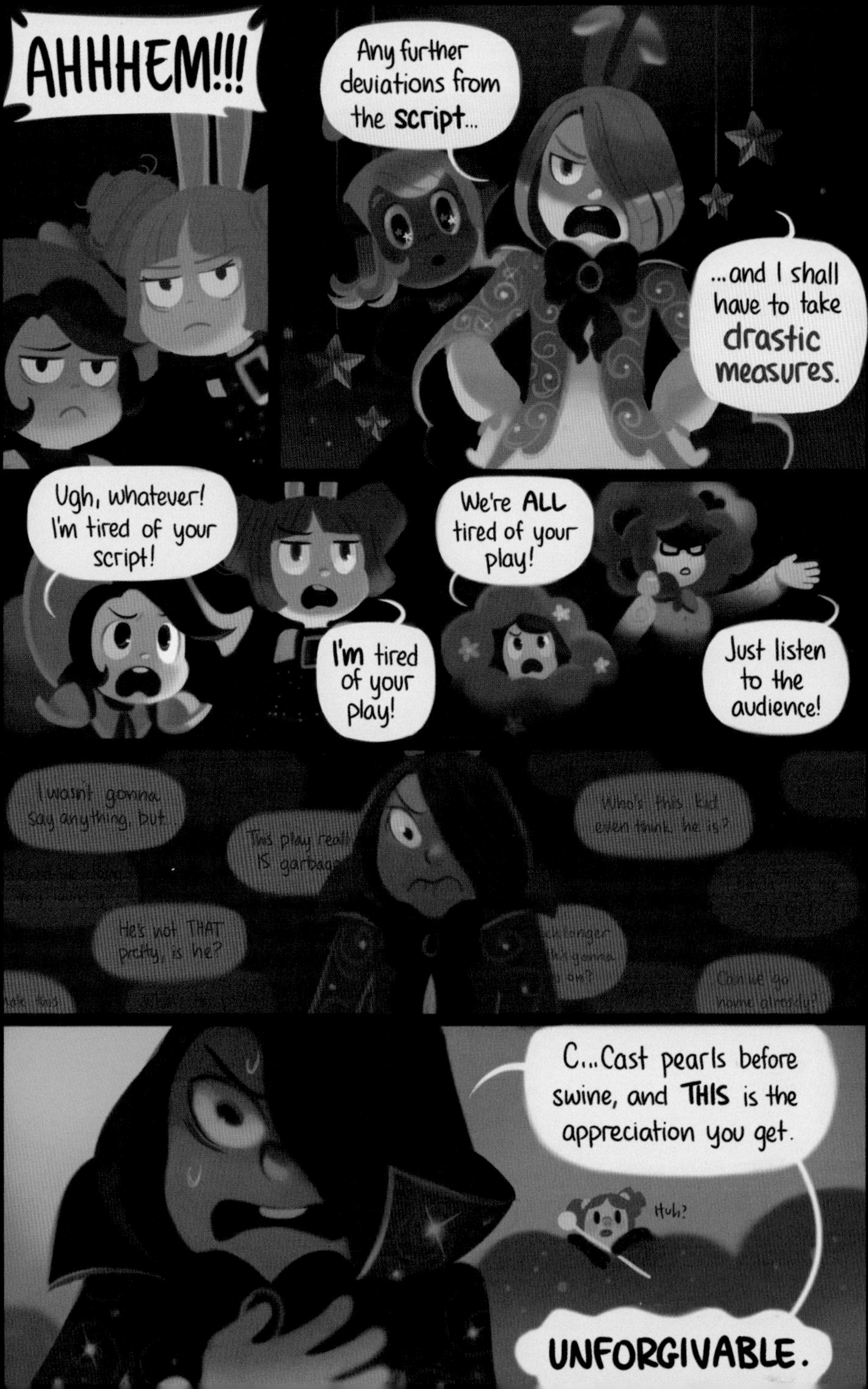
AHHHEM!!!
Any further deviations from the script...
...and I shall have to take drastic measures.
Ugh, whatever! I'm tired of your script!
I'm tired of your play!
We're ALL tired of your play!
Just listen to the audience!
I wasn't gonna say anything, but...
Who's this kid even think he is?
He's not THAT pretty, is he?
Can we go home already?
C...Cast pearls before swine, and THIS is the appreciation you get.
Huh?
UNFORGIVABLE.

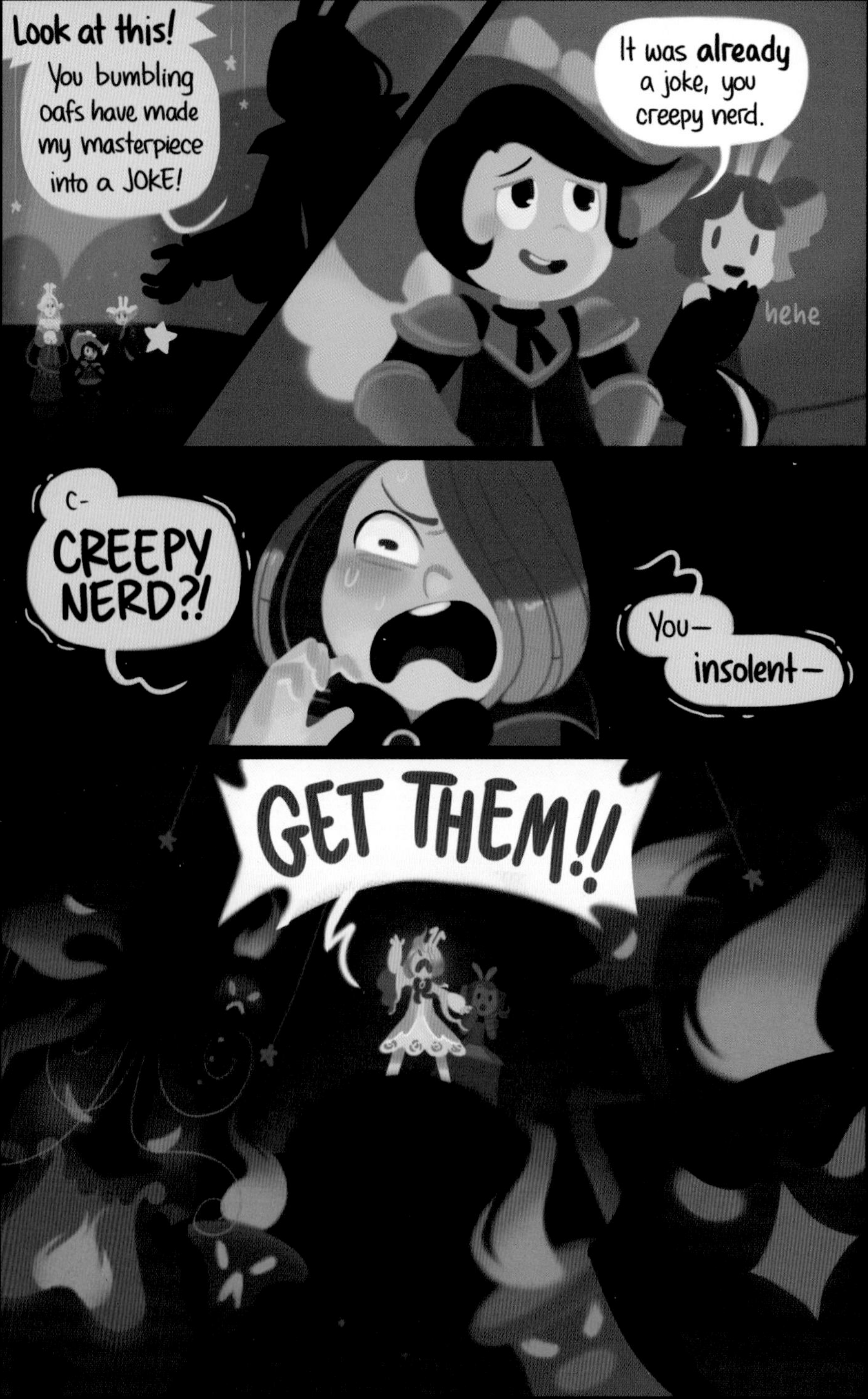
Look at this! You bumbling oafs have made my masterpiece into a JOKE!
It was already a joke, you creepy nerd.
hehe
C- CREEPY NERD?!
You— insolent—
GET THEM!!

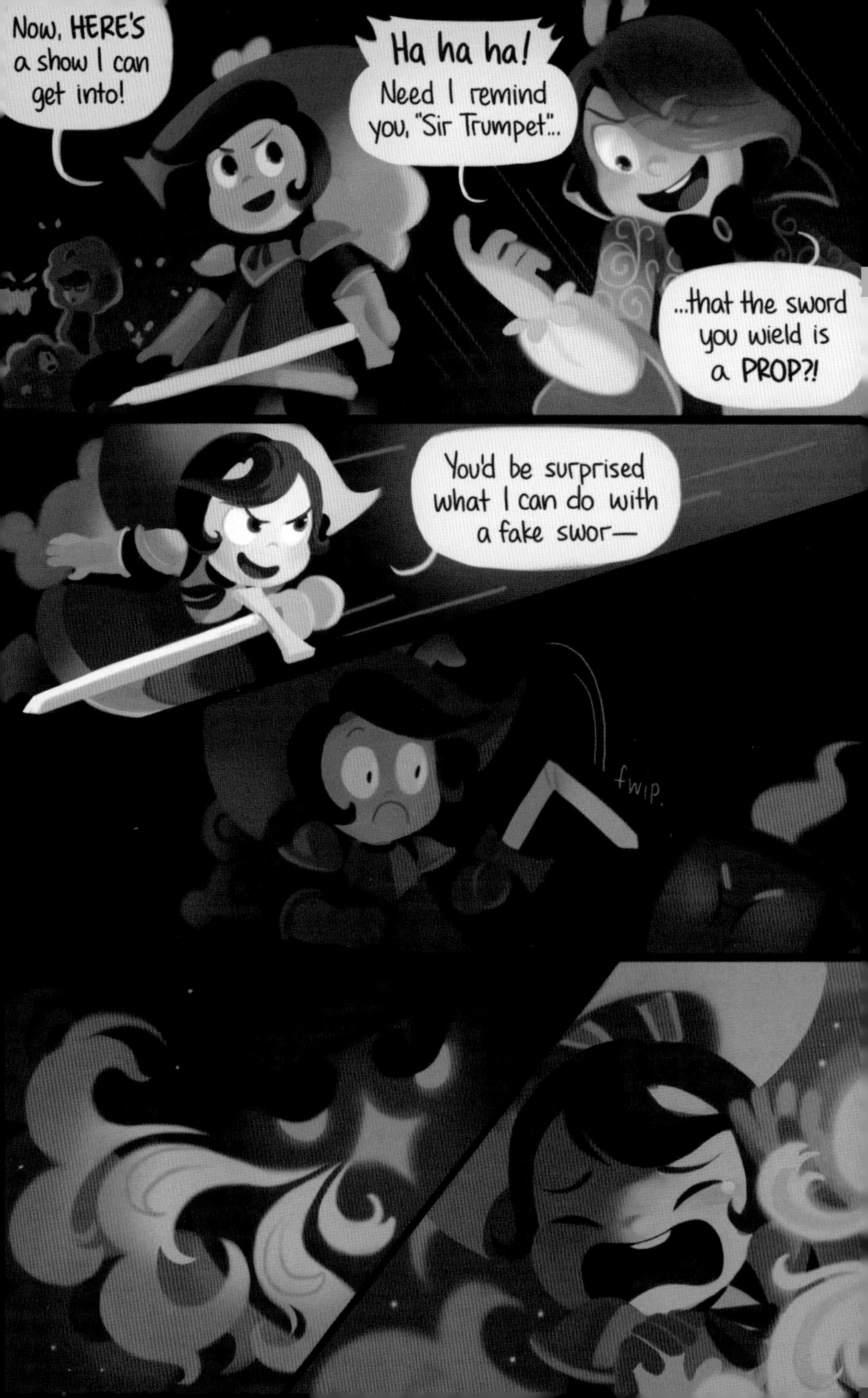
Now, HERE'S a show I can get into!
Ha ha ha! Need I remind you, "Sir Trumpet"...
...that the sword you wield is a PROP?!
You'd be surprised what I can do with a fake swor—
fwip.

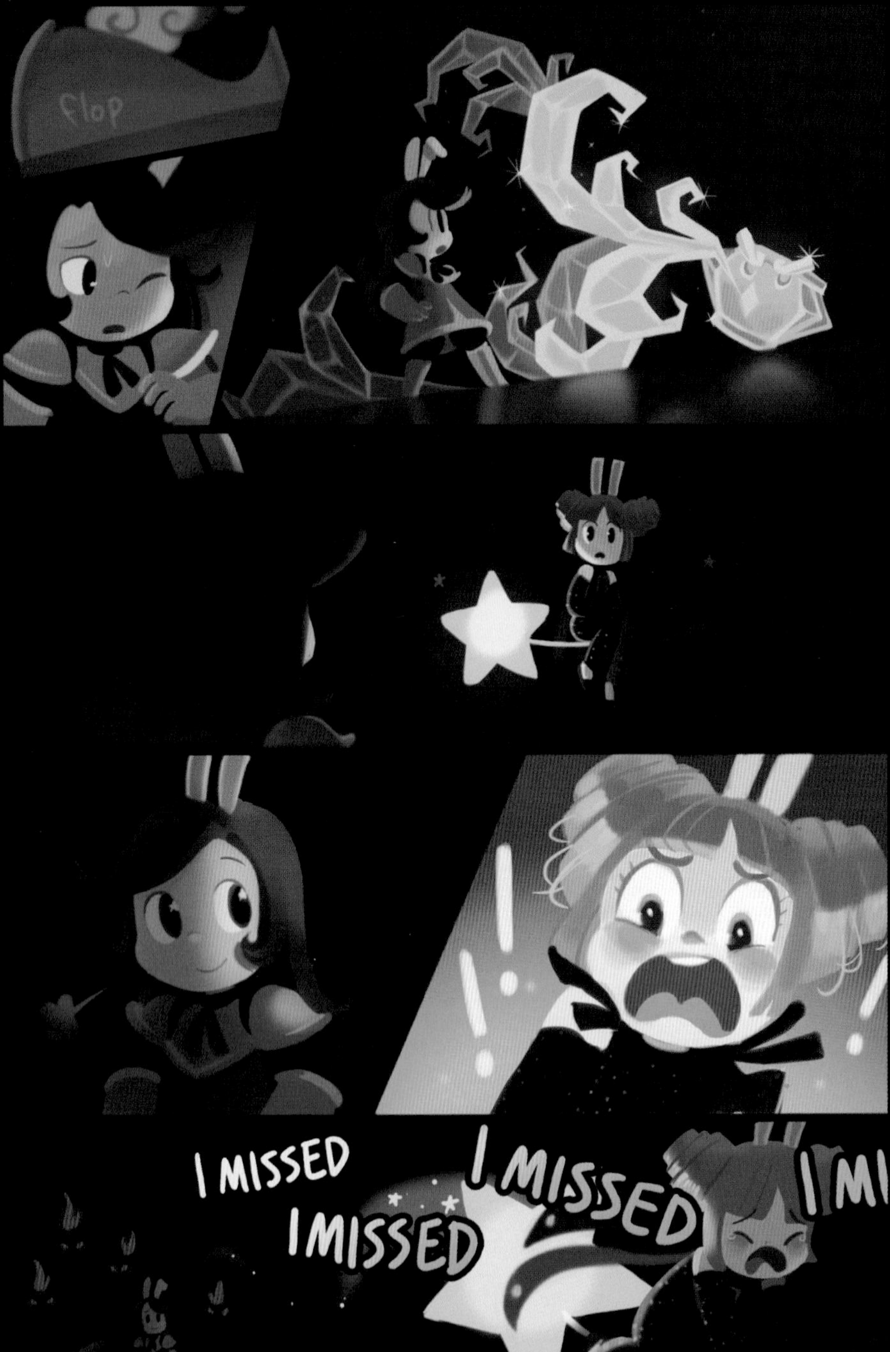
flop
I MISSED
I MISSED
I MISSED
I MI

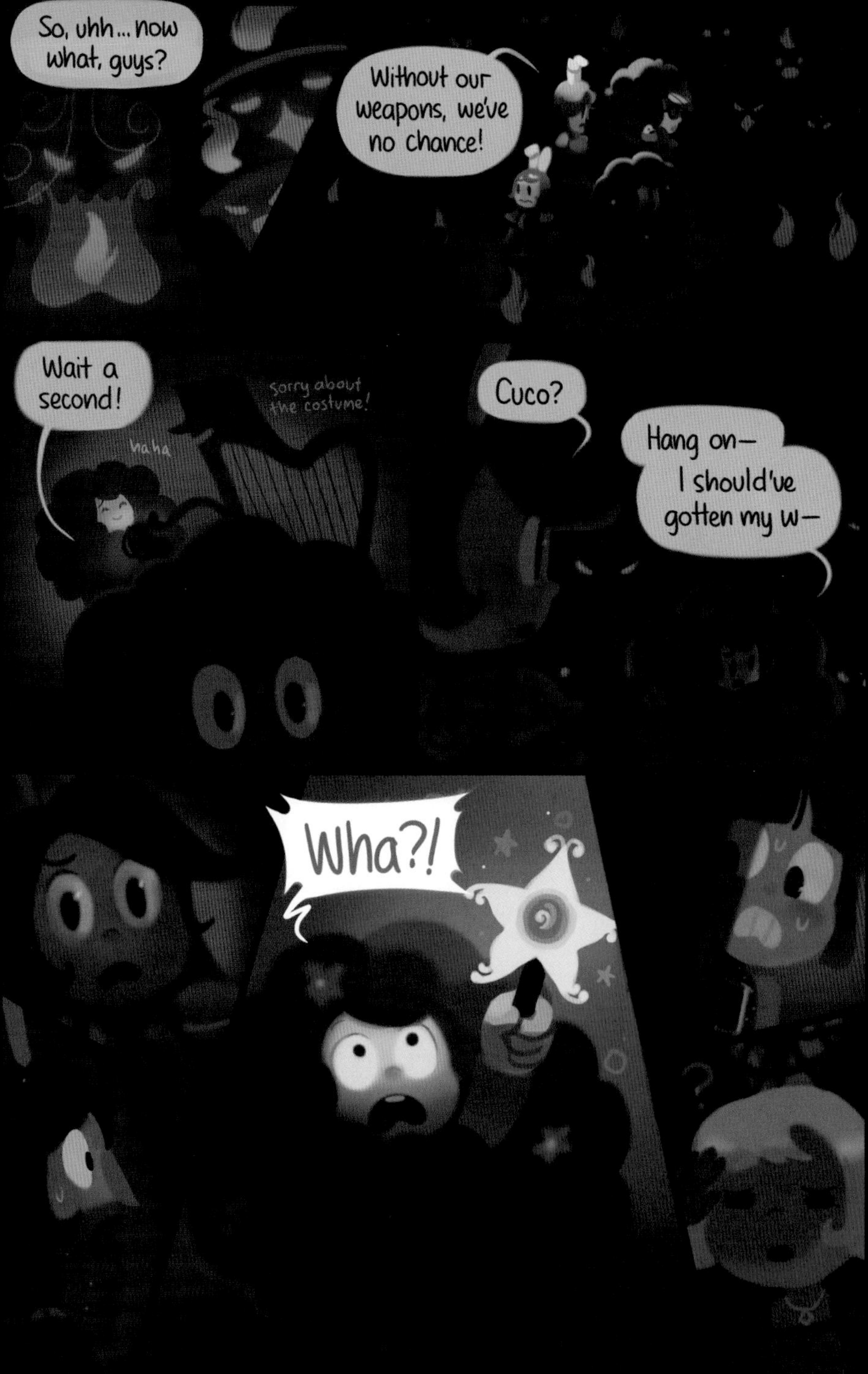
So, uhh... now what, guys?
Without our weapons, we've no chance!
Wait a second!
sorry about the costume!
haha
Cuco?
Hang on— I should've gotten my w—
Wha?!

Isn't this Splashmaster's...?
Hey!
Gonna use that, or what?
R-Right!
KSSHHHHHHHHH!!
What?!

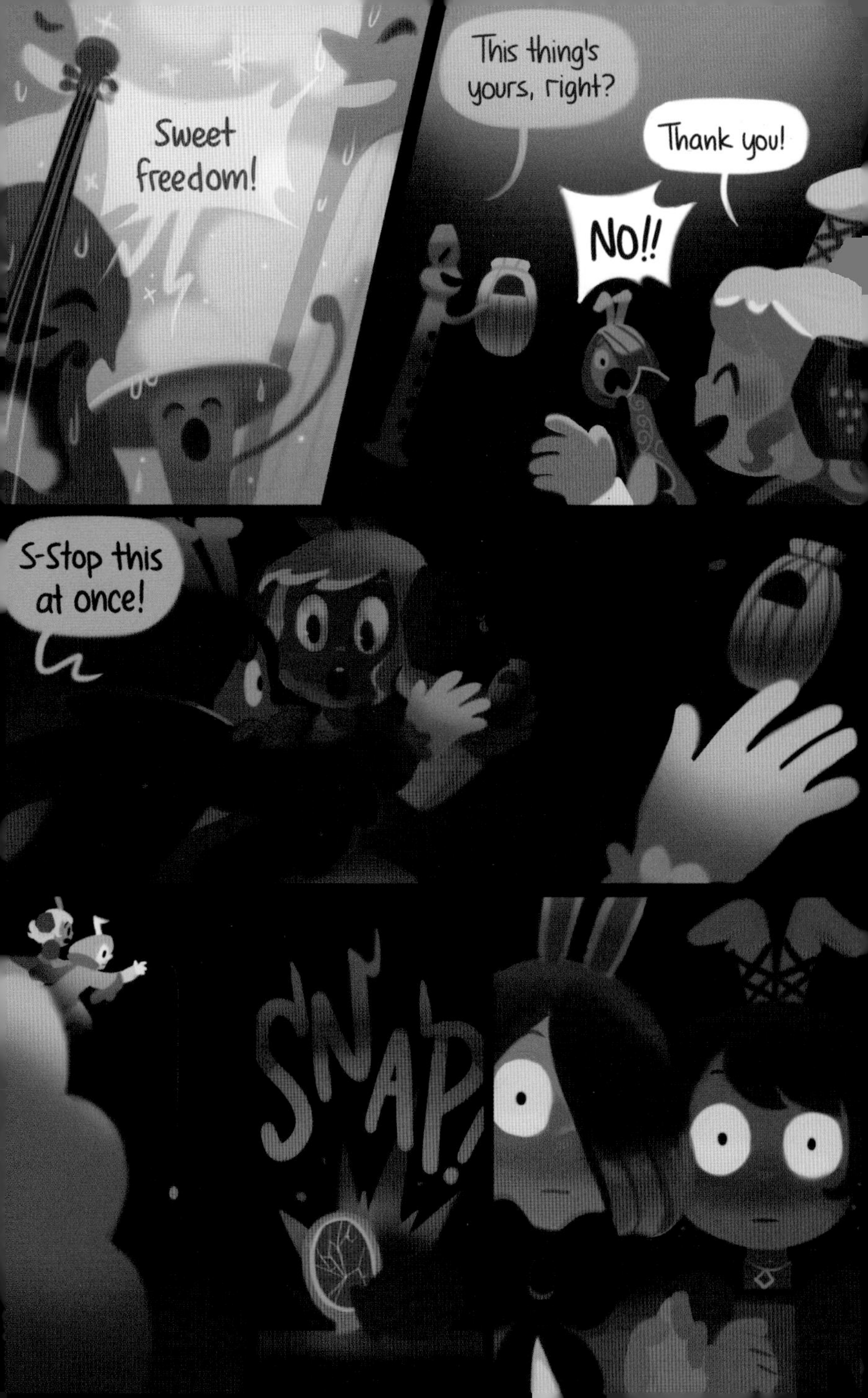
Sweet freedom!
This thing's yours, right?
Thank you!
NO!!
S-Stop this at once!
SNAP!

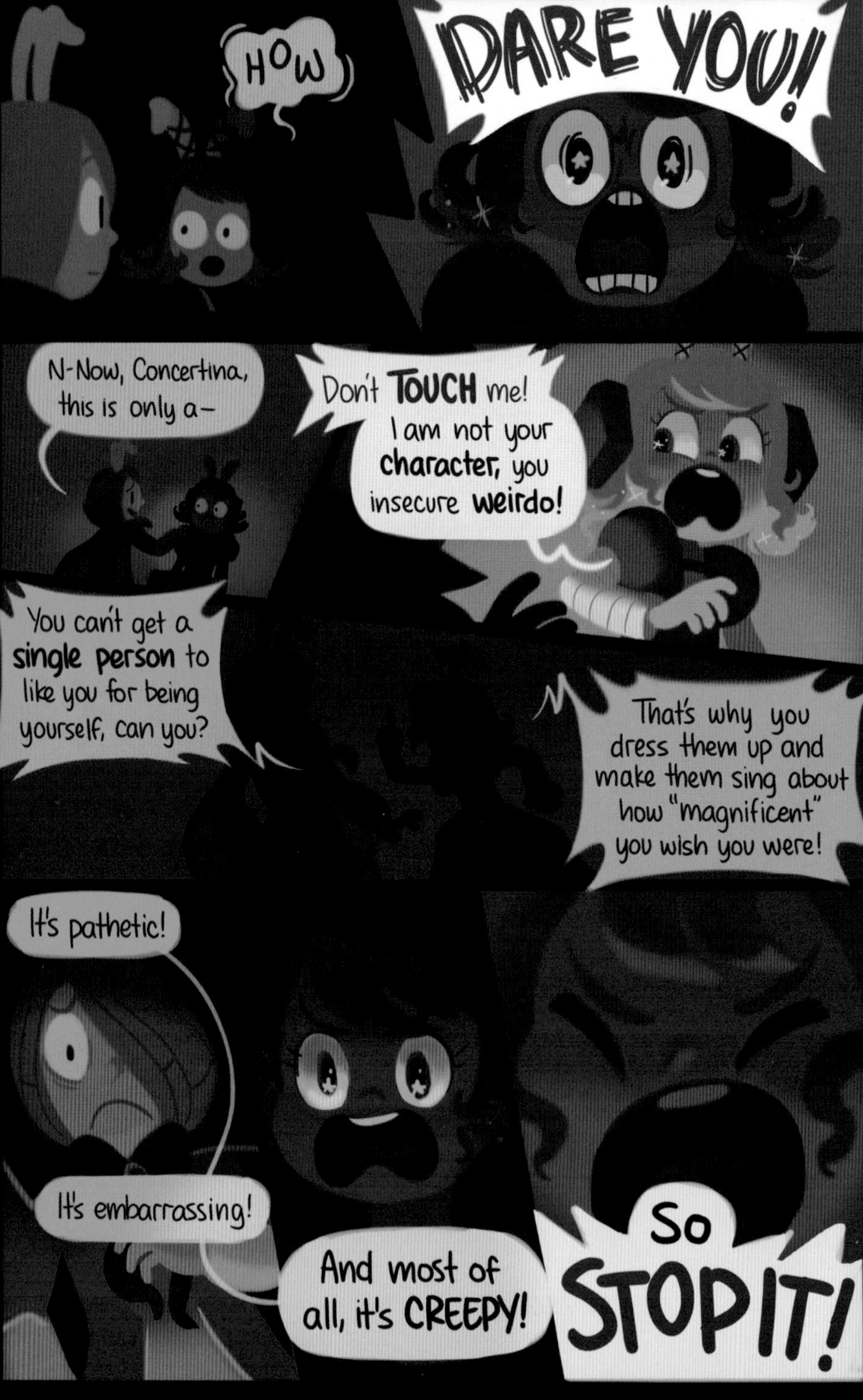
HOW
DARE YOU!
N-Now, Concertina, this is only a—
Don't TOUCH me! I am not your character, you insecure weirdo!
You can't get a single person to like you for being yourself, can you?
That's why you dress them up and make them sing about how "magnificent" you wish you were!
It's pathetic!
It's embarrassing!
And most of all, it's CREEPY!
So STOP IT!

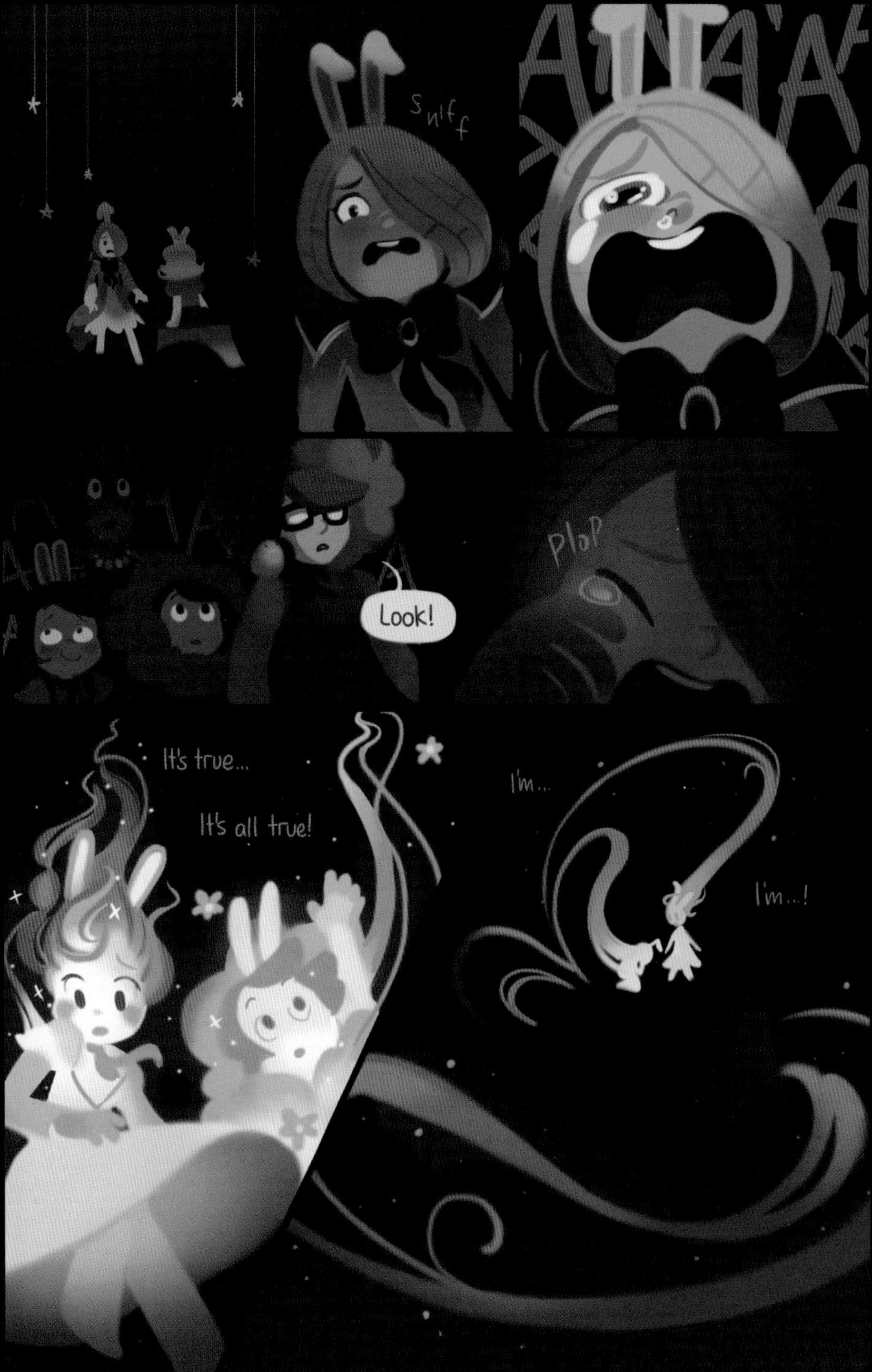
sniff
AAAA'A'
Look!
PLOP
It's true...
It's all true!
I'm...
I'm...!

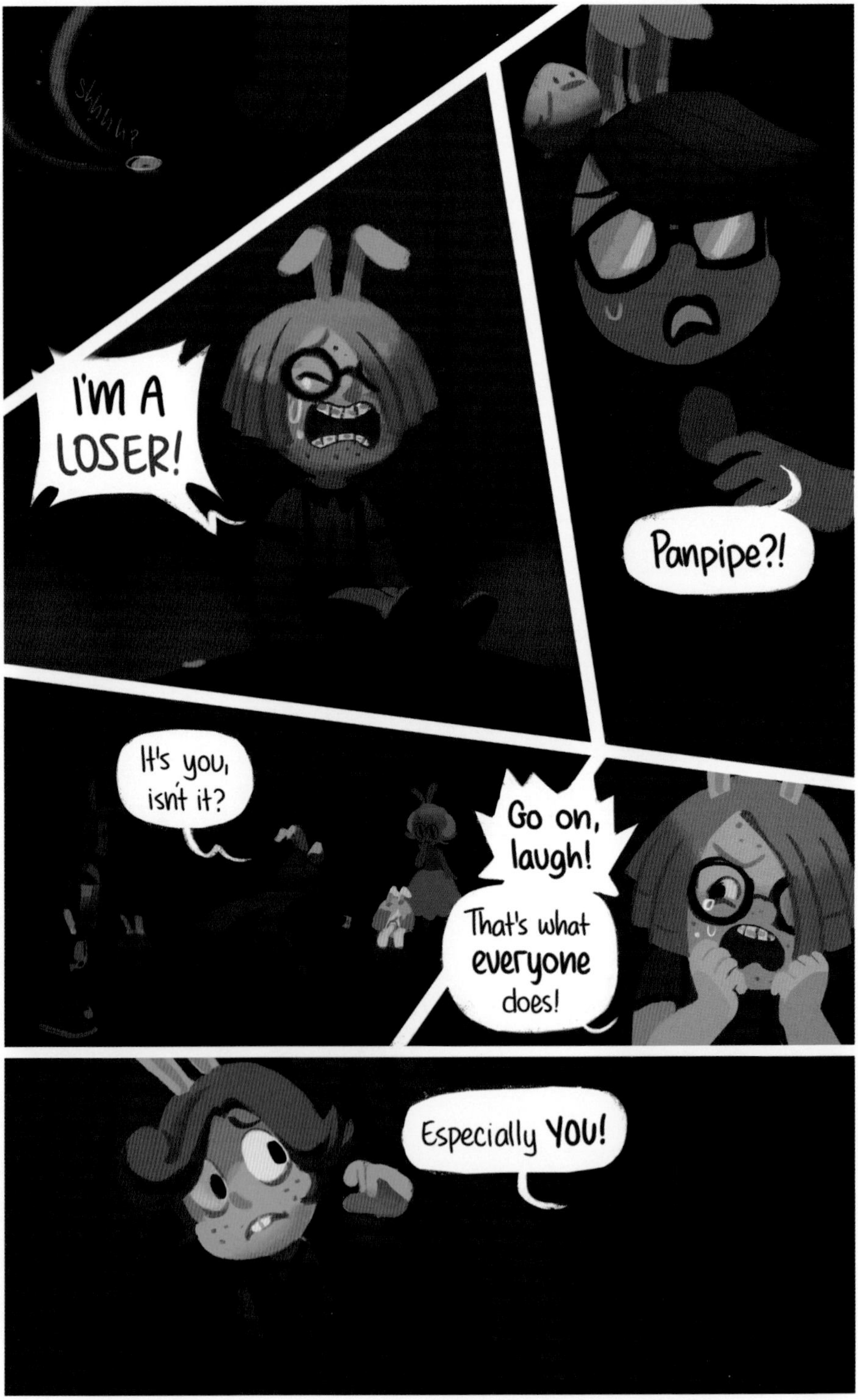
Shhhh?
I'M A LOSER!
Panpipe?!
It's you, isn't it?
Go on, laugh!
That's what everyone does!
Especially YOU!

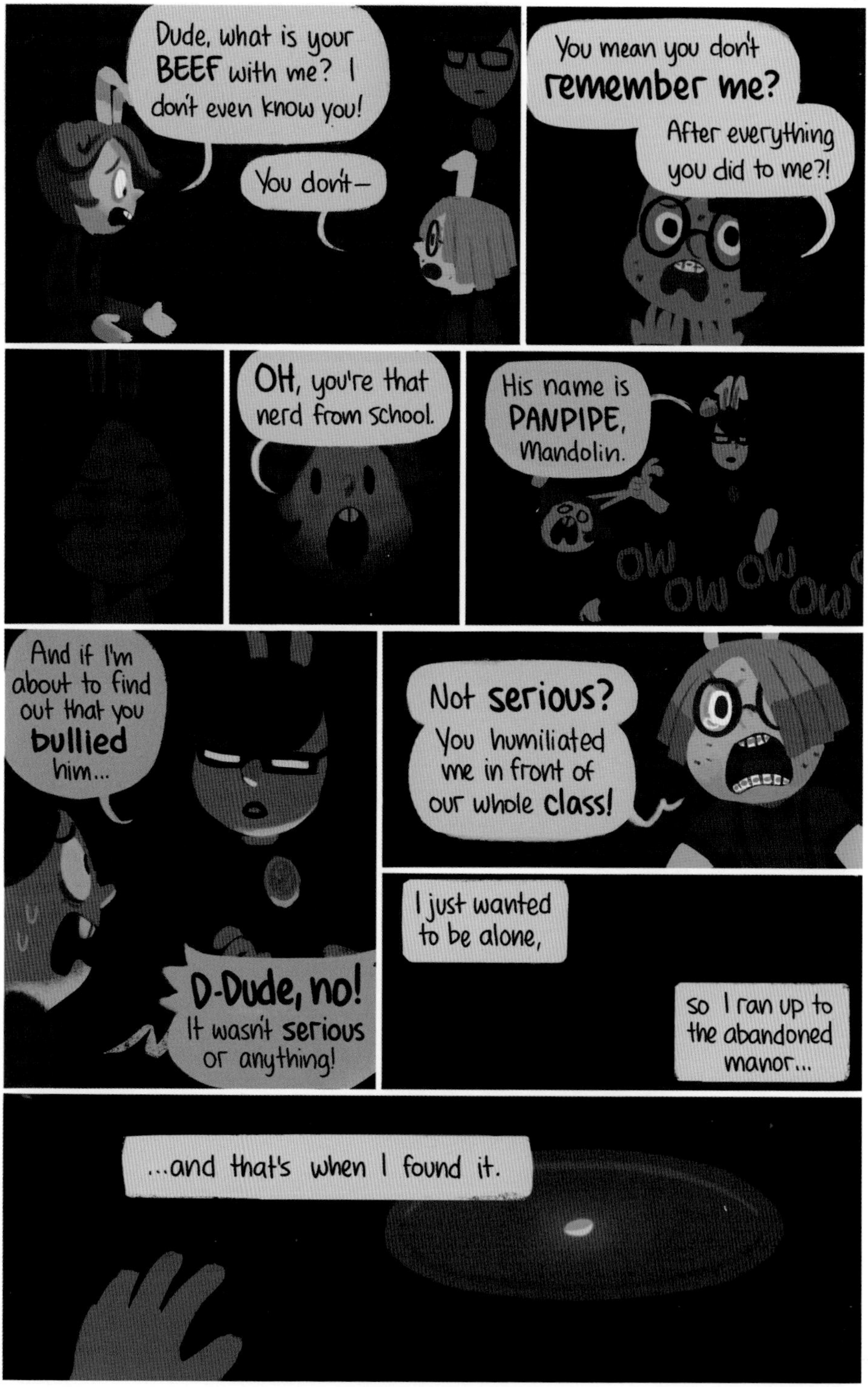
Dude, what is your BEEF with me? I don't even know you!
You don't—
You mean you don't remember me?
After everything you did to me?!
OH, you're that nerd from school.
His name is PANPIPE, Mandolin.
OW OW OW OW
And if I'm about to find out that you bullied him...
D-Dude, no! It wasn't serious or anything!
Not serious? You humiliated me in front of our whole class!
I just wanted to be alone,
so I ran up to the abandoned manor...
...and that's when I found it.

This little thing, huh?

WHOA!

No touching unless you want an encore, kid!

That's... Huh? A contact lens turned him into Legato?

Look, the count was... eccentric.

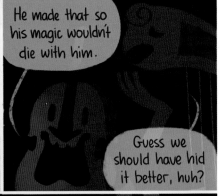

He made that so his magic wouldn't die with him.

Guess we should have hid it better, huh?

Geez, dude, I'm **SORRY**.

If I knew you were so sensitive—

I didn't raise a bully,

and I **know** I didn't raise a bully who can't **apologize**.

AGAGAGAGA

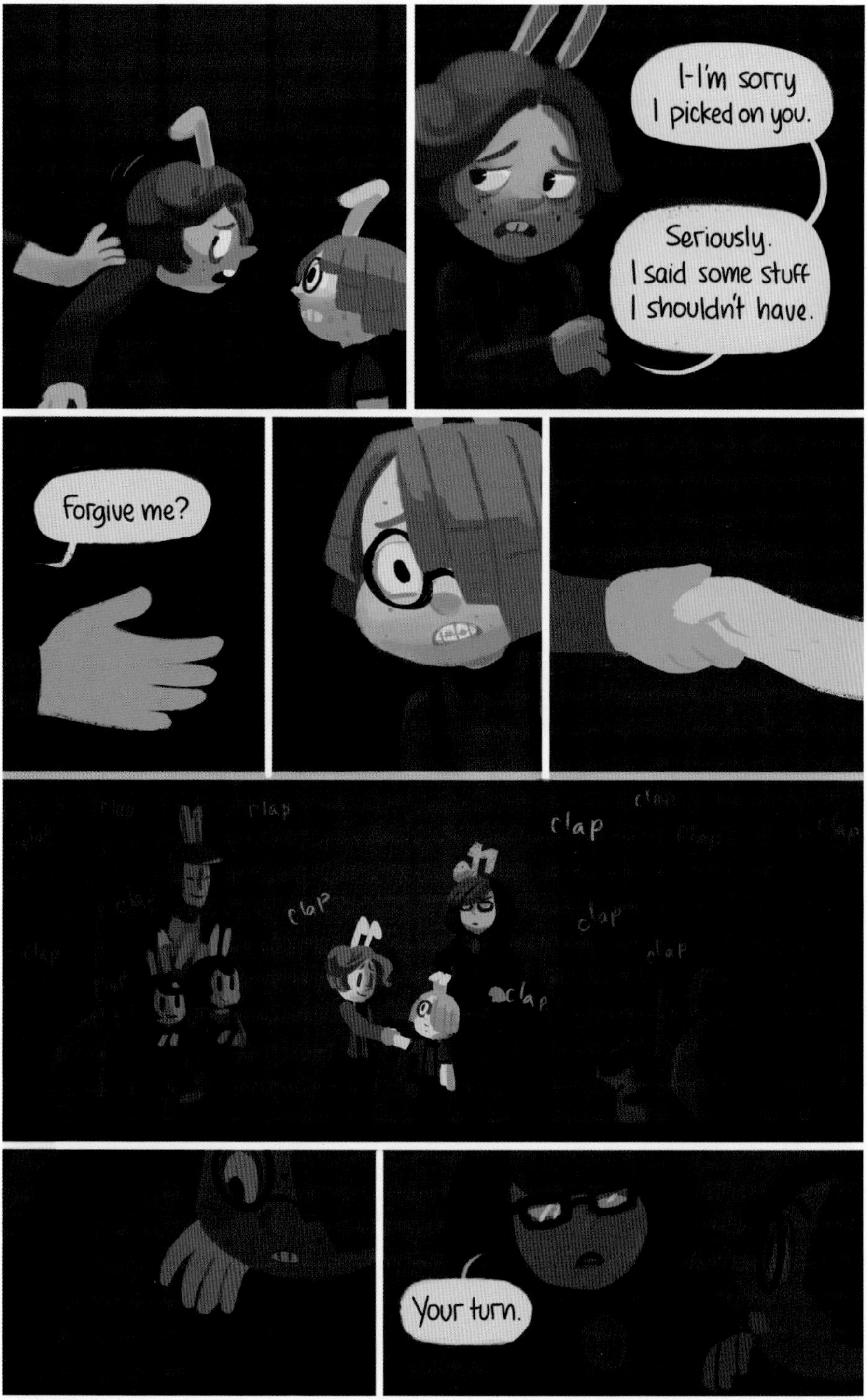
I-I'm sorry
I picked on you.
Seriously.
I said some stuff
I shouldn't have.
Forgive me?
clap
clap
clap
clap
clap
clap
clap
clap
Your turn.

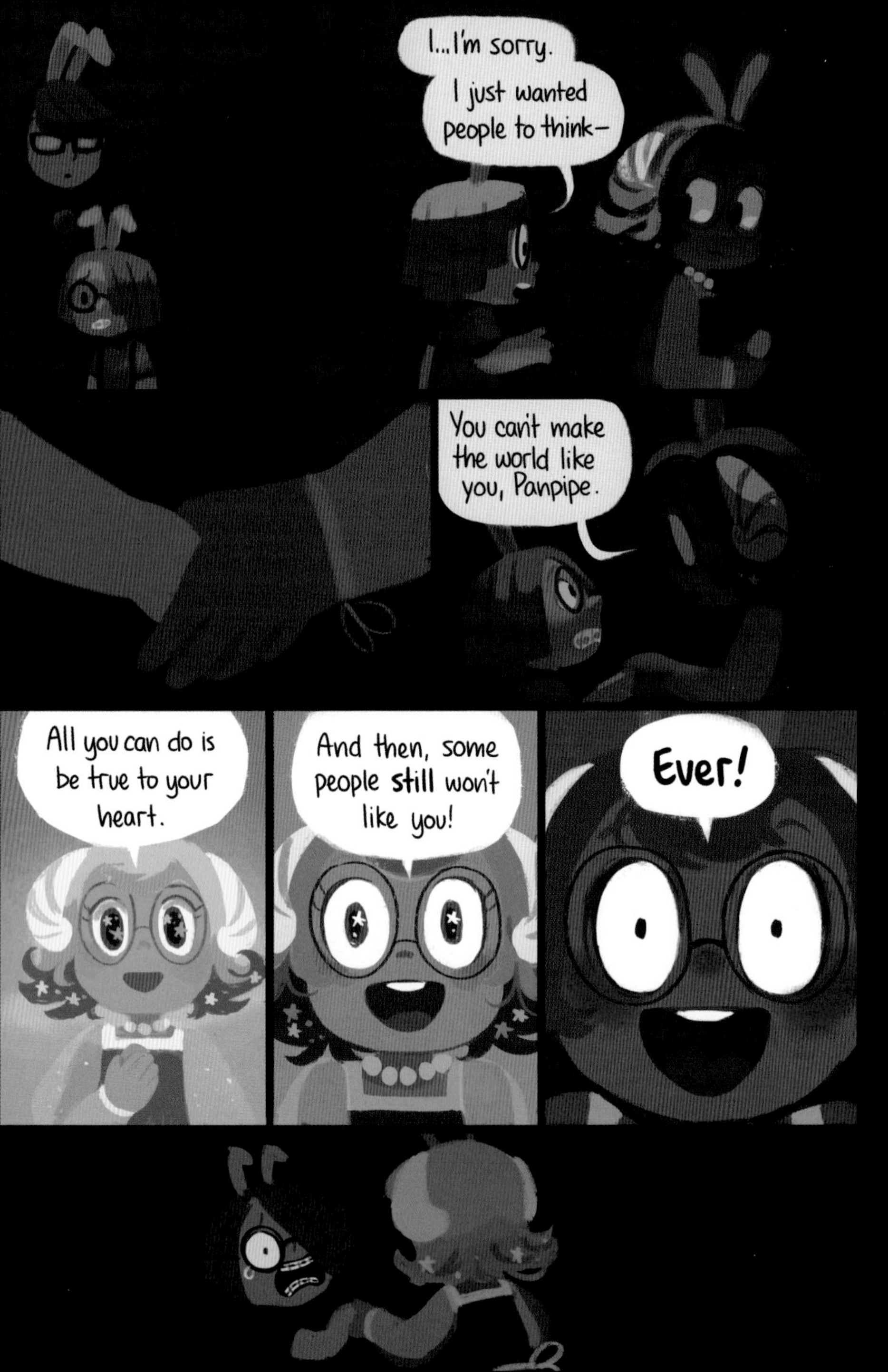
I...I'm sorry.
I just wanted people to think–
You can't make the world like you, Panpipe.
All you can do is be true to your heart.
And then, some people **still** won't like you!
Ever!

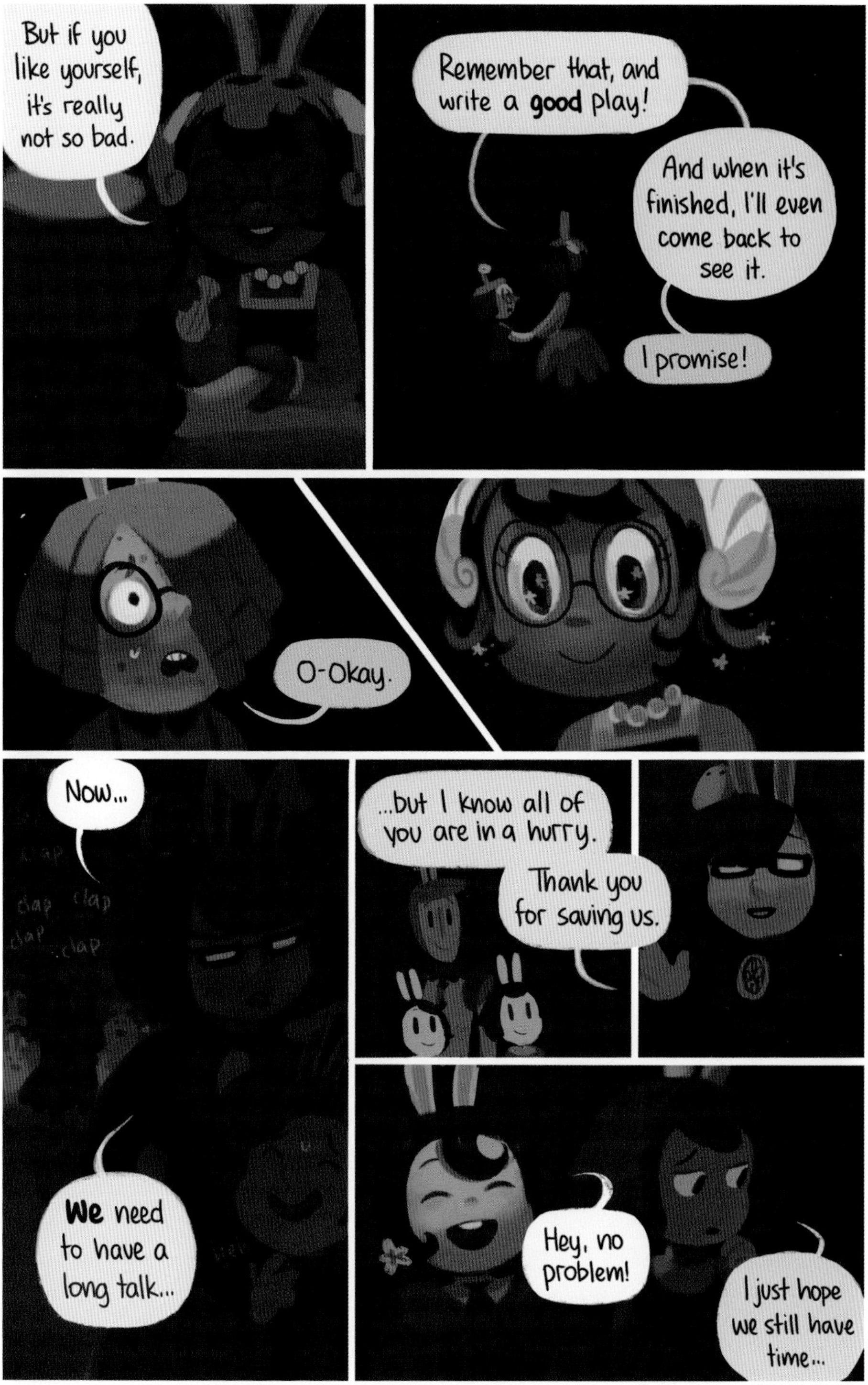
But if you like yourself, it's really not so bad.
Remember that, and write a **good** play!
And when it's finished, I'll even come back to see it.
I promise!
O-Okay.
Now...
...but I know all of you are in a hurry.
Thank you for saving us.
We need to have a long talk...
Hey, no problem!
I just hope we still have time...

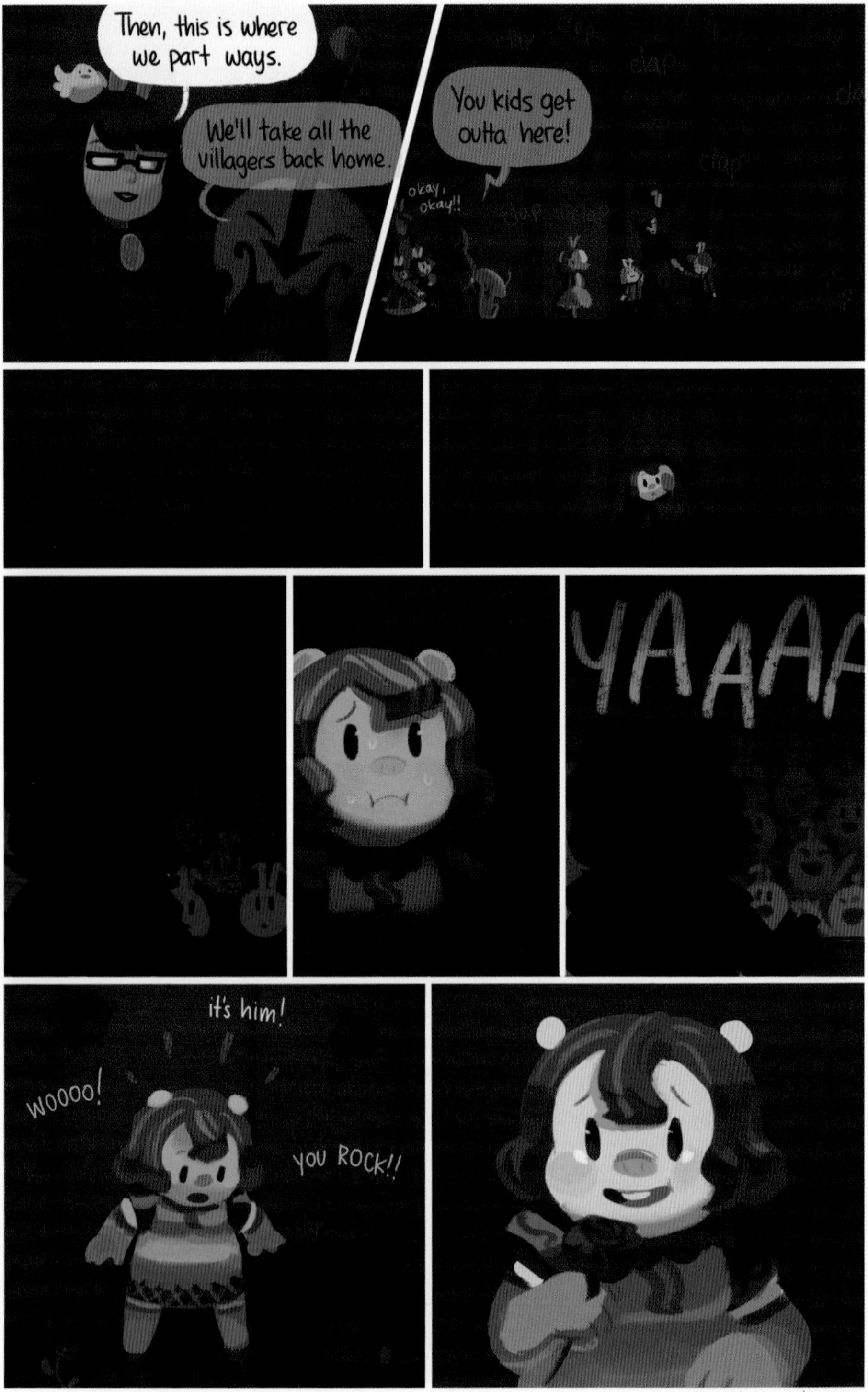
Then, this is where we part ways.
We'll take all the villagers back home.
You kids get outta here!
okay, okay!!
YAAAA
it's him!
WOOOO!
YOU ROCK!!

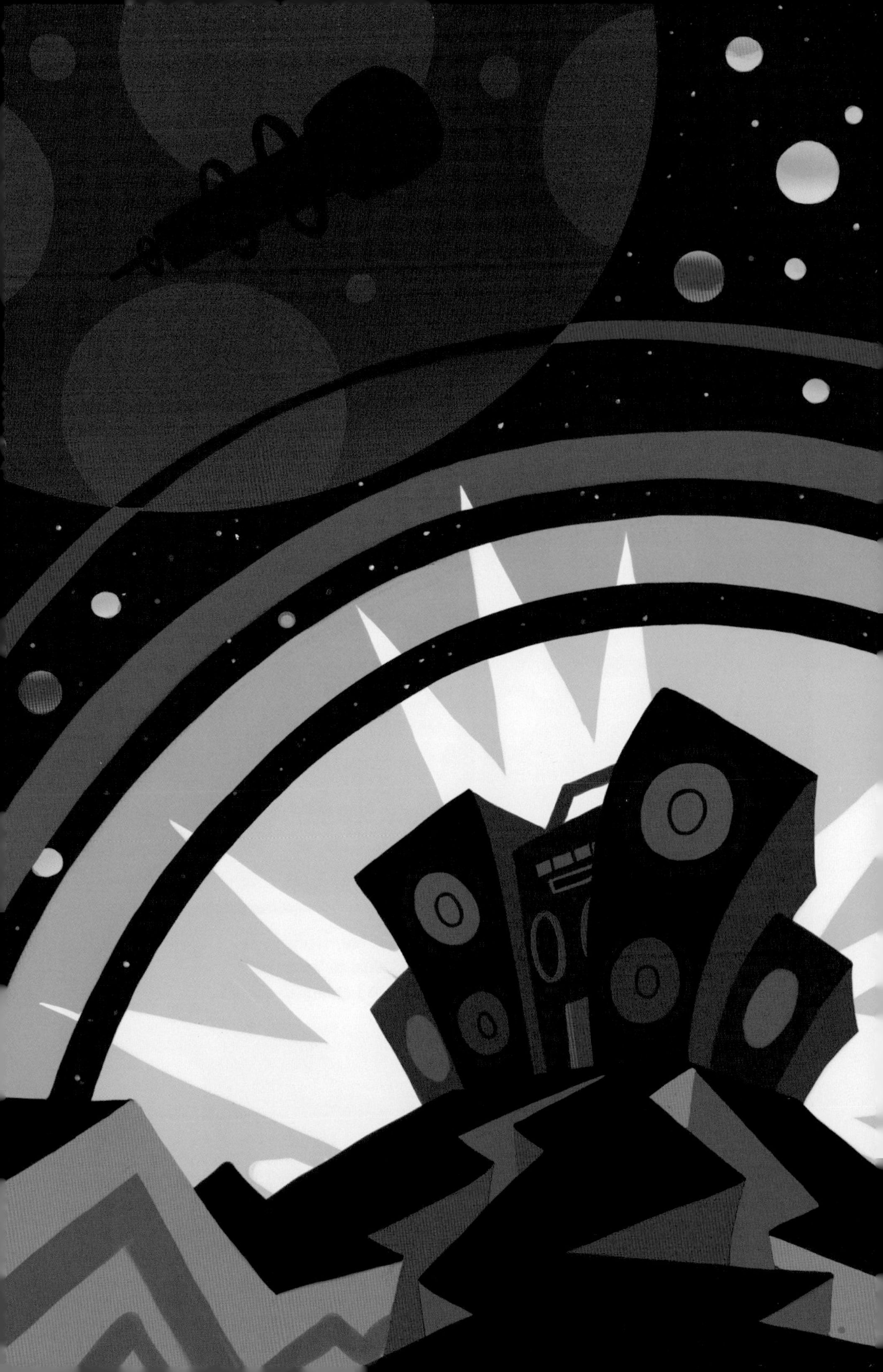

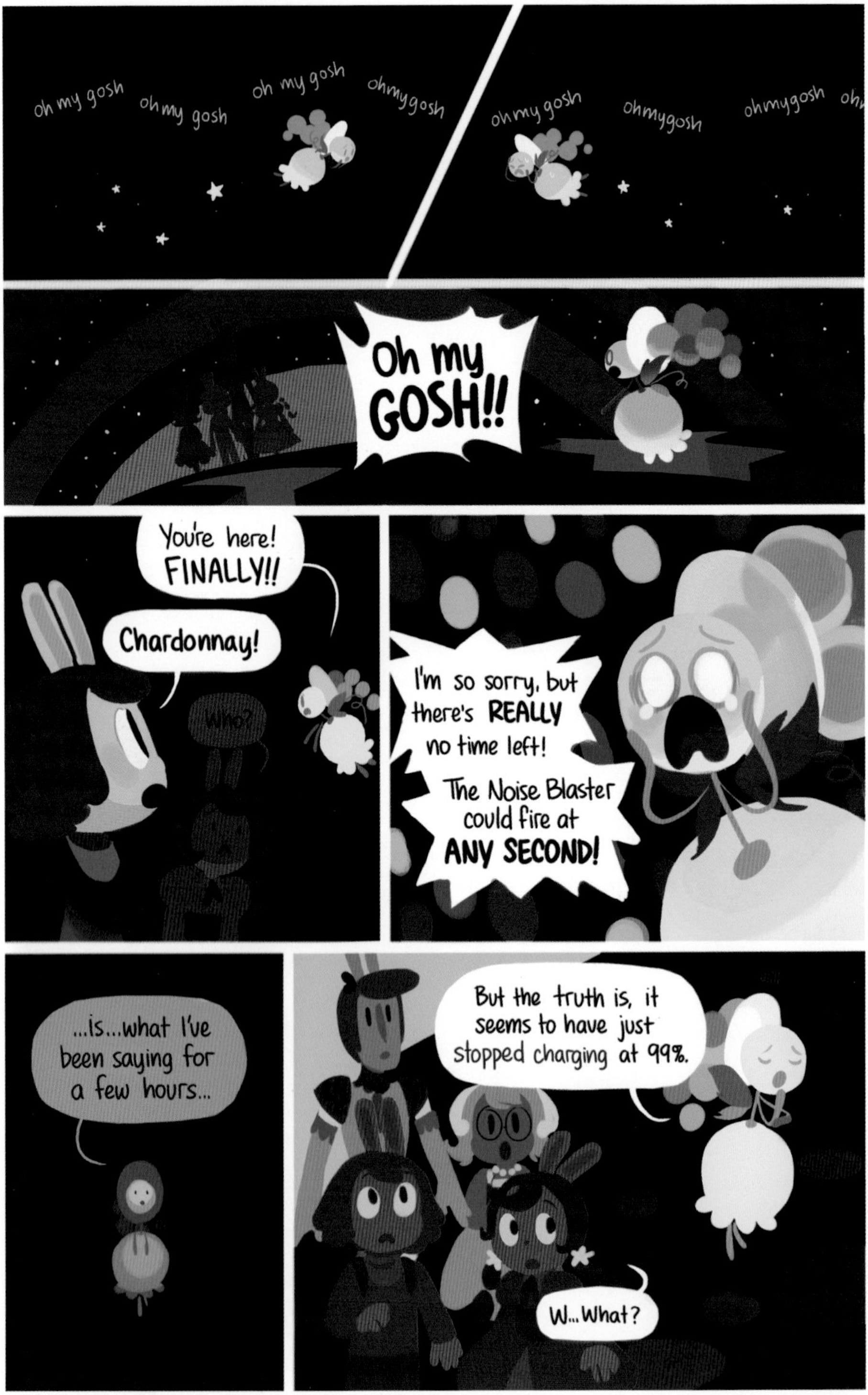
oh my gosh
oh my gosh
oh my gosh
ohmygosh
oh my gosh
ohmygosh
ohmygosh
Oh my GOSH!!
You're here! FINALLY!!
Chardonnay!
Who?
I'm so sorry, but there's REALLY no time left!
The Noise Blaster could fire at ANY SECOND!
...is...what I've been saying for a few hours...
But the truth is, it seems to have just stopped charging at 99%.
W...What?

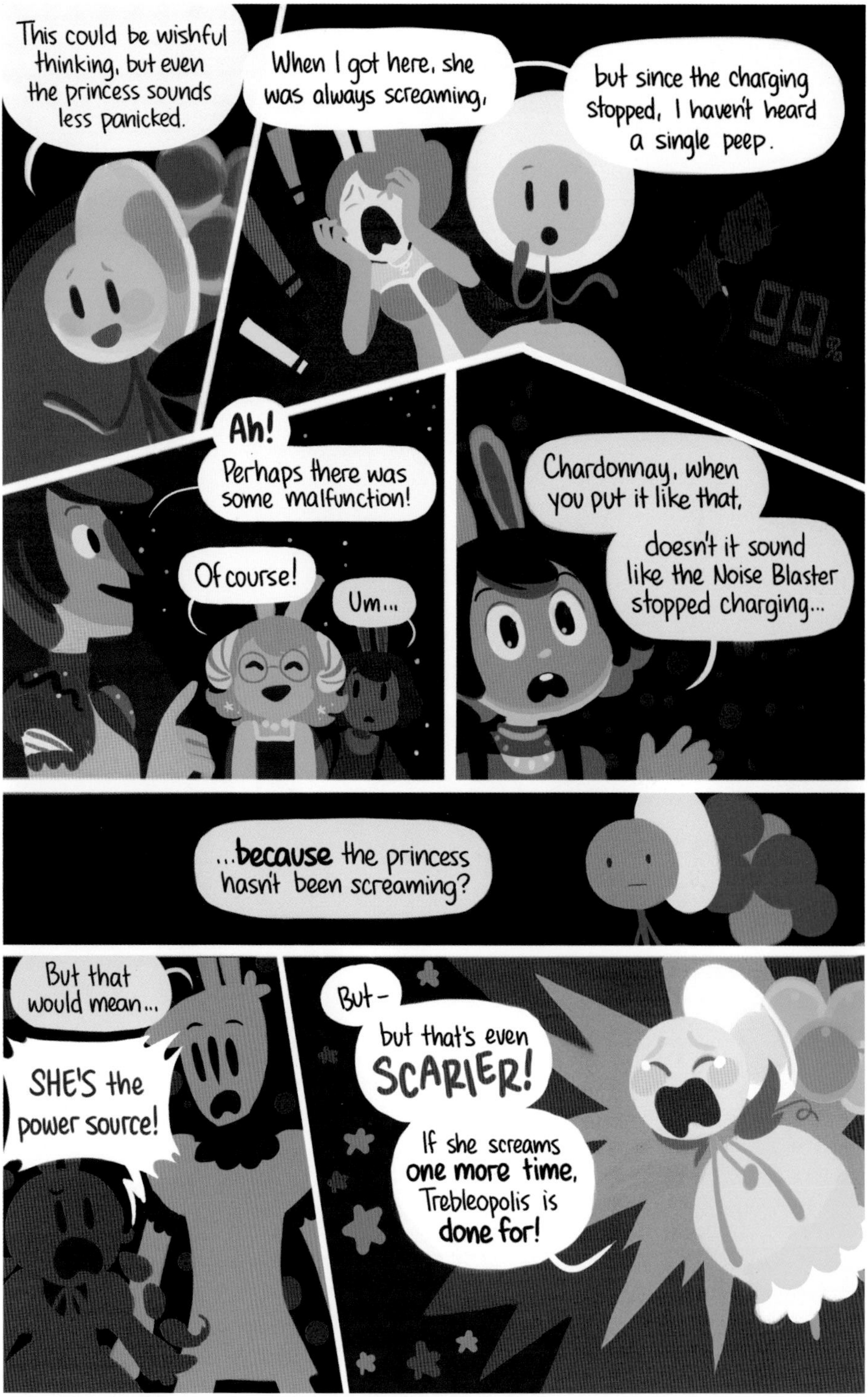
This could be wishful thinking, but even the princess sounds less panicked.
When I got here, she was always screaming,
but since the charging stopped, I haven't heard a single peep.
99%
Ah!
Perhaps there was some malfunction!
Of course!
Um...
Chardonnay, when you put it like that,
doesn't it sound like the Noise Blaster stopped charging...
...**because** the princess hasn't been screaming?
But that would mean...
SHE'S the power source!
But-
but that's even SCARIER!
If she screams **one more time**, Trebleopolis is **done for!**

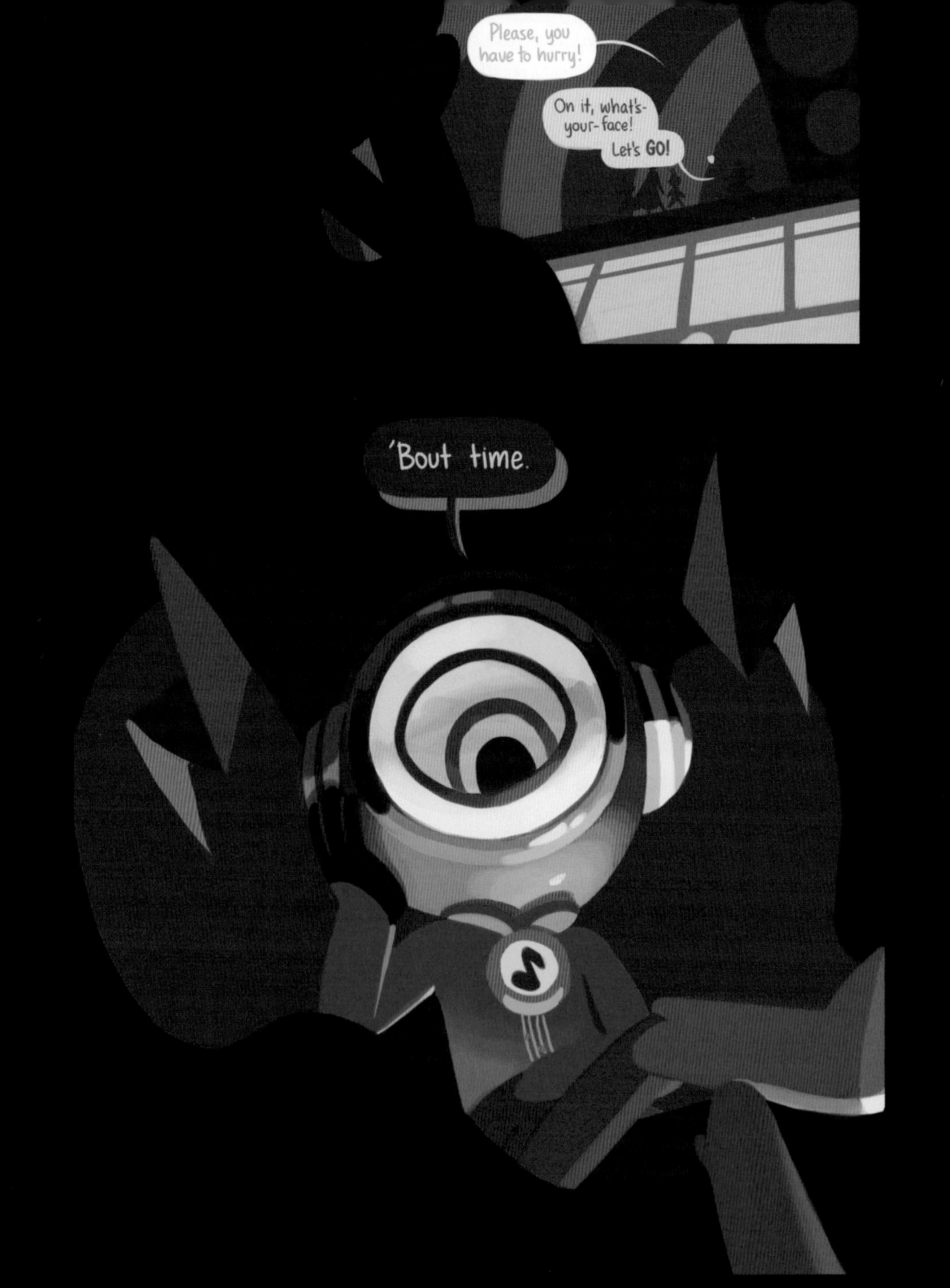
Please, you have to hurry!
On it, what's-your-face!
Let's **GO!**
'Bout time.

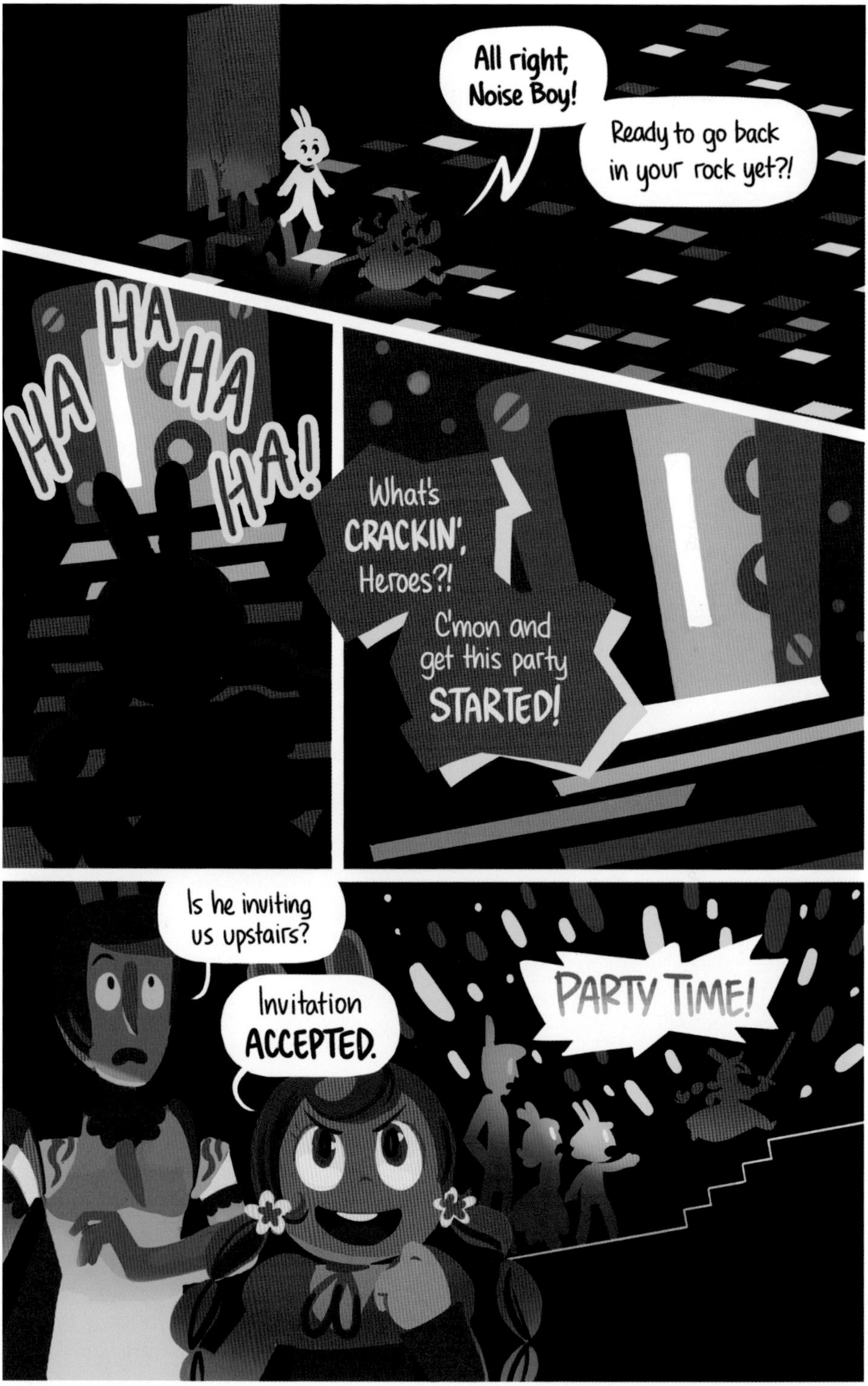
All right, Noise Boy!
Ready to go back in your rock yet?!
HA HA HA HA HA!
What's CRACKIN', Heroes?!
C'mon and get this party STARTED!
Is he inviting us upstairs?
Invitation ACCEPTED.
PARTY TIME!

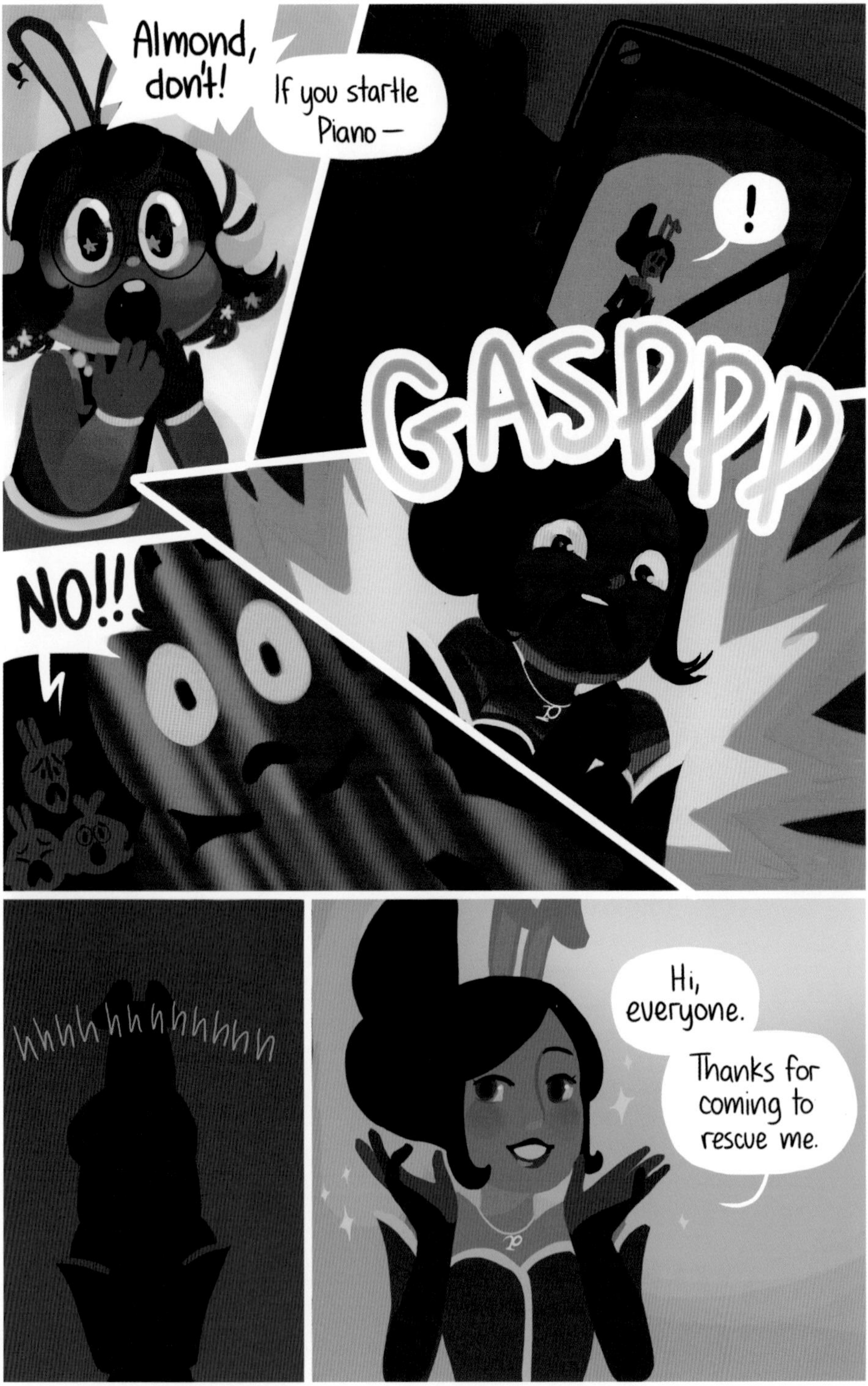
Almond, don't!
If you startle Piano —
!
GASPPP
NO!!
hhhhhhhhhhhh
Hi, everyone.
Thanks for coming to rescue me.

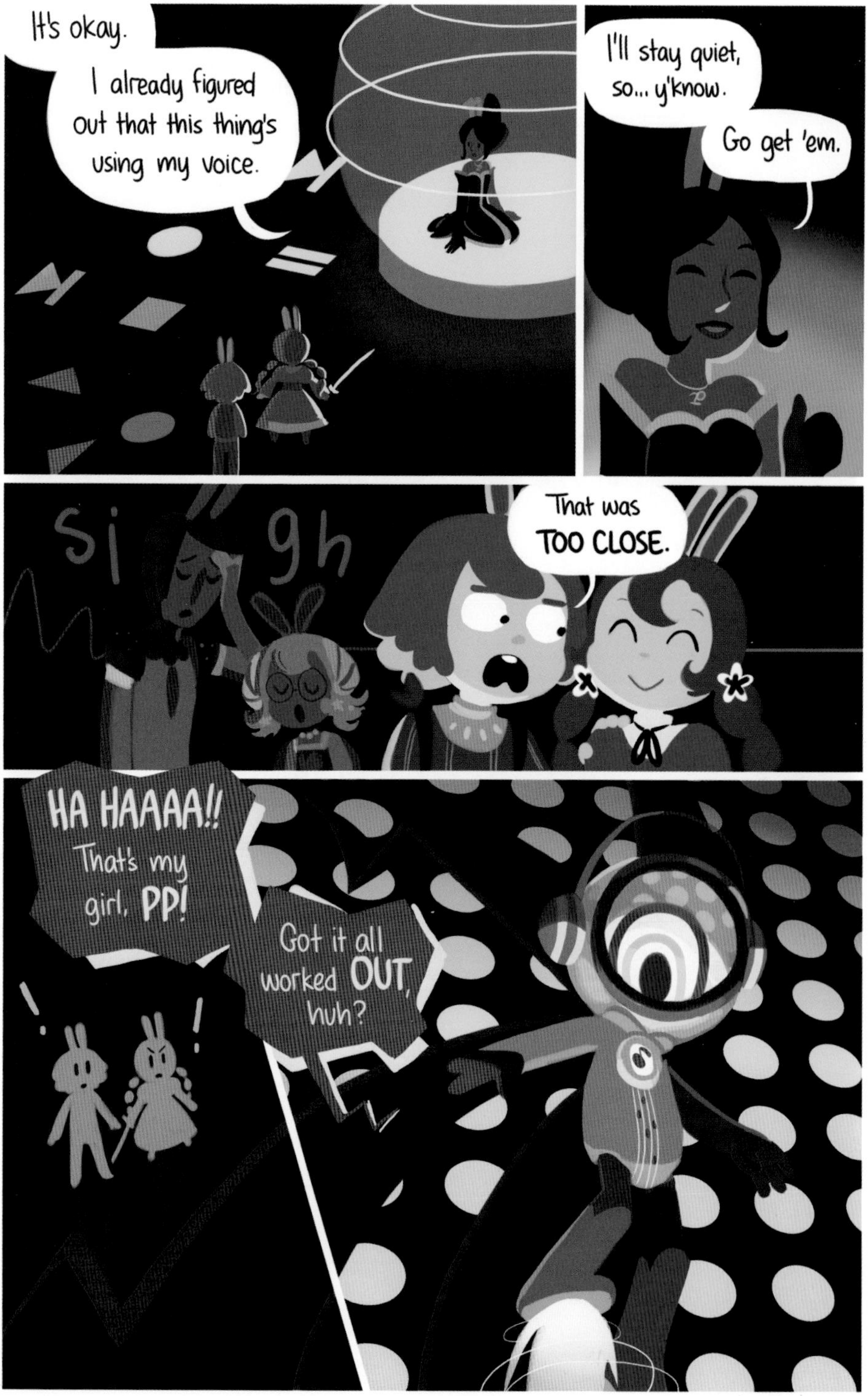
It's okay.
I already figured out that this thing's using my voice.
I'll stay quiet, so... y'know.
Go get 'em.
si gh
That was TOO CLOSE.
HA HAAAA!! That's my girl, PP!
Got it all worked OUT, huh?
!
!

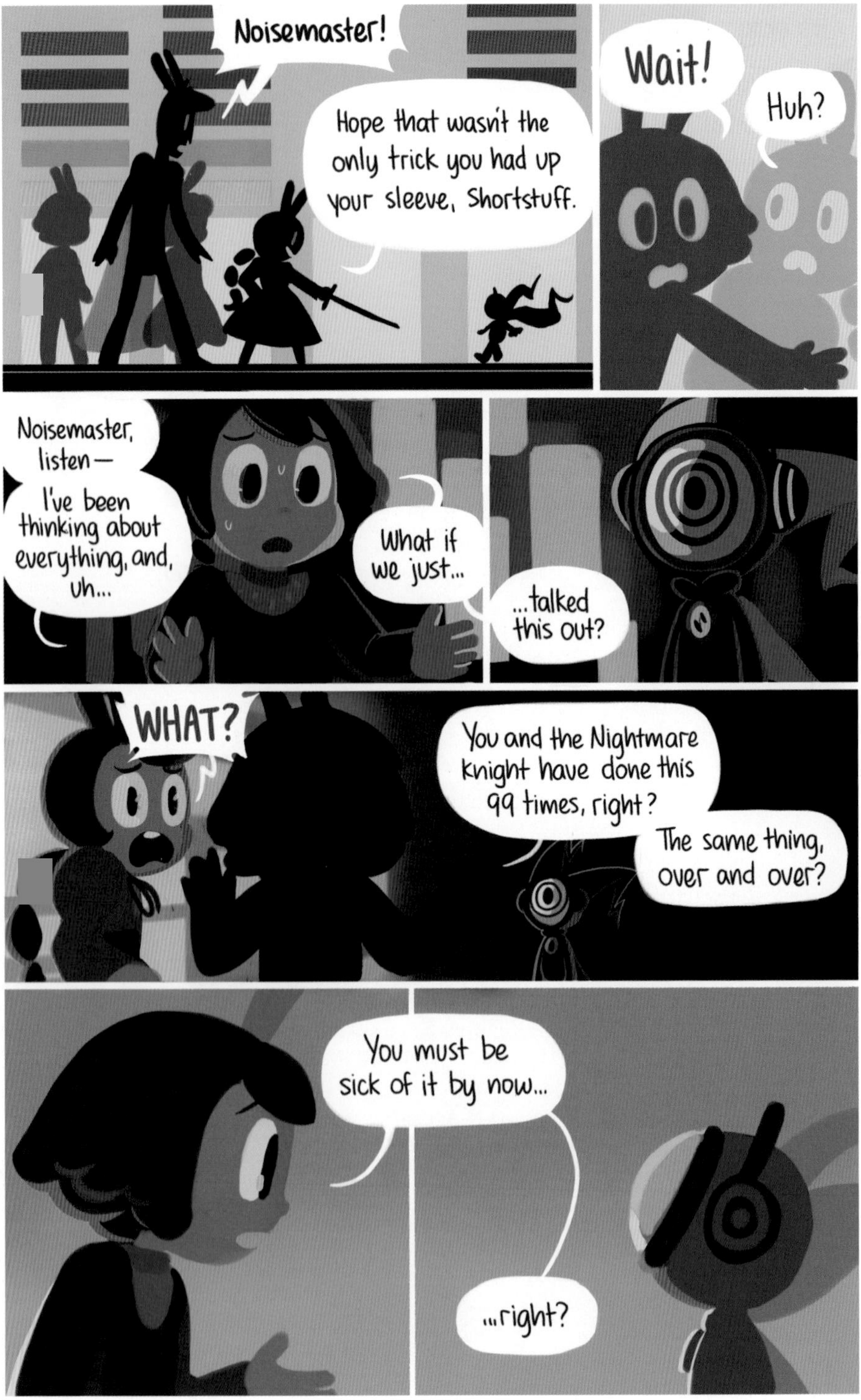
Noisemaster!
Hope that wasn't the only trick you had up your sleeve, Shortstuff.
Wait!
Huh?
Noisemaster, listen—
I've been thinking about everything, and, uh...
What if we just...
...talked this out?
WHAT?
You and the Nightmare Knight have done this 99 times, right?
The same thing, over and over?
You must be sick of it by now...
...right?

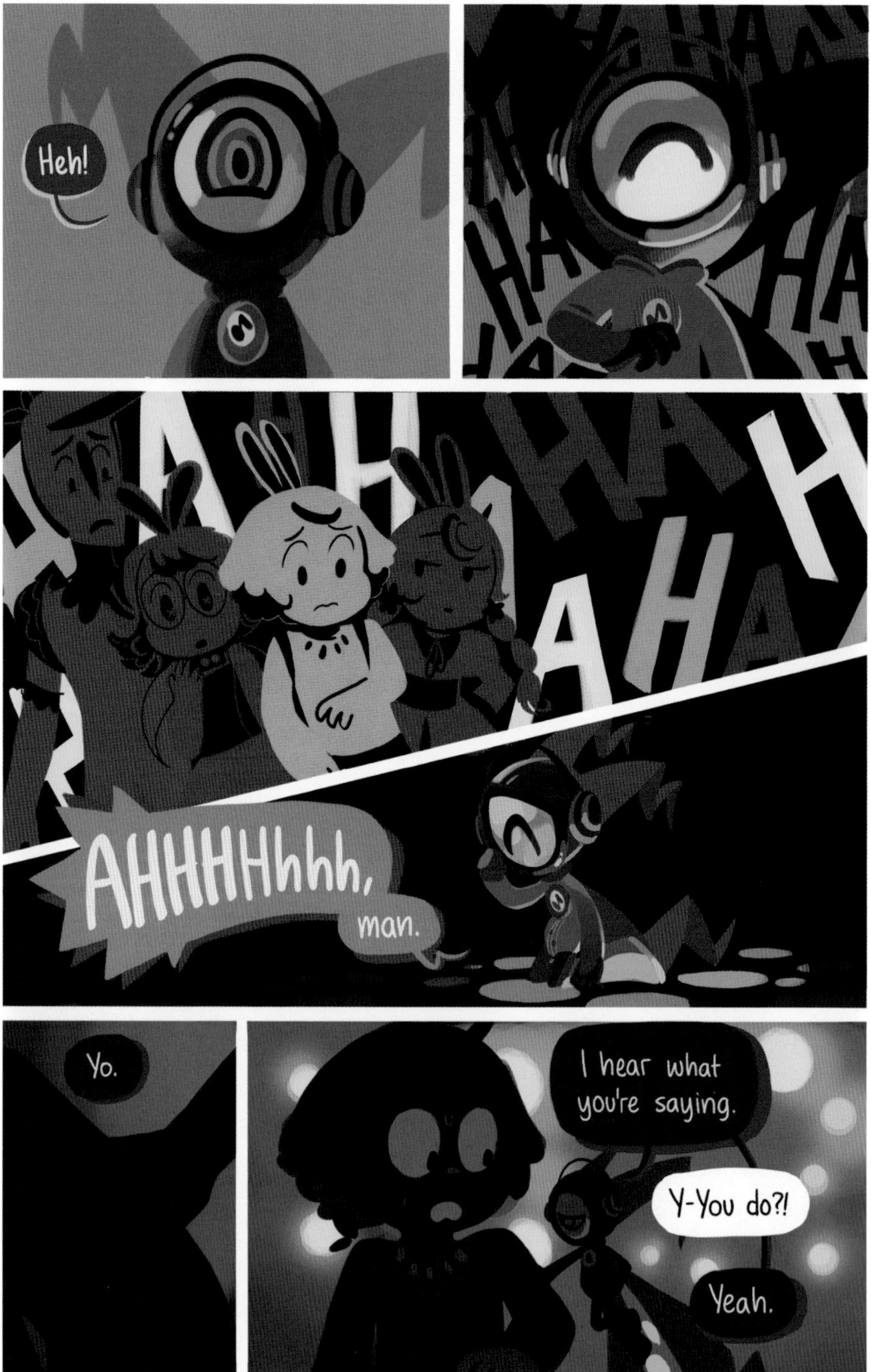
Heh!
AHHHHhhh,
man.
Yo.
I hear what you're saying.
Y-You do?!
Yeah.

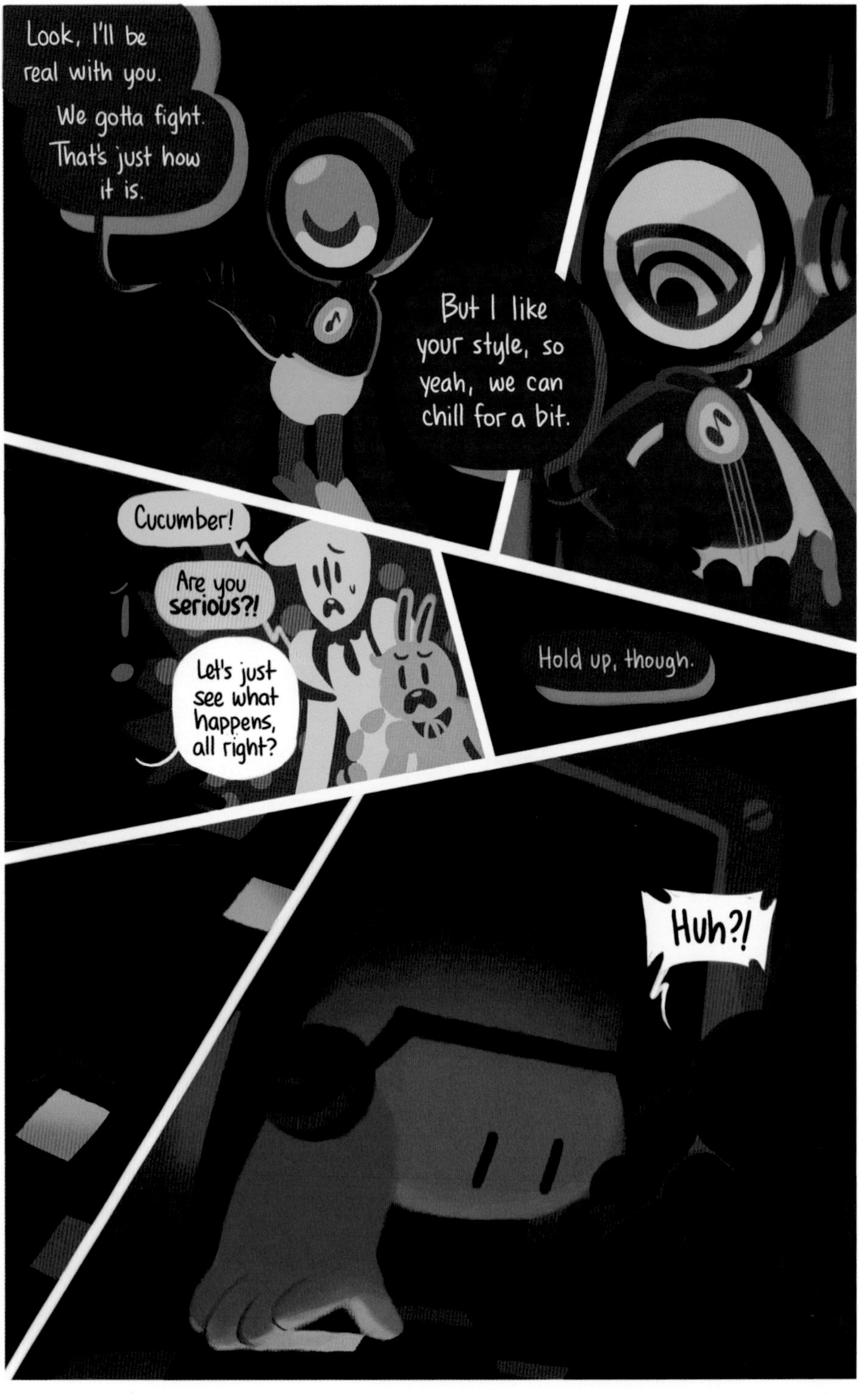
Look, I'll be real with you.
We gotta fight. That's just how it is.
But I like your style, so yeah, we can chill for a bit.
Cucumber!
Are you serious?!
Let's just see what happens, all right?
Hold up, though.
Huh?!

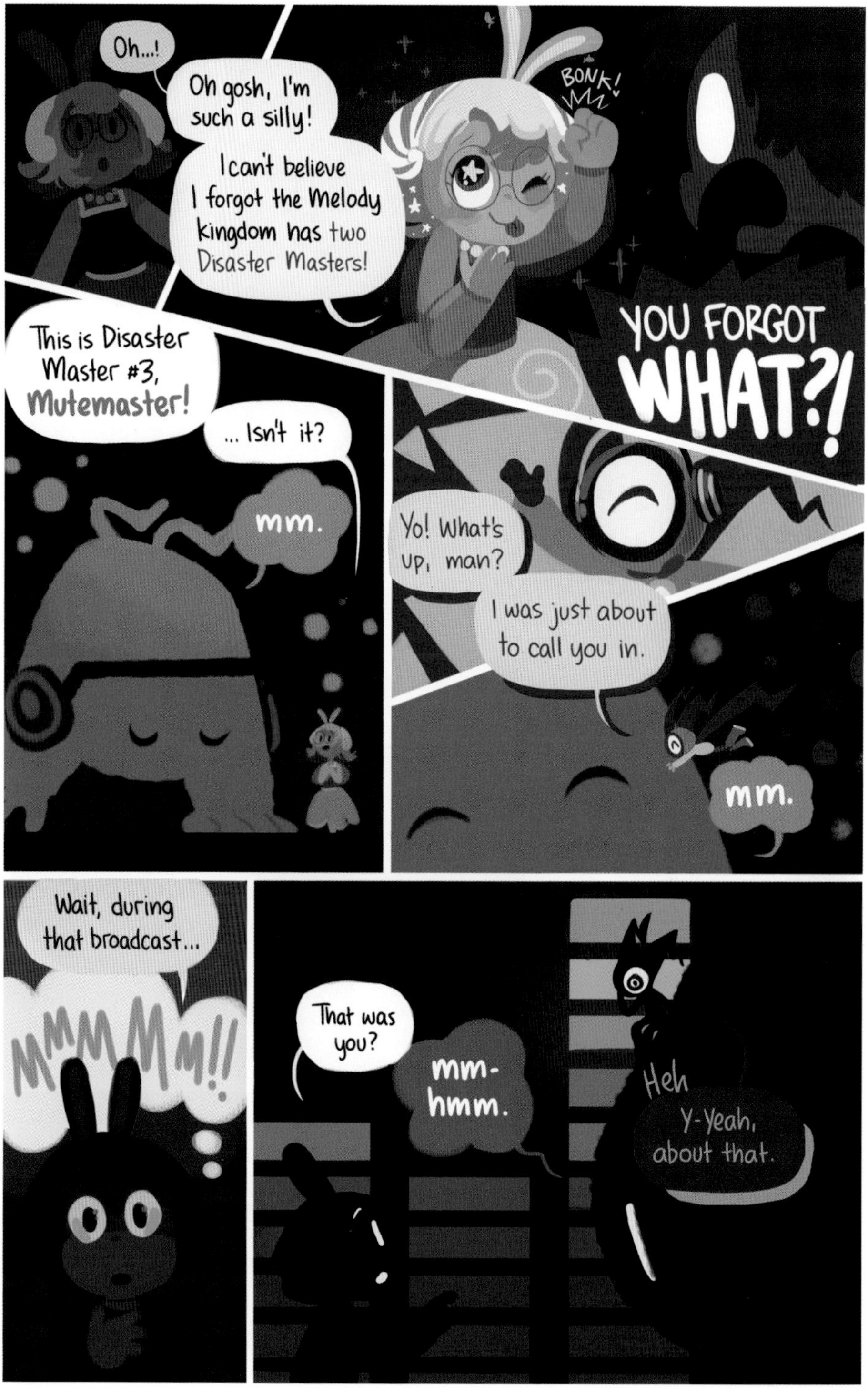
Oh...!
Oh gosh, I'm such a silly!
I can't believe I forgot the Melody kingdom has two Disaster Masters!
BONK!
YOU FORGOT WHAT?!
This is Disaster Master #3, Mutemaster!
... Isn't it?
mm.
Yo! What's up, man?
I was just about to call you in.
mm.
Wait, during that broadcast...
MMMMM!!
That was you?
mm-hmm.
Heh
Y-Yeah, about that.

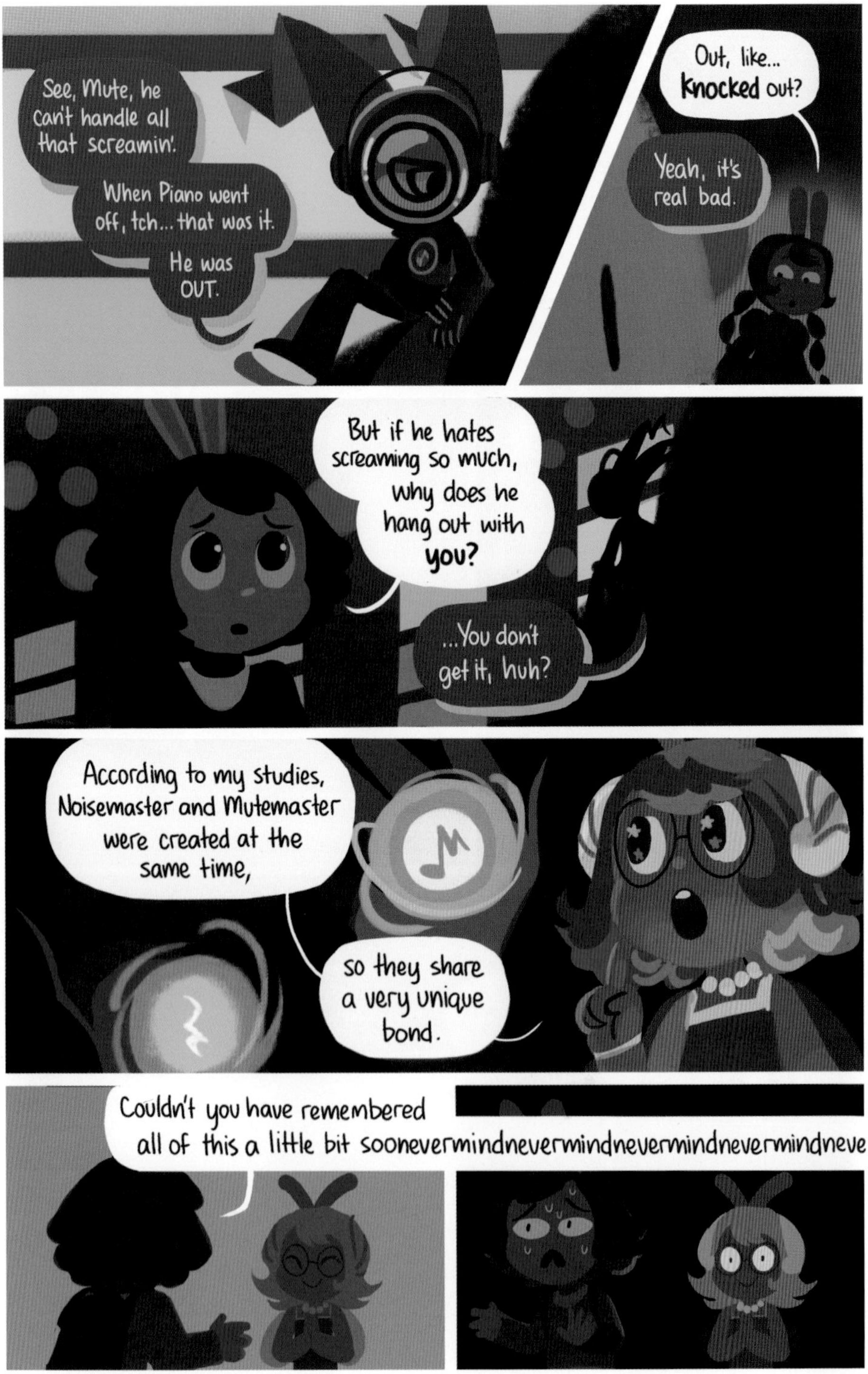
See, Mute, he can't handle all that screamin'.
When Piano went off, tch... that was it.
He was OUT.
Out, like... Knocked out?
Yeah, it's real bad.
But if he hates screaming so much, why does he hang out with you?
...You don't get it, huh?
According to my studies, Noisemaster and Mutemaster were created at the same time,
so they share a very unique bond.
Couldn't you have remembered all of this a little bit soonevermindnevermindnevermindnevermindneve

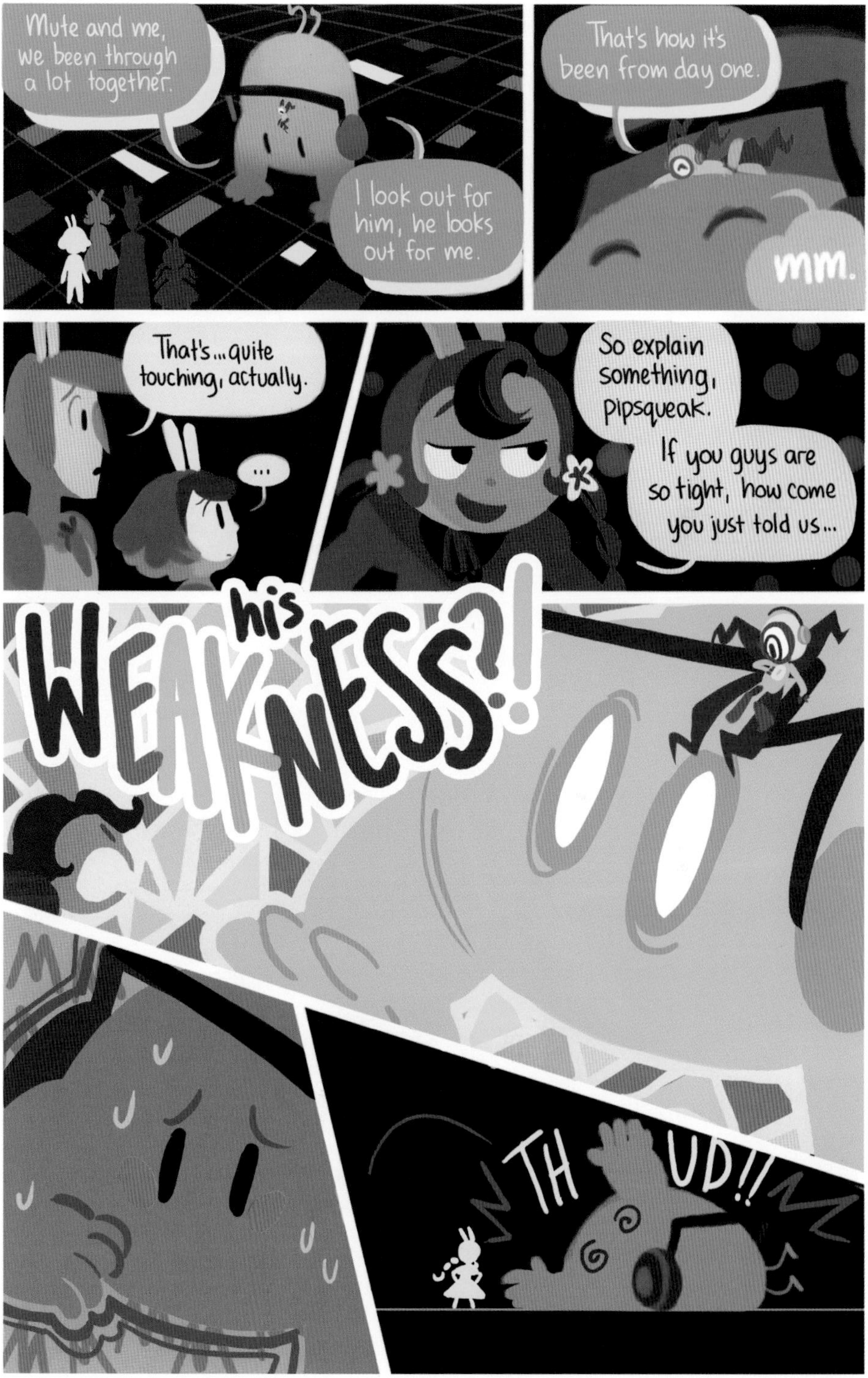

Mute and me, we been through a lot together.
I look out for him, he looks out for me.
That's how it's been from day one.
mm.
That's...quite touching, actually.
...
So explain something, pipsqueak.
If you guys are so tight, how come you just told us...
his WEAKNESS?!
THUD!!

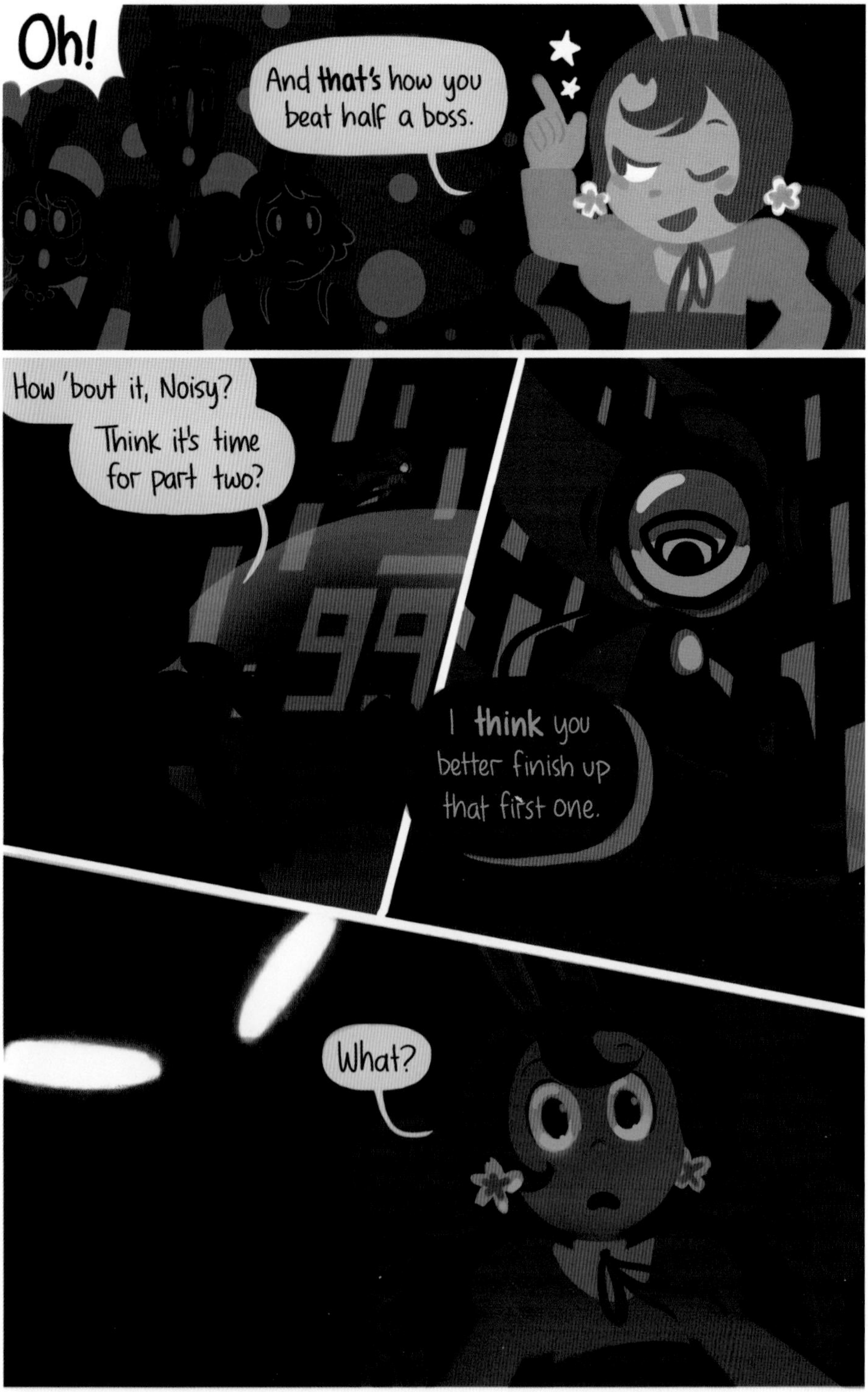
Oh!
And that's how you beat half a boss.
How 'bout it, Noisy?
Think it's time for part two?
I think you better finish up that first one.
What?

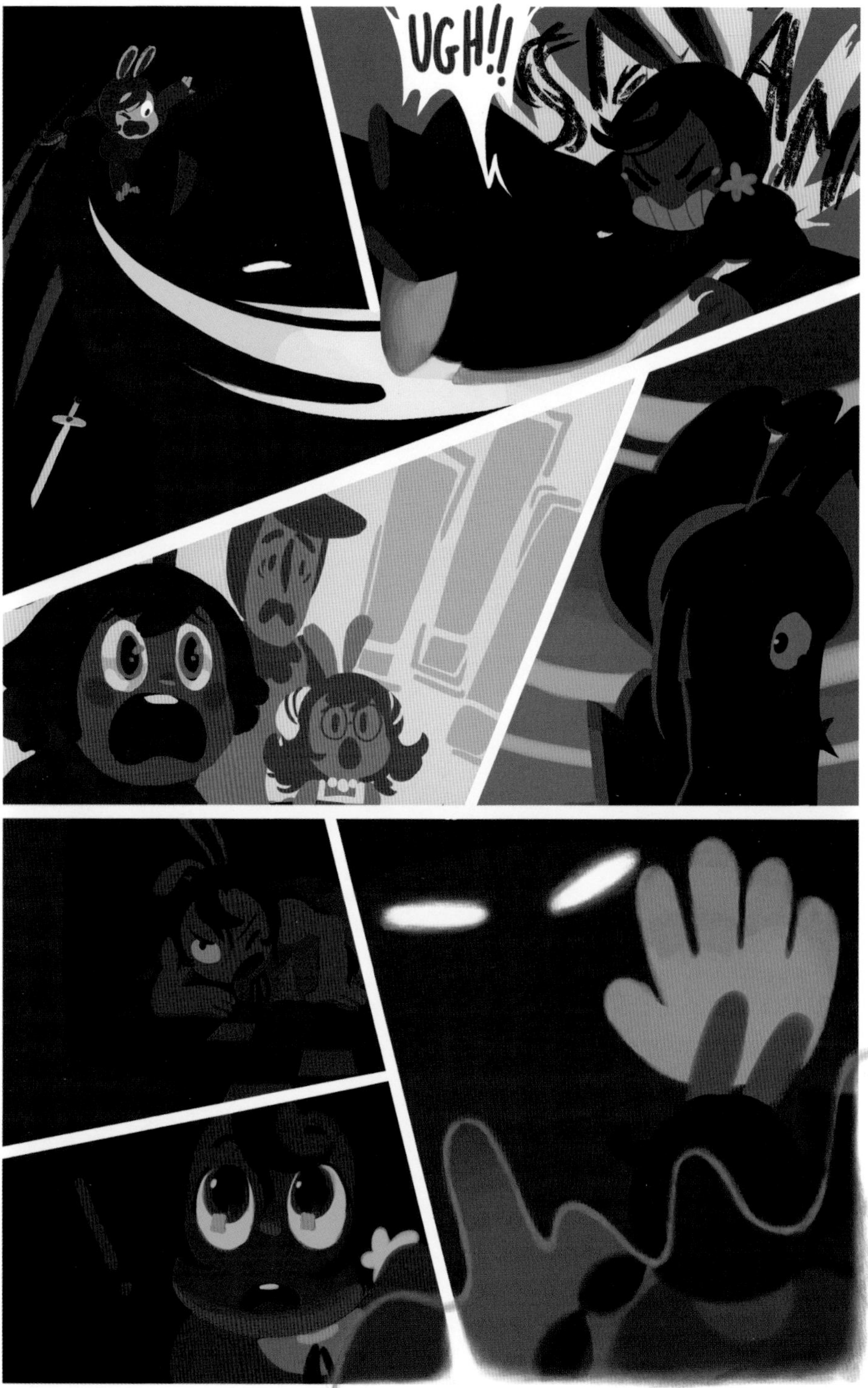
UGH!!

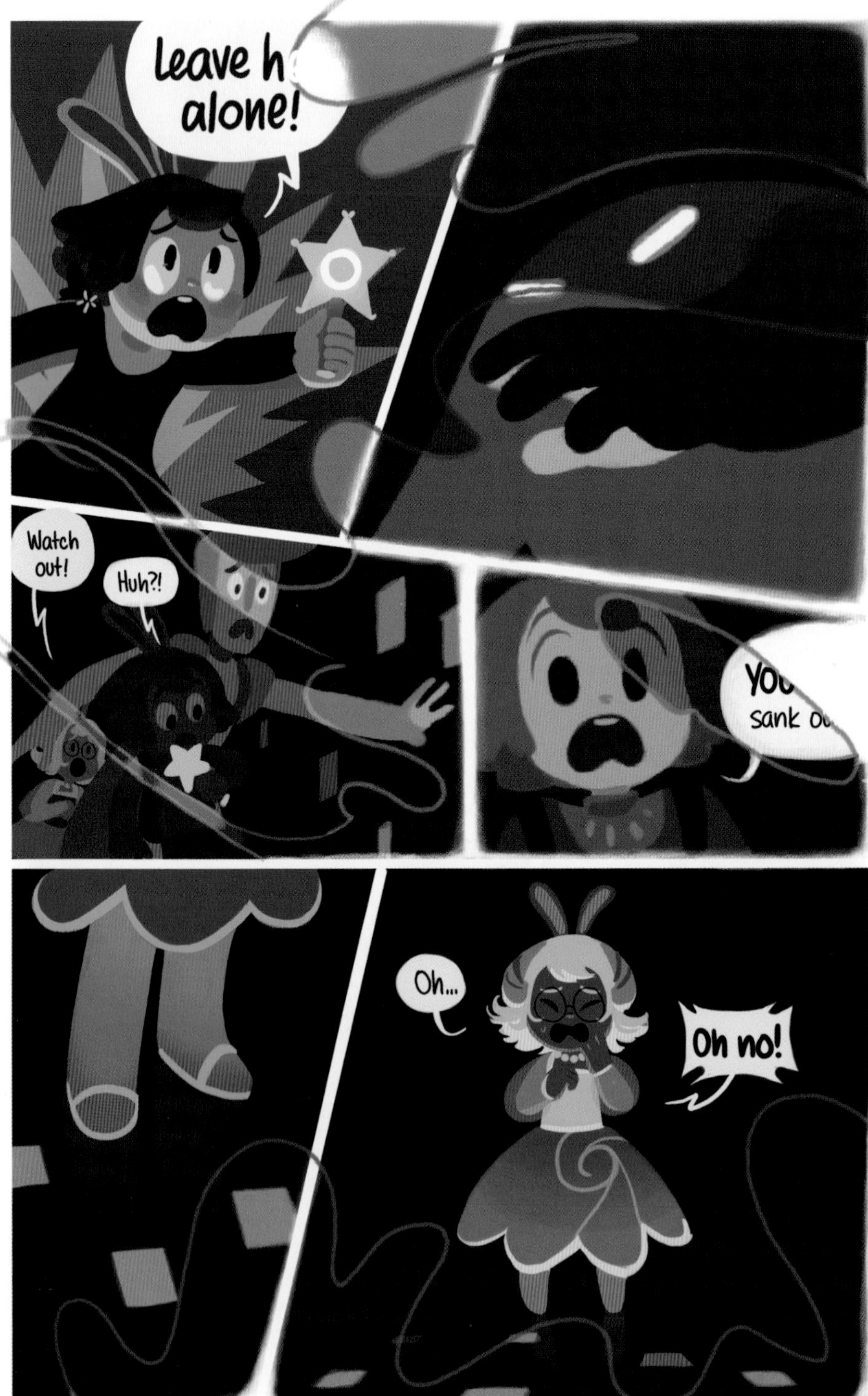
Leave h
alone!
Watch out!
Huh?!
sank ou
Oh...
Oh no!

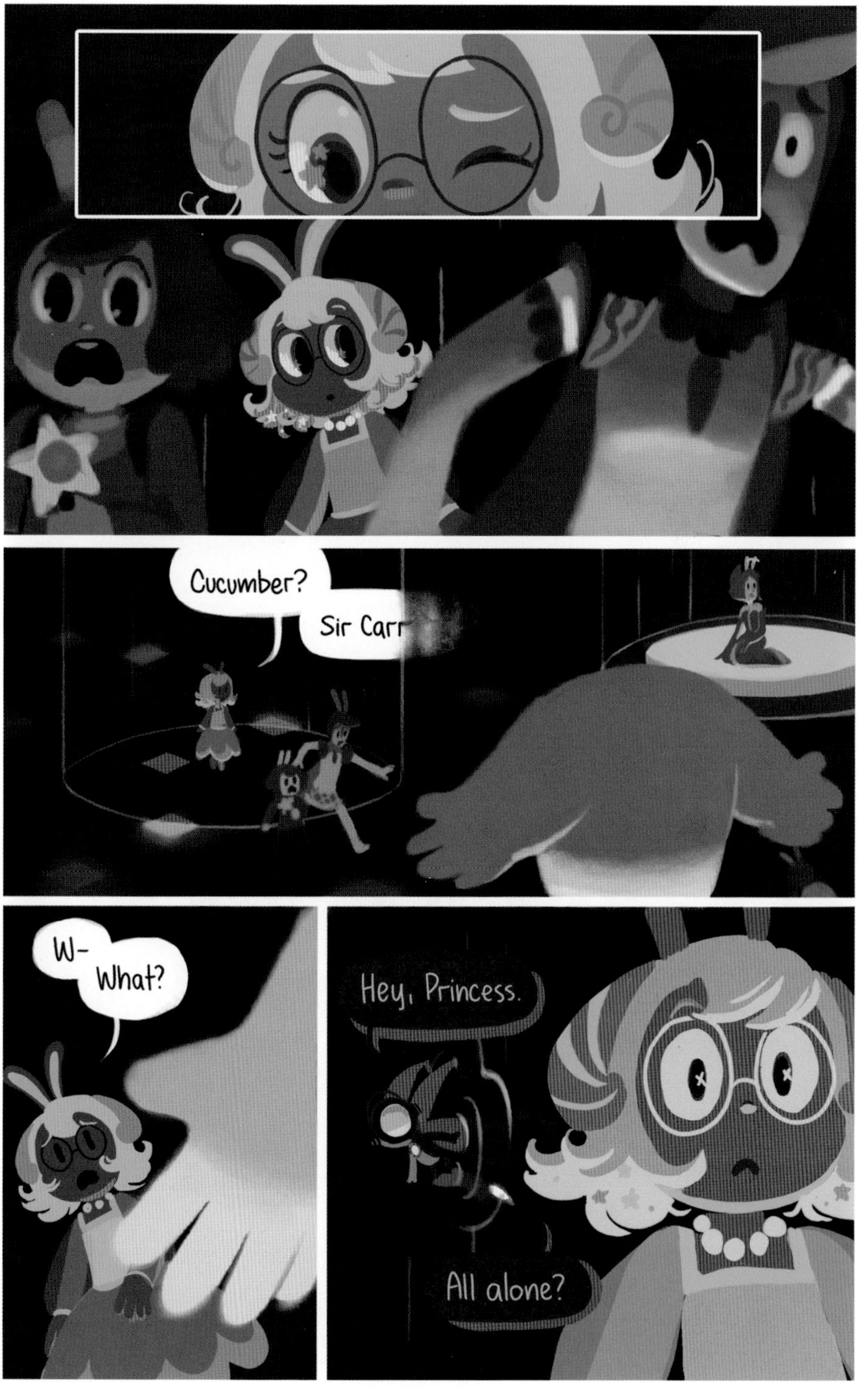
Cucumber?
Sir Carr
W- What?
Hey, Princess.
All alone?

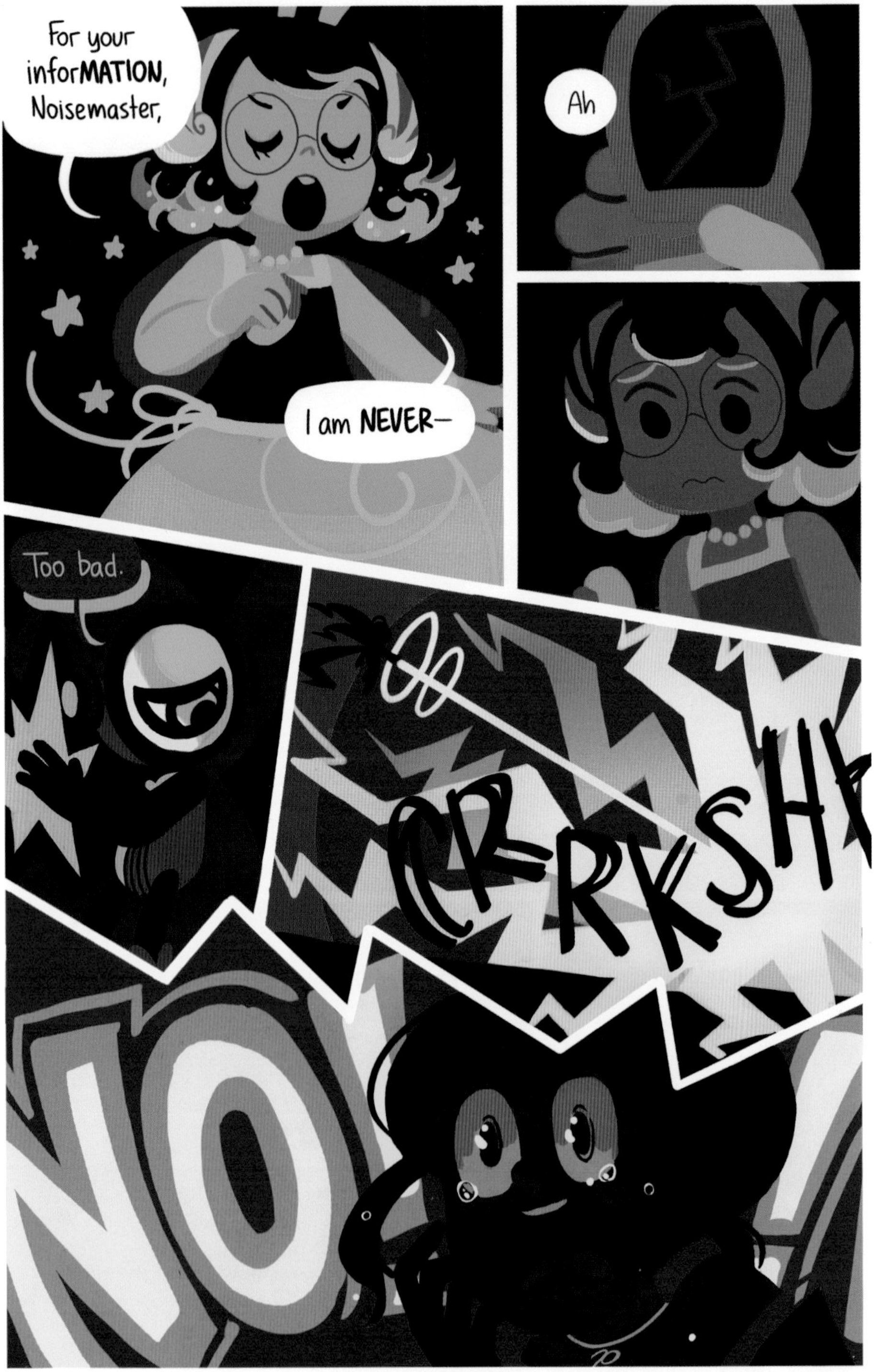

For your inforMATION, Noisemaster,
Ah
I am NEVER—
Too bad.
CRRKSH
NO!

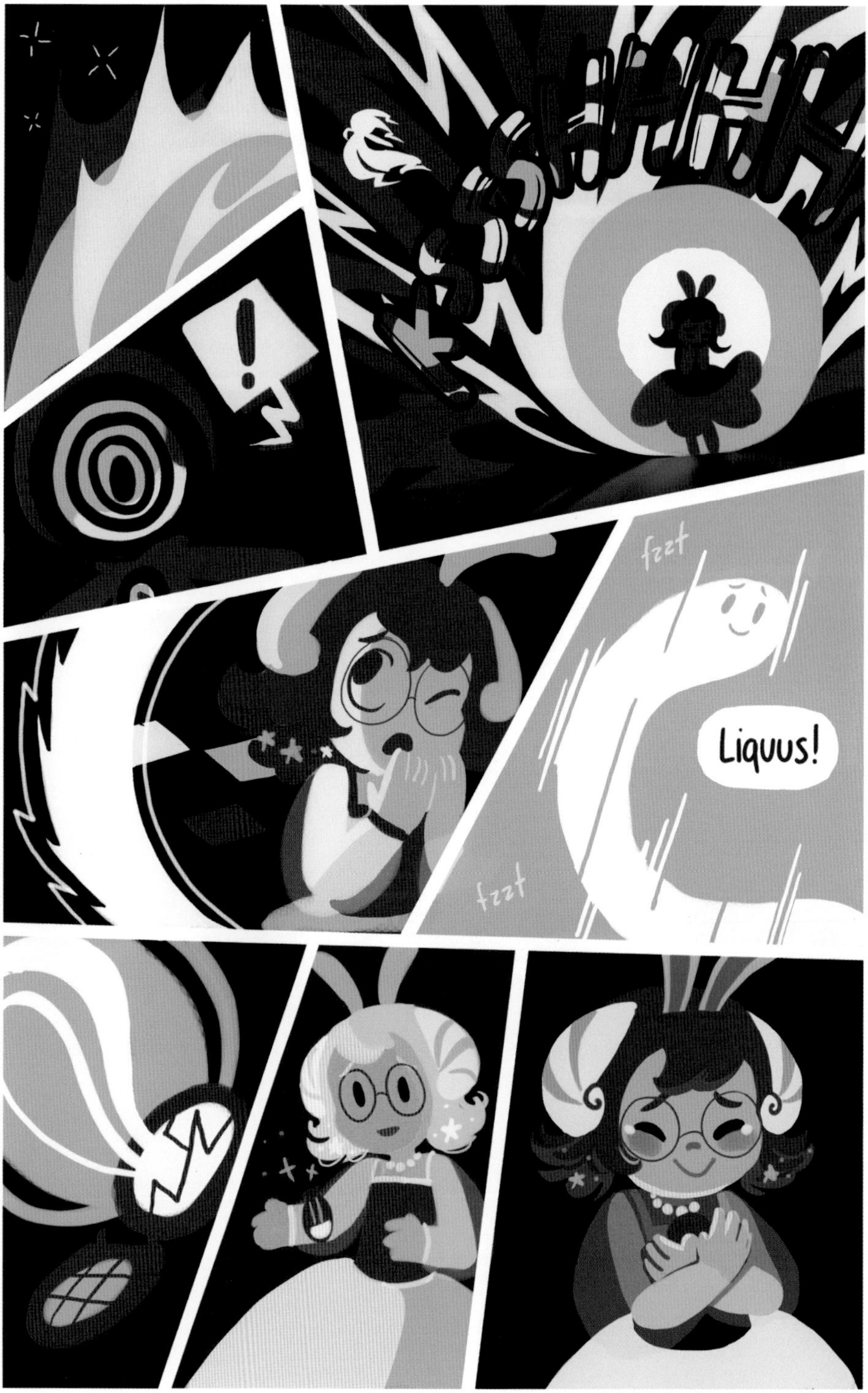
!
fzzt
Liquus!
fzzt

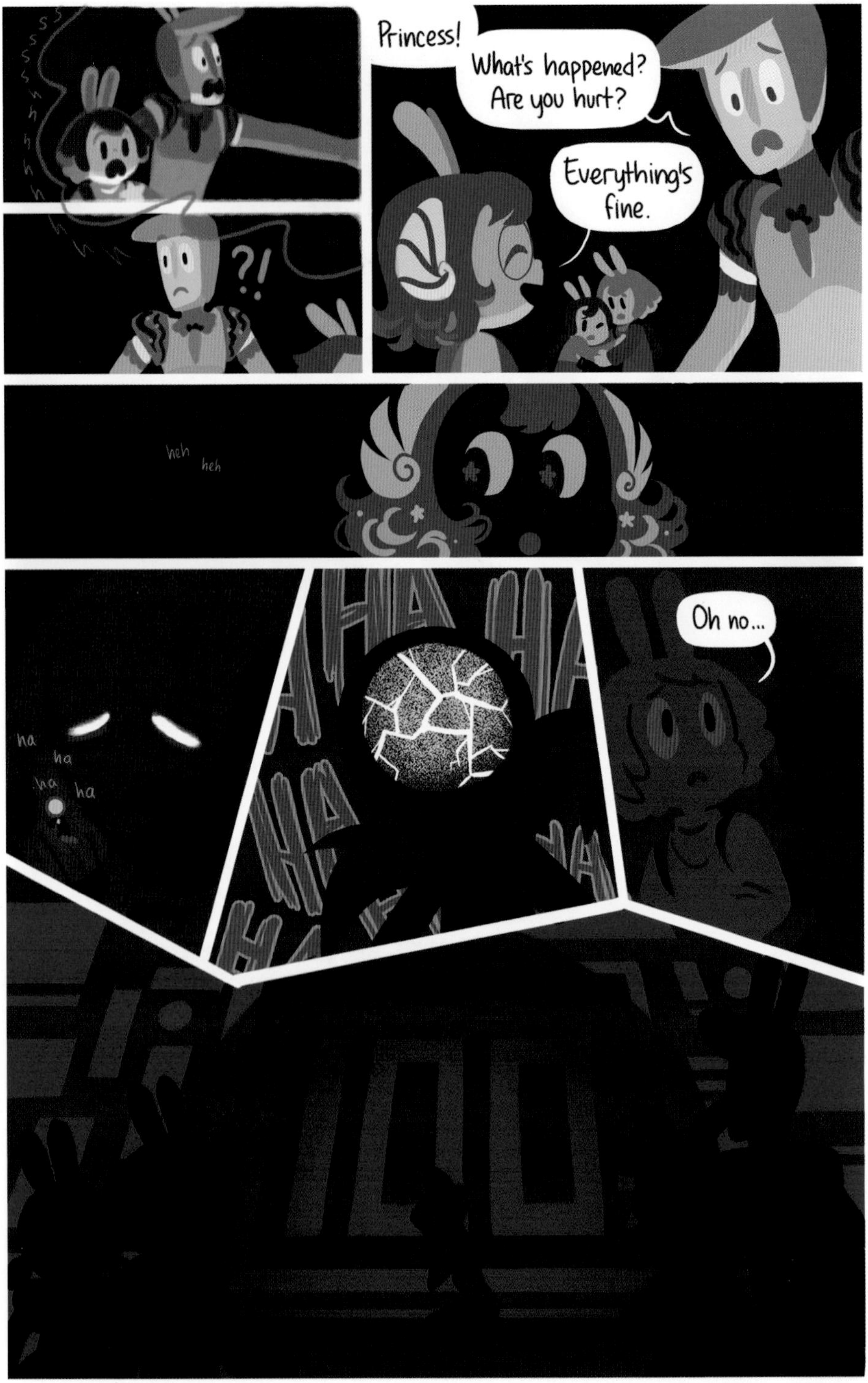
sssshhhhhhh
?!
Princess!
What's happened? Are you hurt?
Everything's fine.
heh heh
ha ha ha ha
HA HA HA HA HA HA HA
Oh no...

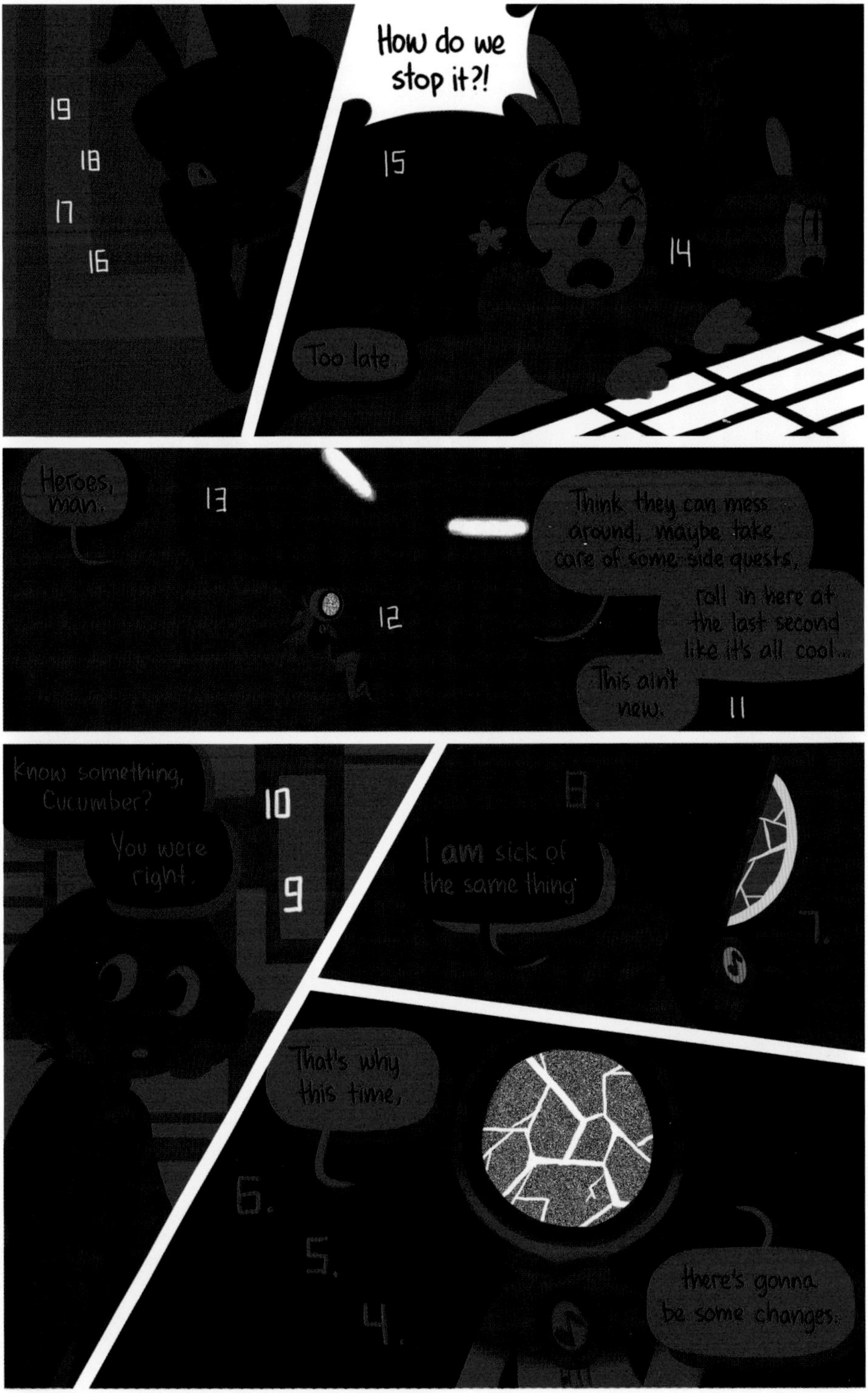

19
18
17
16
How do we stop it?!
15
14
Too late.
Heroes, man.
13
Think they can mess around, maybe take care of some side quests,
roll in here at the last second like it's all cool...
12
This ain't new.
11
Know something, Cucumber?
You were right.
10
9
8.
I am sick of the same thing.
7.
That's why this time,
6.
5.
4.
there's gonna be some changes.

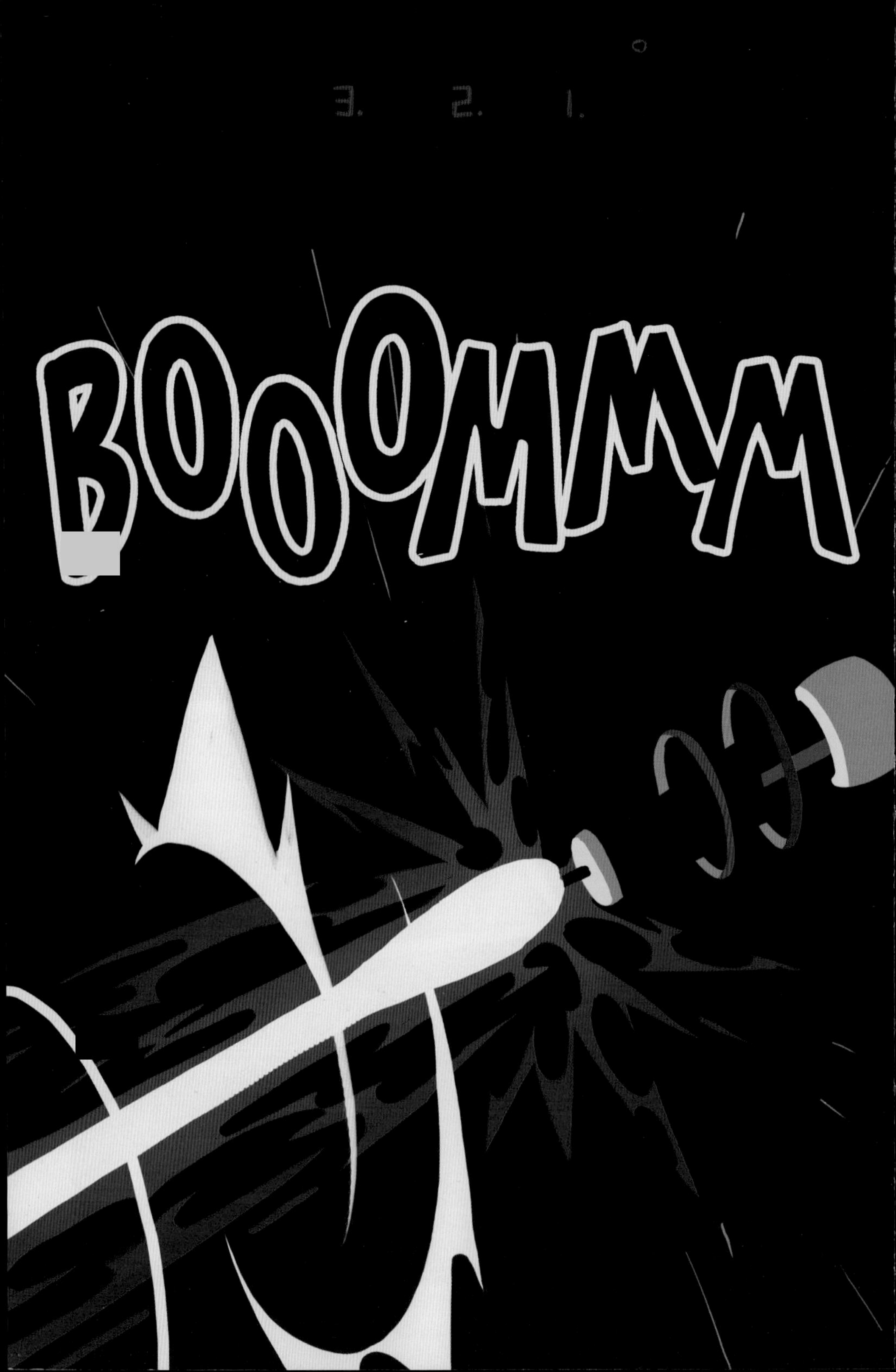
3. 2. 1.
BOOOMMM

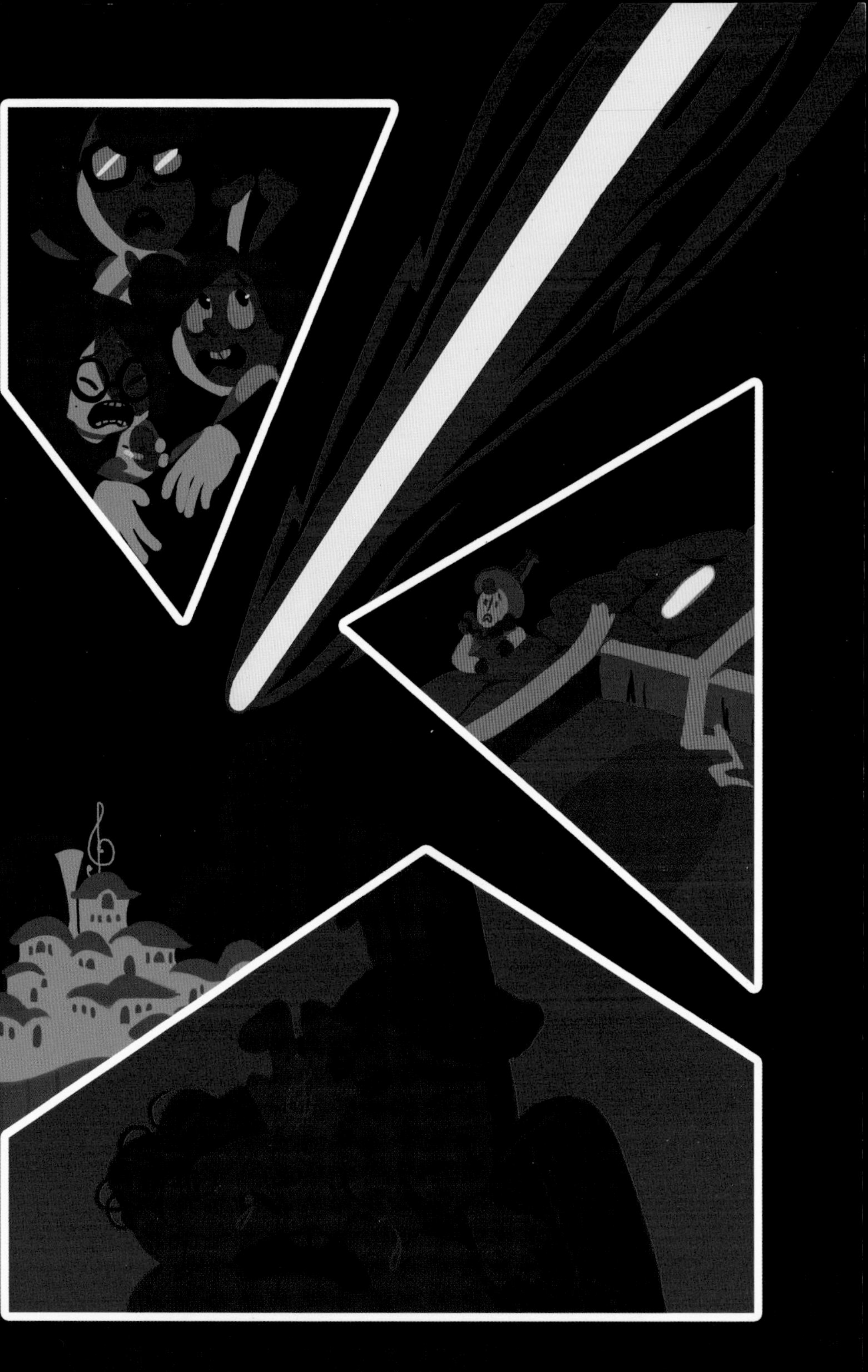

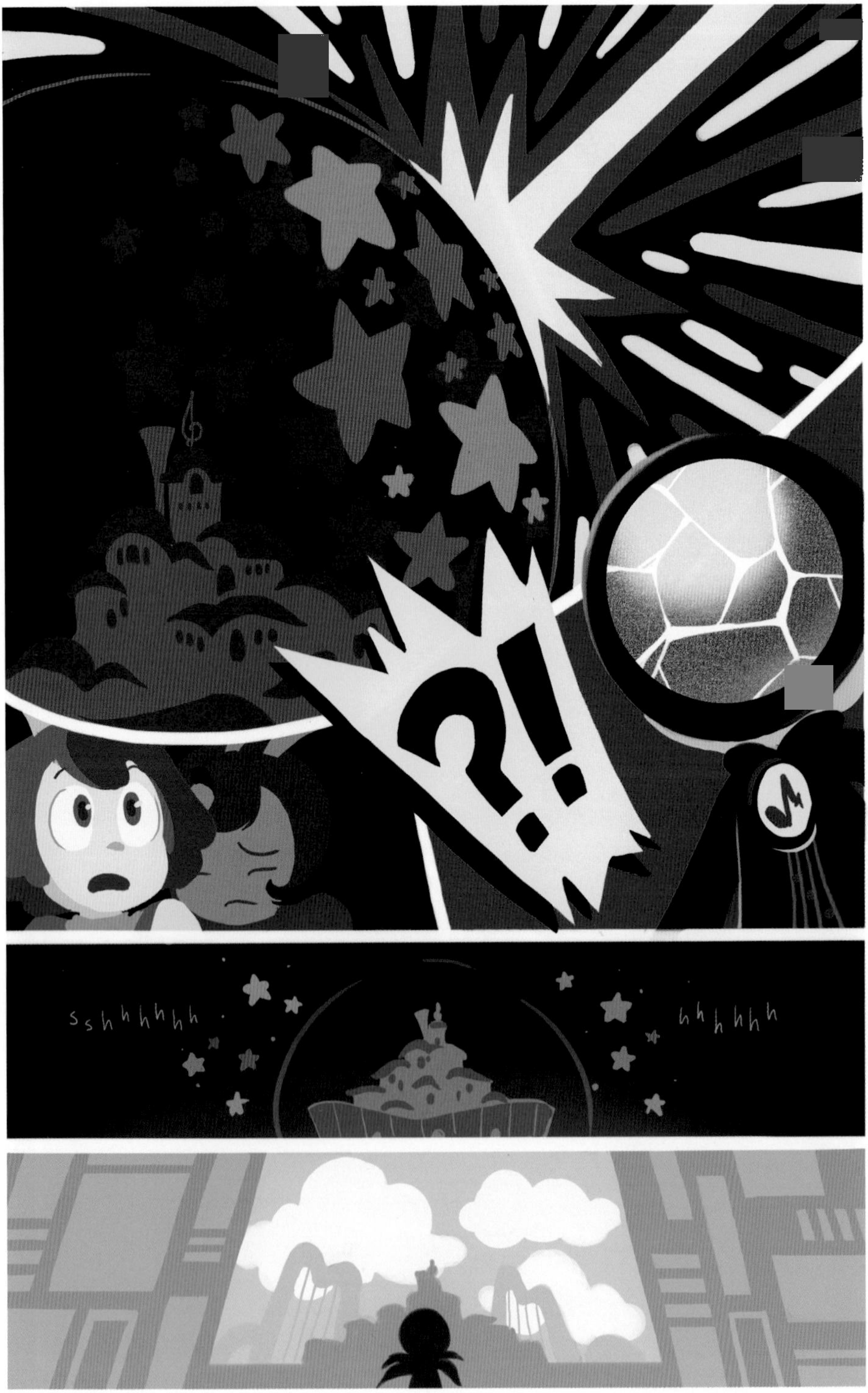
?!
sshhhhhh
hhhhhh

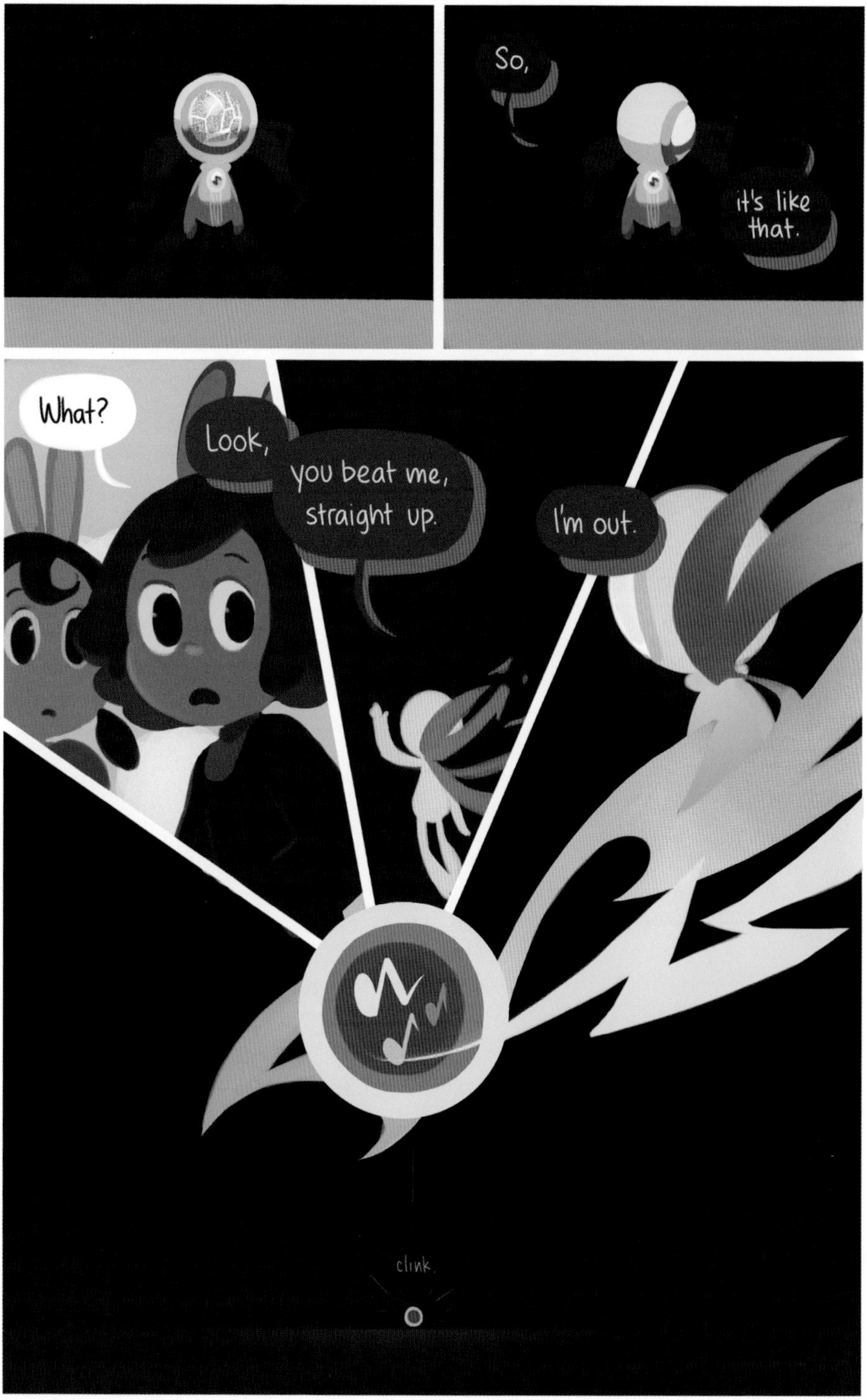
So,
it's like that.
What?
Look,
you beat me, straight up.
I'm out.
clink.

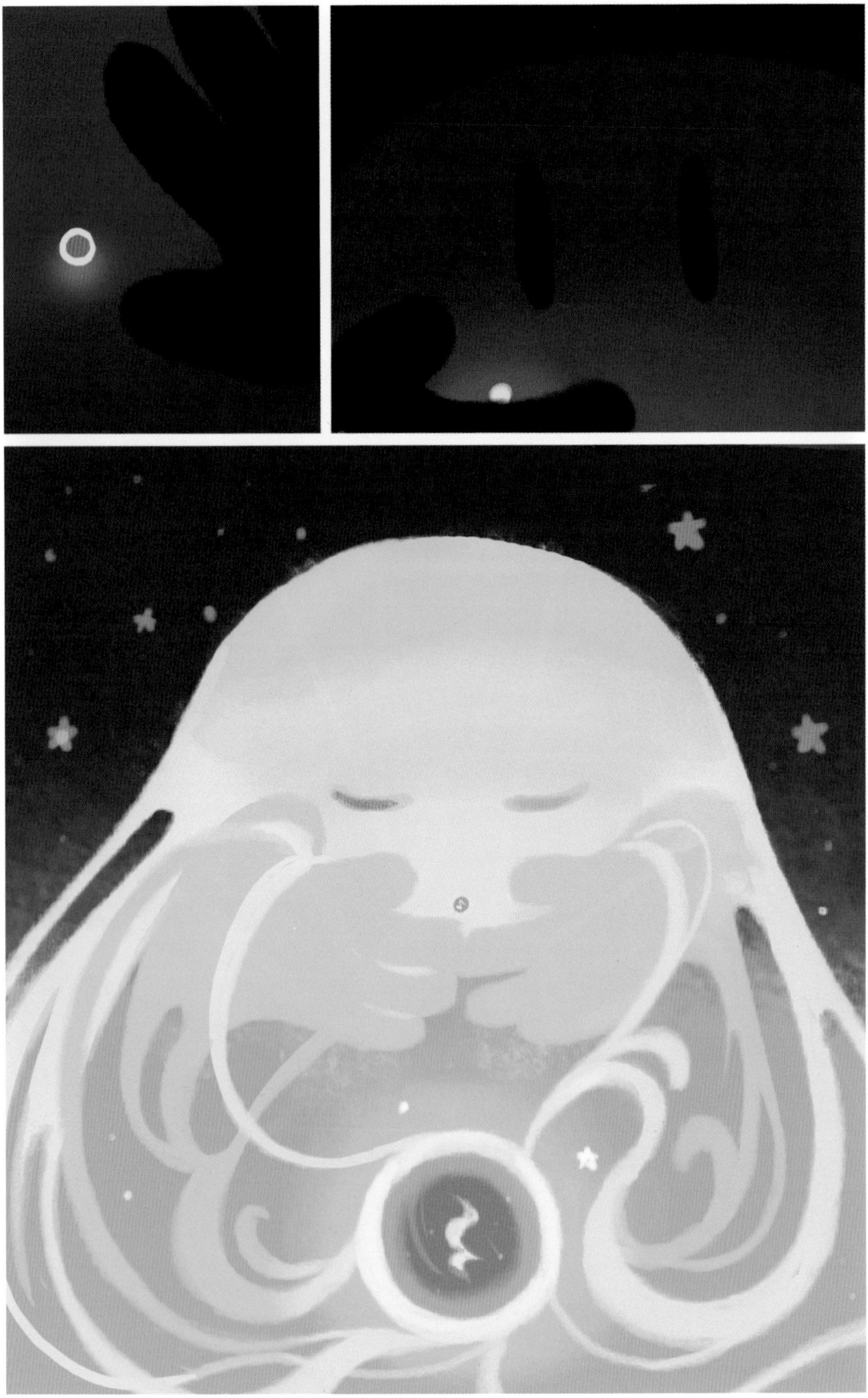

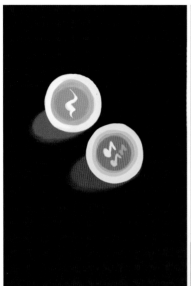

What...

...was **THAT?!**

Have we won?

I-I don't know...

It doesn't really feel like it.

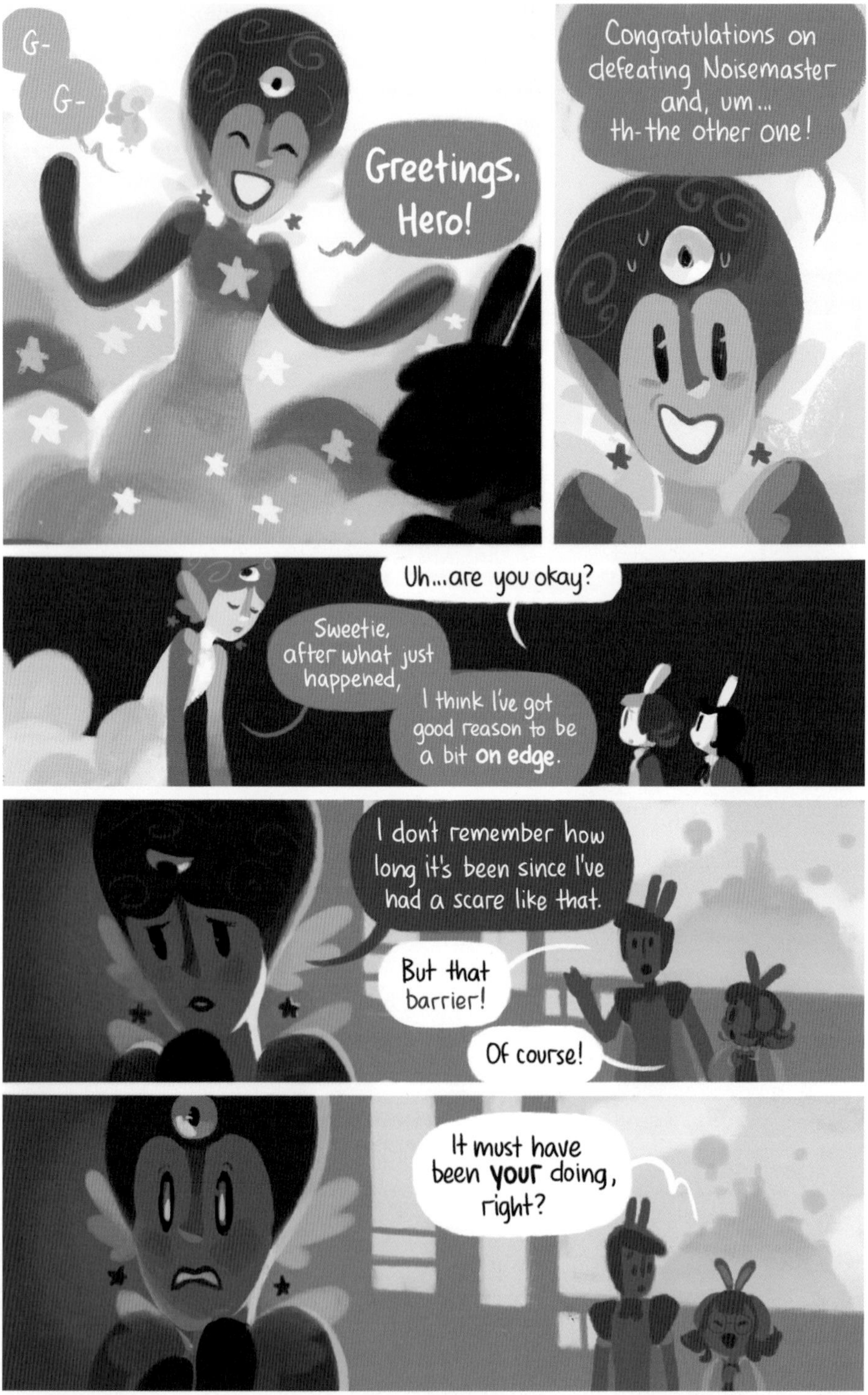
G-
G-
Greetings, Hero!
Congratulations on defeating Noisemaster and, um... th-the other one!
Uh...are you okay?
Sweetie, after what just happened,
I think I've got good reason to be a bit **on edge**.
I don't remember how long it's been since I've had a scare like that.
But that barrier!
Of course!
It must have been **your** doing, right?

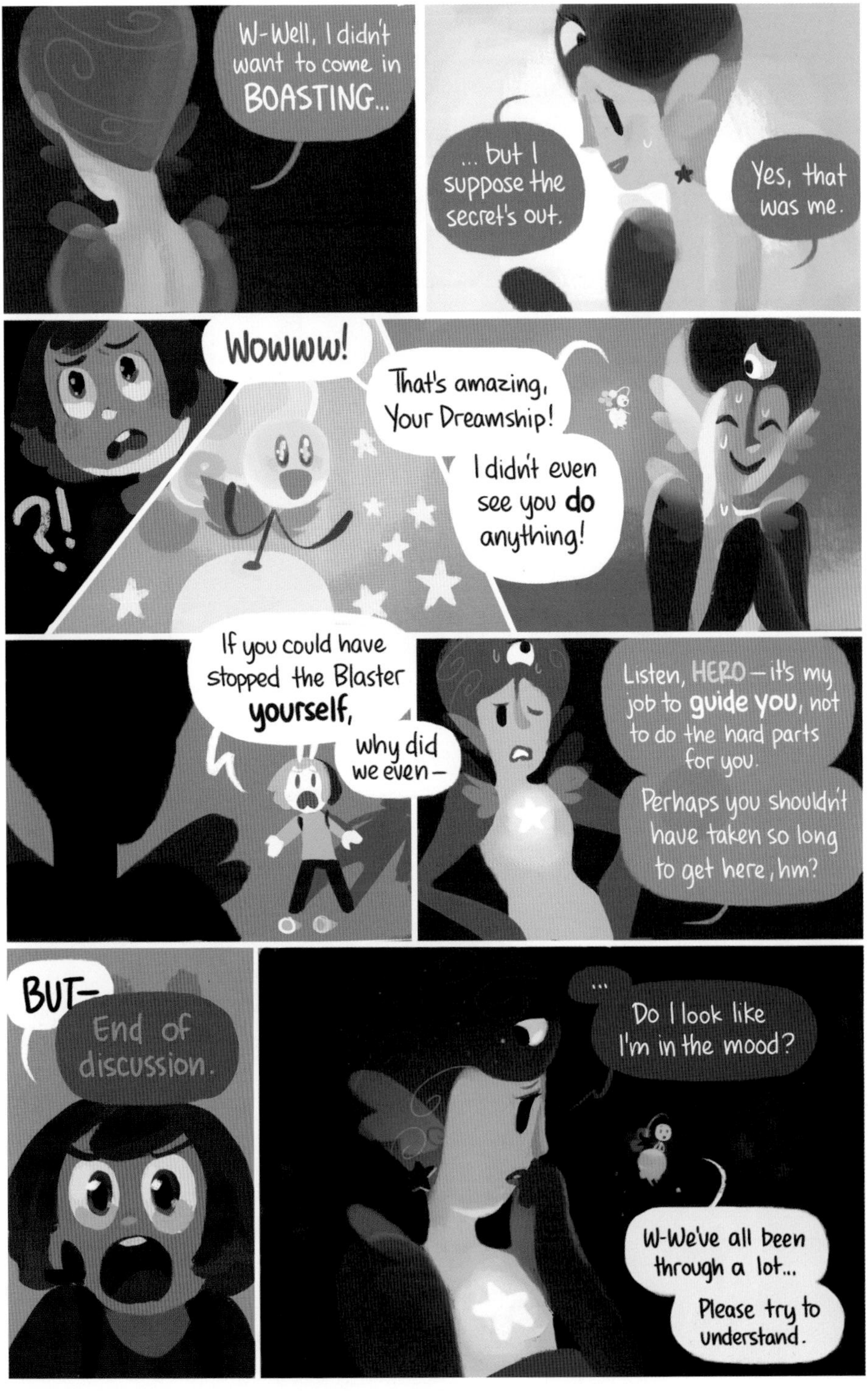
W-Well, I didn't want to come in BOASTING...
... but I suppose the secret's out.
Yes, that was me.
WOWWW!
?!
That's amazing, Your Dreamship!
I didn't even see you do anything!
If you could have stopped the Blaster yourself,
why did we even—
Listen, HERO—it's my job to guide you, not to do the hard parts for you.
Perhaps you shouldn't have taken so long to get here, hm?
BUT—
End of discussion.
...
Do I look like I'm in the mood?
W-We've all been through a lot...
Please try to understand.

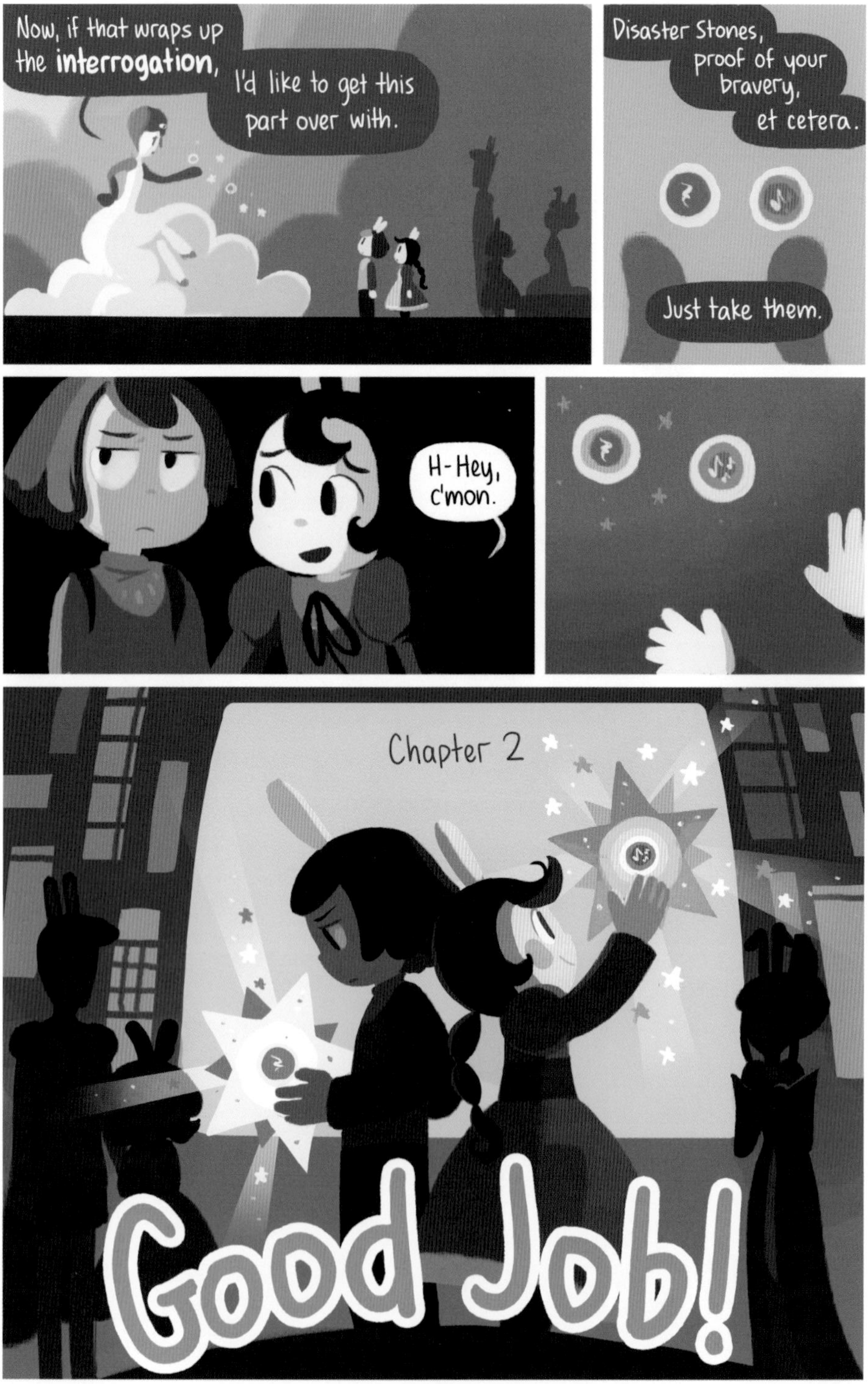
Now, if that wraps up the **interrogation,**
I'd like to get this part over with.
Disaster Stones, proof of your bravery, et cetera.
Just take them.
H-Hey, c'mon.
Chapter 2
Good Job!

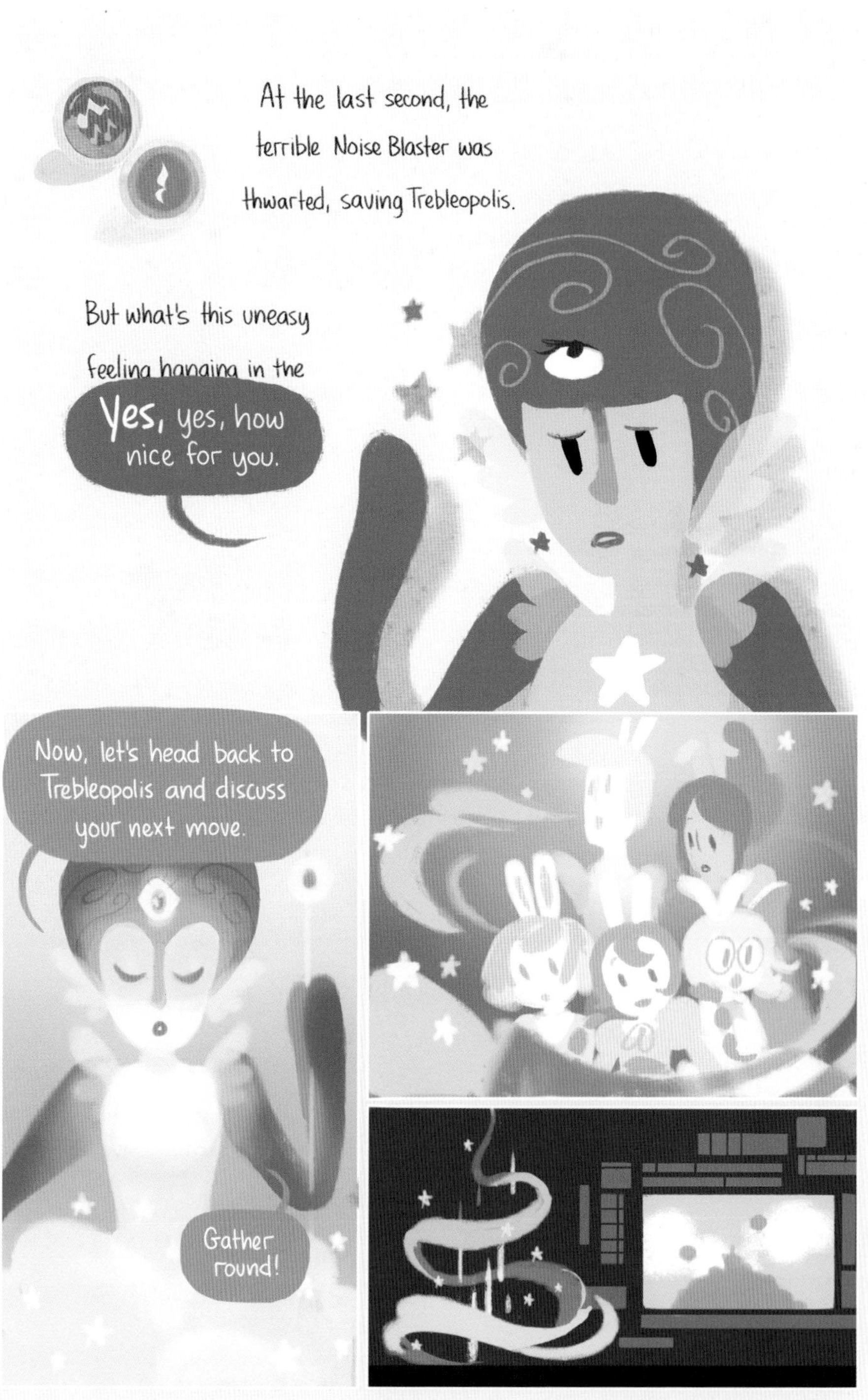

At the last second, the terrible Noise Blaster was thwarted, saving Trebleopolis.
But what's this uneasy feeling hanging in the
Yes, yes, how nice for you.
Now, let's head back to Trebleopolis and discuss your next move.
Gather round!

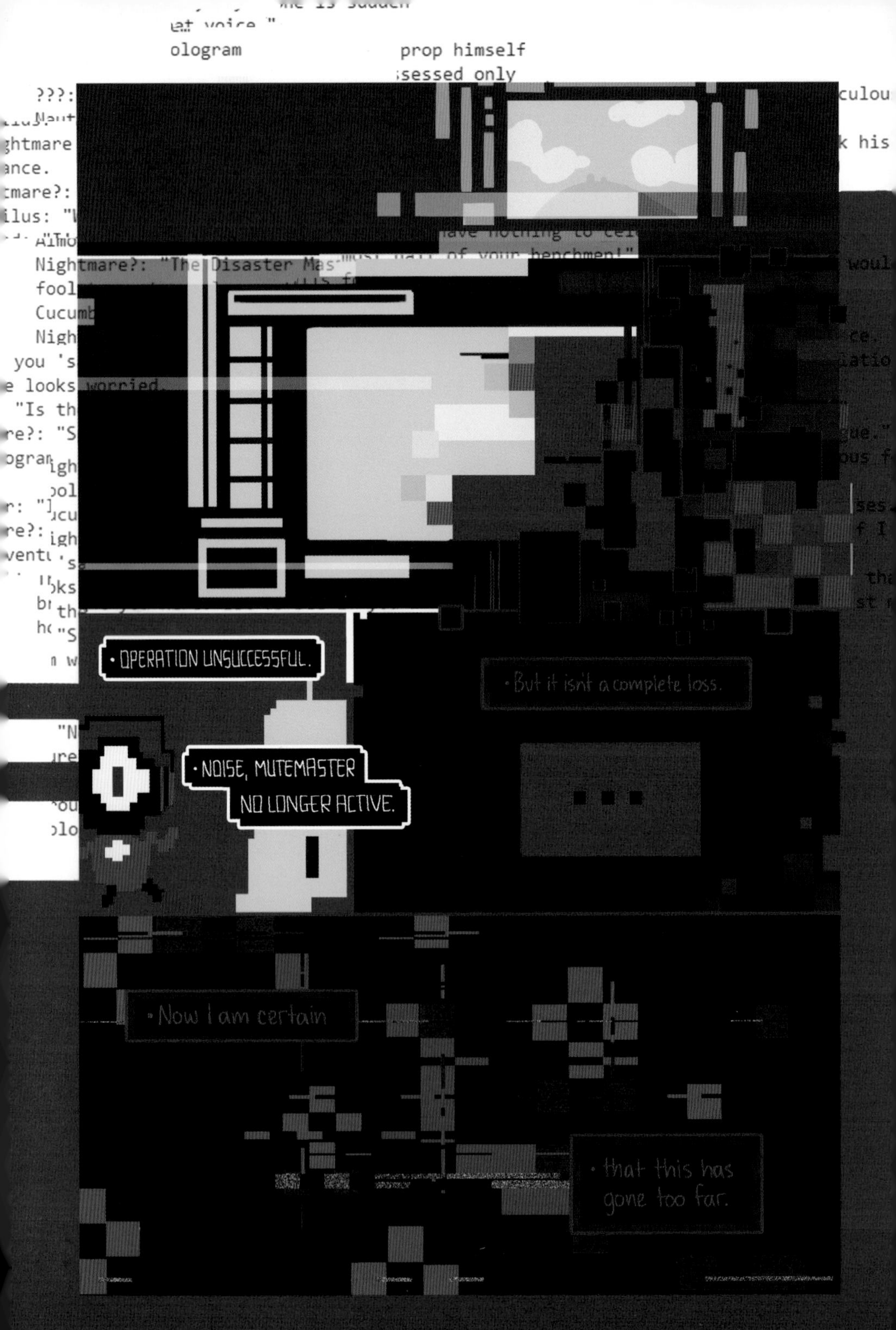
• OPERATION UNSUCCESSFUL.
• But it isn't a complete loss.
• NOISE, MUTEMASTER NO LONGER ACTIVE.
...
• Now I am certain
• that this has gone too far.

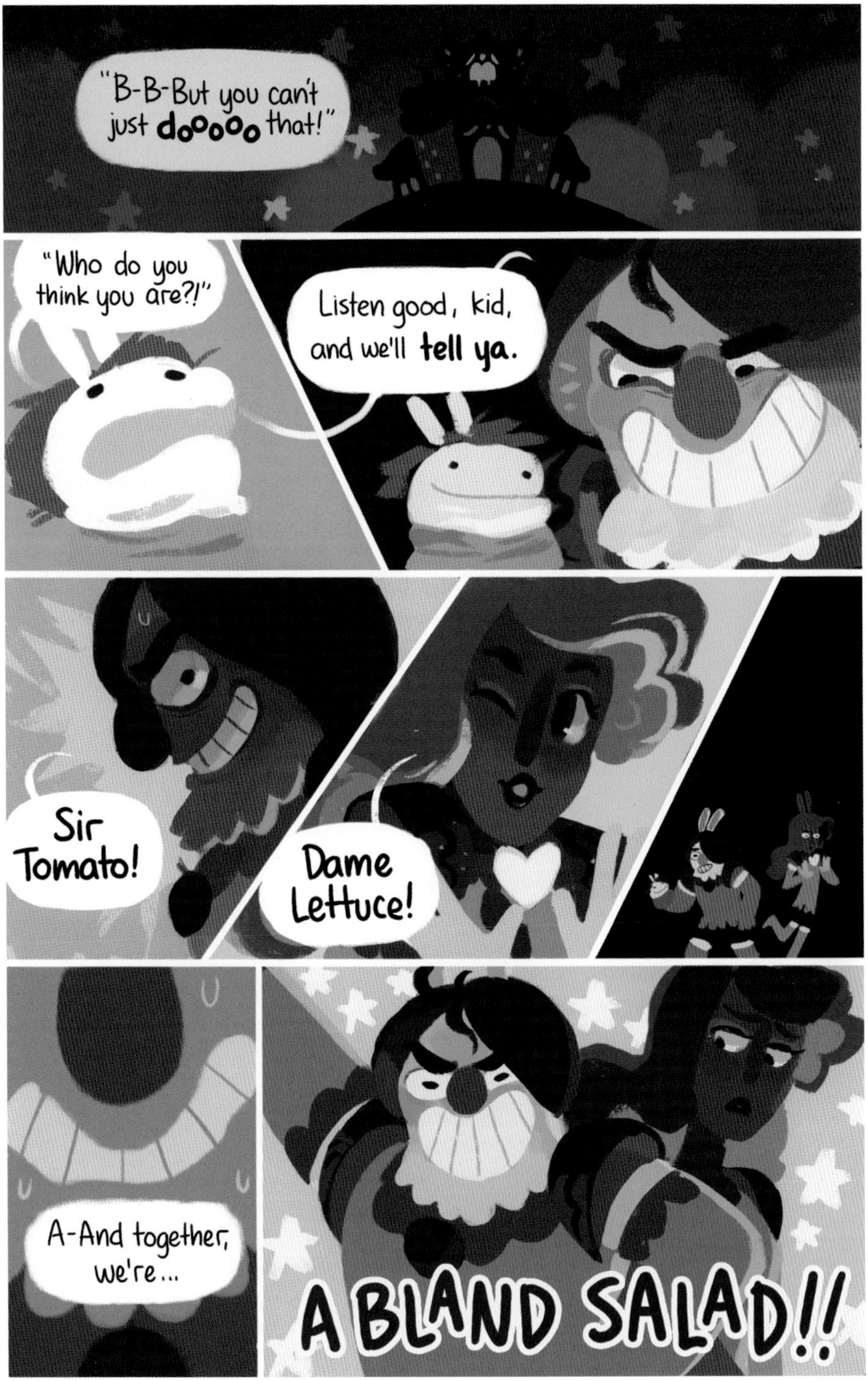
"B-B-But you can't just doOooo that!"
"Who do you think you are?!"
Listen good, kid, and we'll **tell ya.**
Sir Tomato!
Dame Lettuce!
A-And together, we're...
A BLAND SALAD!!

We need a new member.

I dunno, like...

I think it's okay with just us—

It's not **WORKING**, Lettuce!

Sure, I know I'm both cool **and** manly enough to make my **OWN** entrance,

but losing a sidekick's really throwing my balance off, y'know?

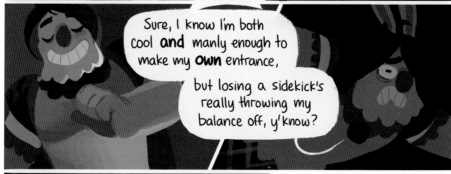

Well, maybe you should have **thought** about that before you went totally nutso on Bacon or, like, whatever??

HEEEEEEELP!!

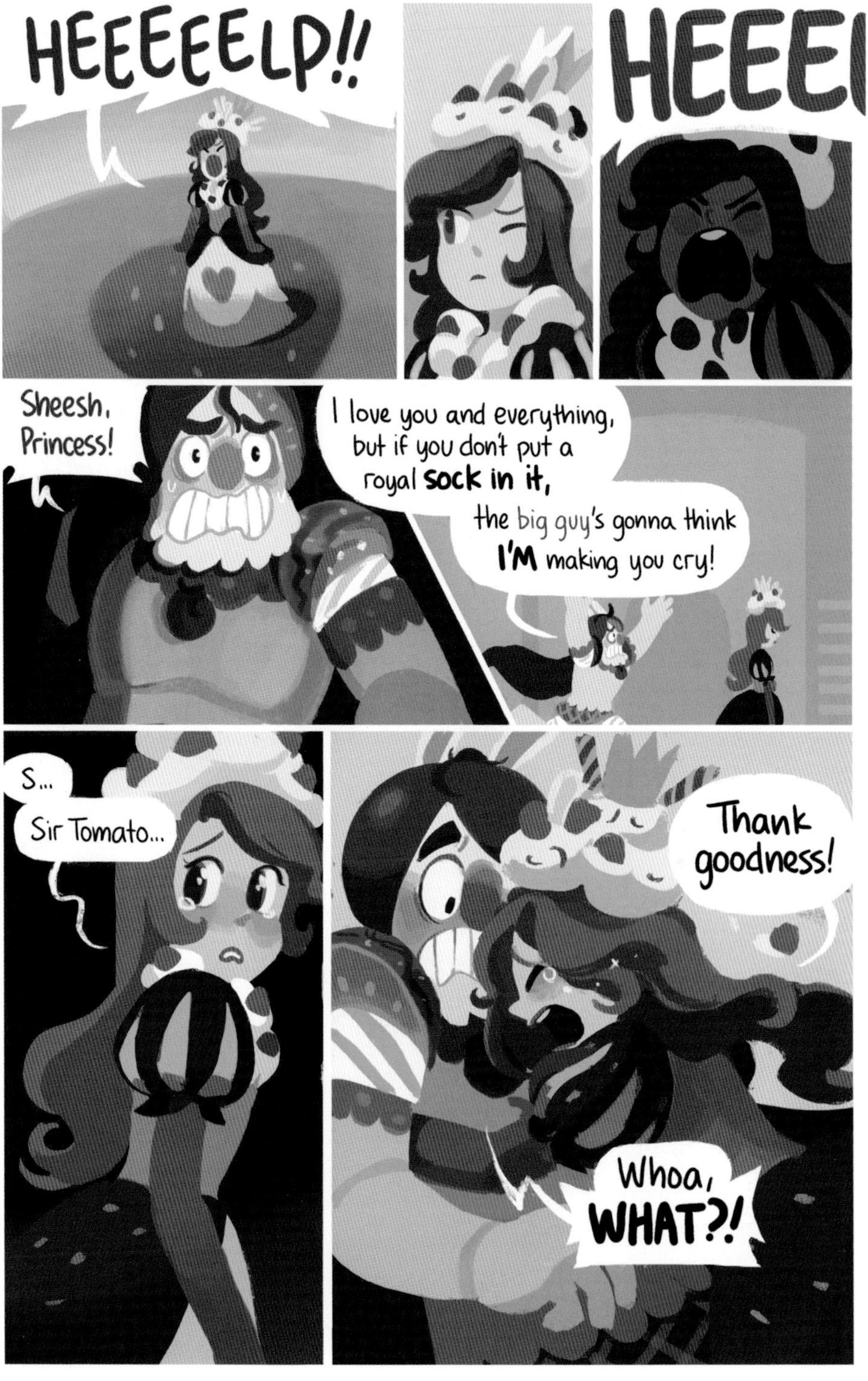
HEEEEELP!!
HEEEE
Sheesh, Princess!
I love you and everything, but if you don't put a royal SOCK IN IT,
the big guy's gonna think I'M making you cry!
S... Sir Tomato...
Thank goodness!
Whoa, WHAT?!

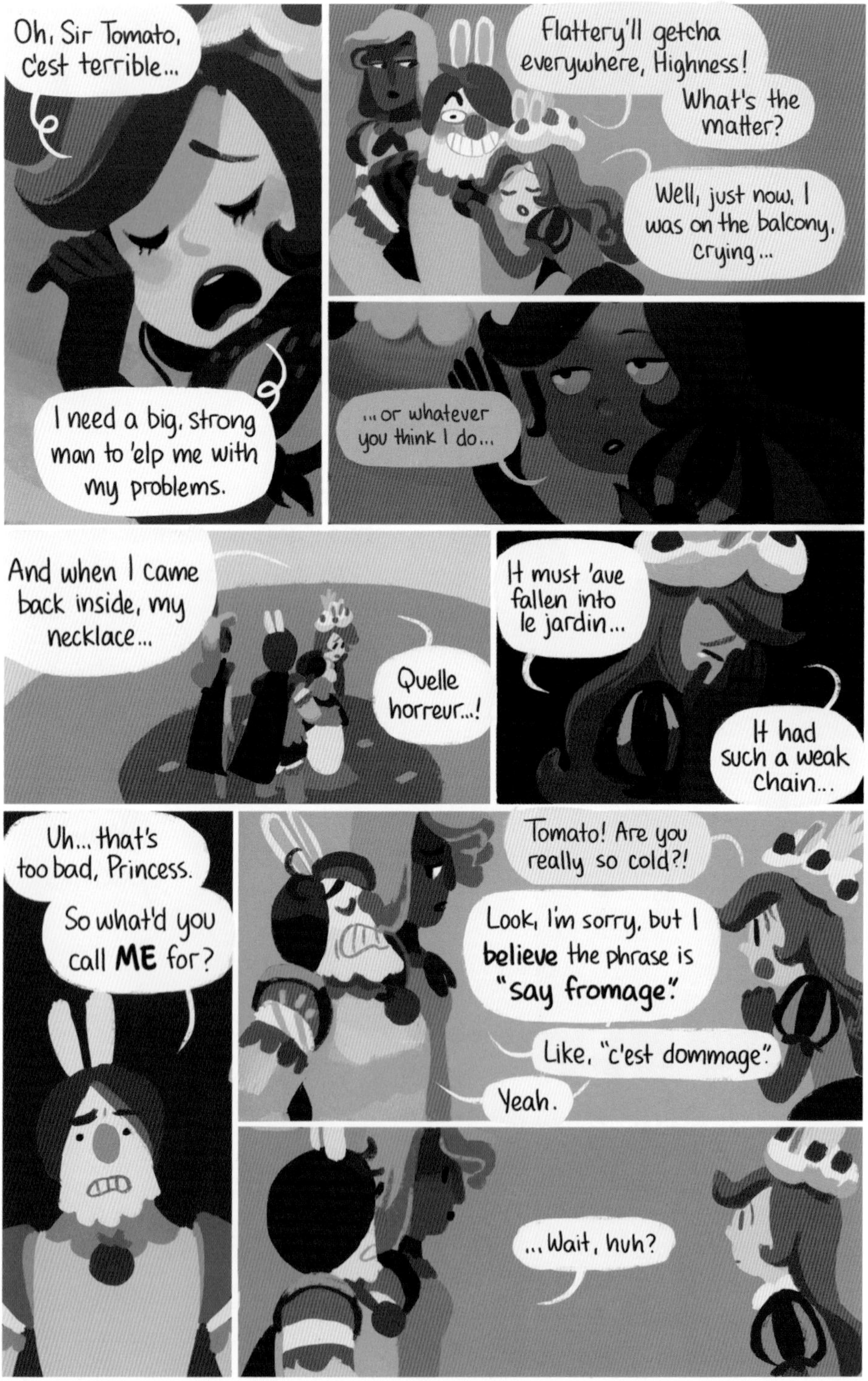
Oh, Sir Tomato, c'est terrible...
I need a big, strong man to 'elp me with my problems.
Flattery'll getcha everywhere, Highness!
What's the matter?
Well, just now, I was on the balcony, crying...
...or whatever you think I do...
And when I came back inside, my necklace...
Quelle horreur...!
It must 'ave fallen into le jardin...
It had such a weak chain...
Uh... that's too bad, Princess.
So what'd you call **ME** for?
Tomato! Are you really so cold?!
Look, I'm sorry, but I **believe** the phrase is **"say fromage."**
Like, "c'est dommage."
Yeah.
...Wait, huh?

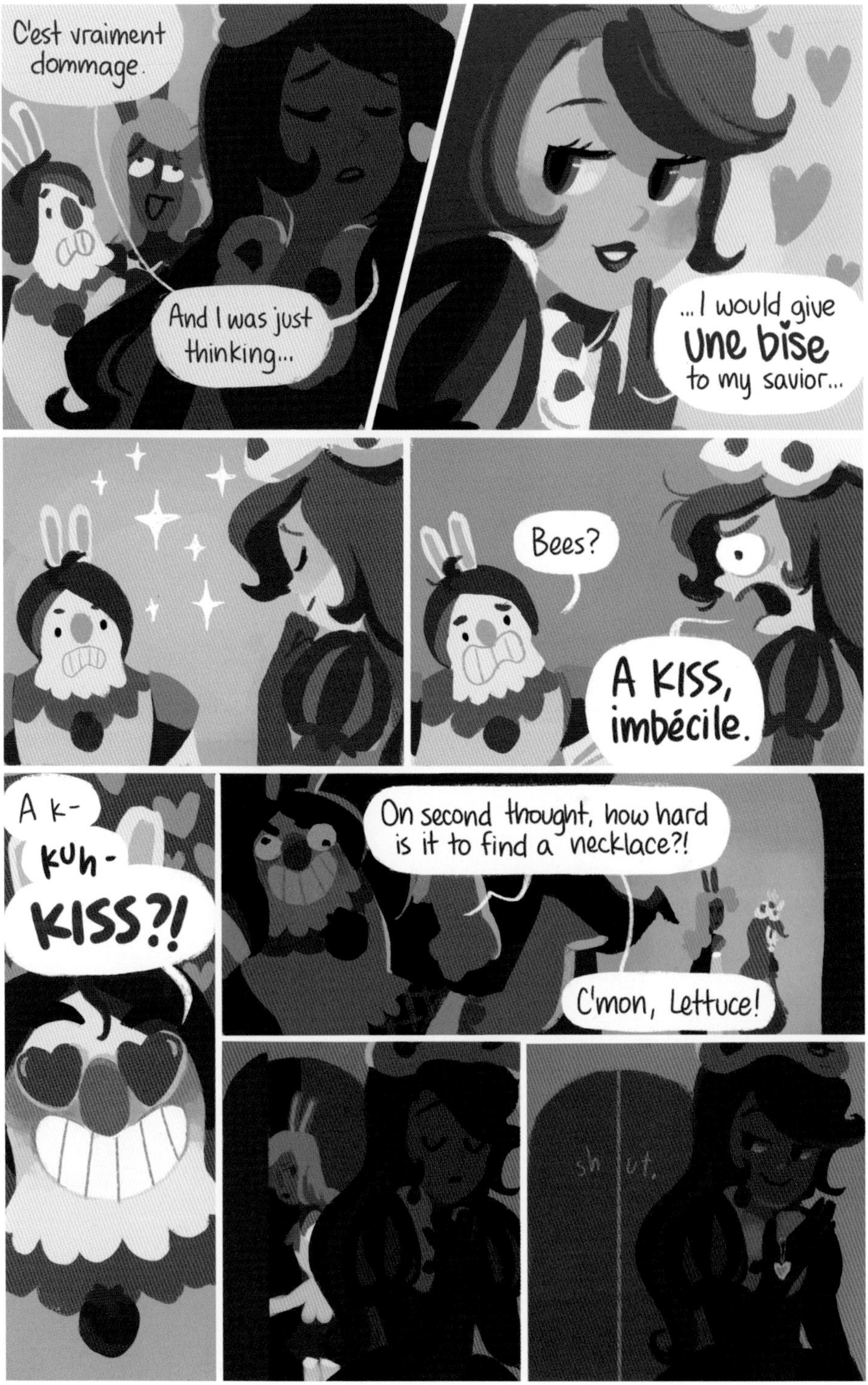
C'est vraiment dommage.
And I was just thinking...
...I would give une bise to my savior...
Bees?
A KISS, imbécile.
A k- kuh- KISS?!
On second thought, how hard is it to find a necklace?!
C'mon, Lettuce!
shut.

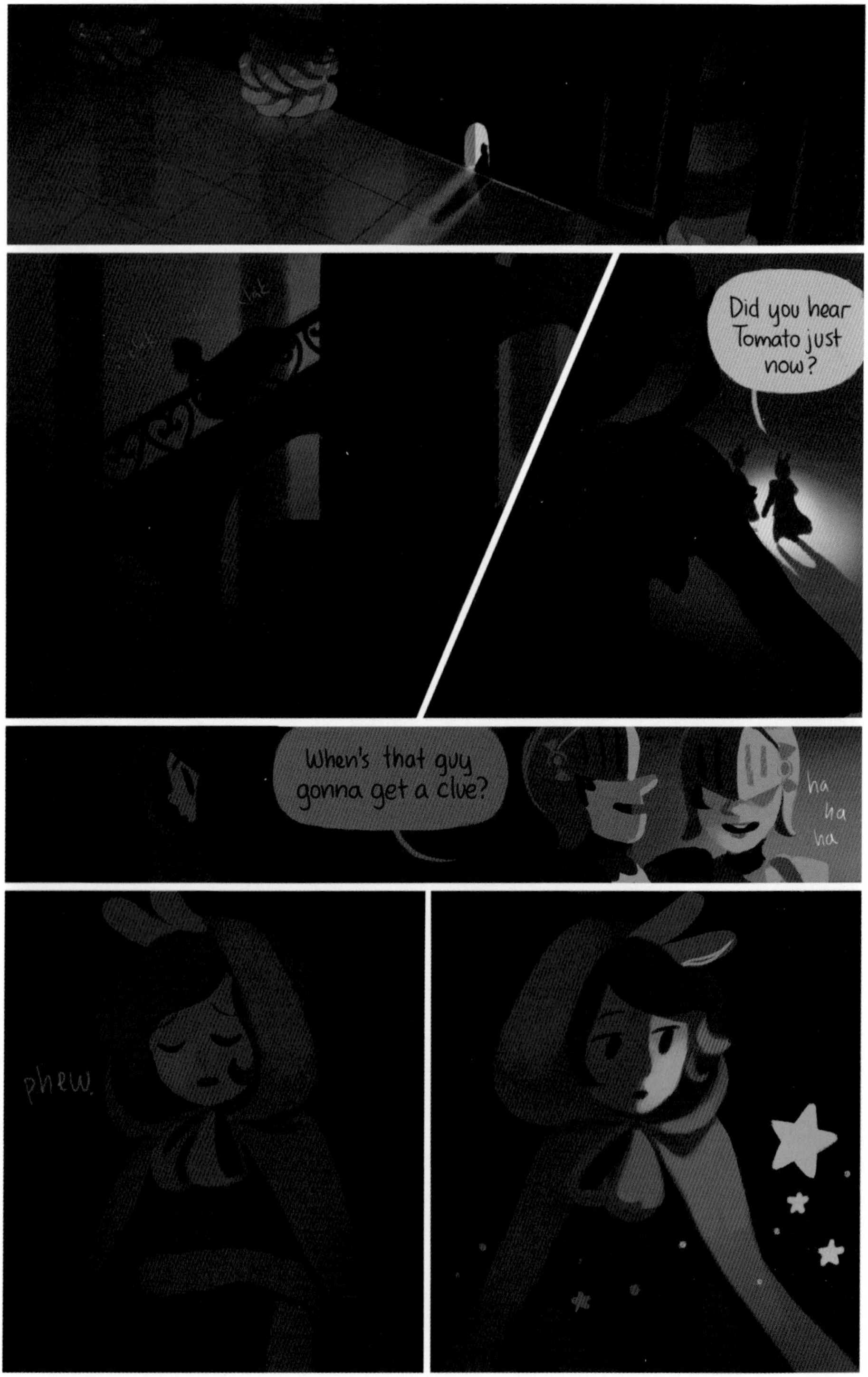
Did you hear Tomato just now?
When's that guy gonna get a clue?
ha ha ha
phew

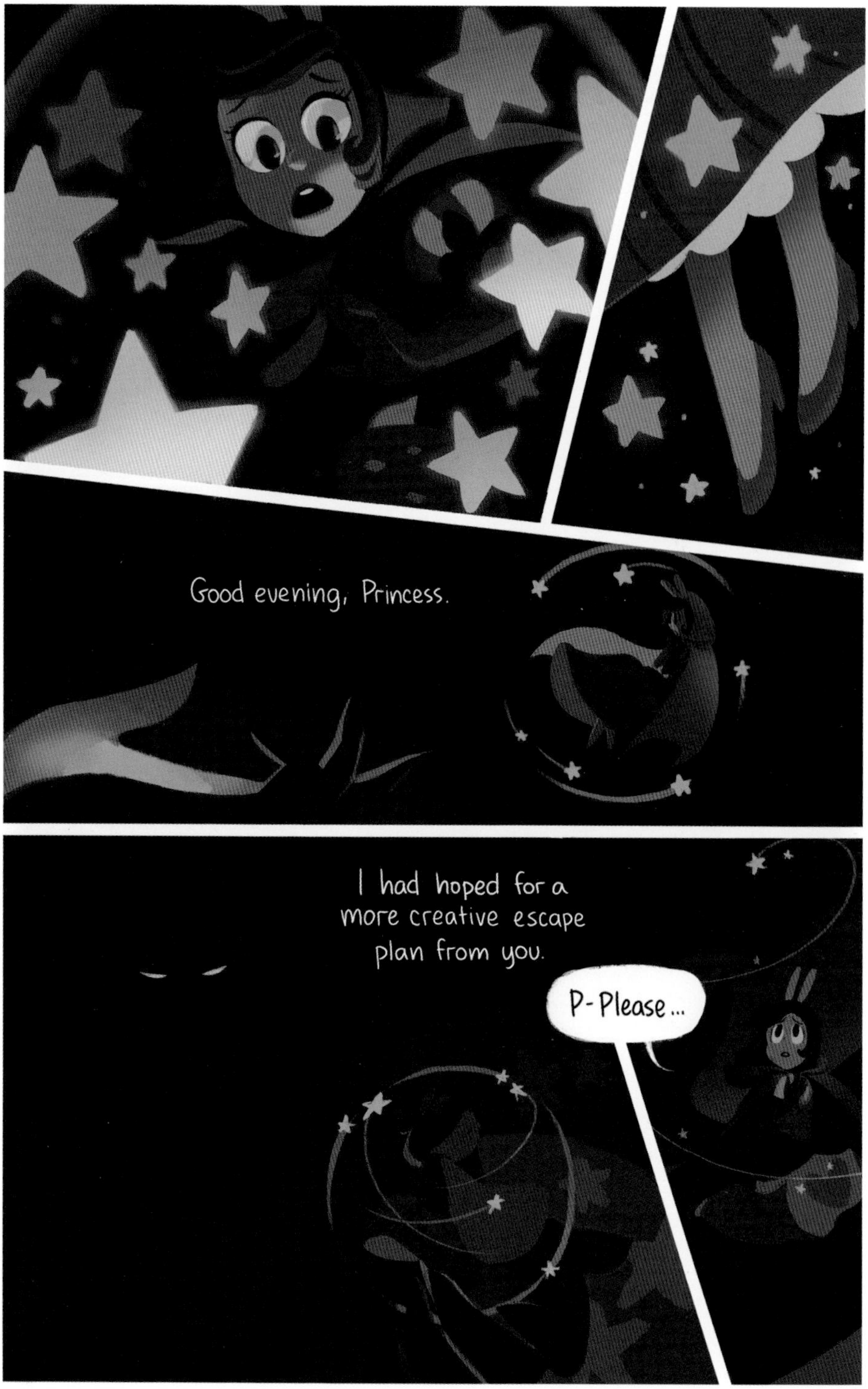
Good evening, Princess.
I had hoped for a more creative escape plan from you.
P-Please...

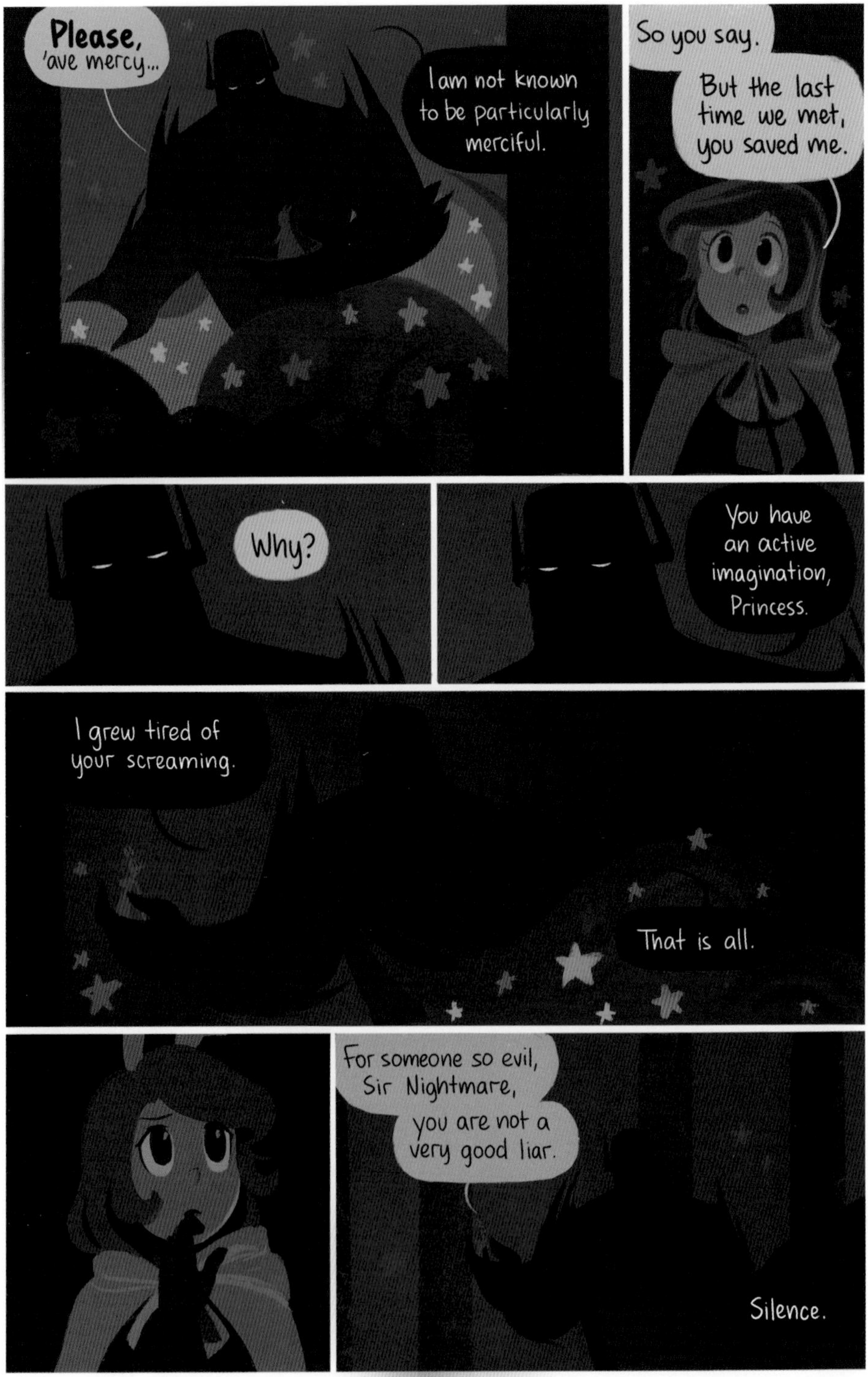
Please, 'ave mercy...
I am not known to be particularly merciful.
So you say.
But the last time we met, you saved me.
Why?
You have an active imagination, Princess.
I grew tired of your screaming.
That is all.
For someone so evil, Sir Nightmare,
you are not a very good liar.
Silence.

Your room, Princess.

creeeeeeeeeeeak

Do not attempt this again.

Oui, d'accord...

...

But—wait.

P-Please.

I—

Being locked away like this every day, with no one but Tomato to talk to...

I've never felt more alone.

I understand if you won't let me go,

but...

Will you at least stay and listen to me?

Just for a few minutes?

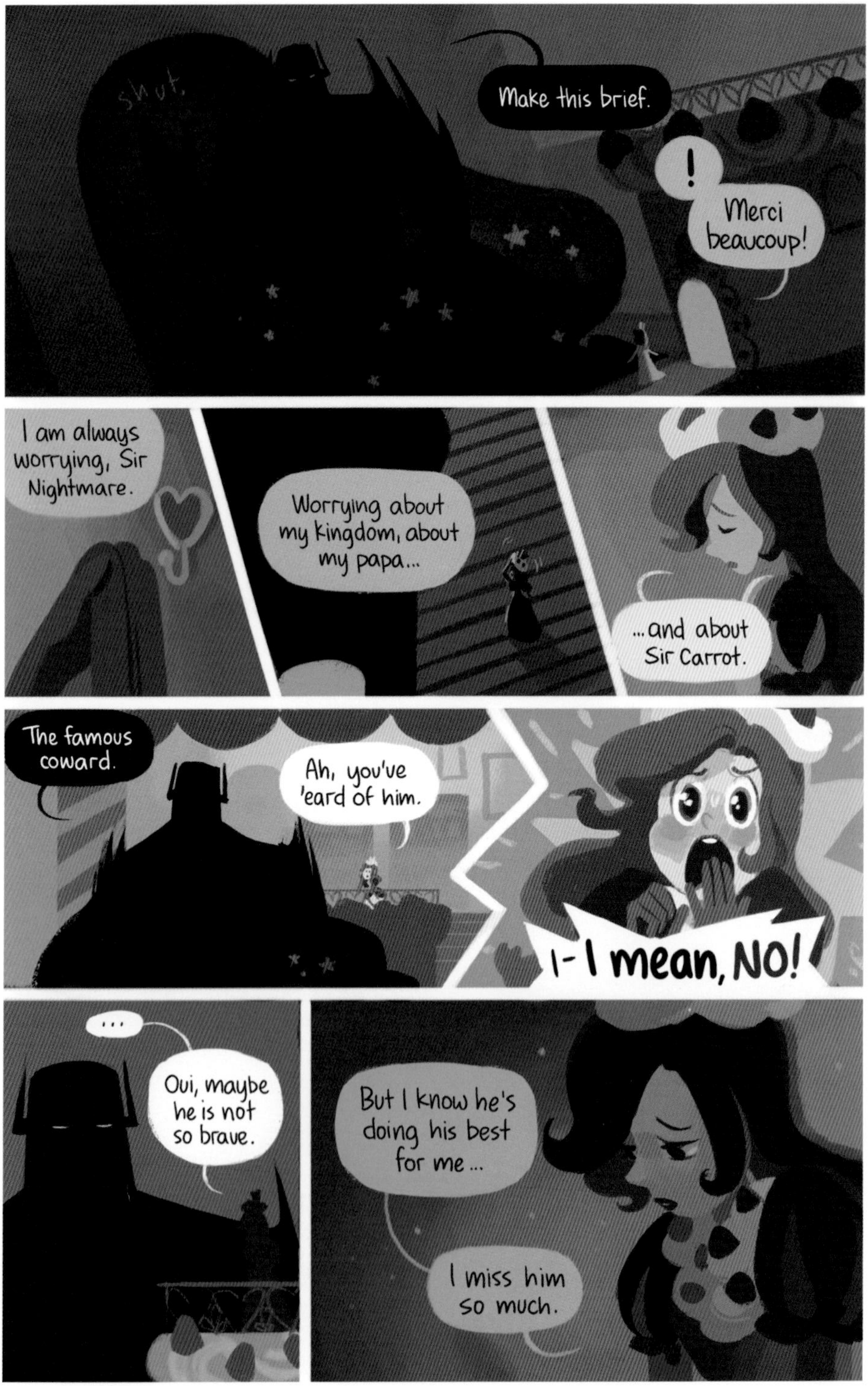
shut.
Make this brief.
!
Merci beaucoup!
I am always worrying, Sir Nightmare.
Worrying about my kingdom, about my papa...
...and about Sir Carrot.
The famous coward.
Ah, you've 'eard of him.
I- I mean, NO!
...
Oui, maybe he is not so brave.
But I know he's doing his best for me...
I miss him so much.

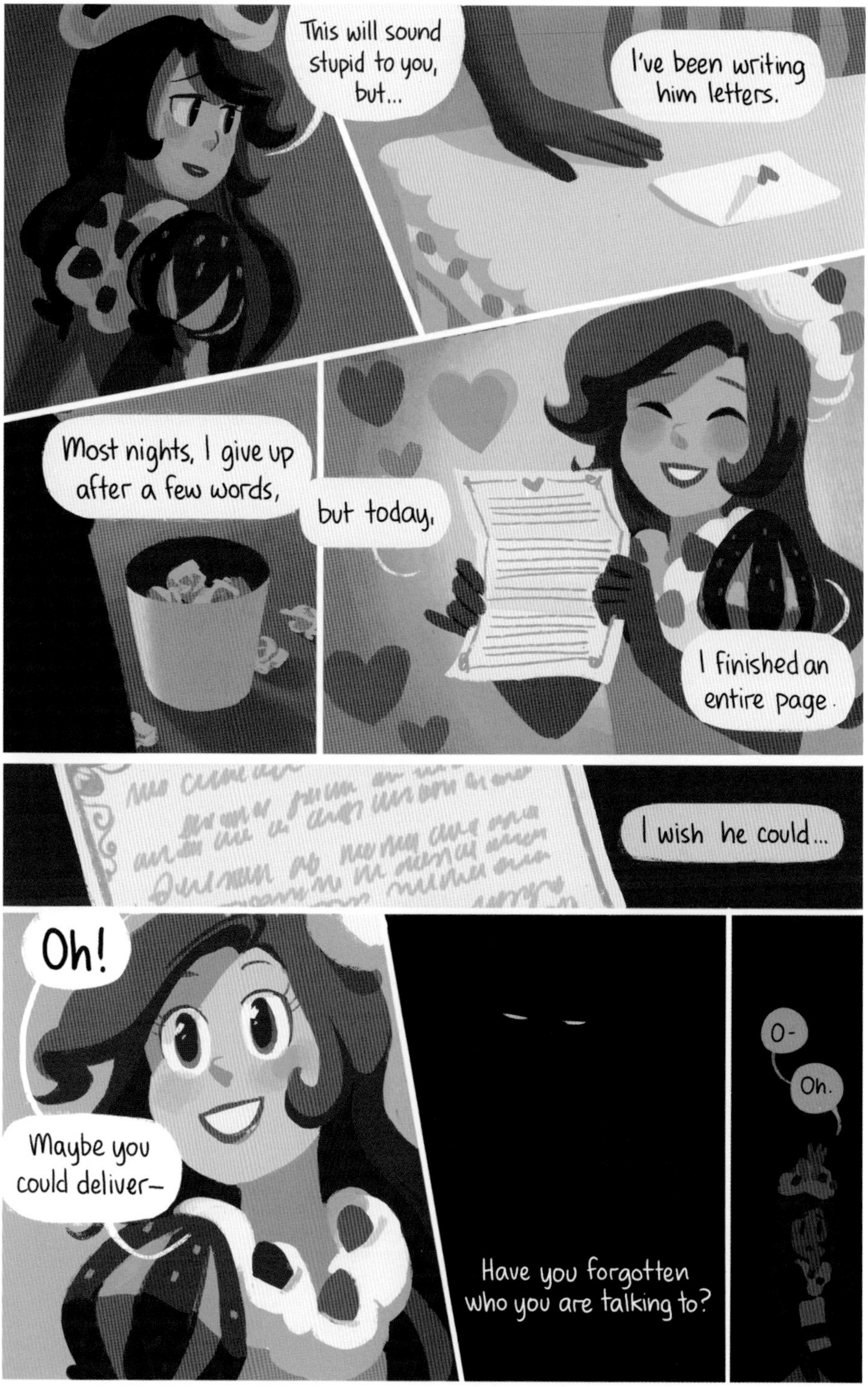

This will sound stupid to you, but...
I've been writing him letters.
Most nights, I give up after a few words,
but today,
I finished an entire page.
I wish he could...
Oh!
Maybe you could deliver—
Have you forgotten who you are talking to?
O-
Oh.

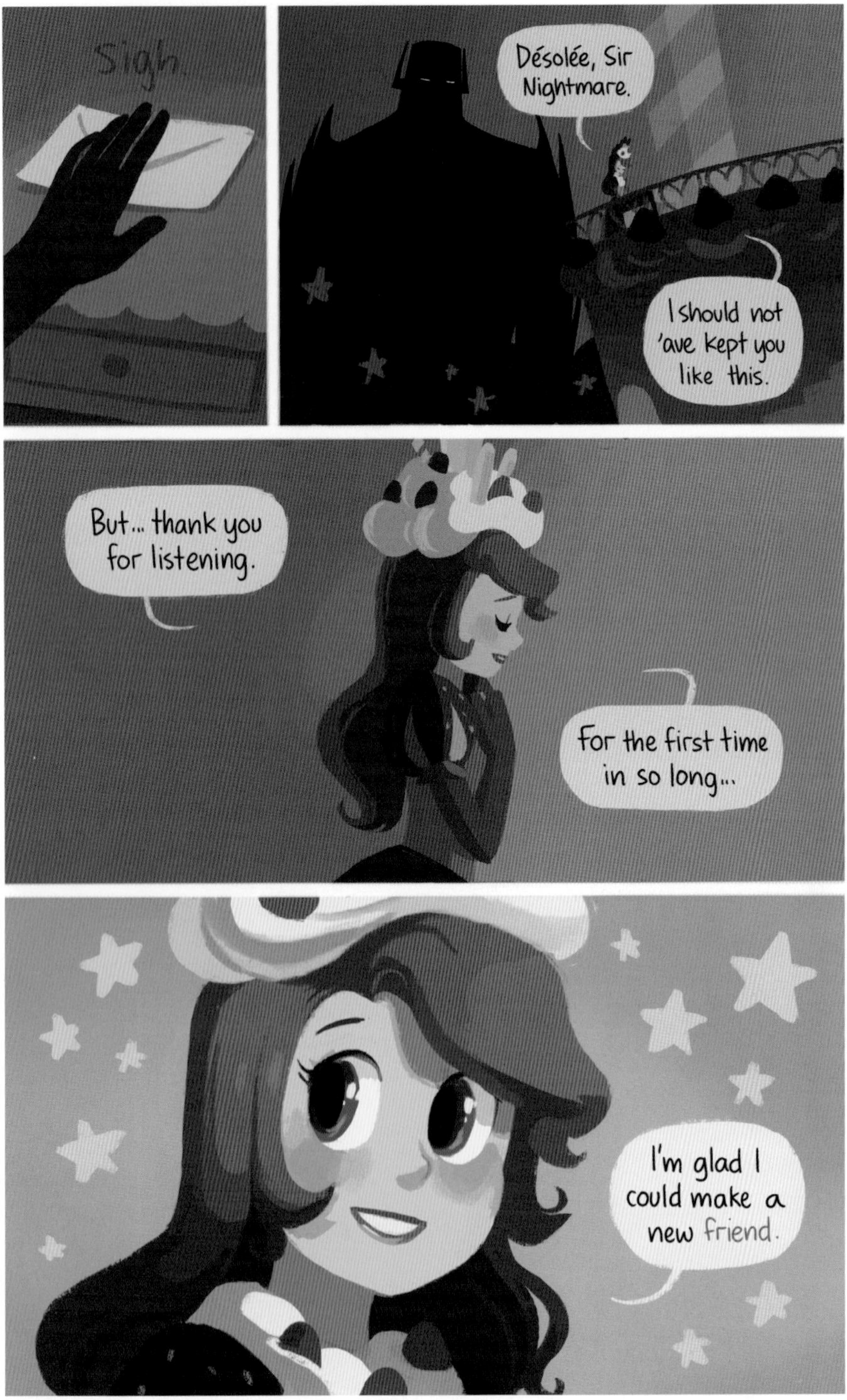
Sigh.
Désolée, Sir Nightmare.
I should not 'ave kept you like this.
But... thank you for listening.
For the first time in so long...
I'm glad I could make a new friend.

a what

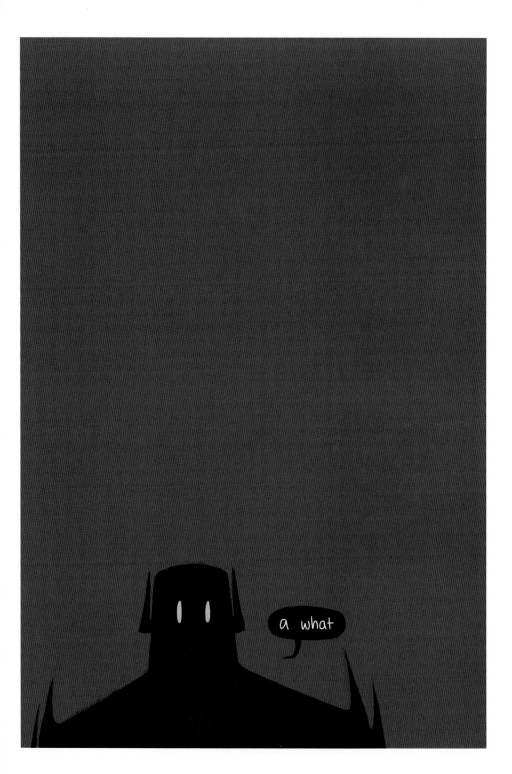

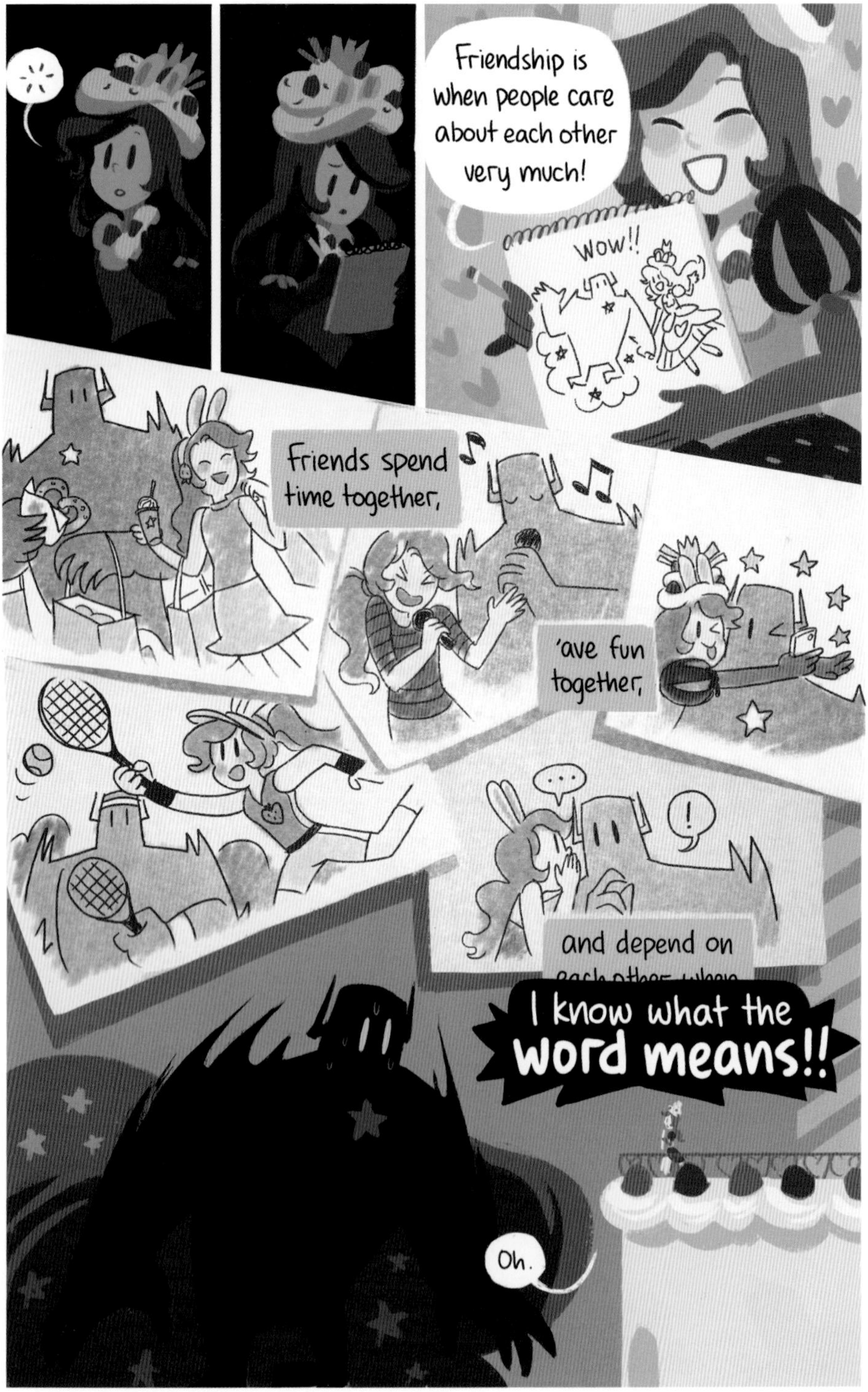
Friendship is when people care about each other very much!
WOW!!
Friends spend time together,
'ave fun together,
and depend on
I know what the word means!!
Oh.

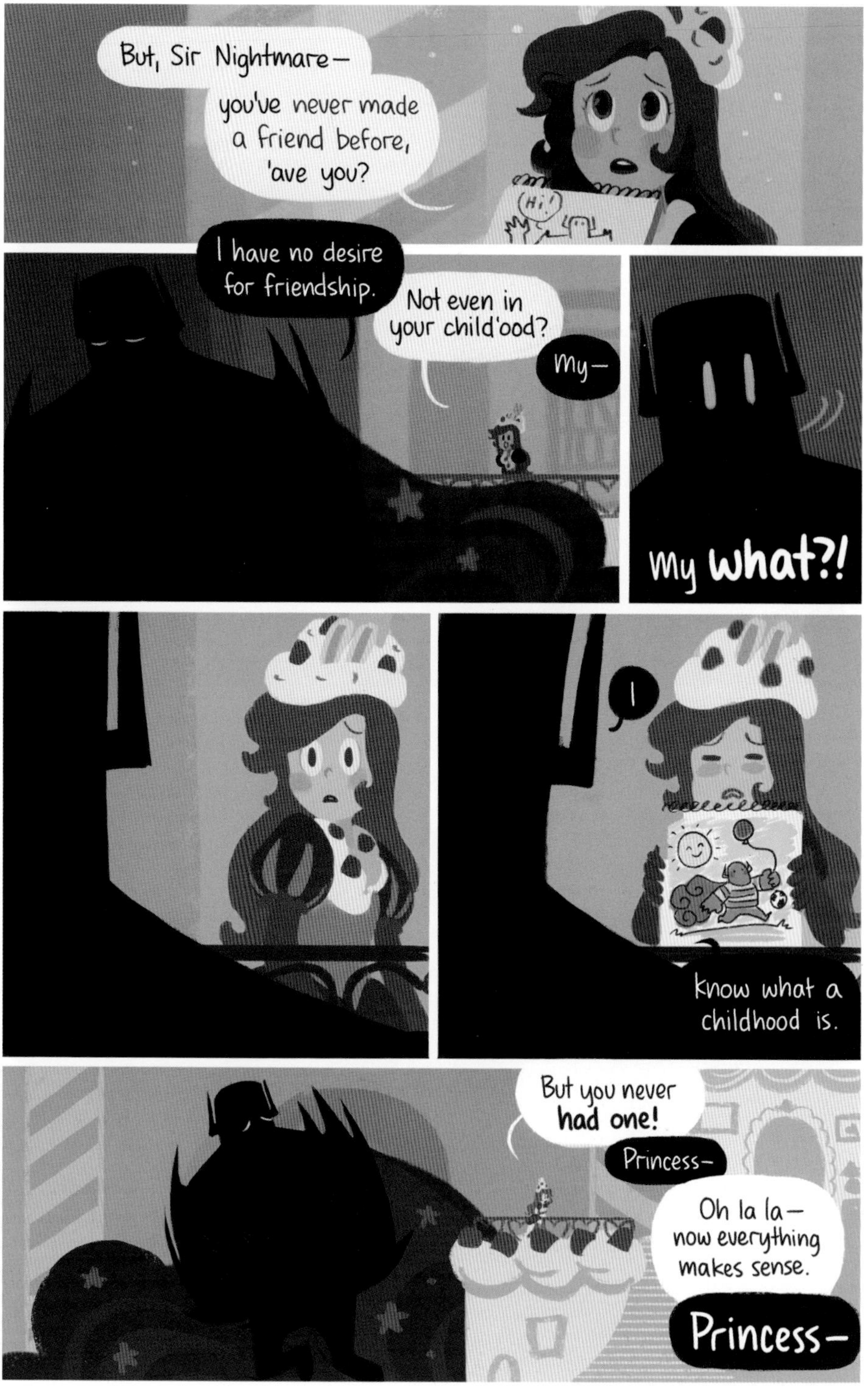

But, Sir Nightmare—
you've never made a friend before, 'ave you?
I have no desire for friendship.
Not even in your child'ood?
My—
My what?!
I
know what a childhood is.
But you never had one!
Princess—
Oh la la— now everything makes sense.
Princess—

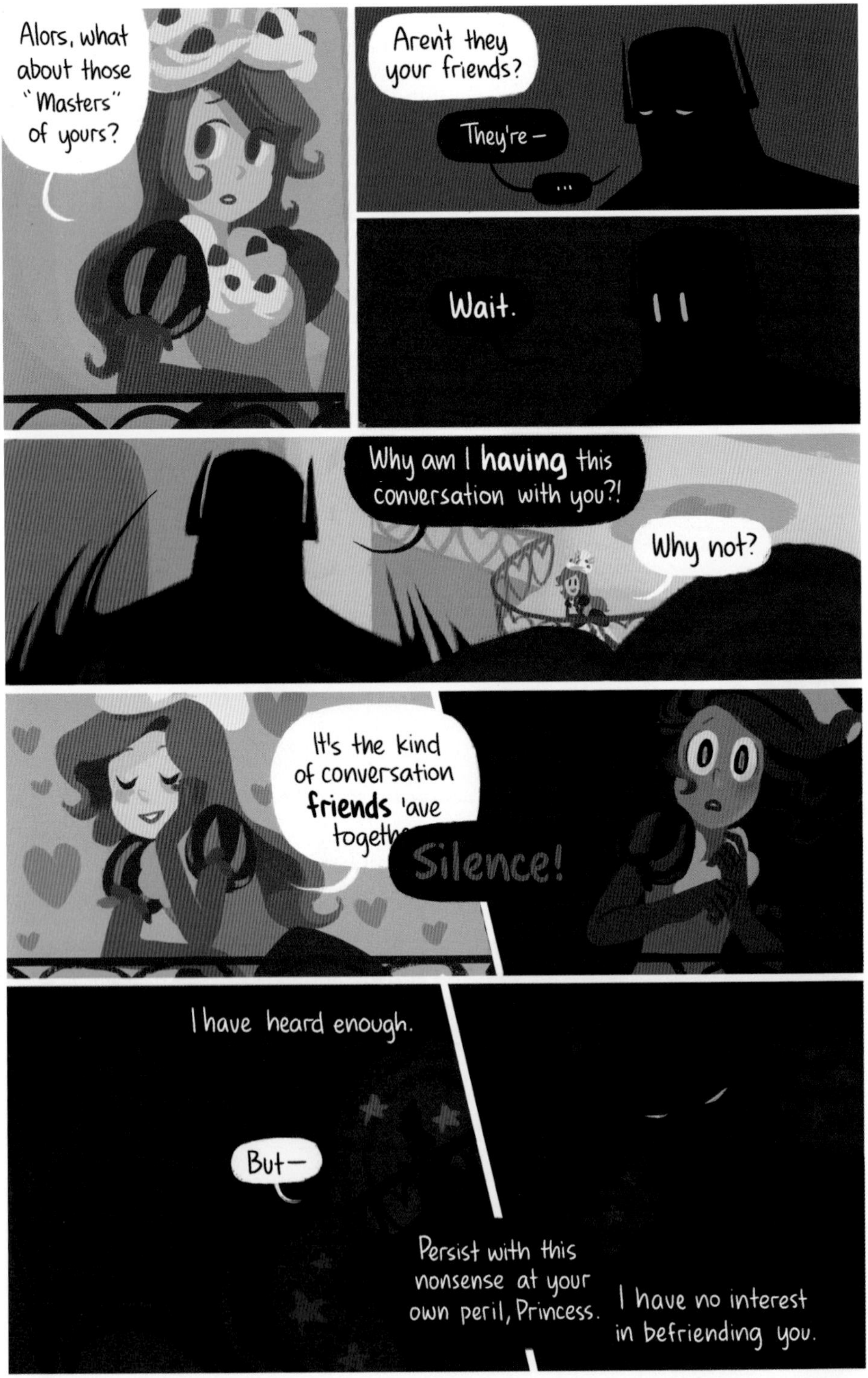
Alors, what about those "Masters" of yours?
Aren't they your friends?
They're —
...
Wait.
Why am I **having** this conversation with you?!
Why not?
It's the kind of conversation **friends** 'ave togeth
Silence!
I have heard enough.
But—
Persist with this nonsense at your own peril, Princess.
I have no interest in befriending you.

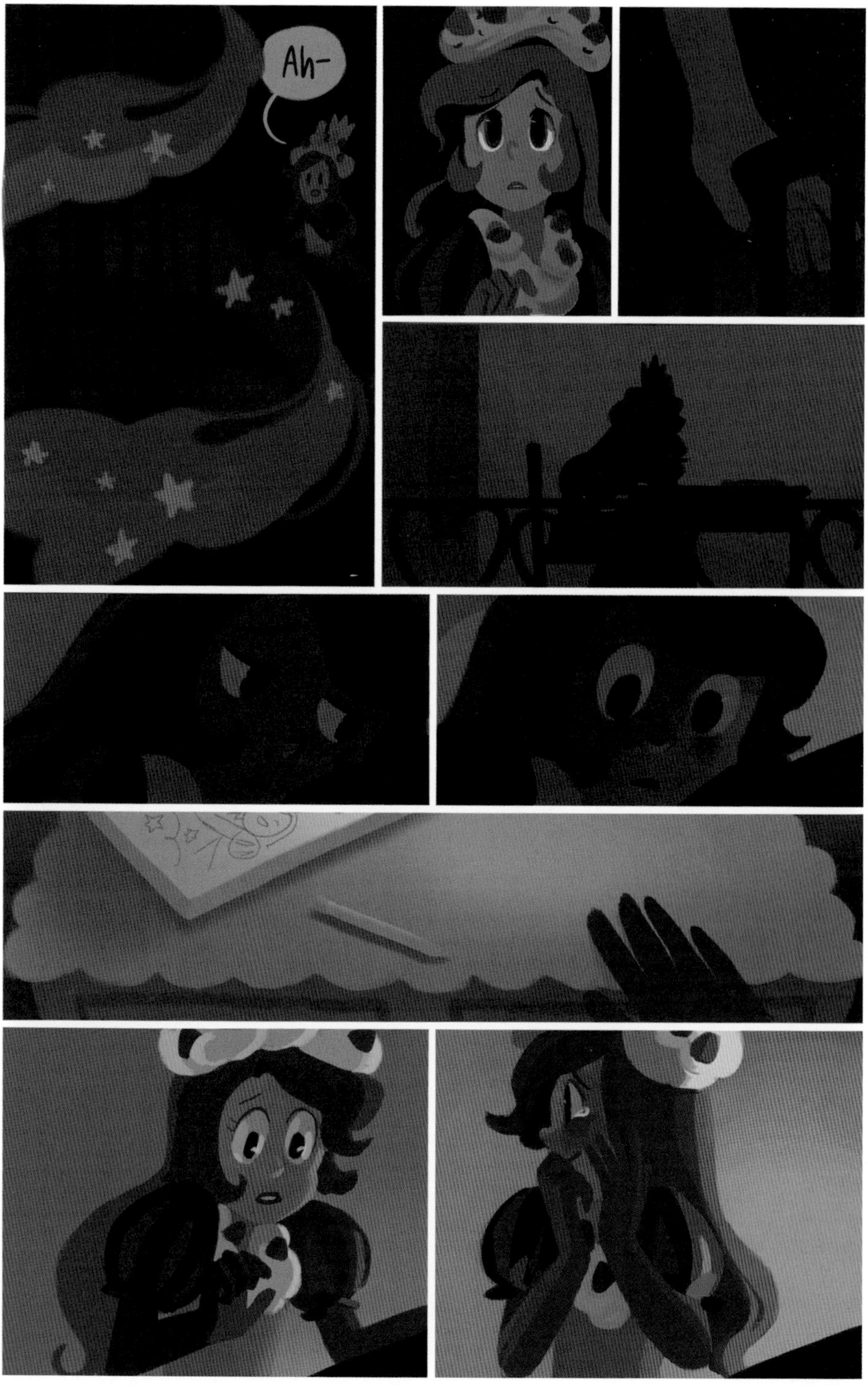
Ah-

Mon cher Carrot,

My letters to you never seem to turn out right. Sometimes I see you reading the mushy things I write, and I get embarrassed... Other times, I imagine you worrying about me, and then I just end up crying.

This letter is already mushy, and I am already crying, so I guess I have nothing else to be afraid of! 🐰

Do you remember the night that shooting star fell <u>onto</u> my balcony? He said the pendants he gave us would keep us together even when we were far apart. I thought it was a little silly at the time, but I still wear mine every day.

I know you — you just reached for yours, didn't you? ːᷧꙨᷧː

In truth, I know that you will probably never read this letter... But if some miracle really has brought it to your hands, there is something I want you to know...

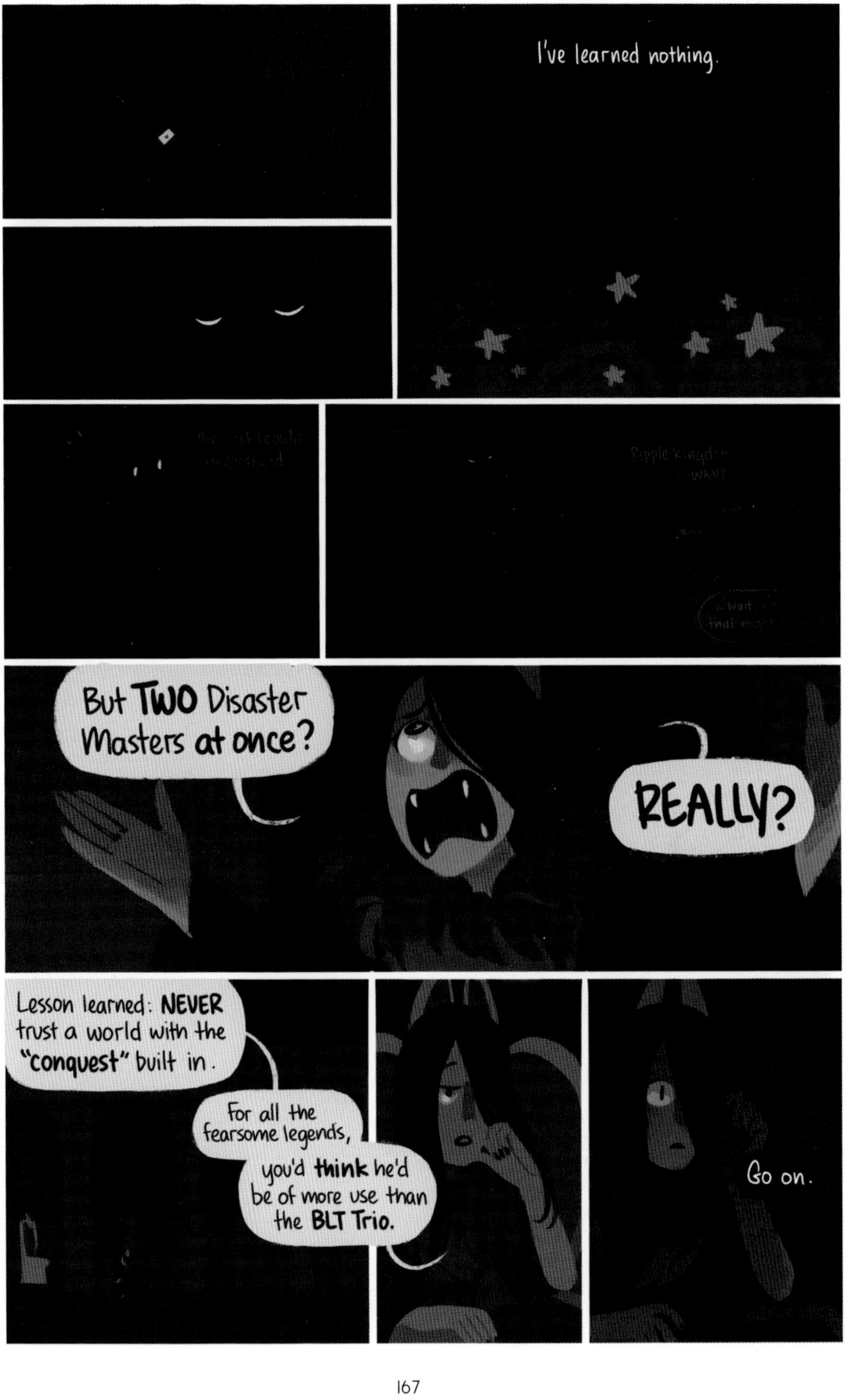

I've learned nothing.
But TWO Disaster Masters at once?
REALLY?
Lesson learned: NEVER trust a world with the "conquest" built in.
For all the fearsome legends,
you'd think he'd be of more use than the BLT Trio.
Go on.

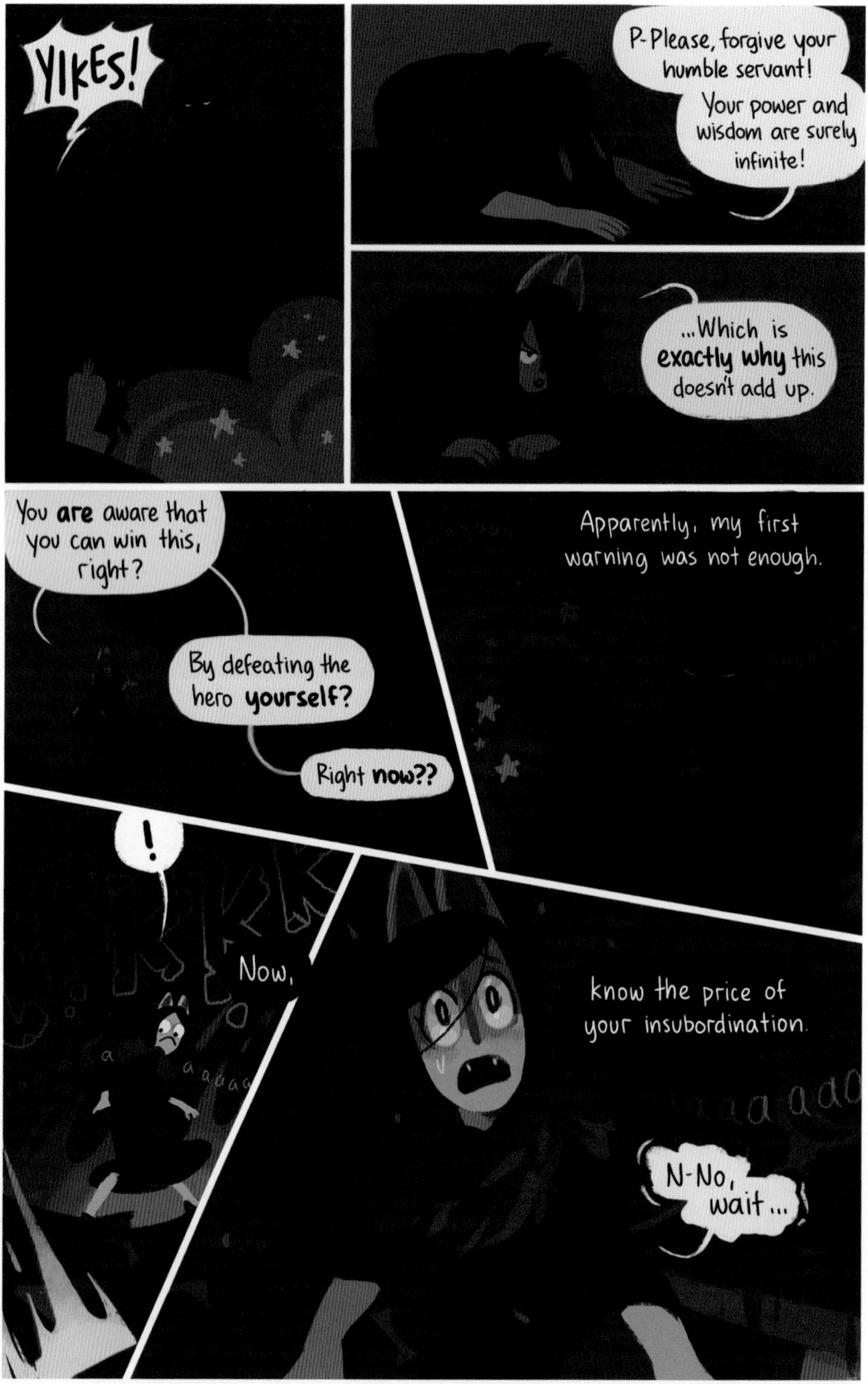

YIKES!
P-Please, forgive your humble servant!
Your power and wisdom are surely infinite!
...Which is **exactly why** this doesn't add up.
You **are** aware that you can win this, right?
By defeating the hero **yourself?**
Right **now??**
Apparently, my first warning was not enough.
!
Now,
know the price of your insubordination.
aaaaa
N-No, wait...

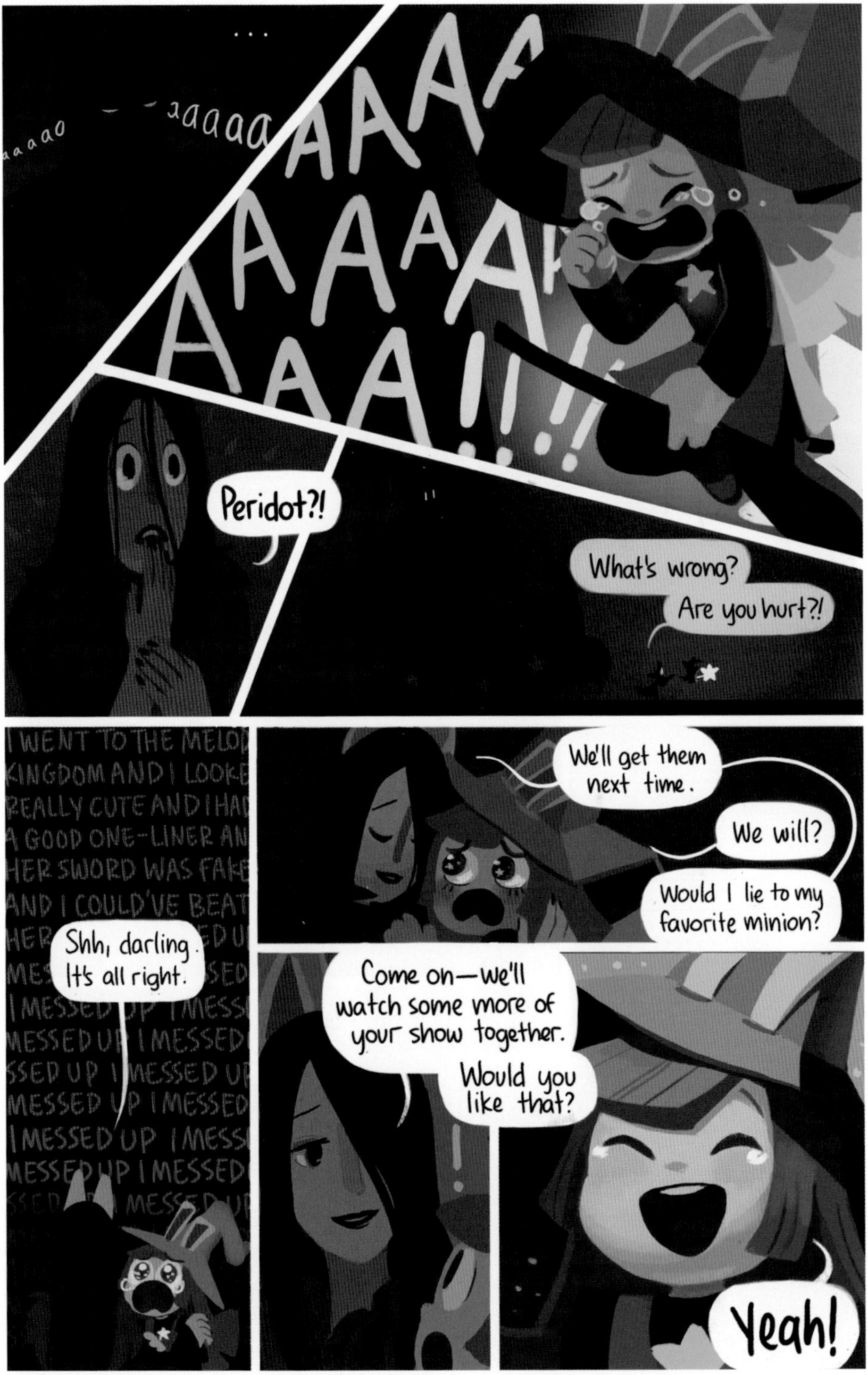
...
aaaao — —aaaaa
AAAAAAAAAAAAA!!!!
Peridot?!
What's wrong?
Are you hurt?!
I WENT TO THE MELOD KINGDOM AND I LOOKE REALLY CUTE AND I HAD A GOOD ONE-LINER AN HER SWORD WAS FAKE AND I COULD'VE BEAT HER
I MESSED UP I MESSED UP I MESSED UP I MESSED UP I MESSED UP I MESSED UP I MESSED UP I MESSED UP
Shh, darling. It's all right.
We'll get them next time.
We will?
Would I lie to my favorite minion?
Come on—we'll watch some more of your show together.
Would you like that?
Yeah!

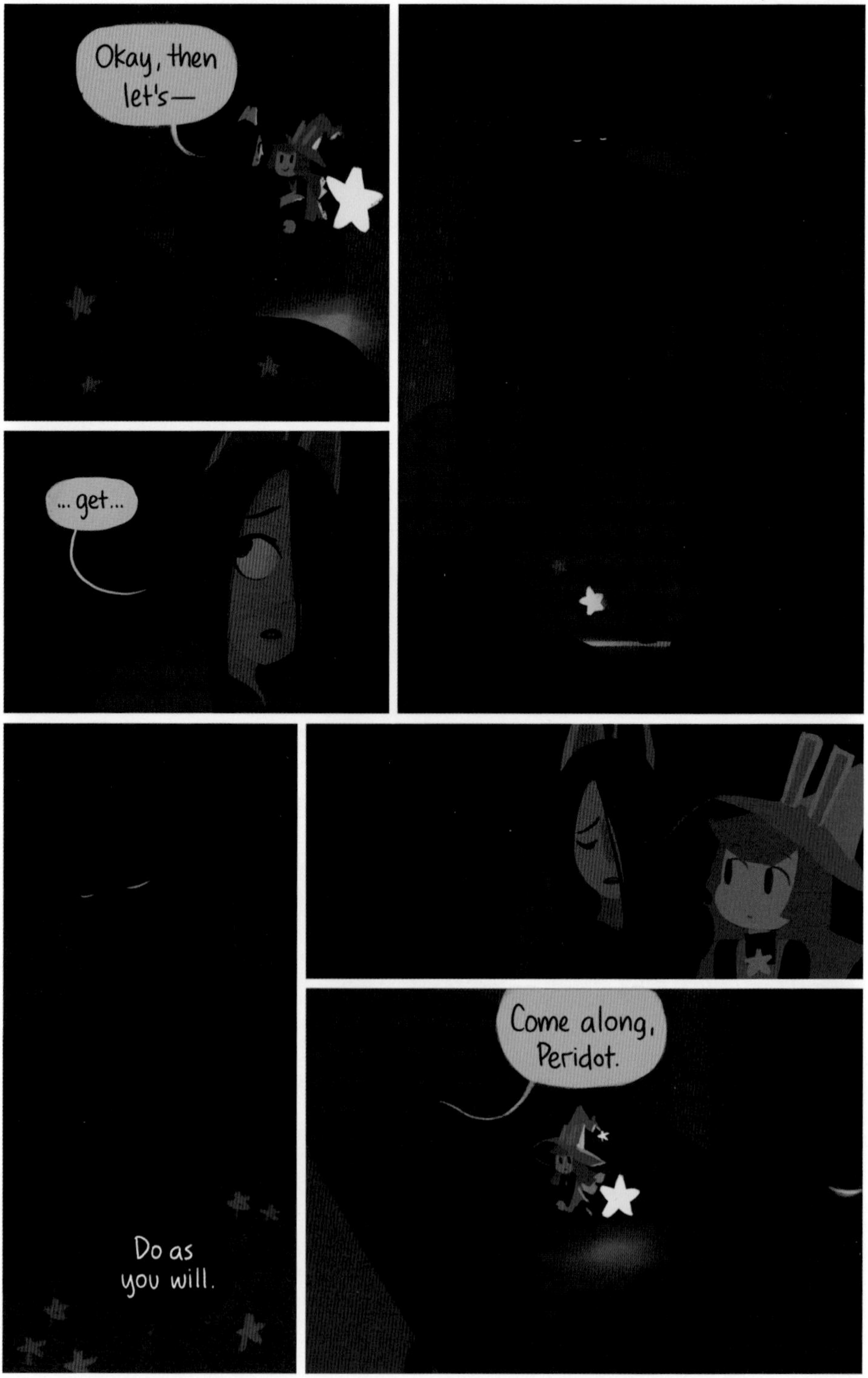

Okay, then let's—
... get...
Do as you will.
Come along, Peridot.

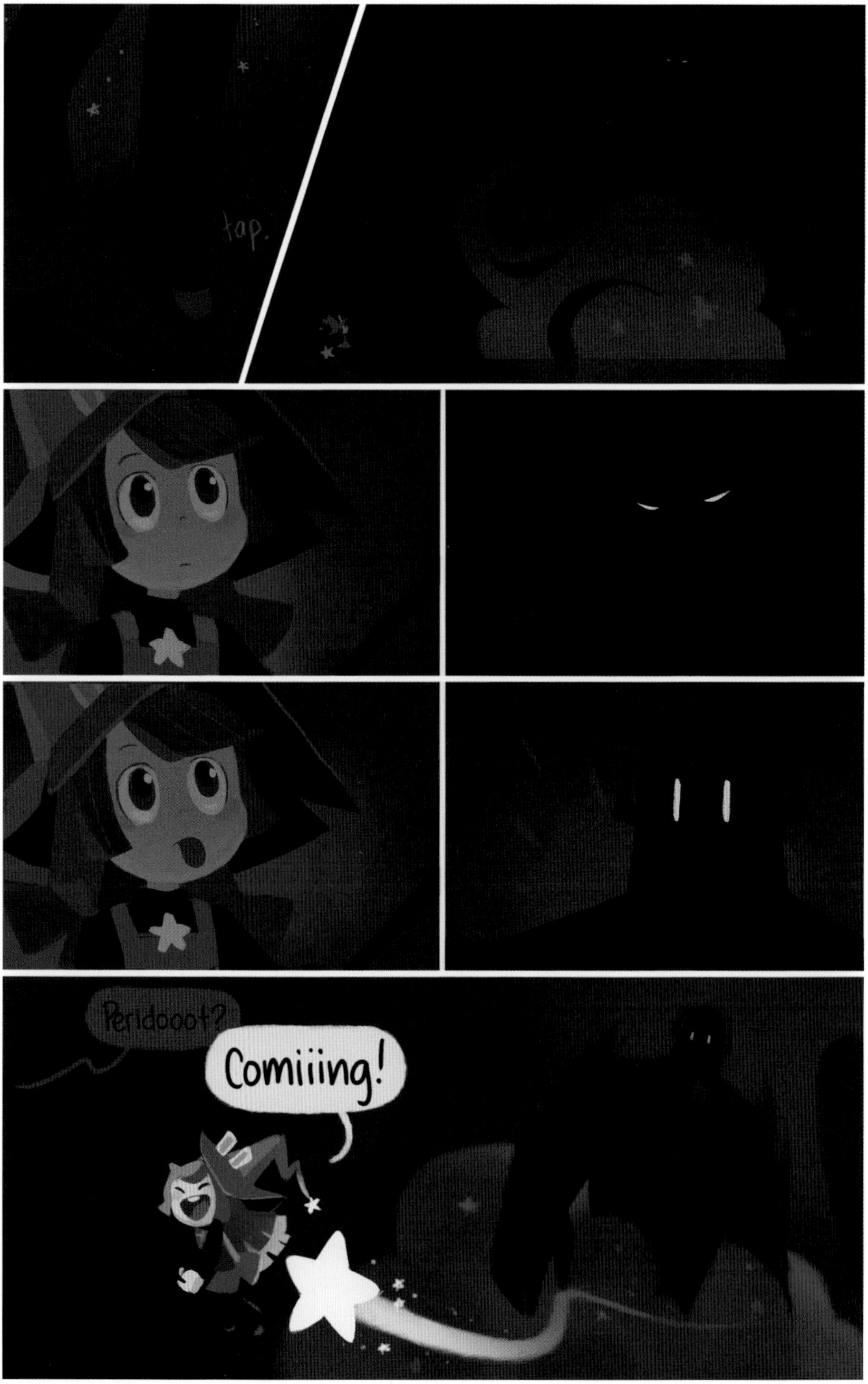
tap.
Peridooot?
Comiiing!

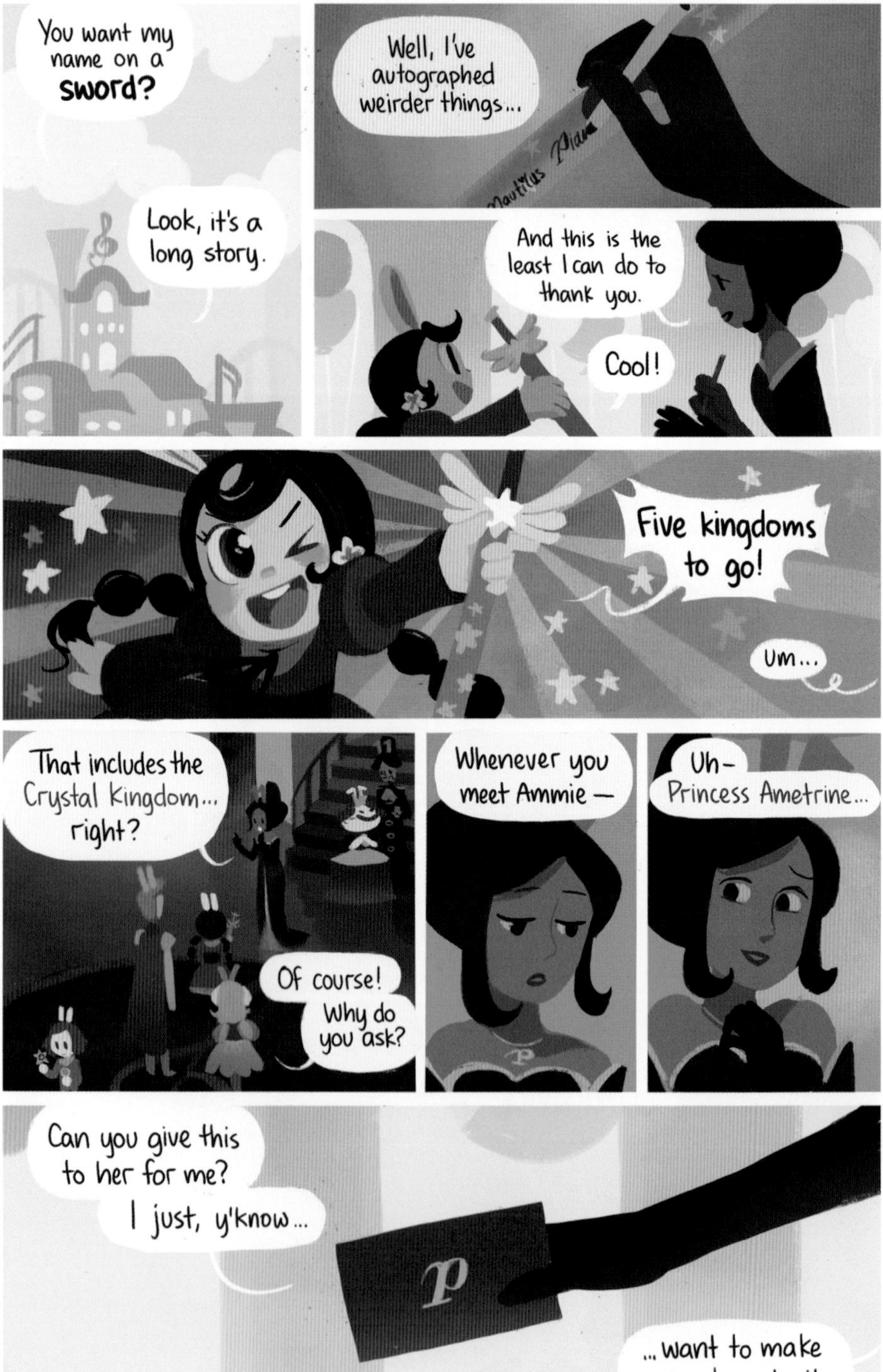
You want my name on a **sword?**
Look, it's a long story.
Well, I've autographed weirder things...
Nautilus Piano
And this is the least I can do to thank you.
Cool!
Five kingdoms to go!
Um...
That includes the Crystal Kingdom... right?
Of course! Why do you ask?
Whenever you meet Ammie —
Uh- Princess Ametrine...
Can you give this to her for me?
I just, y'know...
...want to make sure she gets it.

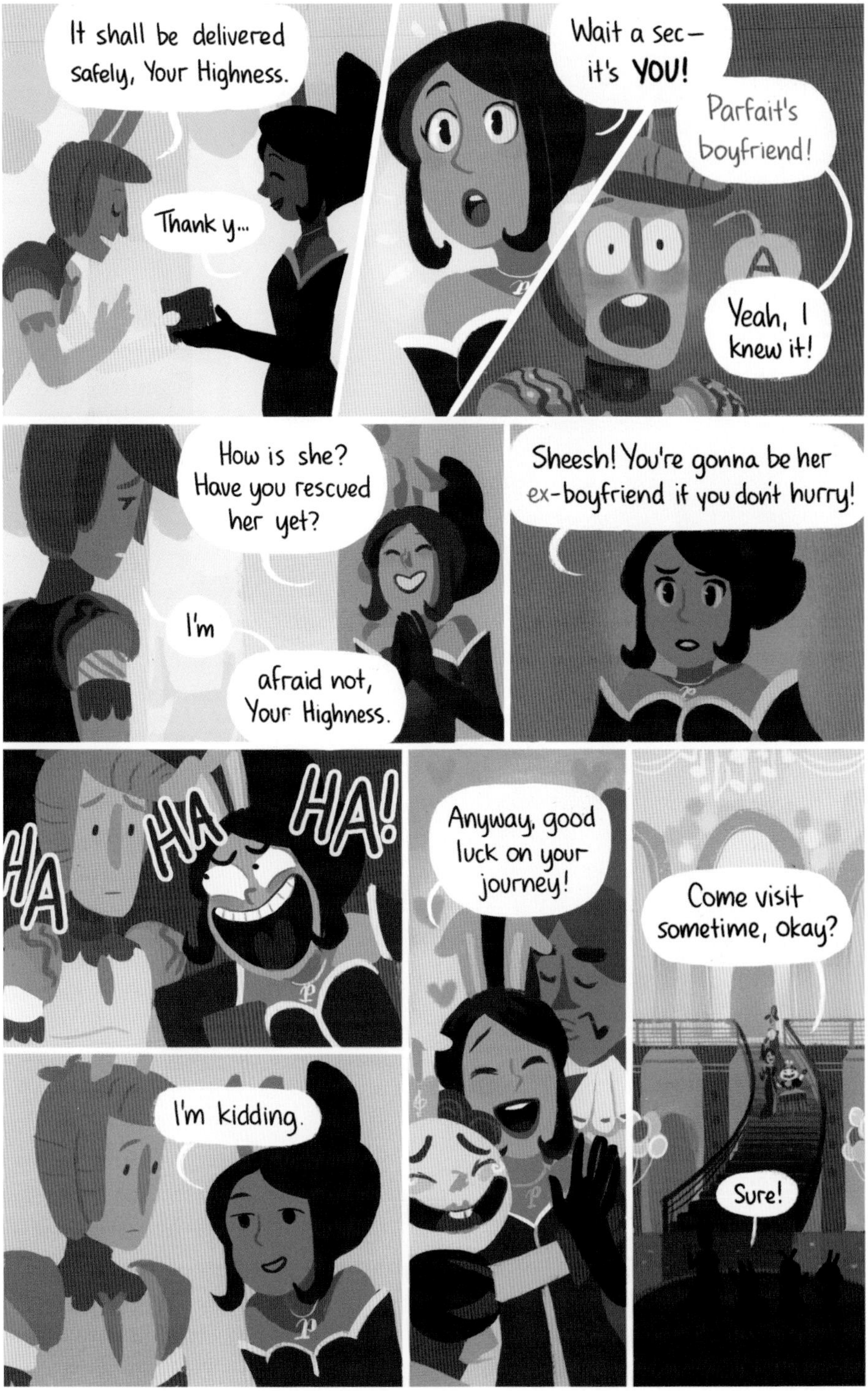
It shall be delivered safely, Your Highness.
Thank y...
Wait a sec— it's **YOU!**
Parfait's boyfriend!
Yeah, I knew it!
How is she? Have you rescued her yet?
I'm
afraid not, Your Highness.
Sheesh! You're gonna be her ex-boyfriend if you don't hurry!
HA HA HA!
I'm kidding.
Anyway, good luck on your journey!
Come visit sometime, okay?
Sure!

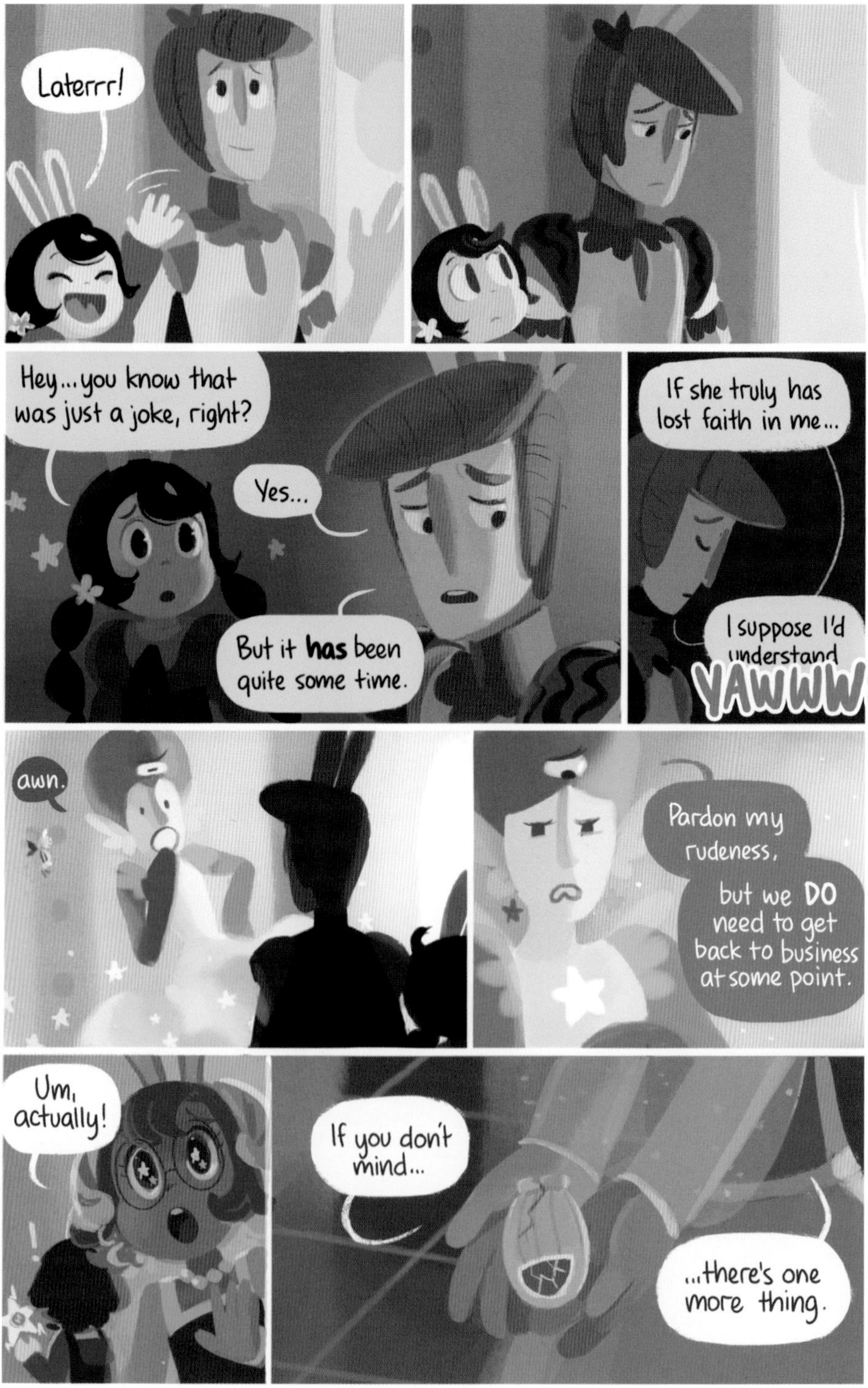
Laterrr!
Hey...you know that was just a joke, right?
Yes...
But it **has** been quite some time.
If she truly has lost faith in me...
I suppose I'd understand
YAWWW
awn.
Pardon my rudeness,
but we **DO** need to get back to business at some point.
Um, actually!
If you don't mind...
...there's one more thing.

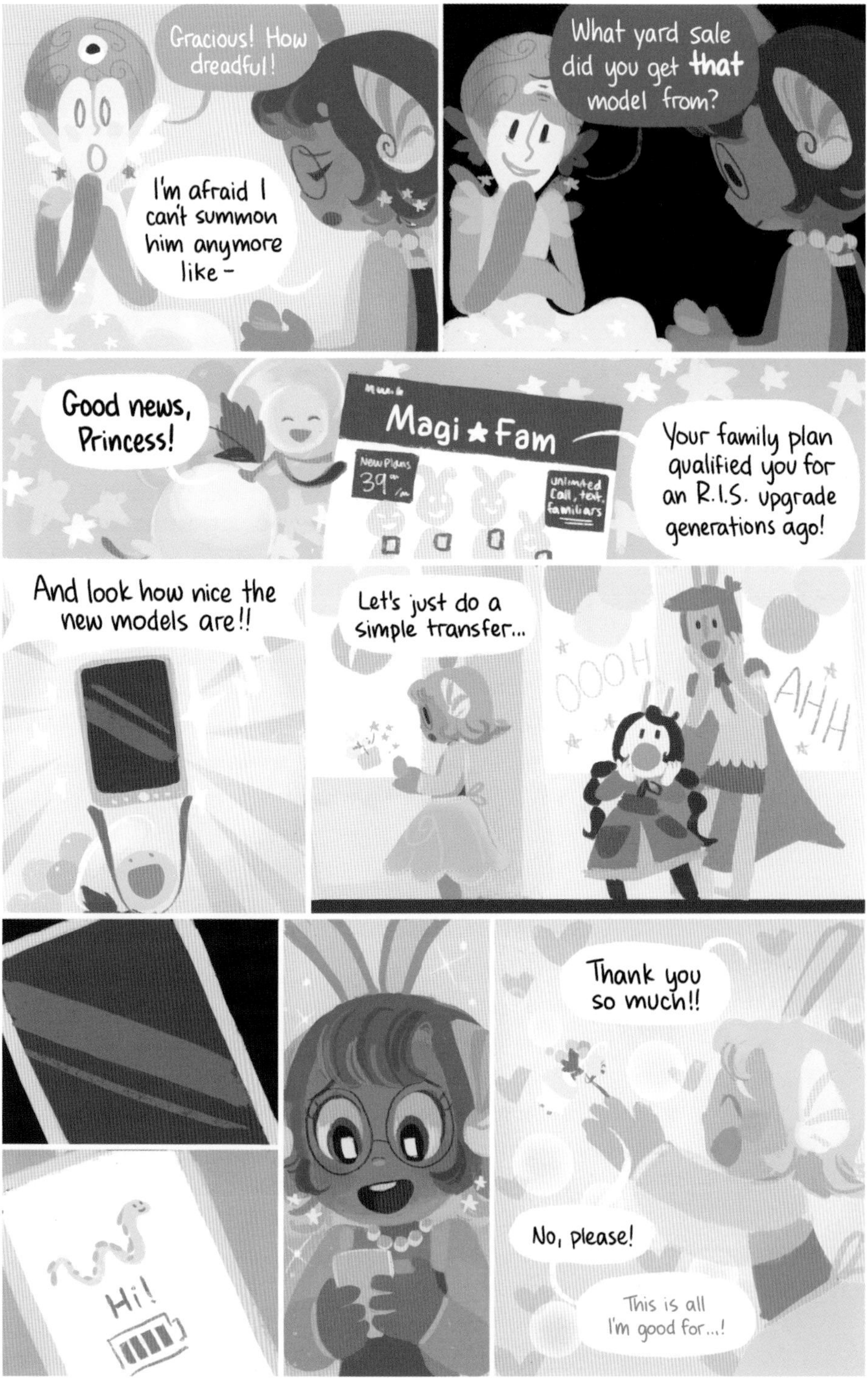
Gracious! How dreadful!
I'm afraid I can't summon him anymore like-
What yard sale did you get **that** model from?
Good news, Princess!
Magi★Fam
New Plans 39
Unlimited Call, text, familiars
Your family plan qualified you for an R.I.S. upgrade generations ago!
And look how nice the new models are!!
Let's just do a simple transfer...
OOOH
AHH
Hi!
Thank you so much!!
No, please!
This is all I'm good for...!

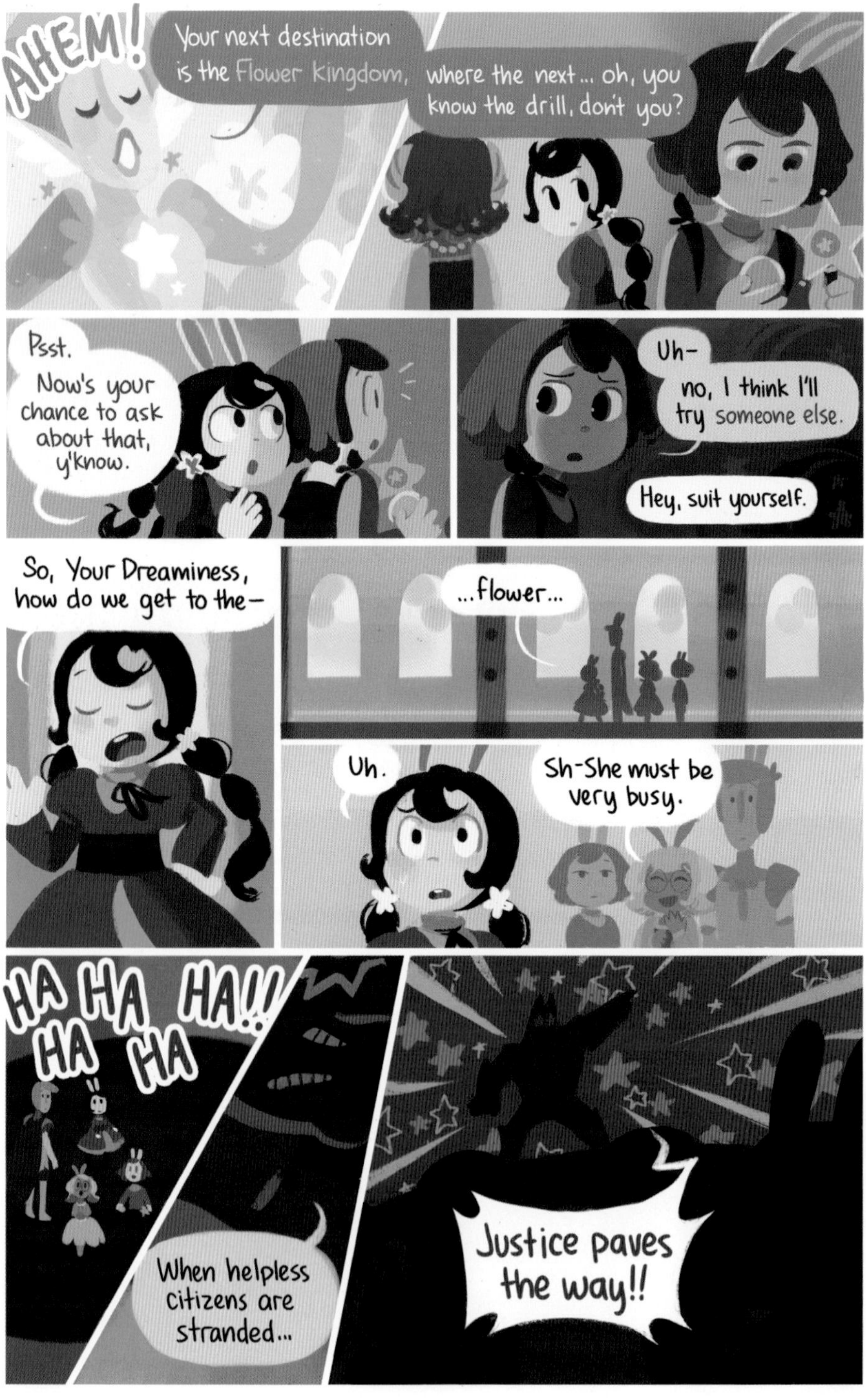
AHEM!
Your next destination is the Flower Kingdom,
where the next... oh, you know the drill, don't you?
Psst.
Now's your chance to ask about that, y'know.
Uh-
no, I think I'll try someone else.
Hey, suit yourself.
So, Your Dreaminess, how do we get to the-
...flower...
Uh.
Sh-She must be very busy.
HA HA HA HA HA!!
When helpless citizens are stranded...
Justice paves the way!!

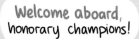

Welcome aboard, honorary champions!

Now that my ship has been refueled,

your "Flow-er king-dom" should be only a few short minutes away!

Whoa, cool!

But...you're still headed for Caketown, right?

Isn't this a little out of the way for you?

Crazy talk, Cucumber!

This is the least I can do for a fellow ally of justice!

Or a test subject.

Oho! Well, we **ARE** certainly—

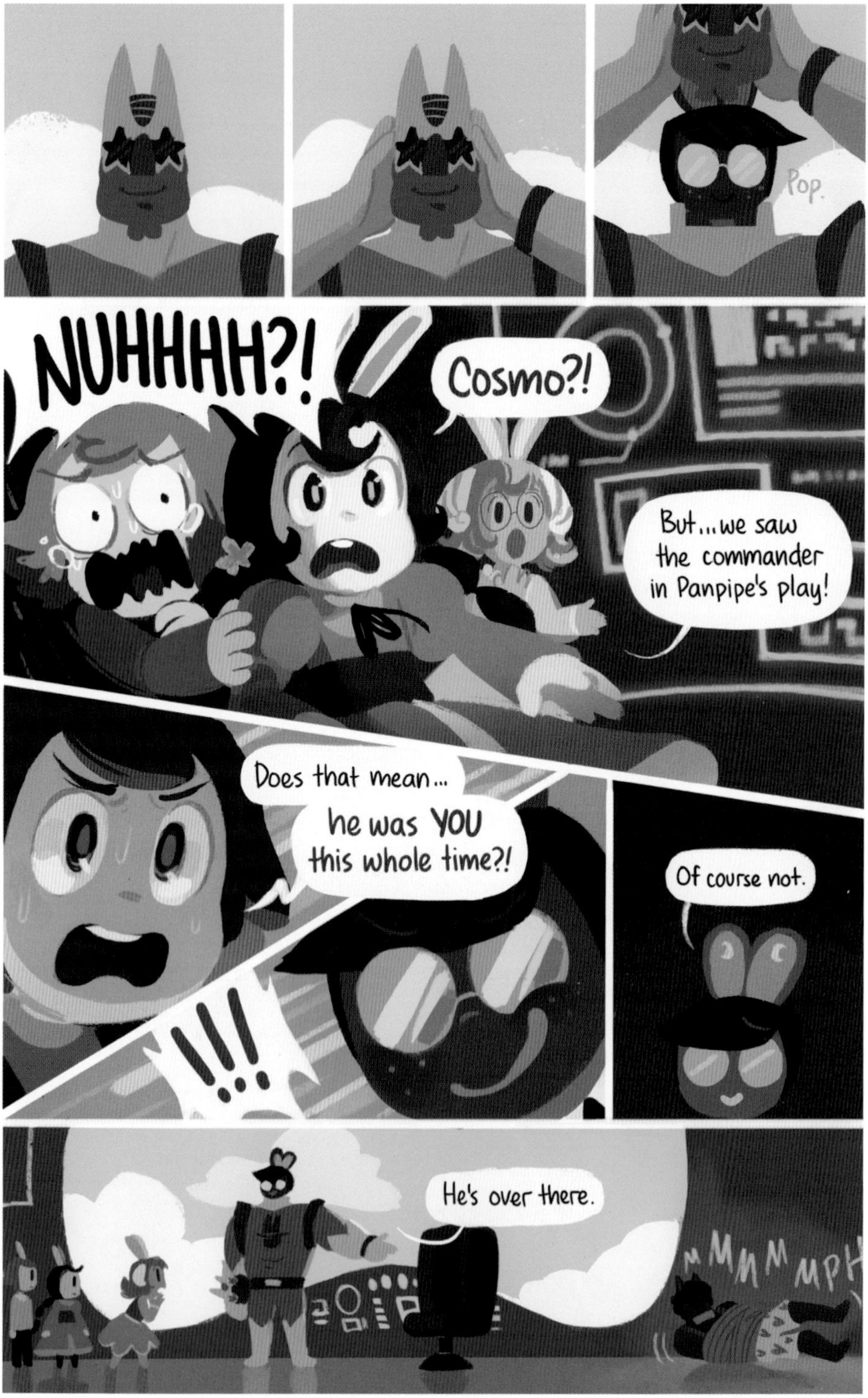
Pop.
NUHHHH?!
Cosmo?!
But...we saw the commander in Panpipe's play!
Does that mean...
he was YOU this whole time?!
!!!
Of course not.
He's over there.
MMMMMPH

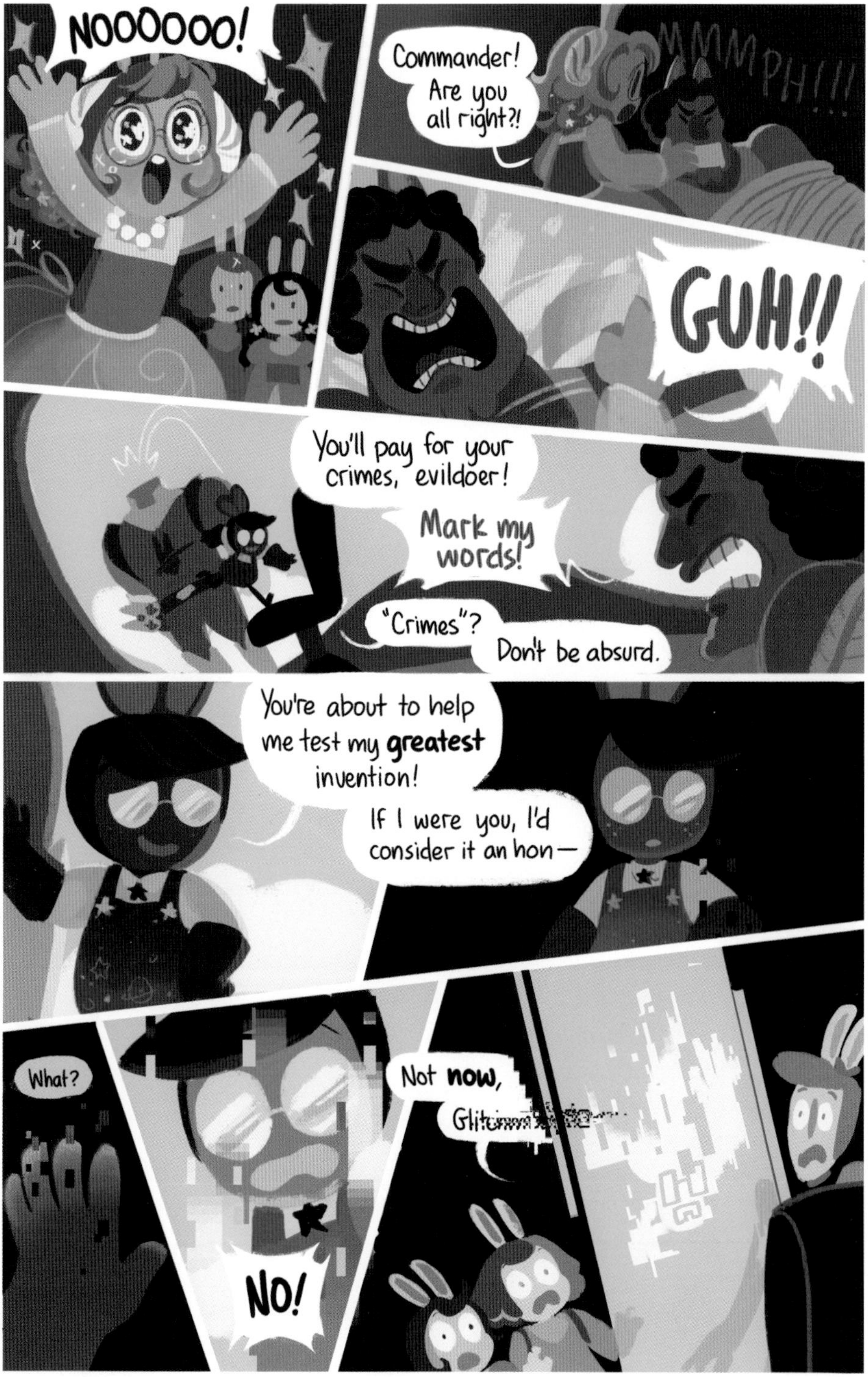
NOOOOOO!
Commander! Are you all right?!
MMMMPH!!!
GUH!!
You'll pay for your crimes, evildoer!
Mark my words!
"Crimes"?
Don't be absurd.
You're about to help me test my **greatest** invention!
If I were you, I'd consider it an hon—
What?
NO!
Not **now**,

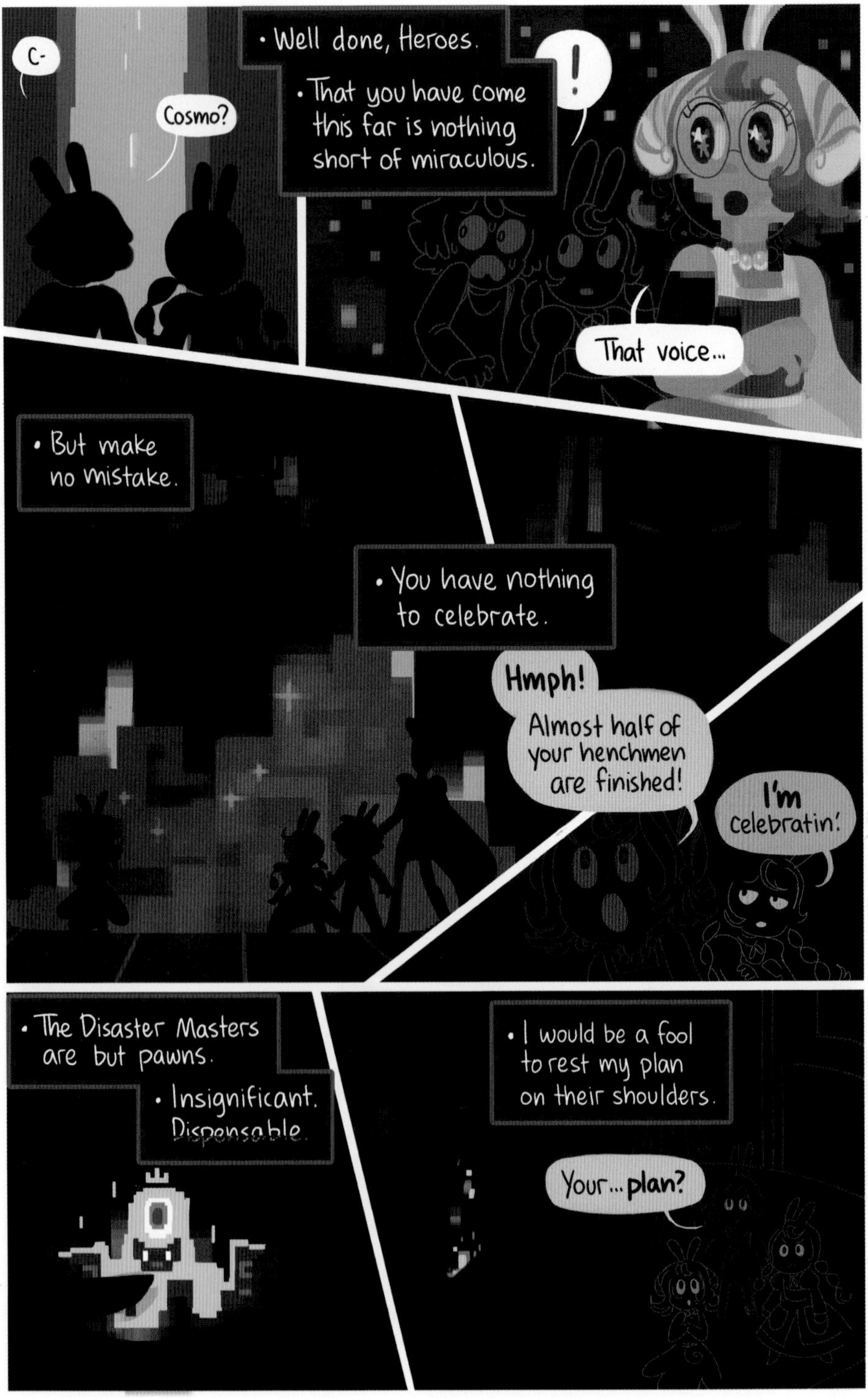

C-
Cosmo?
• Well done, Heroes.
• That you have come this far is nothing short of miraculous.
!
That voice...
• But make no mistake.
• You have nothing to celebrate.
Hmph!
Almost half of your henchmen are finished!
I'm celebratin'!
• The Disaster Masters are but pawns.
• Insignificant. Dispensable.
• I would be a fool to rest my plan on their shoulders.
Your... plan?

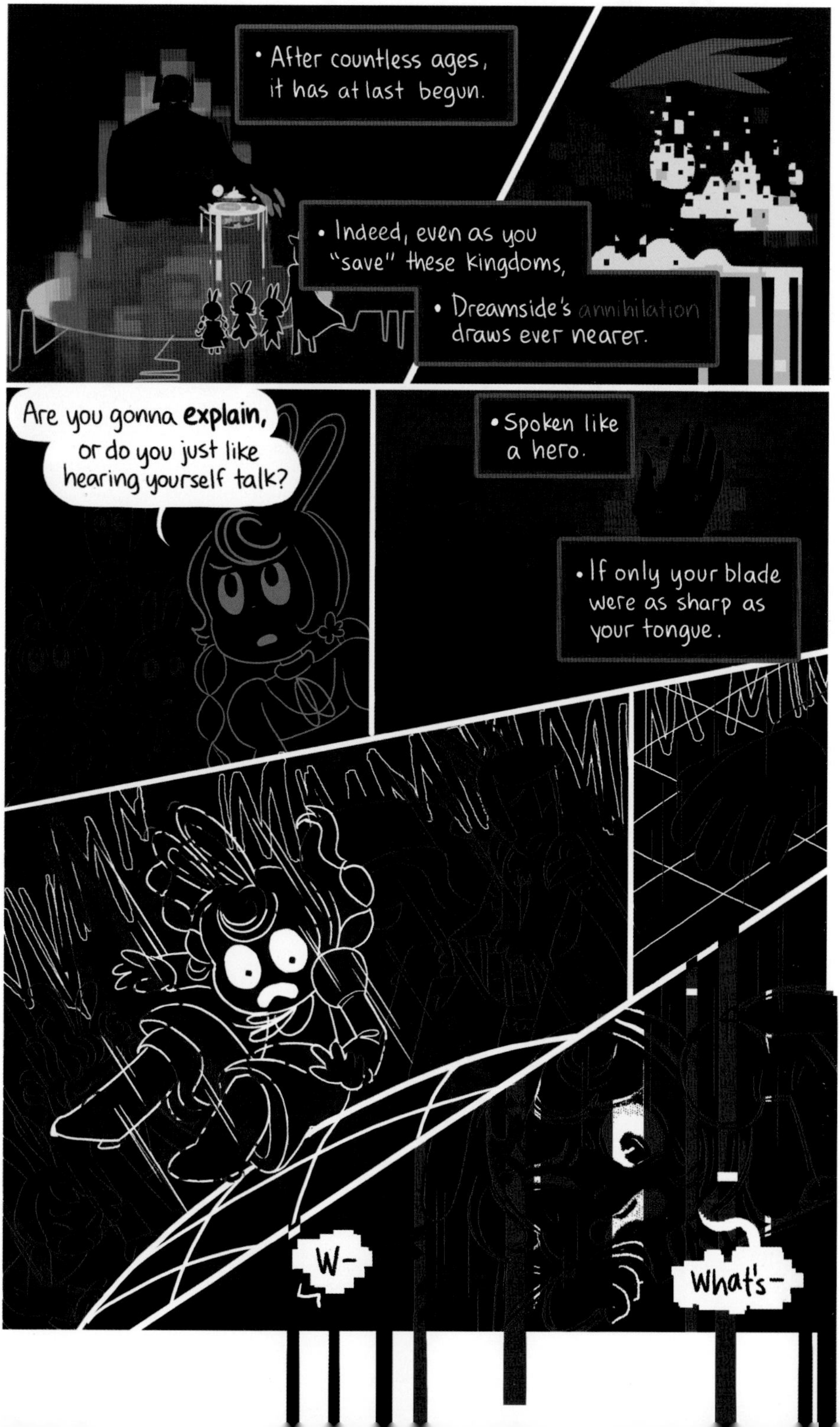
• After countless ages, it has at last begun.
• Indeed, even as you "save" these kingdoms,
• Dreamside's annihilation draws ever nearer.
Are you gonna **explain,** or do you just like hearing yourself talk?
• Spoken like a hero.
• If only your blade were as sharp as your tongue.
W-
What's-

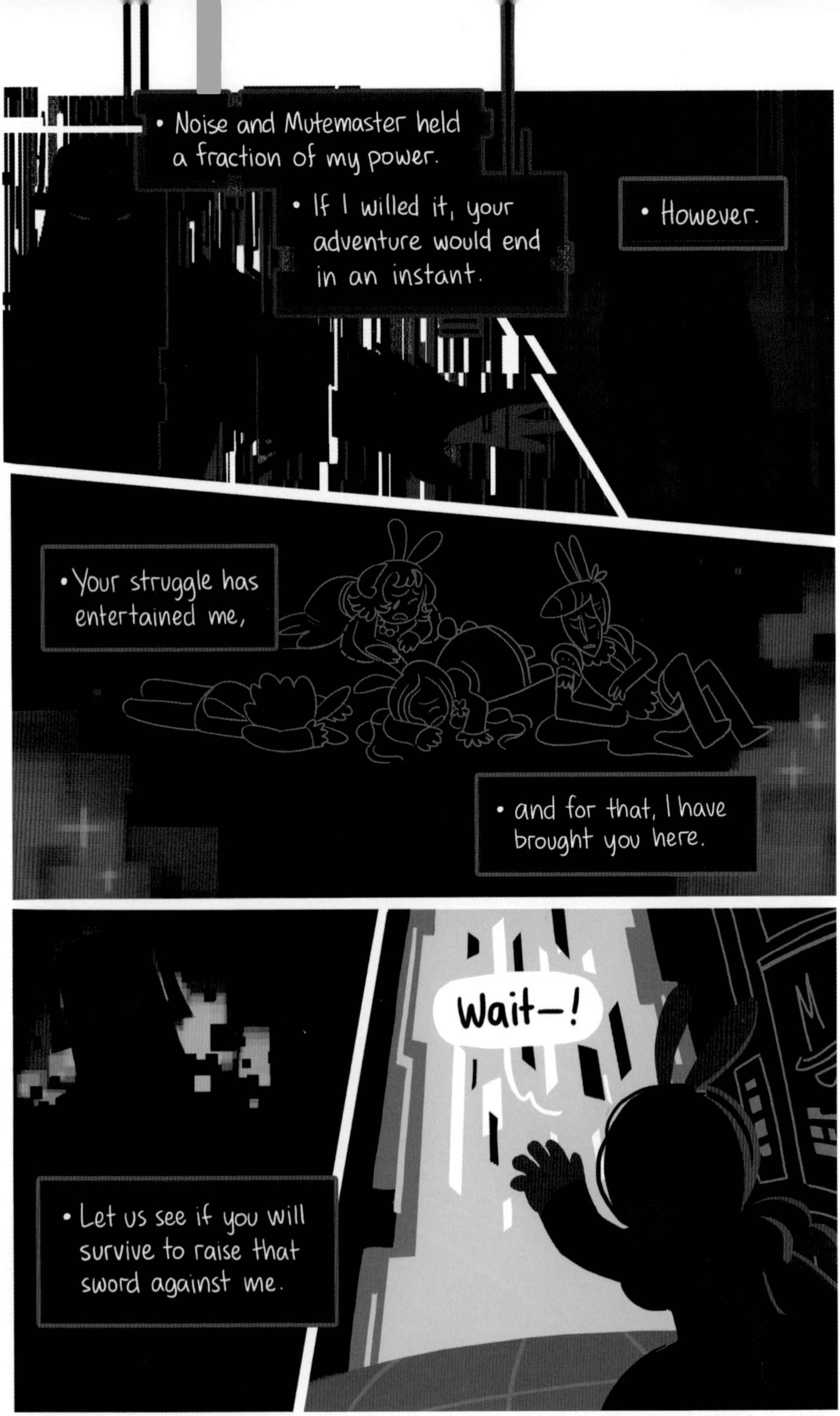

• Noise and Mutemaster held a fraction of my power.
• If I willed it, your adventure would end in an instant.
• However.
• Your struggle has entertained me,
• and for that, I have brought you here.
• Let us see if you will survive to raise that sword against me.
Wait—!

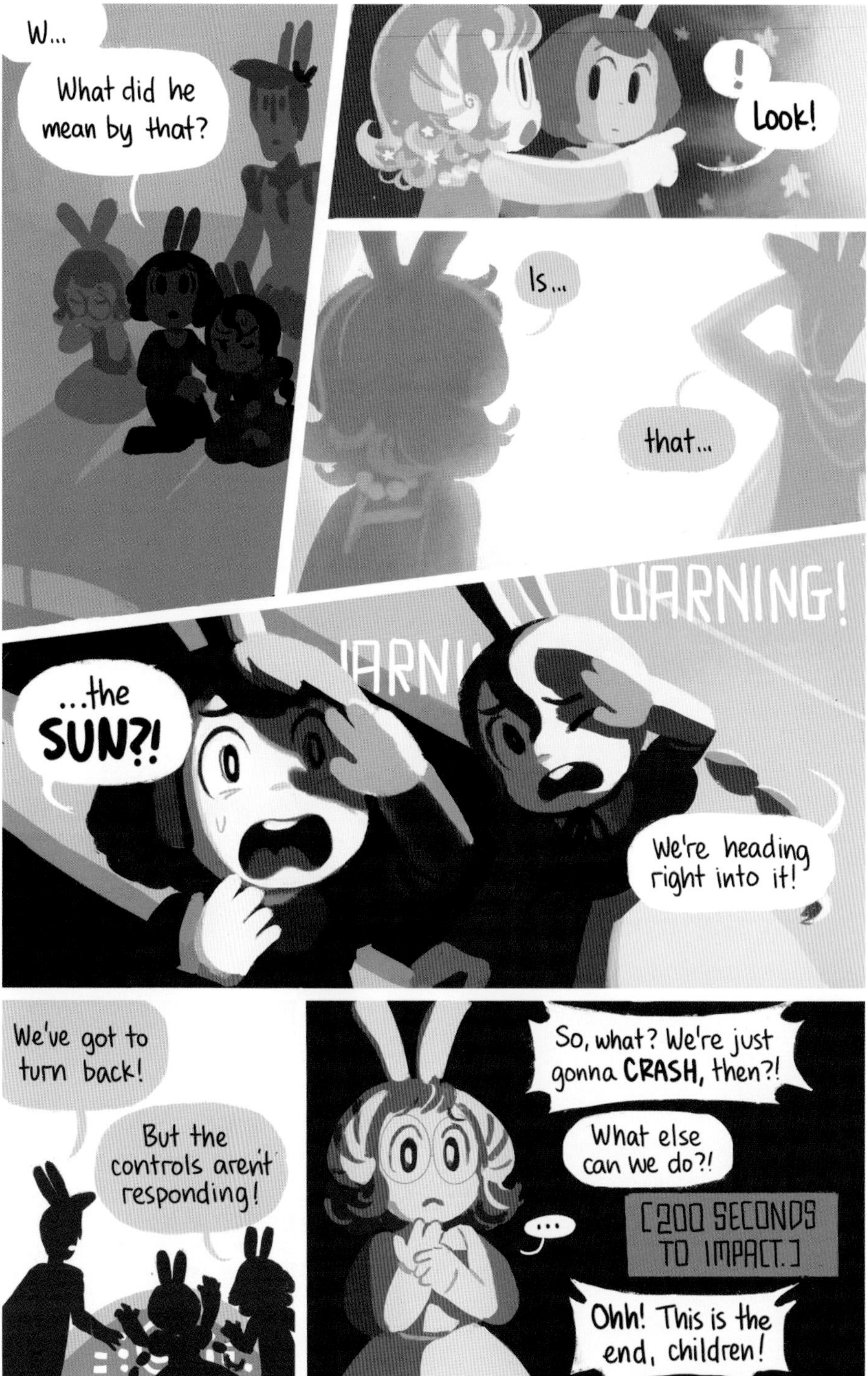
W...
What did he mean by that?
!
Look!
Is...
that...
WARNING!
...the SUN?!
We're heading right into it!
We've got to turn back!
But the controls aren't responding!
So, what? We're just gonna CRASH, then?!
What else can we do?!
...
[200 SECONDS TO IMPACT.]
Ohh! This is the end, children!

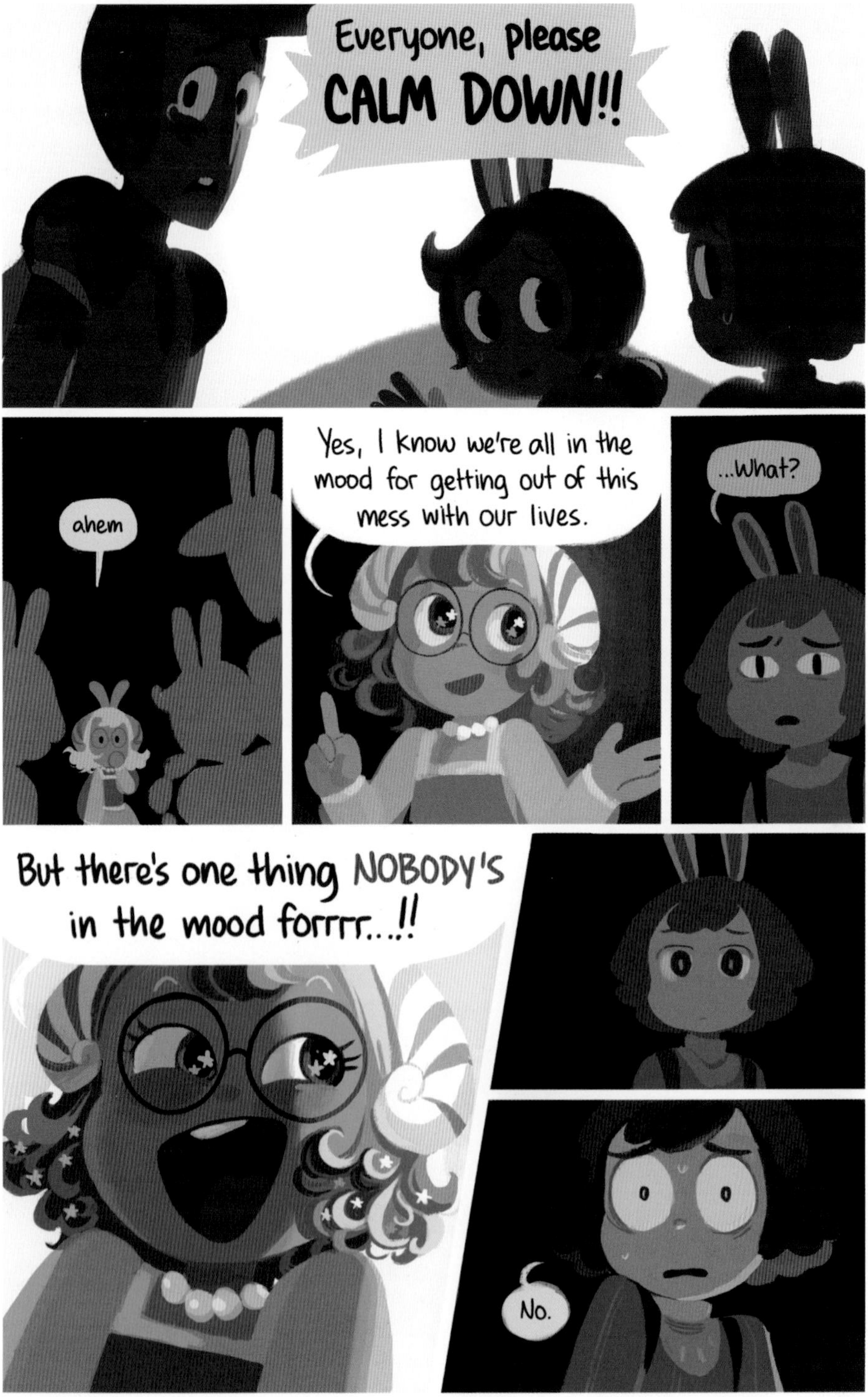
Everyone, please
CALM DOWN!!
ahem
Yes, I know we're all in the mood for getting out of this mess with our lives.
...What?
But there's one thing NOBODY's in the mood forrrr...!!
No.

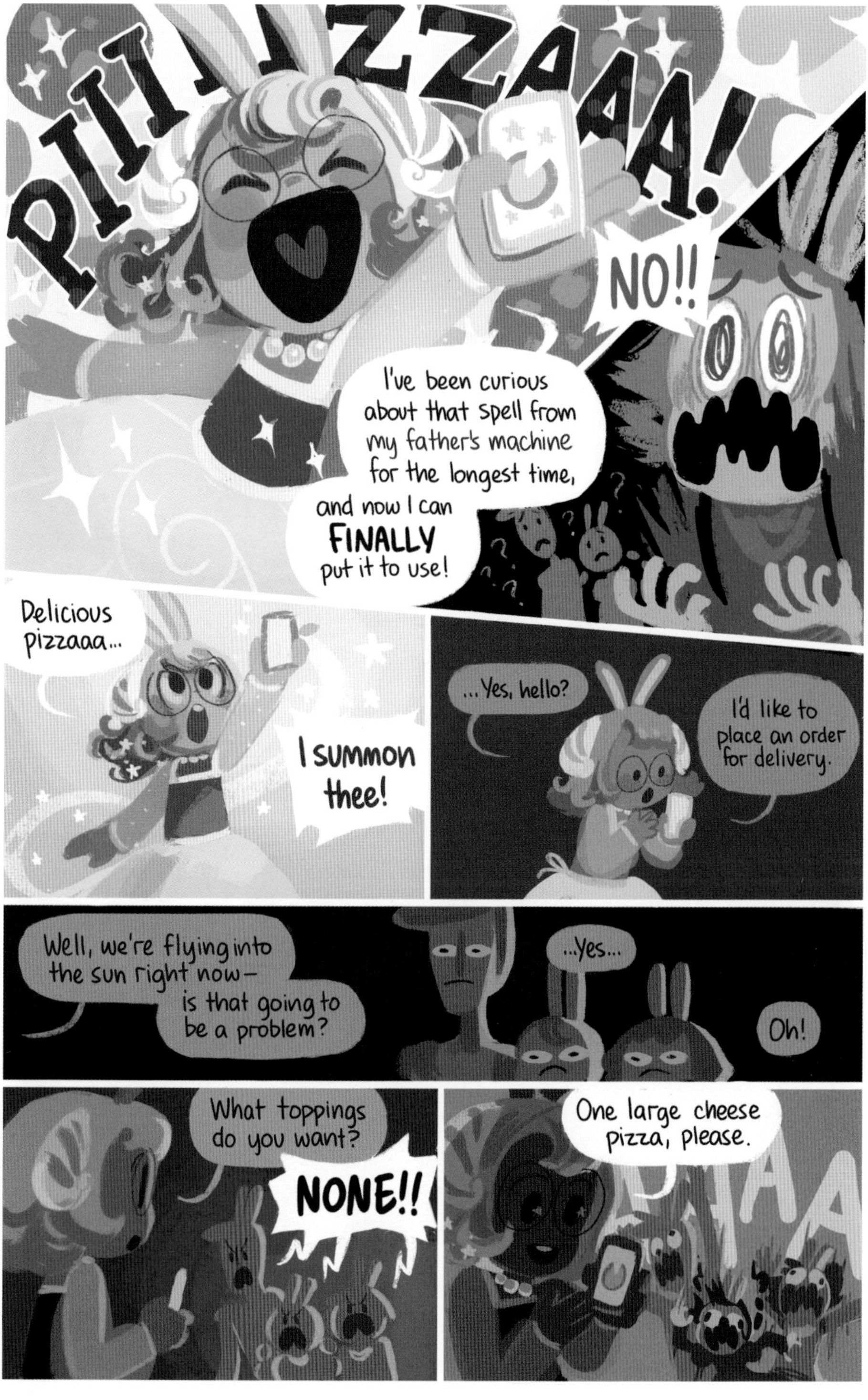
PIIIIZZZAAAA!
NO!!
I've been curious about that spell from my father's machine for the longest time,
and now I can FINALLY put it to use!
Delicious pizzaaa...
I summon thee!
...Yes, hello?
I'd like to place an order for delivery.
Well, we're flying into the sun right now—
is that going to be a problem?
...Yes...
Oh!
What toppings do you want?
NONE!!
One large cheese pizza, please.

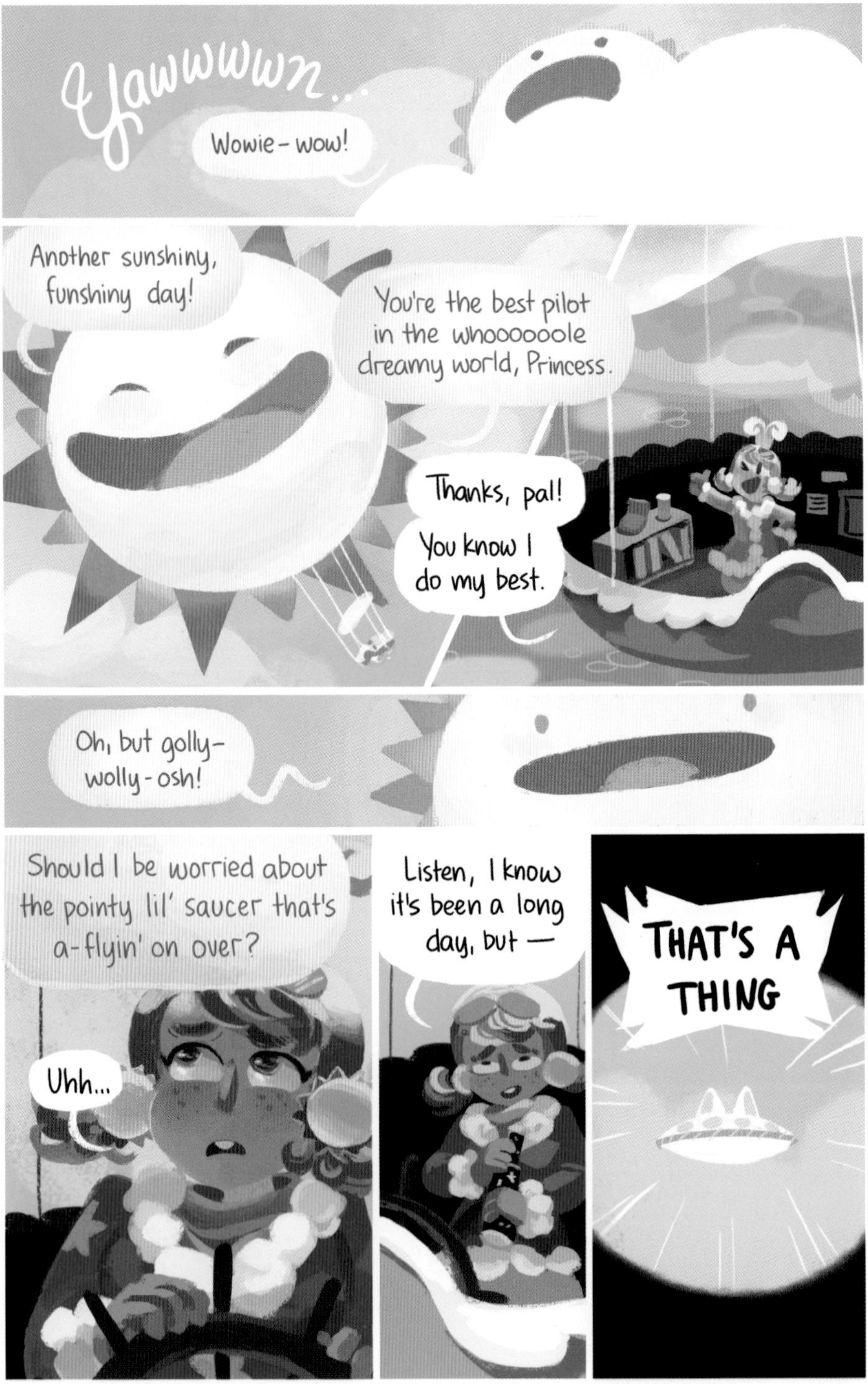
Yawwwwn...
Wowie-wow!
Another sunshiny, funshiny day!
You're the best pilot in the whoooooole dreamy world, Princess.
Thanks, pal!
You know I do my best.
Oh, but golly-wolly-osh!
Should I be worried about the pointy lil' saucer that's a-flyin' on over?
Uhh...
Listen, I know it's been a long day, but —
THAT'S A THING

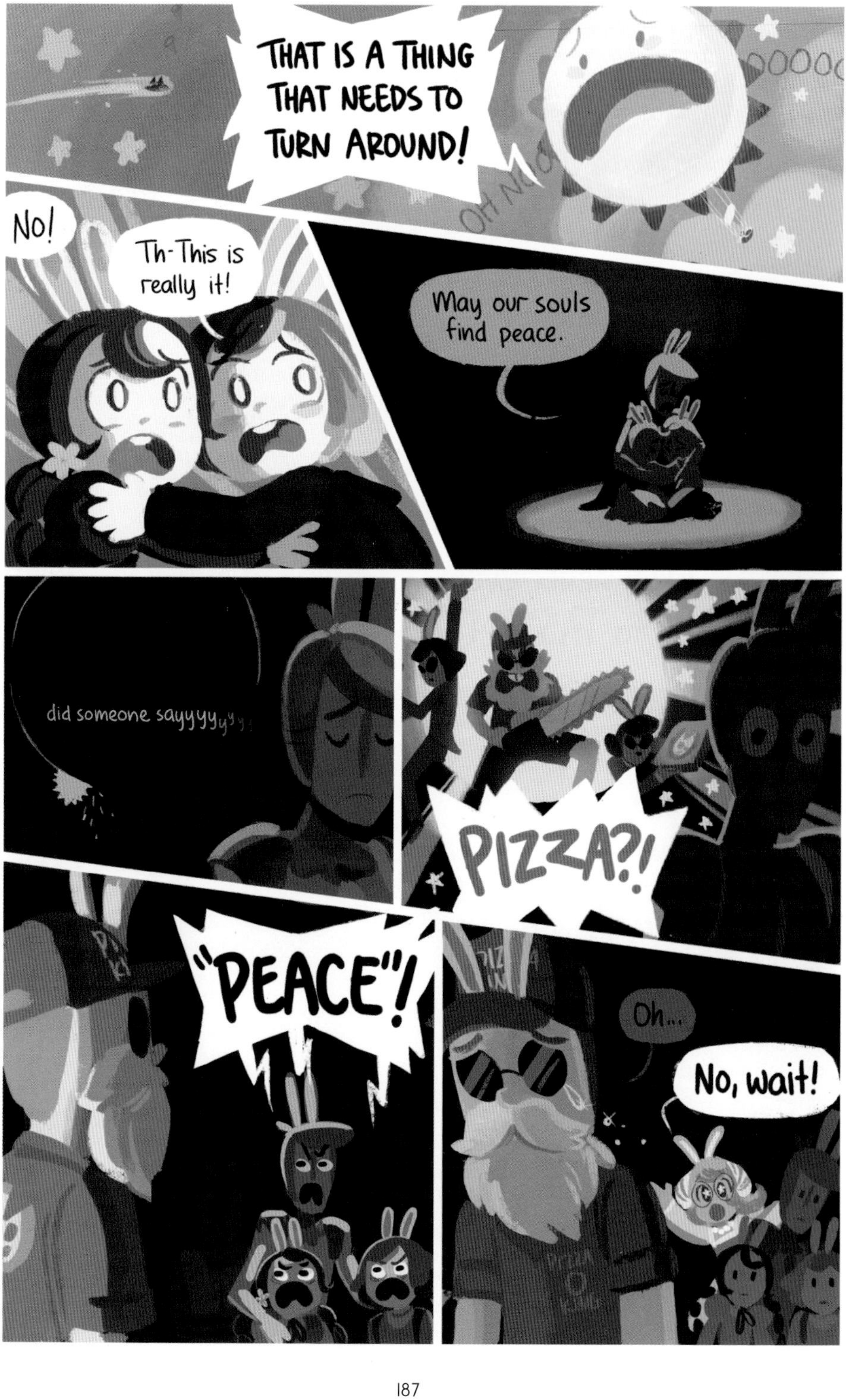
THAT IS A THING THAT NEEDS TO TURN AROUND!
OH NO
No!
Th-This is really it!
May our souls find peace.
did someone sayyyyyyy
PIZZA?!
"PEACE"!
Oh...
No, wait!

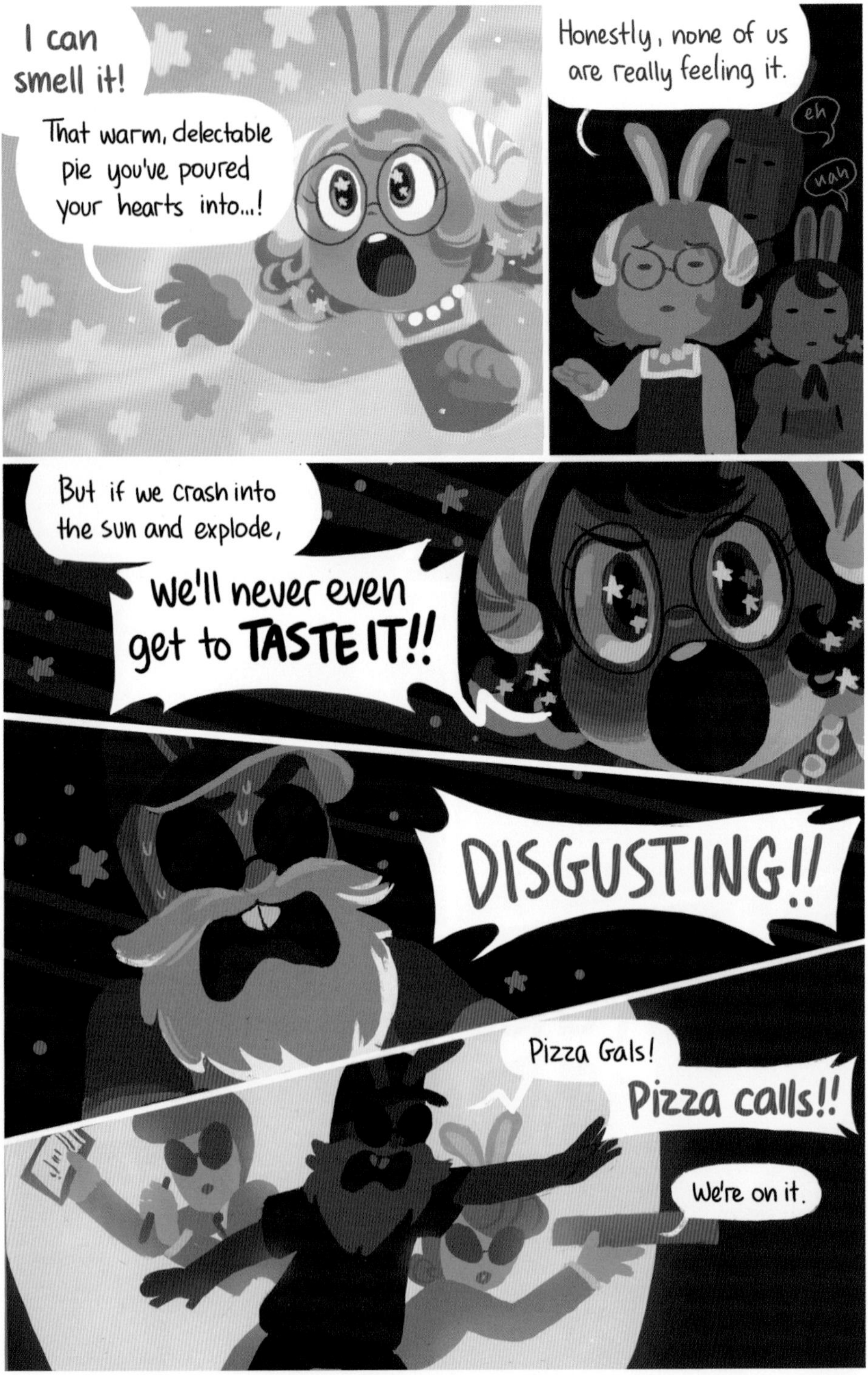
I can smell it!
That warm, delectable pie you've poured your hearts into...!
Honestly, none of us are really feeling it.
eh
nah
But if we crash into the sun and explode,
we'll never even get to TASTE IT!!
DISGUSTING!!
Pizza Gals!
Pizza calls!!
We're on it.

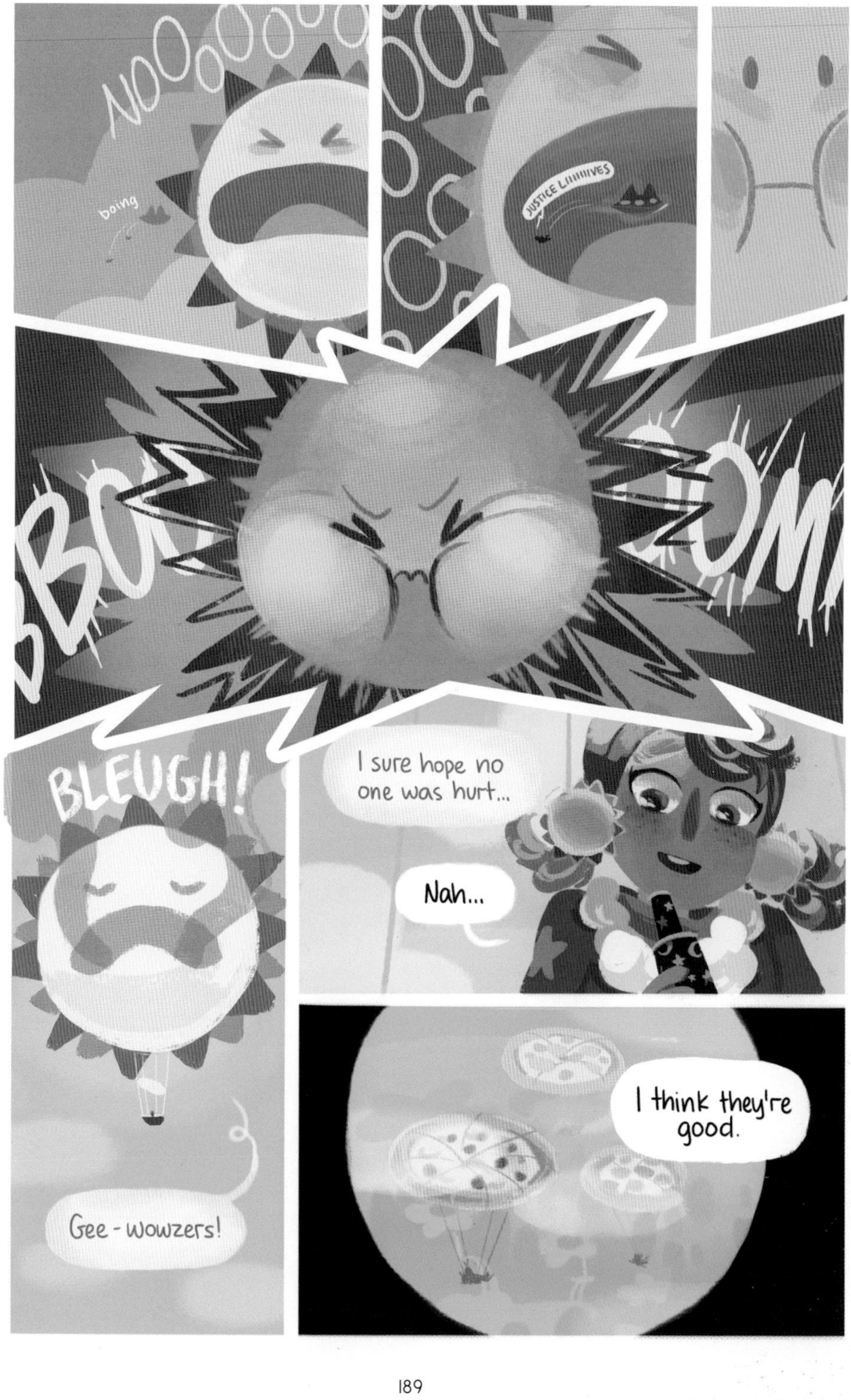
NOOOOOOOOOOO
doing
JUSTICE LIIIIIIVES
BBOOOM!
BLEUGH!
Gee-wowzers!
I sure hope no one was hurt...
Nah...
I think they're good.

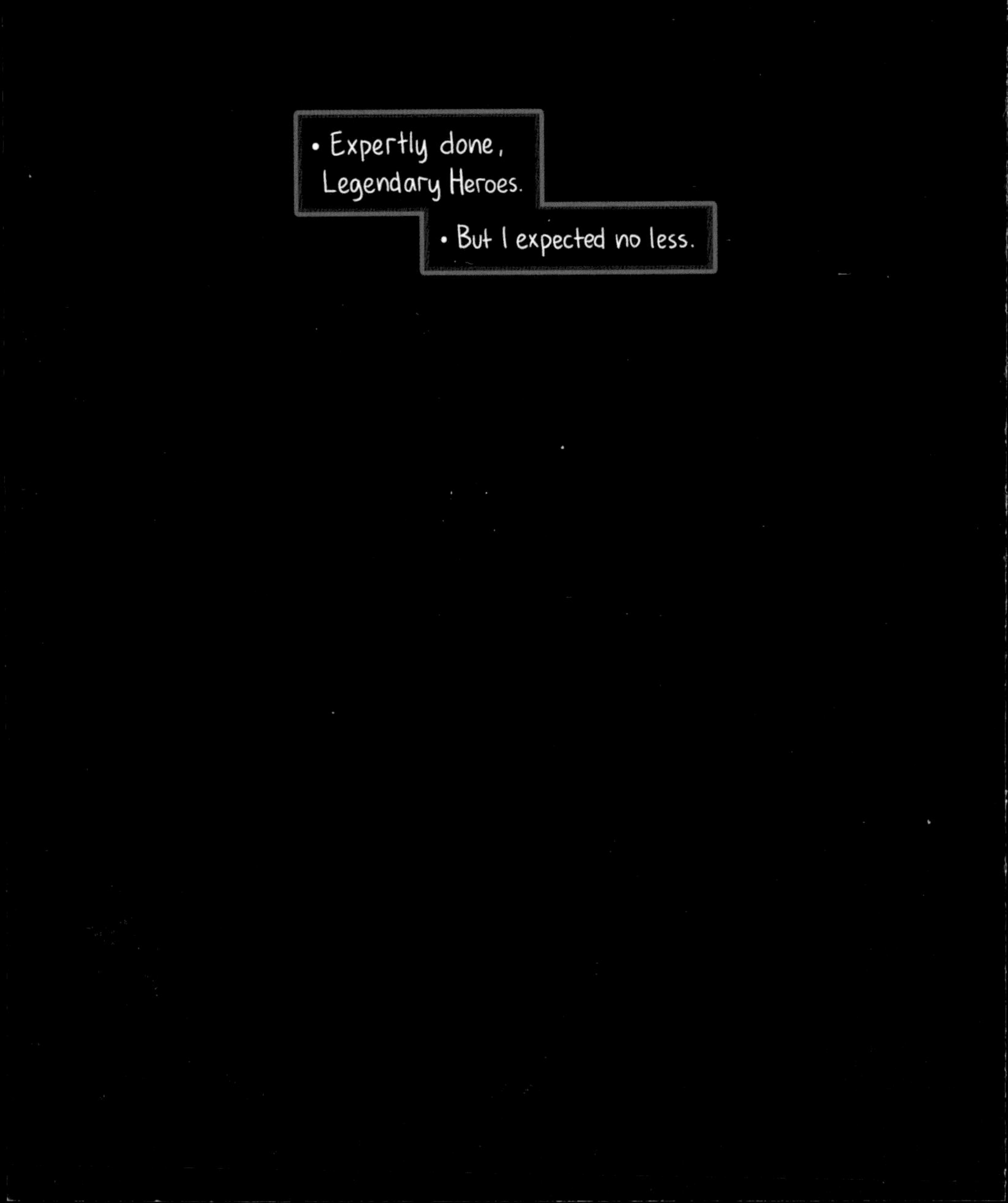
• Expertly done, Legendary Heroes.
• But I expected no less.

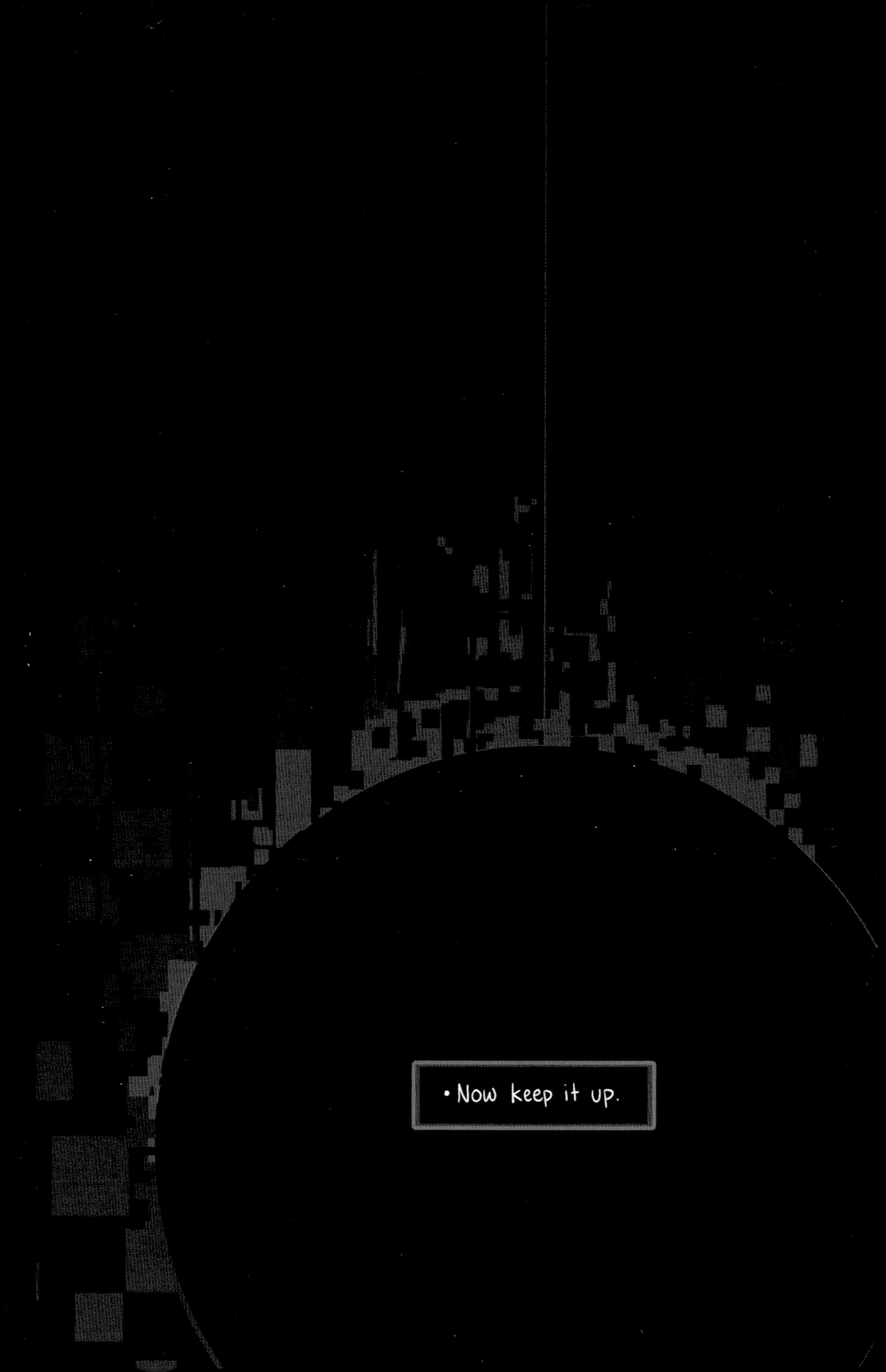
• Now keep it up.

To be continued in...

Cucumber
QUEST 4

The Flower Kingdom

Peridot Fact #1

Cresceeeendo~
Cresceeeendo~
So then, I'll go out, and I'm gonna be like—
"Sorry, Prince Crescen**dork**— me and your knight have unfinished business."
Isn't that cool?!
"Your knight and I."
Huh?
It's "your knight and I," darling.
HUH?!
once me and cordelia
have the Nightmare
Knight on our
side, your
!!
am I gonna look dumb if I say it wrong
Peridot
IS SHE GONNA
THINK I'M DUMB IF

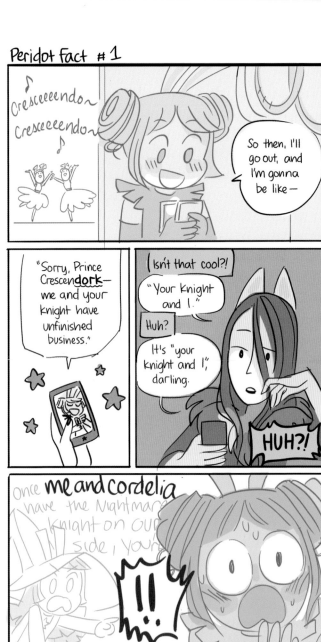

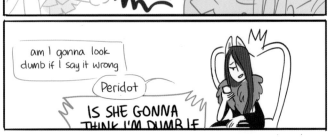

Peridot Fact #2

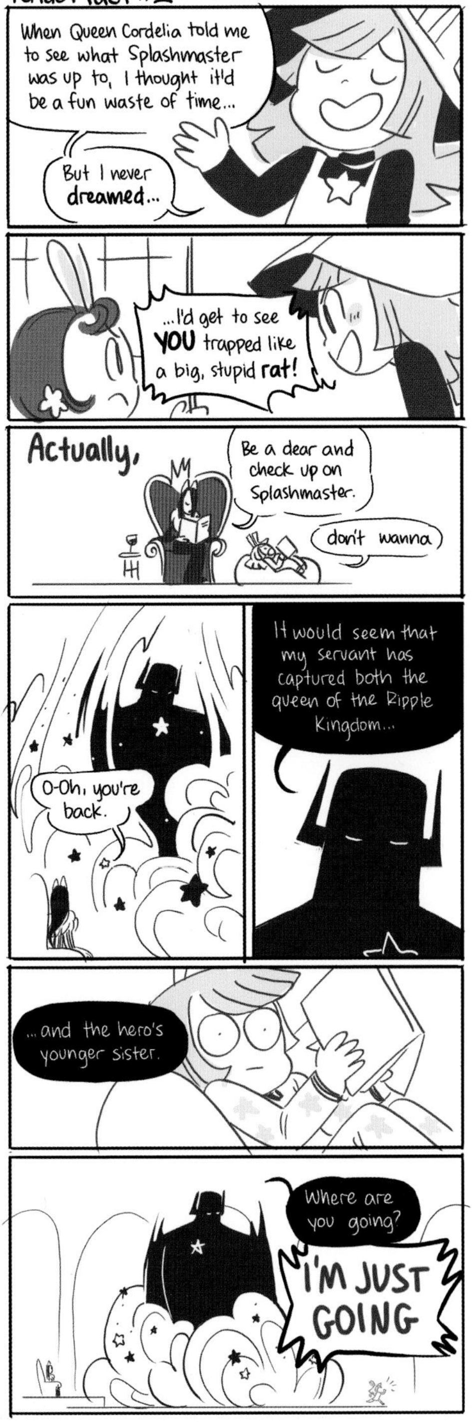

When Queen Cordelia told me to see what Splashmaster was up to, I thought it'd be a fun waste of time...
But I never **dreamed**...
...I'd get to see **YOU** trapped like a big, stupid **rat**!
Actually,
Be a dear and check up on Splashmaster.
don't wanna
O-Oh, you're back.
It would seem that my servant has captured both the queen of the Ripple Kingdom...
...and the hero's younger sister.
Where are you going?
I'M JUST GOING

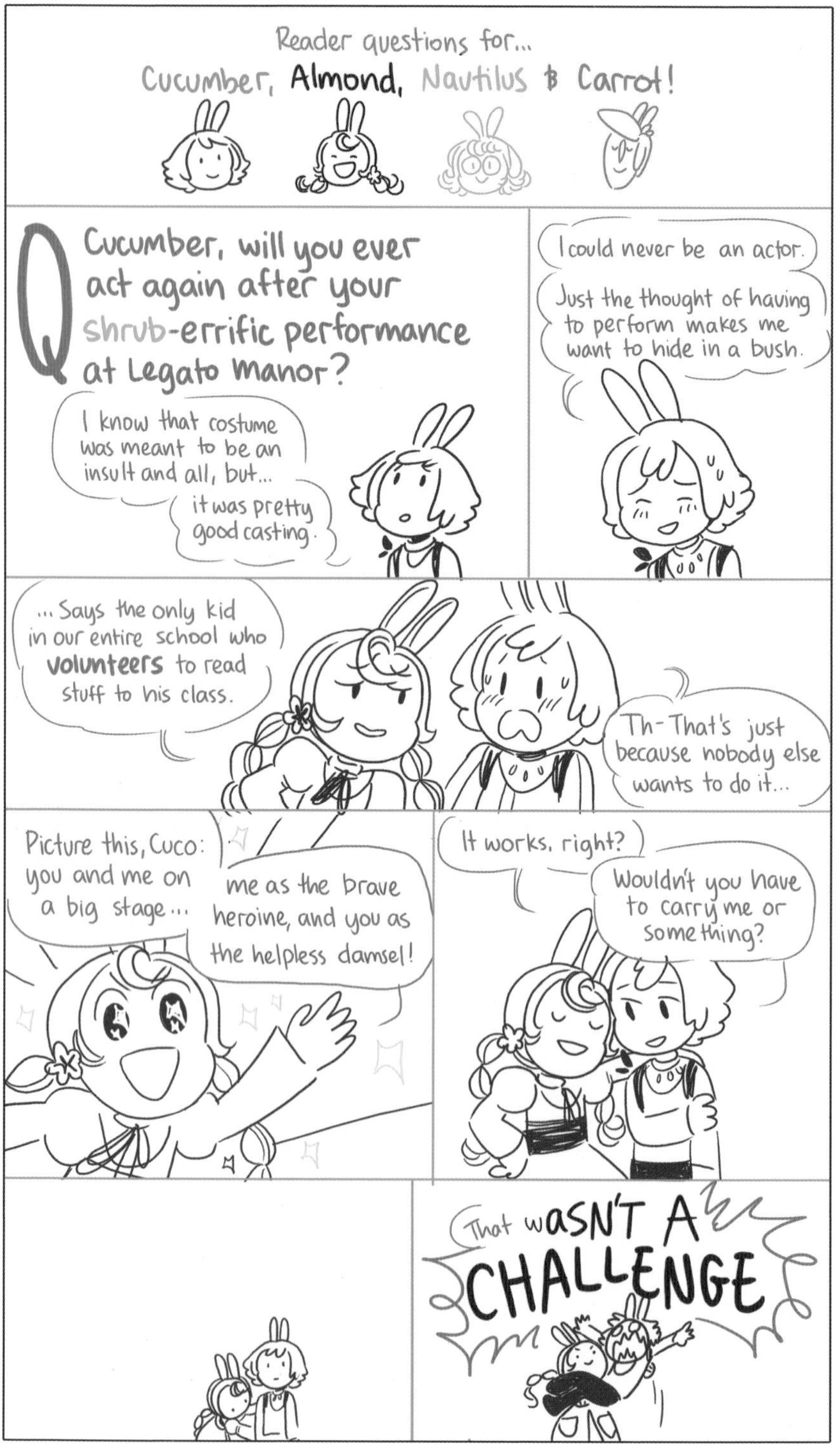
Reader questions for...
Cucumber, Almond, Nautilus & Carrot!
Q Cucumber, will you ever act again after your shrub-errific performance at Legato Manor?
I know that costume was meant to be an insult and all, but...
it was pretty good casting.
I could never be an actor.
Just the thought of having to perform makes me want to hide in a bush.
...Says the only kid in our entire school who volunteers to read stuff to his class.
Th-That's just because nobody else wants to do it...
Picture this, Cuco: you and me on a big stage...
me as the brave heroine, and you as the helpless damsel!
It works, right?
Wouldn't you have to carry me or something?
That wasn't A CHALLENGE

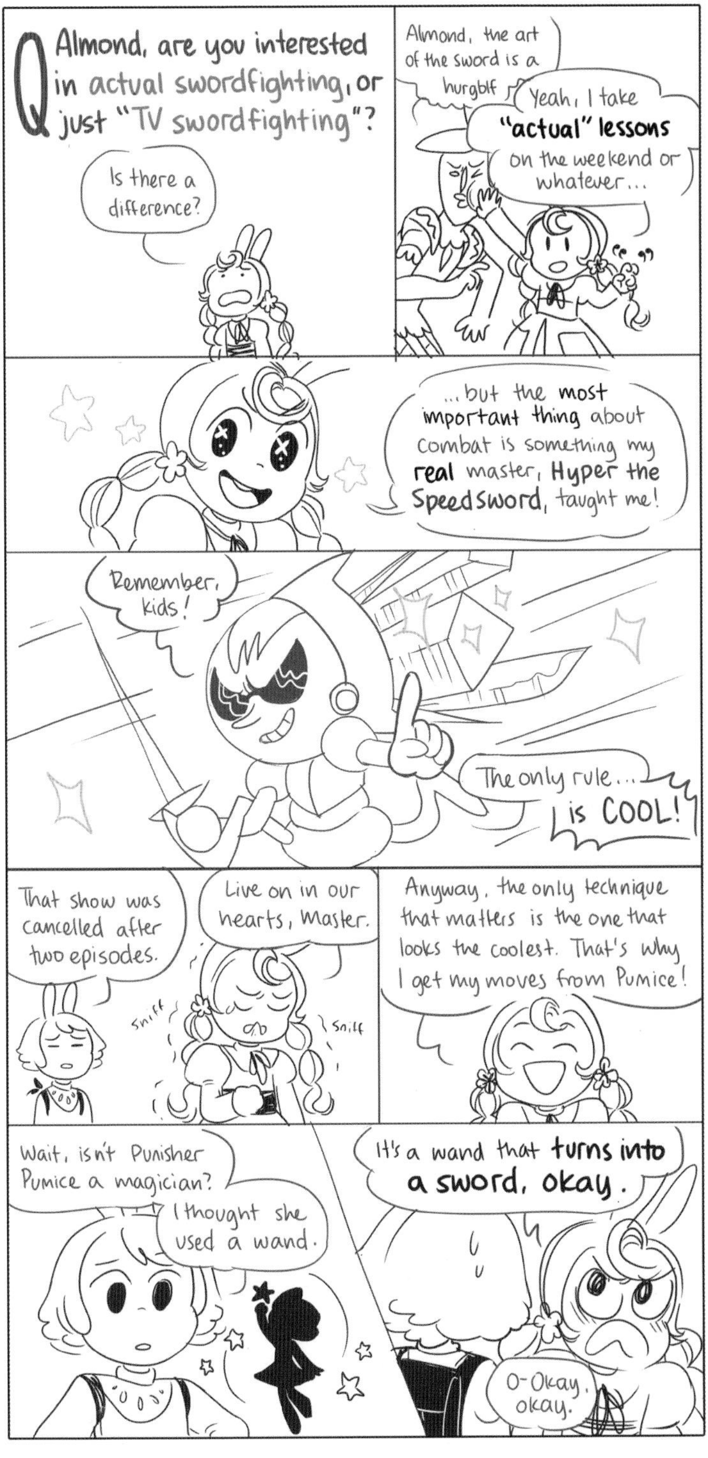
Q Almond, are you interested in actual swordfighting, or just "TV swordfighting"?
Is there a difference?
Almond, the art of the sword is a hurgblf
Yeah, I take "actual" lessons on the weekend or whatever...
...but the most important thing about combat is something my real master, Hyper the Speedsword, taught me!
Remember, kids!
The only rule... is COOL!
That show was cancelled after two episodes.
Live on in our hearts, Master.
Sniff
Sniff
Anyway, the only technique that matters is the one that looks the coolest. That's why I get my moves from Pumice!
Wait, isn't Punisher Pumice a magician?
I thought she used a wand.
It's a wand that turns into a sword, okay.
O-Okay, okay.

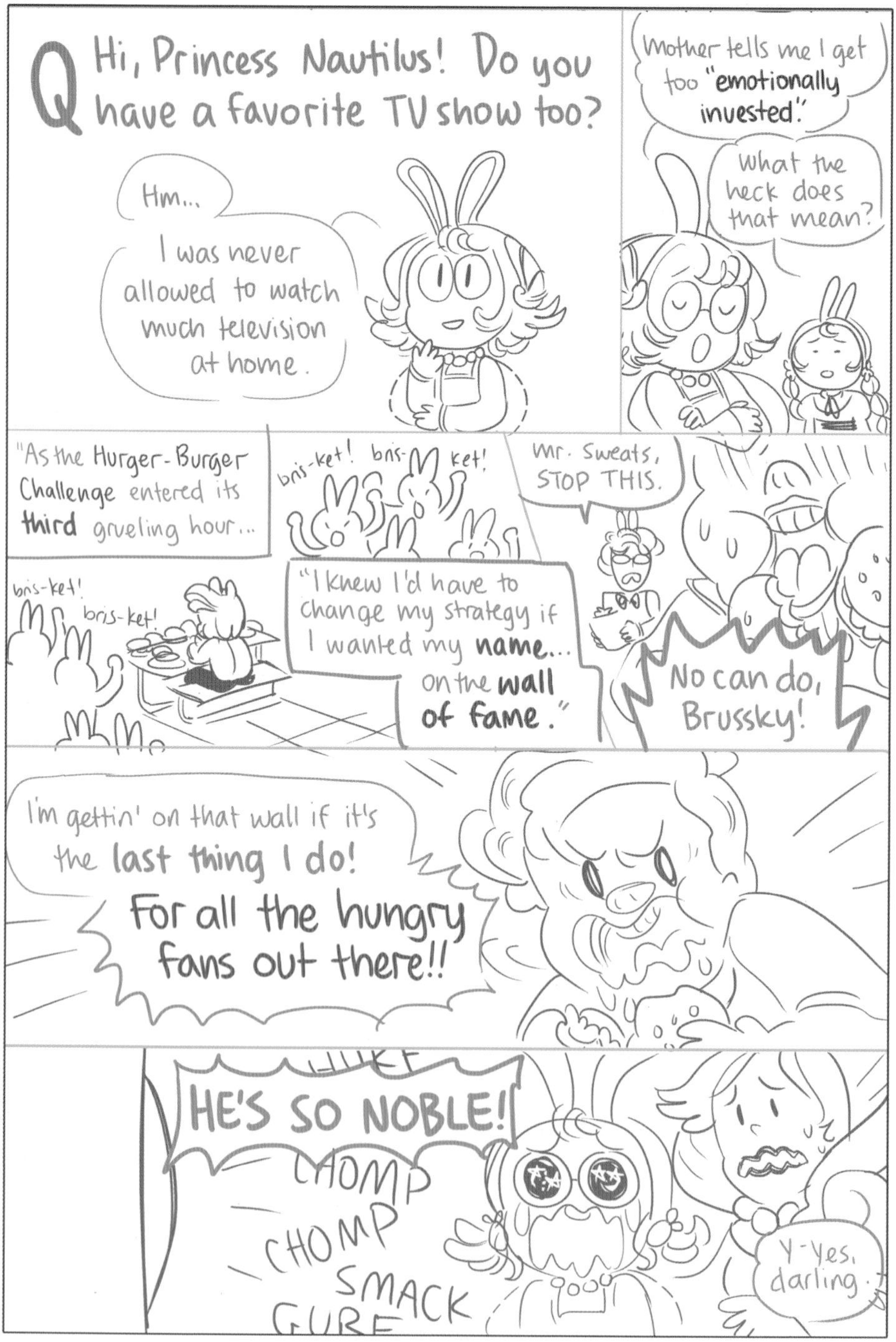
Q Hi, Princess Nautilus! Do you have a favorite TV show too?
Hm...
I was never allowed to watch much television at home.
Mother tells me I get too "emotionally invested."
What the heck does that mean?
"As the Hurger-Burger Challenge entered its third grueling hour...
bris-ket! bris- ket!
bris-ket! bris-ket!
"I knew I'd have to change my strategy if I wanted my name... on the wall of fame."
Mr. Sweats, STOP THIS.
No can do, Brussky!
I'm gettin' on that wall if it's the last thing I do!
For all the hungry fans out there!!
HE'S SO NOBLE!
CHOMP
CHOMP
SMACK
Y-Yes, darling.

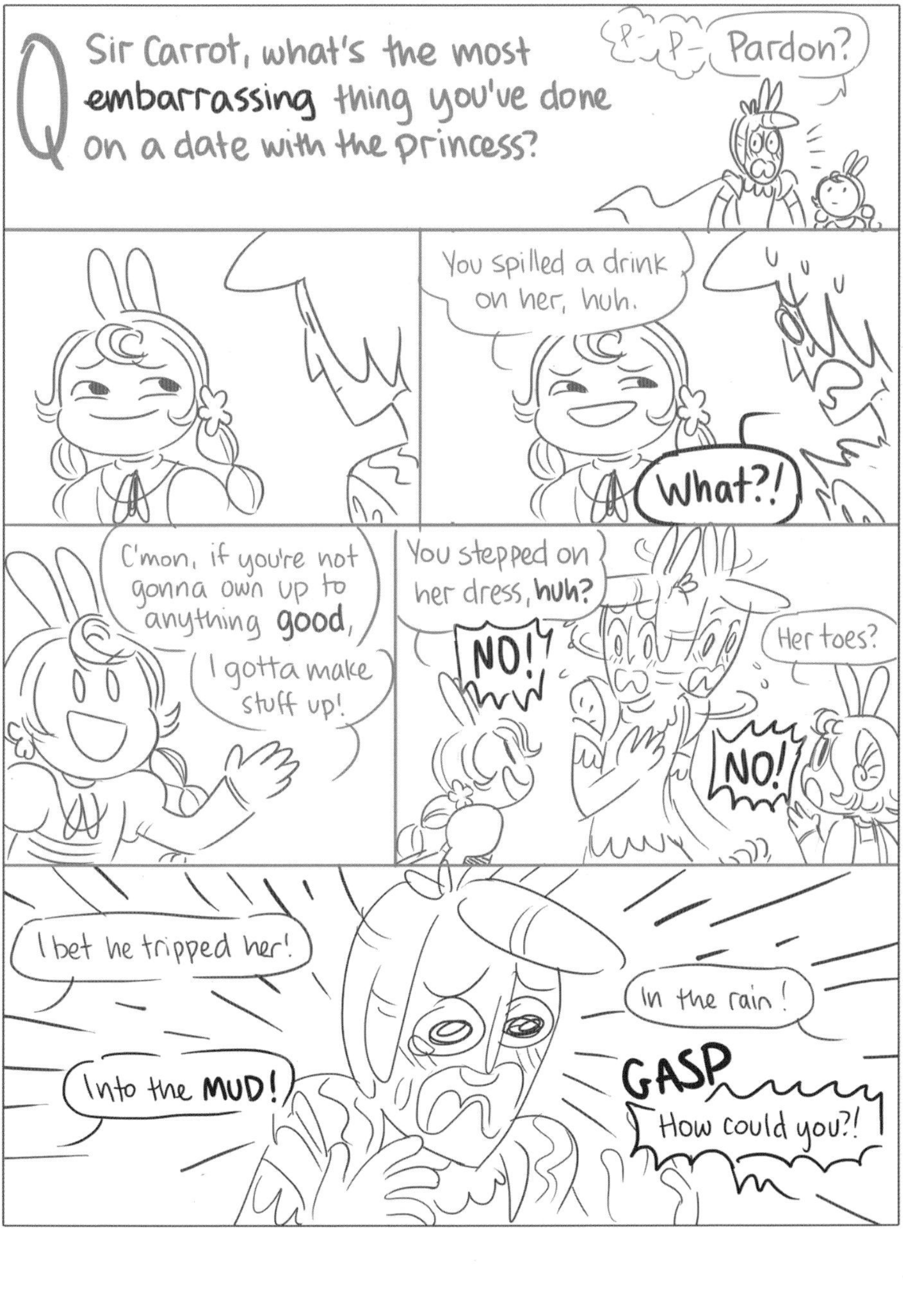
Q
Sir Carrot, what's the most embarrassing thing you've done on a date with the princess?
P- P- Pardon?
You spilled a drink on her, huh.
What?!
C'mon, if you're not gonna own up to anything good,
I gotta make stuff up!
You stepped on her dress, huh?
NO!
Her toes?
NO!
I bet he tripped her!
In the rain!
Into the MUD!
GASP
How could you?!

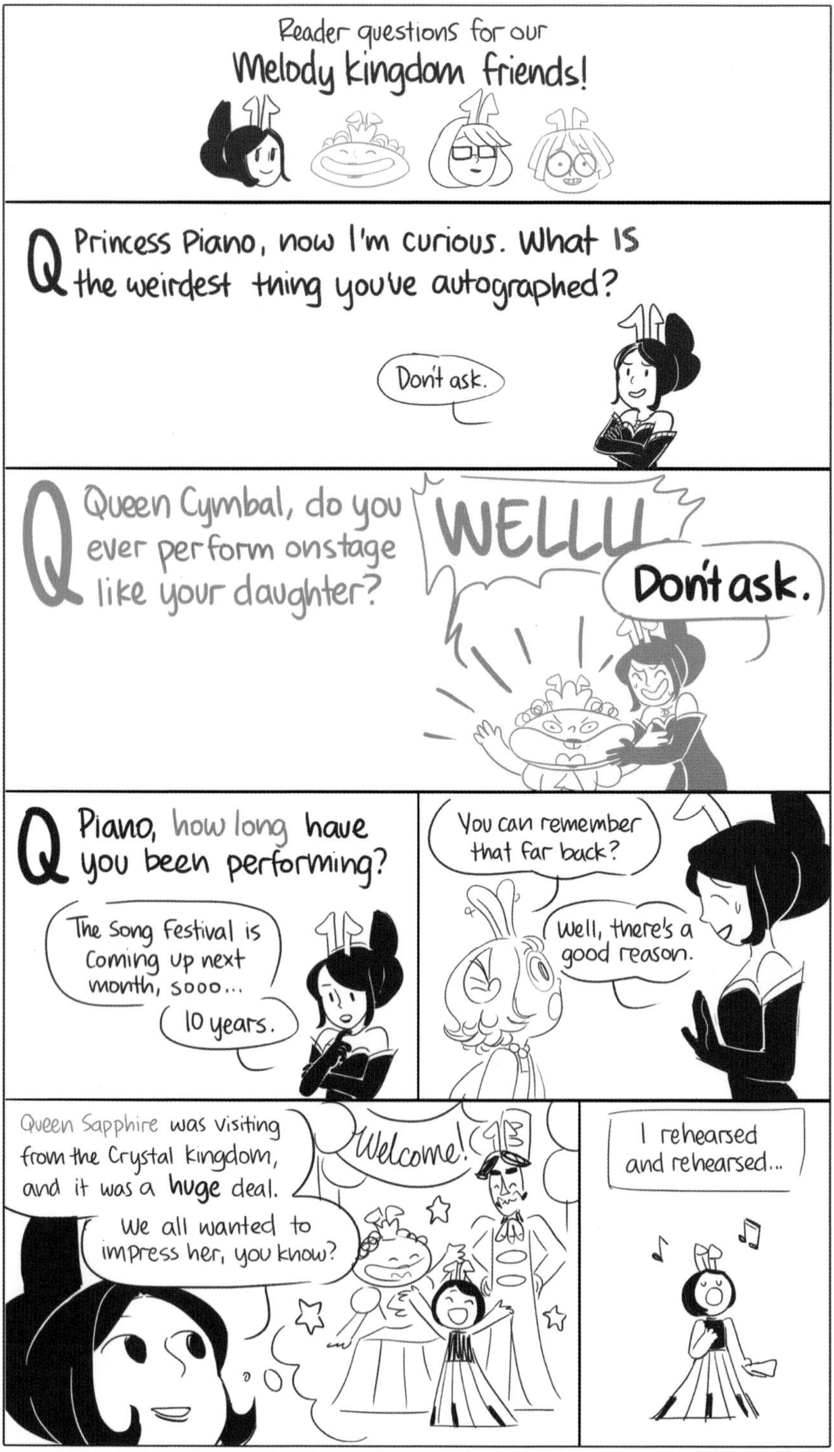

Reader questions for our
Melody kingdom friends!
Q Princess Piano, now I'm curious. What IS the weirdest thing you've autographed?
Don't ask.
Q Queen Cymbal, do you ever perform onstage like your daughter?
WELLL
Don't ask.
Q Piano, how long have you been performing?
The Song Festival is coming up next month, sooo...
10 years.
You can remember that far back?
Well, there's a good reason.
Queen Sapphire was visiting from the Crystal kingdom, and it was a huge deal.
Welcome!
We all wanted to impress her, you know?
I rehearsed and rehearsed...

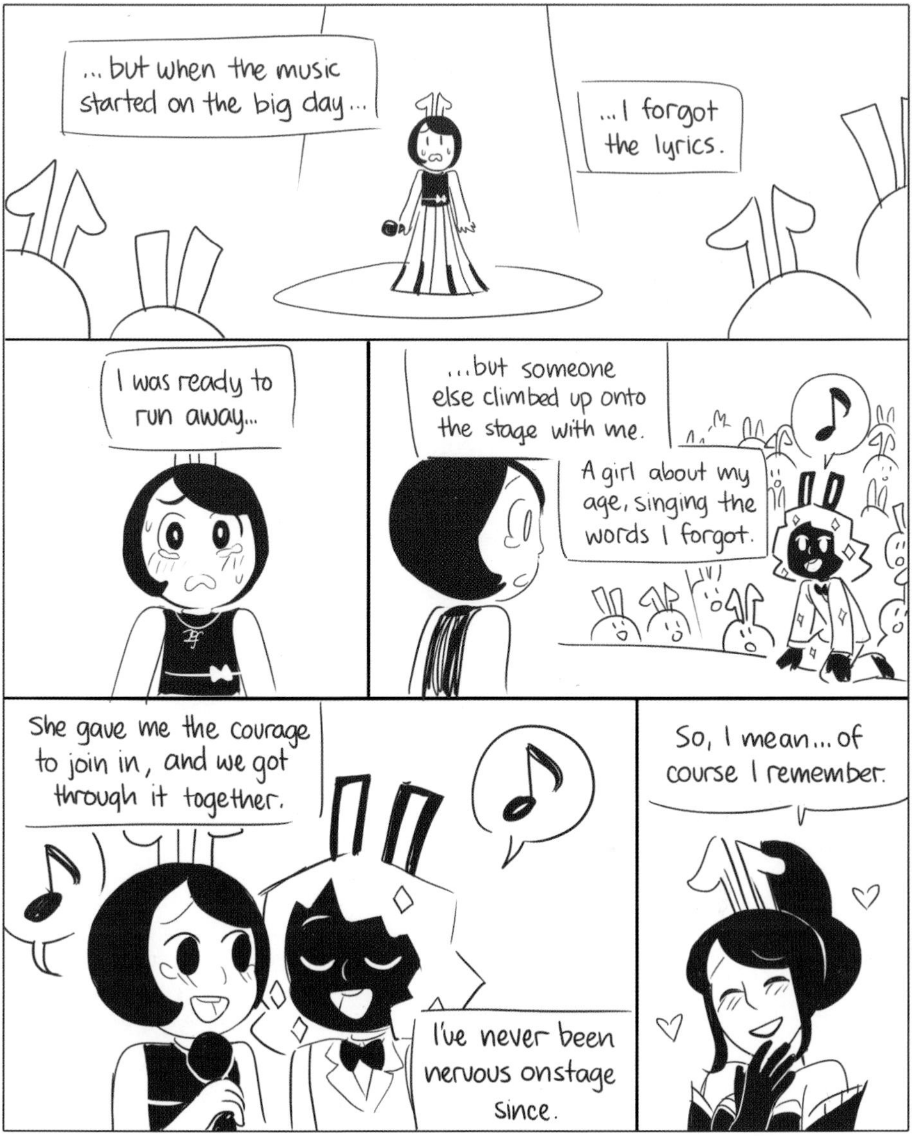

...but when the music started on the big day...
...I forgot the lyrics.
I was ready to run away...
...but someone else climbed up onto the stage with me.
A girl about my age, singing the words I forgot.
She gave me the courage to join in, and we got through it together.
I've never been nervous onstage since.
So, I mean... of course I remember.

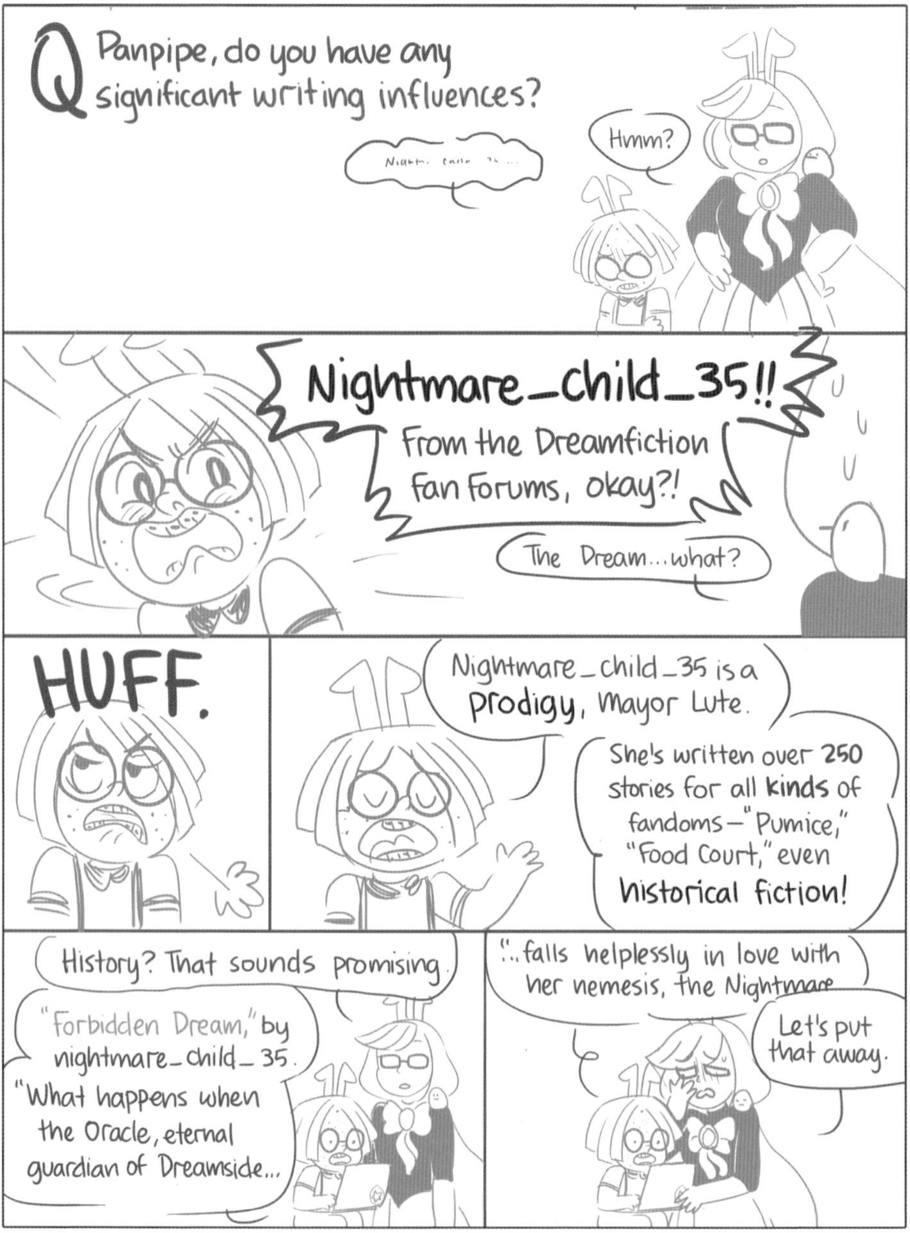
Q Panpipe, do you have any significant writing influences?
Hmm?
Nightmare_child_35!!
From the Dreamfiction fan forums, okay?!
The Dream...what?
HUFF.
Nightmare_child_35 is a prodigy, Mayor Lute.
She's written over 250 stories for all kinds of fandoms—"Pumice," "Food Court," even historical fiction!
History? That sounds promising.
"Forbidden Dream," by nightmare_child_35.
"What happens when the Oracle, eternal guardian of Dreamside...
"...falls helplessly in love with her nemesis, the Nightmare
Let's put that away.

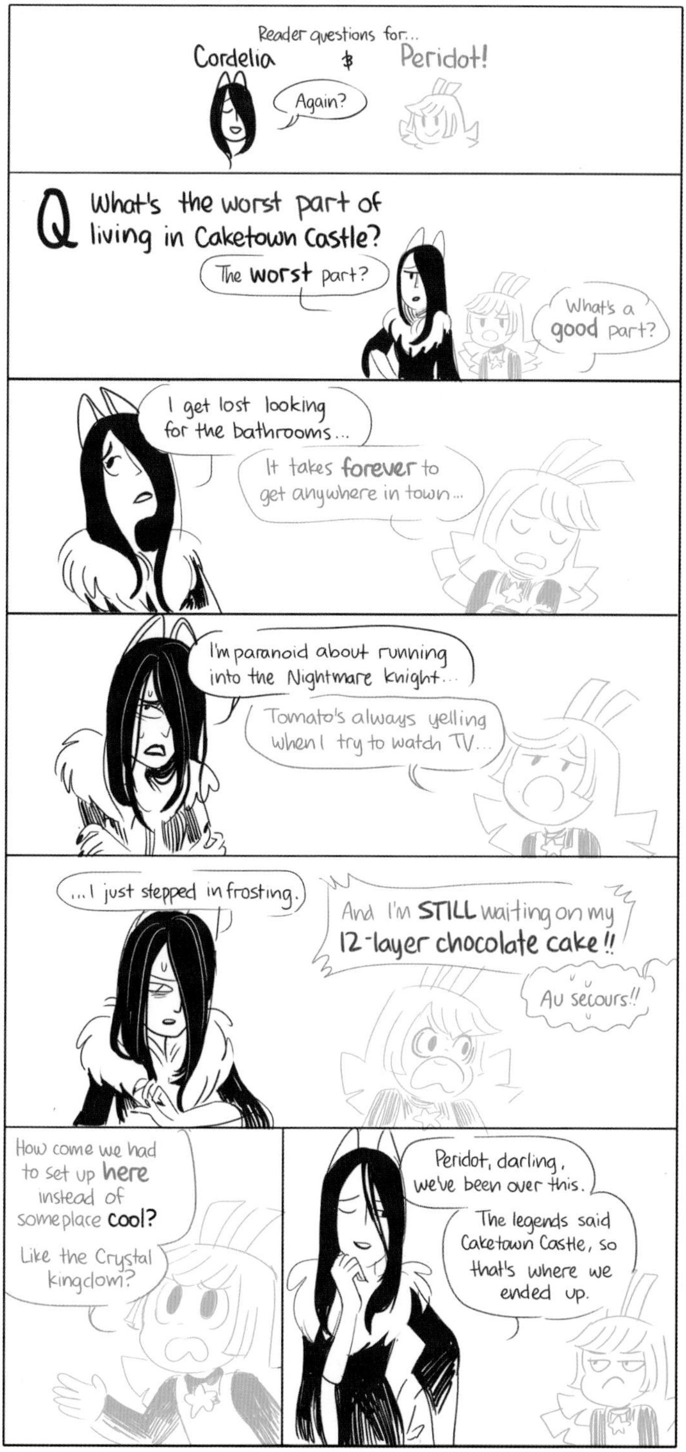
Reader questions for...
Cordelia & Peridot!
Again?
Q What's the worst part of living in Caketown Castle?
The worst part?
What's a good part?
I get lost looking for the bathrooms...
It takes forever to get anywhere in town...
I'm paranoid about running into the Nightmare knight...
Tomato's always yelling when I try to watch TV...
...I just stepped in frosting.
And I'm STILL waiting on my 12-layer chocolate cake!!
Au secours!!
How come we had to set up here instead of someplace cool?
Like the Crystal kingdom?
Peridot, darling, we've been over this.
The legends said Caketown Castle, so that's where we ended up.

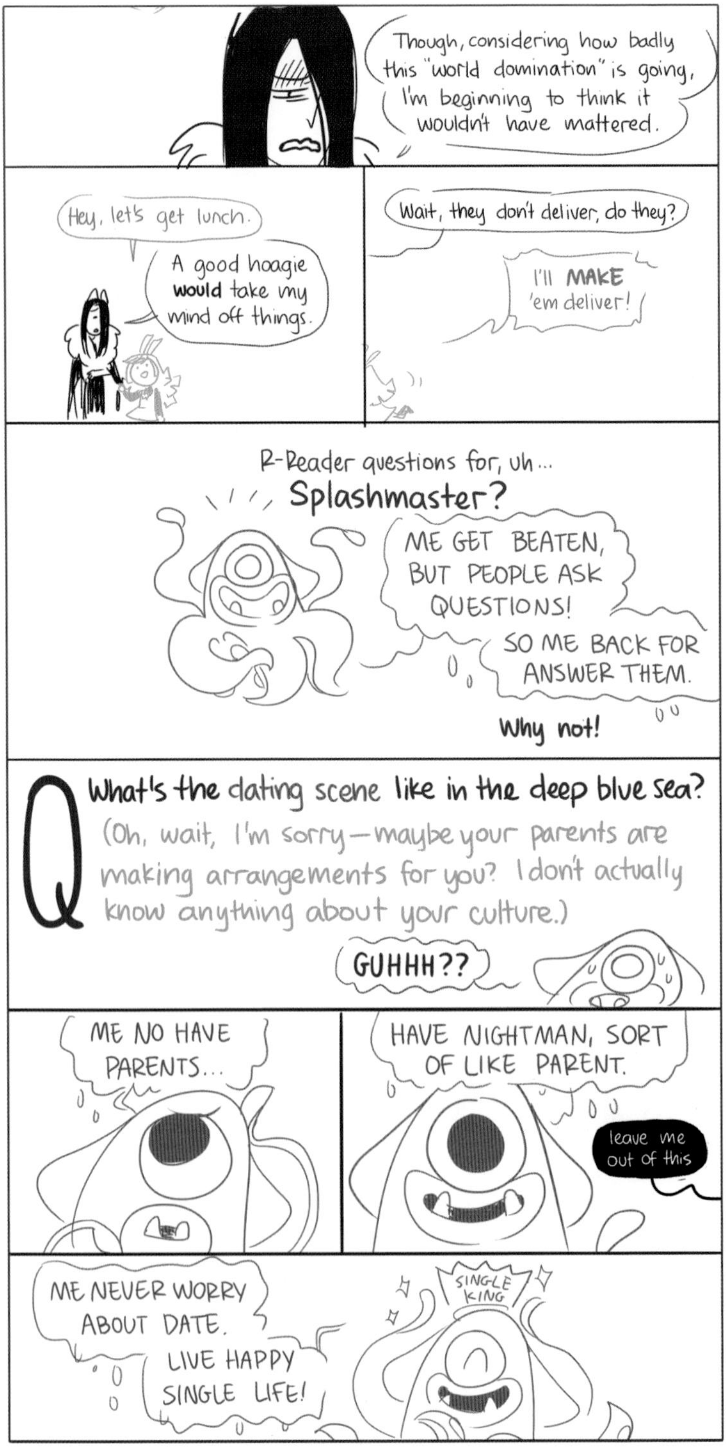
Though, considering how badly this "world domination" is going, I'm beginning to think it wouldn't have mattered.
Hey, let's get lunch.
A good hoagie would take my mind off things.
Wait, they don't deliver, do they?
I'll MAKE 'em deliver!
R-Reader questions for, uh...
Splashmaster?
ME GET BEATEN, BUT PEOPLE ASK QUESTIONS!
SO ME BACK FOR ANSWER THEM.
Why not!
Q
What's the dating scene like in the deep blue sea?
(Oh, wait, I'm sorry—maybe your parents are making arrangements for you? I don't actually know anything about your culture.)
GUHHH??
ME NO HAVE PARENTS...
HAVE NIGHTMAN, SORT OF LIKE PARENT.
leave me out of this
ME NEVER WORRY ABOUT DATE.
LIVE HAPPY SINGLE LIFE!
SINGLE KING

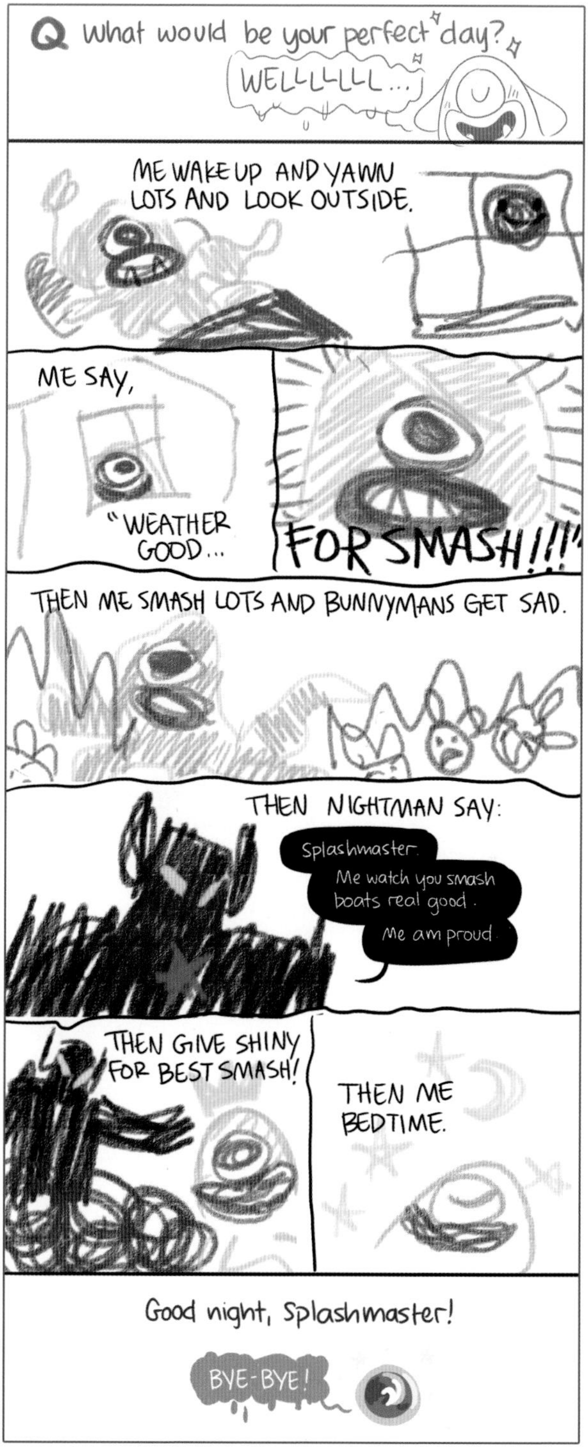
Q What would be your perfect day?
WELLLLLLL...
ME WAKE UP AND YAWN LOTS AND LOOK OUTSIDE.
ME SAY,
"WEATHER GOOD...
FOR SMASH!!!!"
THEN ME SMASH LOTS AND BUNNYMANS GET SAD.
THEN NIGHTMAN SAY:
Splashmaster.
Me watch you smash boats real good.
Me am proud.
THEN GIVE SHINY FOR BEST SMASH!
THEN ME BEDTIME.
Good night, Splashmaster!
BYE-BYE!

Melody Miscellany

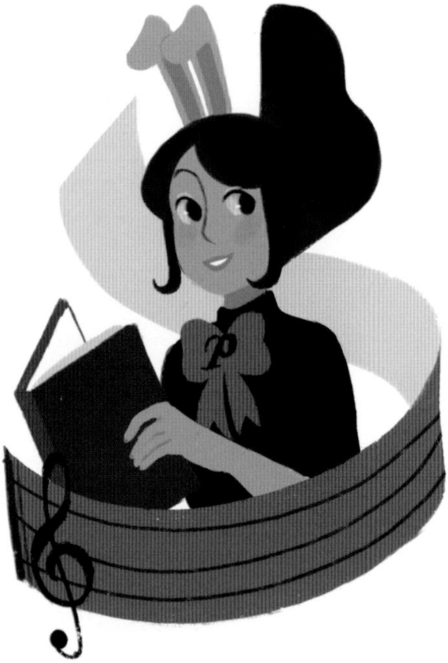

Did you enjoy your time in the Melody Kingdom? Are you itching to learn more about its people, history...and maybe a few things you never wanted to know? Well, itch no more! (And then keep reading.)

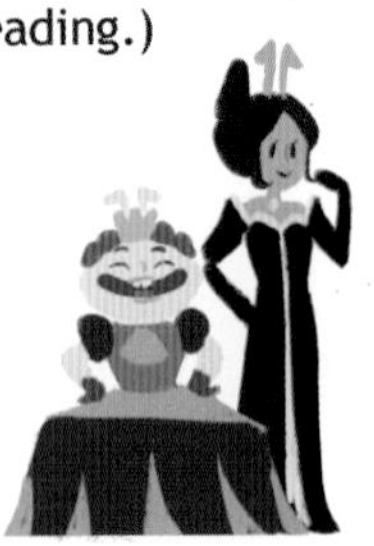

Let's start with the royal family! You remember **Princess Piano** and **Queen Cymbal**, right?

But...

Wait a second, did **King Clarinet** ever introduce himself?

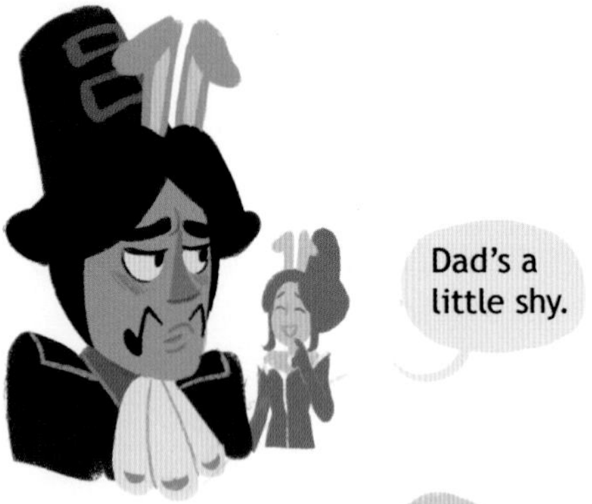
Dad's a little shy.

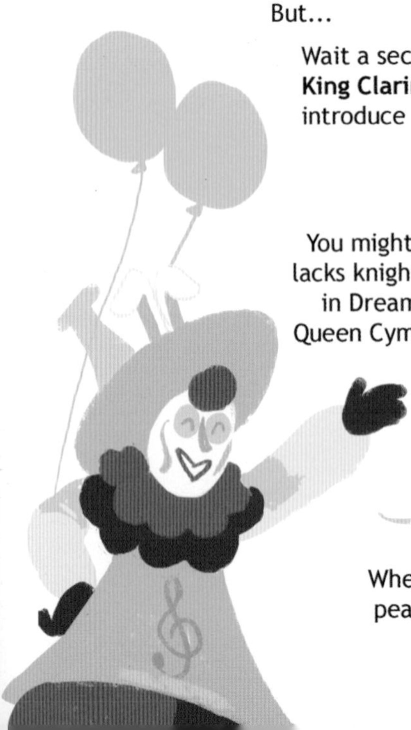

You might have noticed that Trebleopolis lacks knights, unlike most other royal cities in Dreamside. But never fear, because Queen Cymbal's elite **Clown Squad** is here!

...To spread some cheer!

When they aren't keeping the peace in town, they're great for parties.

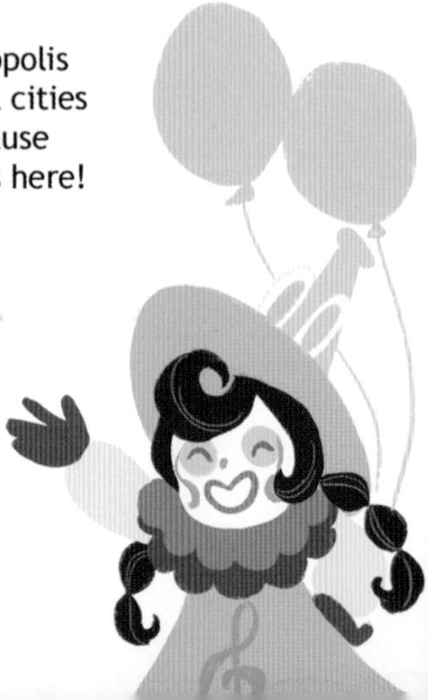

If you're looking to do some sightseeing, hot-air balloons like the ones shown to the right are popular in Trebleopolis, but...

...Queen Cymbal's pride and joy, the *Ocarina Blimp*, is the fastest way to get over the enormous(ly inconvenient) Intermezzo Wall.

Speaking of which, remember the two kings who divided the country over their tastes in music?

King Treble and King Bass were brothers, and they actually got along pretty well otherwise. It's a good thing they could still visit each other from time to time!

You might have guessed that **Trebleopolis** was named after the ancient King Treble. It has always been as cheery (and loud) as it is today!

There was also a city called **Bassville** back then, located near modern-day Rhythm Ridge. King Bass' palace used to be a dark, gloomy place until Noisemaster made it his own during the Nightmare Knight's first conquest.

After Noisemaster's arrival in Bassville, King Bass and his subjects fled deep into Waltz Woods, where they founded a new village called Organetto.

Shortly thereafter, the king was betrayed by his most trusted court magician, a young man named Legato, who seized control of the town and ruled with a (beautifully manicured) iron fist!

It's said that Legato was so powerful that even the spirits haunting Waltz Woods were bound to his will.

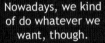

Nowadays, we kind of do whatever we want, though.

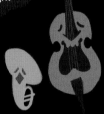

Count Legato was eventually bested by Gherkin, the first legendary hero, on his way to challenge Noise and Mutemaster. At the moment of his defeat, Legato sealed his power into the contact lens we saw in Chapter 2.

Keeping that contact lens hidden away for all eternity is definitely the most responsible thing to do, here.

...But if it could turn little Panpipe into "Prince Crescendo," you have to wonder what it might do to other characters...

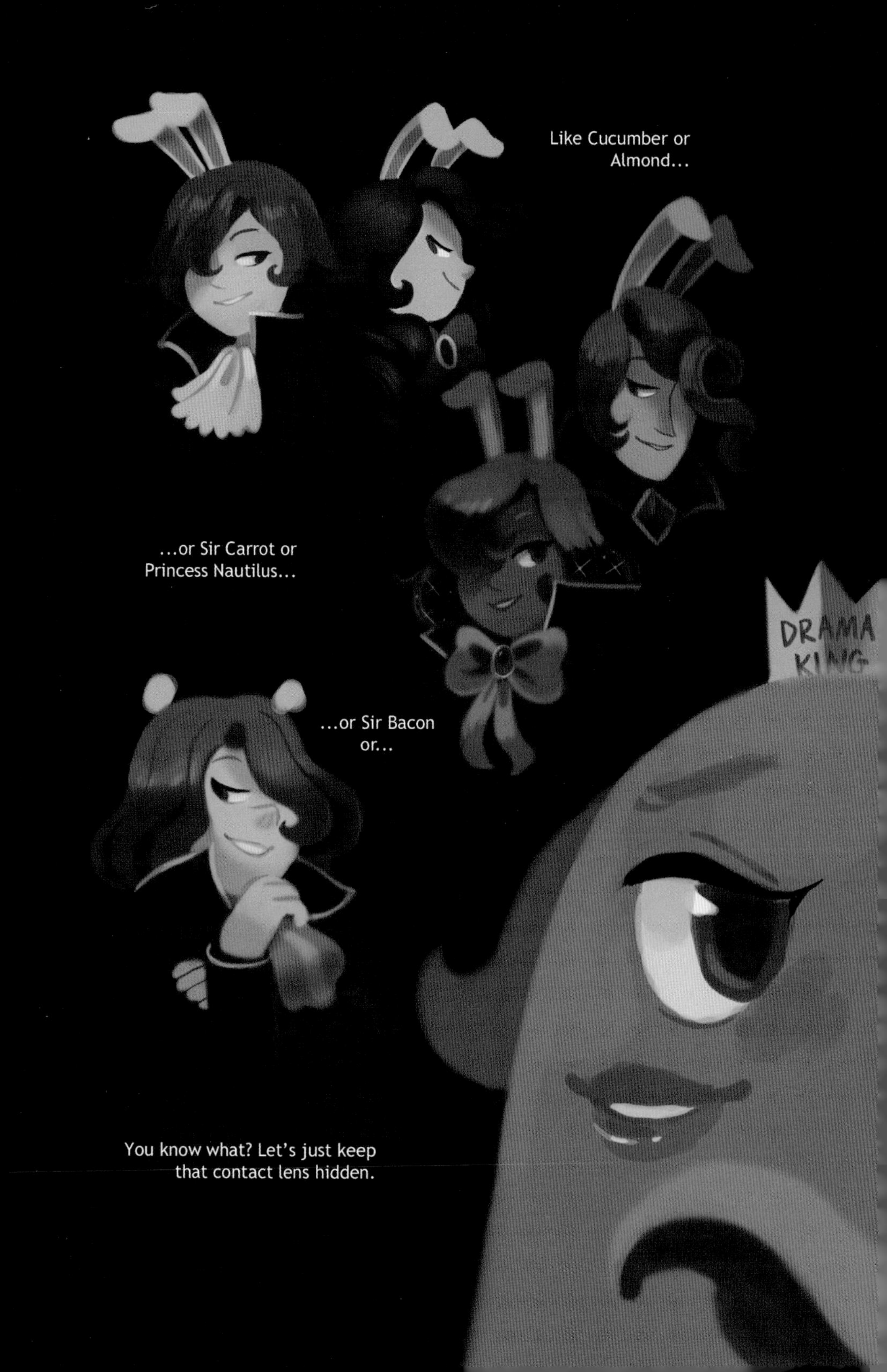

Like Cucumber or Almond...
...or Sir Carrot or Princess Nautilus...
...or Sir Bacon or...
DRAMA KING
You know what? Let's just keep that contact lens hidden.

Princess Piano

Atk ★
Def ★
Sp ★ ★

🎵 "piano" pendant
🎁 farr gifts
✉ red envelope

The Melody Kingdom princess is said to have Dreamside's loveliest voice...when she's not screaming her head off. For some reason, her mind seems to be elsewhere these days. What could be troubling her?

Commander Caboodle

Atk ★ ★ ★ ★
Def ★ ★ ★ ★
Sp ★

🎖 justice navi
⛑ justice helmet
🔑 justice ship key

This space-traveling oddball has made it his mission to defend the defenseless in the name of **JUSTICE!!** Despite his over-the-top, uh...**everything**, he seems like a good guy. But who could he be looking for?

Noisemaster

Atk ★★★★ 🎲 vinyl
Def ★★ 😃 cool phones
Sp ★★★★ 🎻 dysone coffee

Ya boy's in the house! Who's ready to make some **NOISE**?! Don't be fooled by his showmanship — this Master's quick, cunning, and serious when it really matters. How did such a little guy build that huge Noise Blaster, anyway?

Mutemaster

Atk ★★★ light reading
Def ★★★★ gentle earmuffs
Sp ★★★★★+ china collection

The third Disaster Master was created at the same time as Noisemaster, with whom he shares an unbreakable bond. He's usually calm, but once he gets mad, watch out! His Mute Zone power is fearsome, and he's physically tough, too. He'd be unstoppable, if not for...

Concept Art

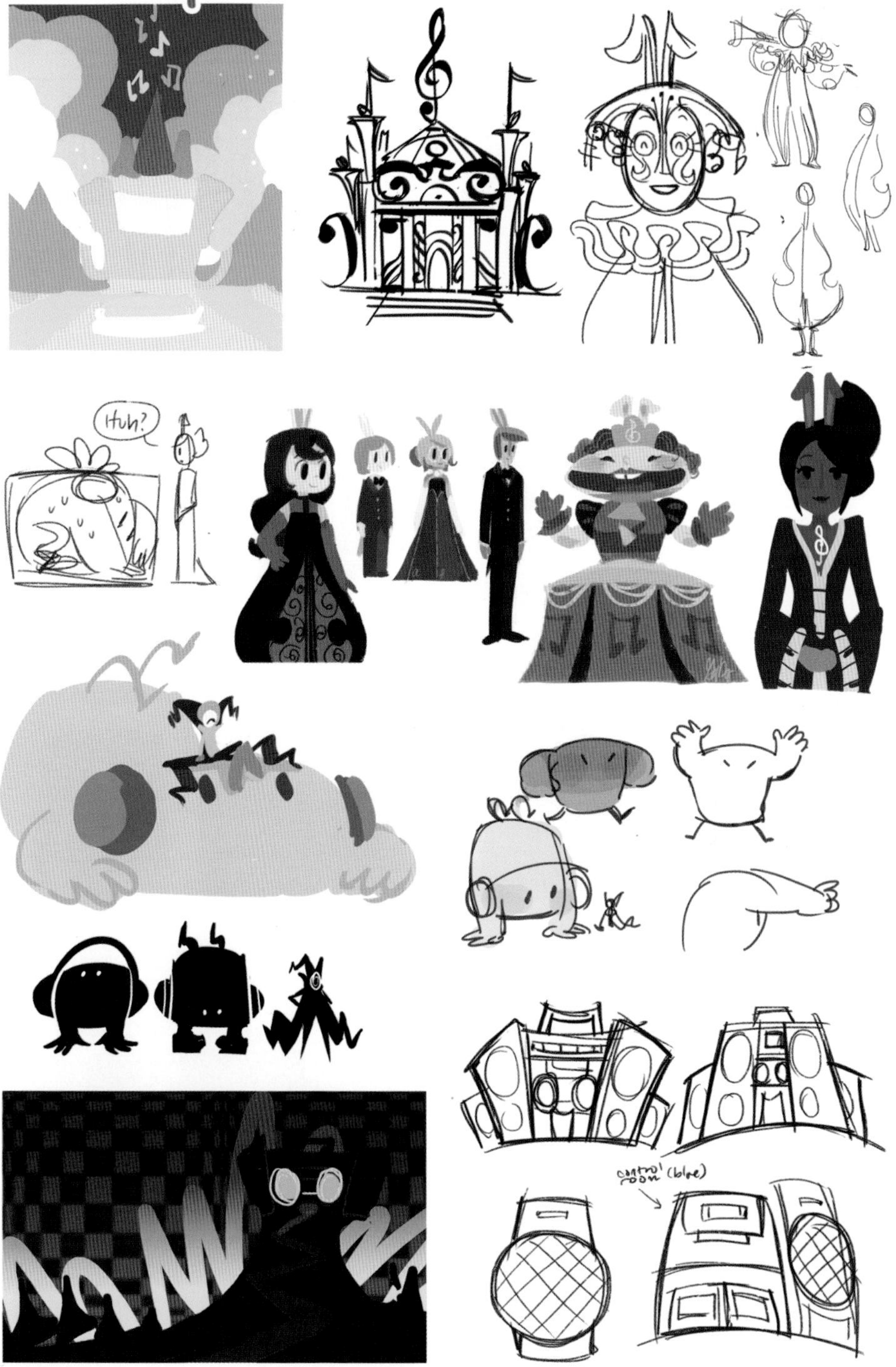

Huh?
control room (blue)

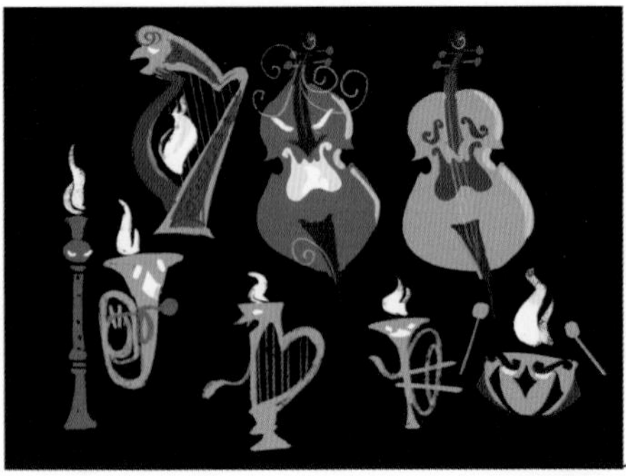

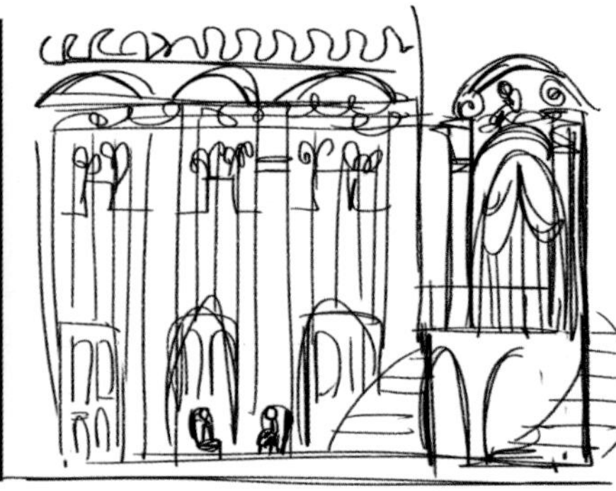

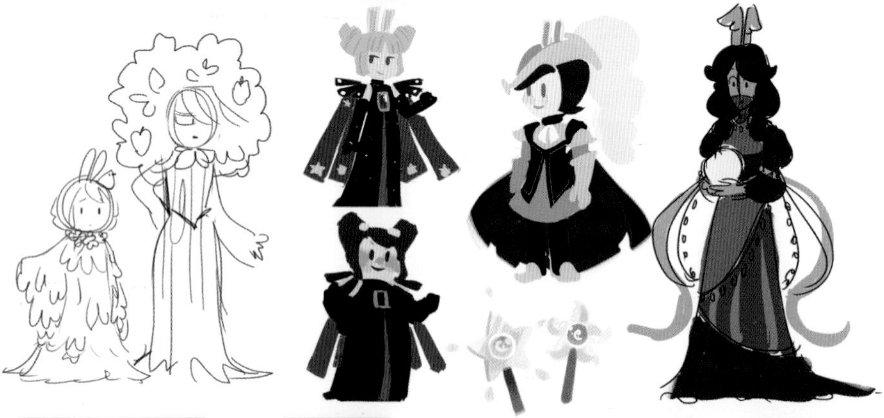

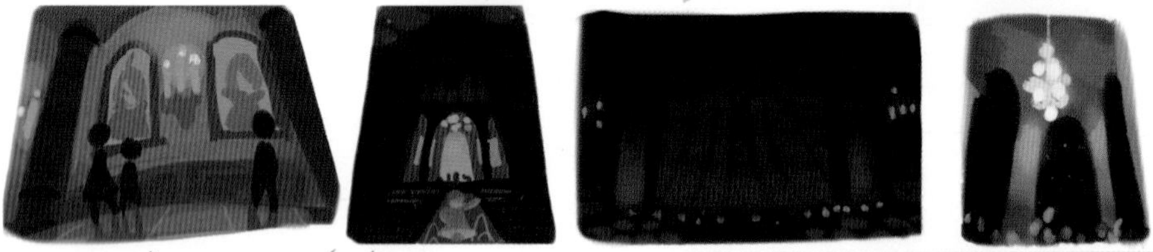

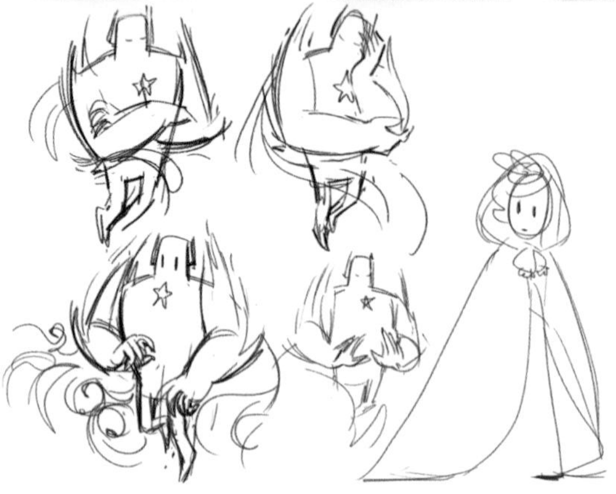

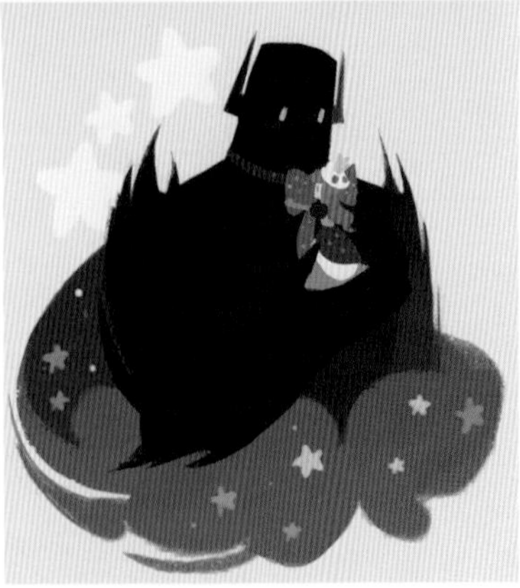

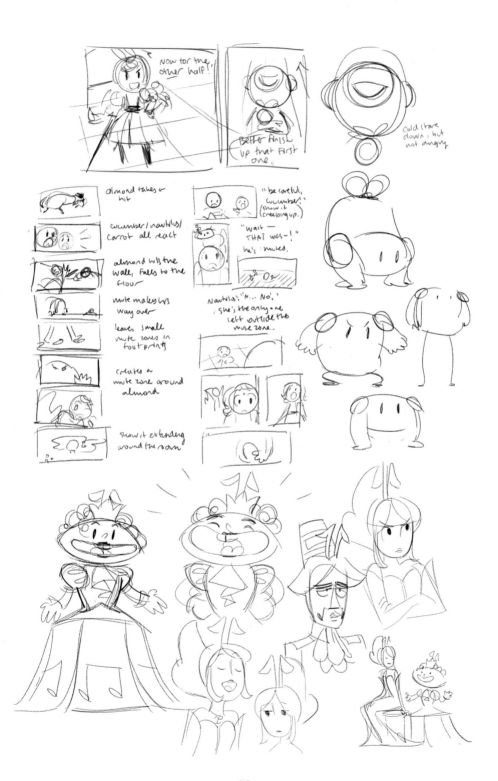

Now for the other half!

Better finish up that first one.

Cold stare down, but not angry

almond takes a hit

cucumber/nautilus/carrot all react

almond hits the wall, falls to the floor

mute makes its way over

leaves small mute zones in footprints

creates a mute zone around almond

show it extending around the room

"be careful, cucumber!" (mute is creeping up.)

"wait — THAT was—!" he's muted.

Nautilus: "n... No," she's the only one left outside the mute zone.

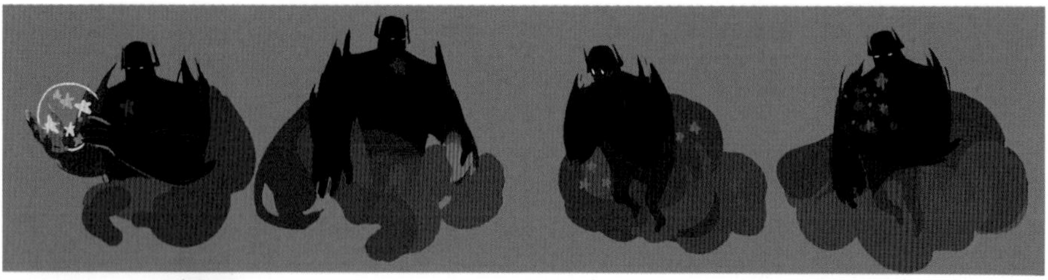

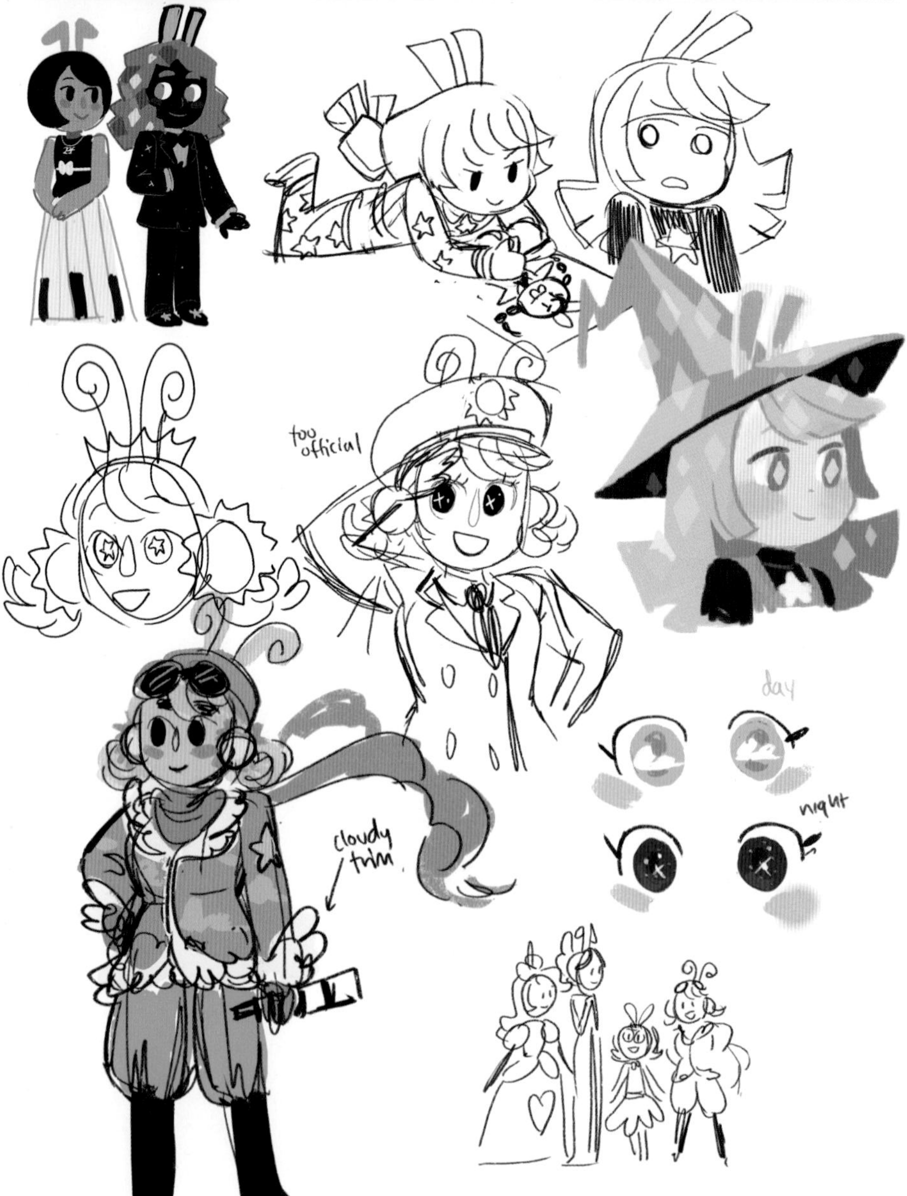
too official
day
night
cloudy trim

Bonus Story 1: Bland Salad

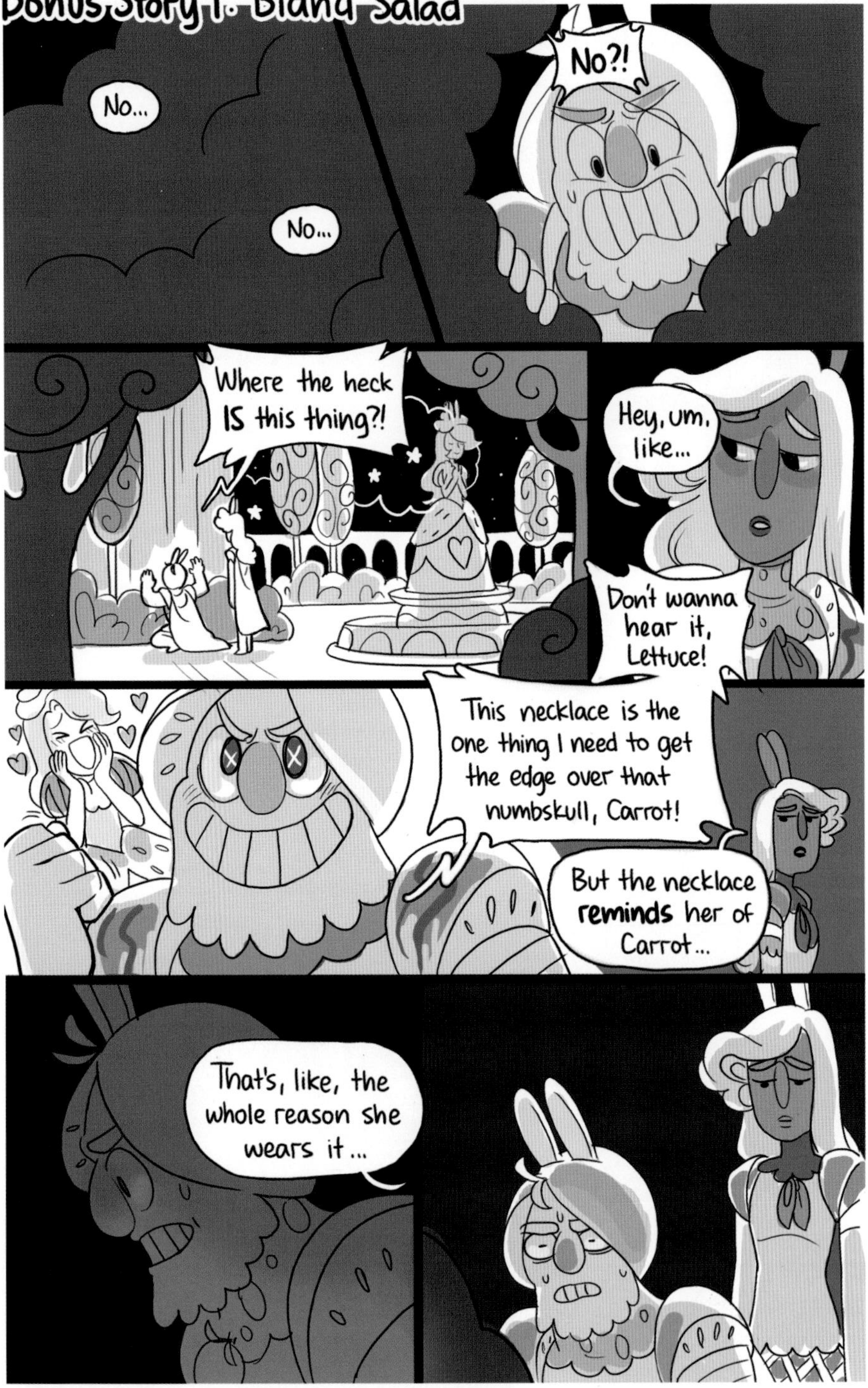

No...
No...
No?!
Where the heck IS this thing?!
Hey, um, like...
Don't wanna hear it, Lettuce!
This necklace is the one thing I need to get the edge over that numbskull, Carrot!
But the necklace reminds her of Carrot...
That's, like, the whole reason she wears it...

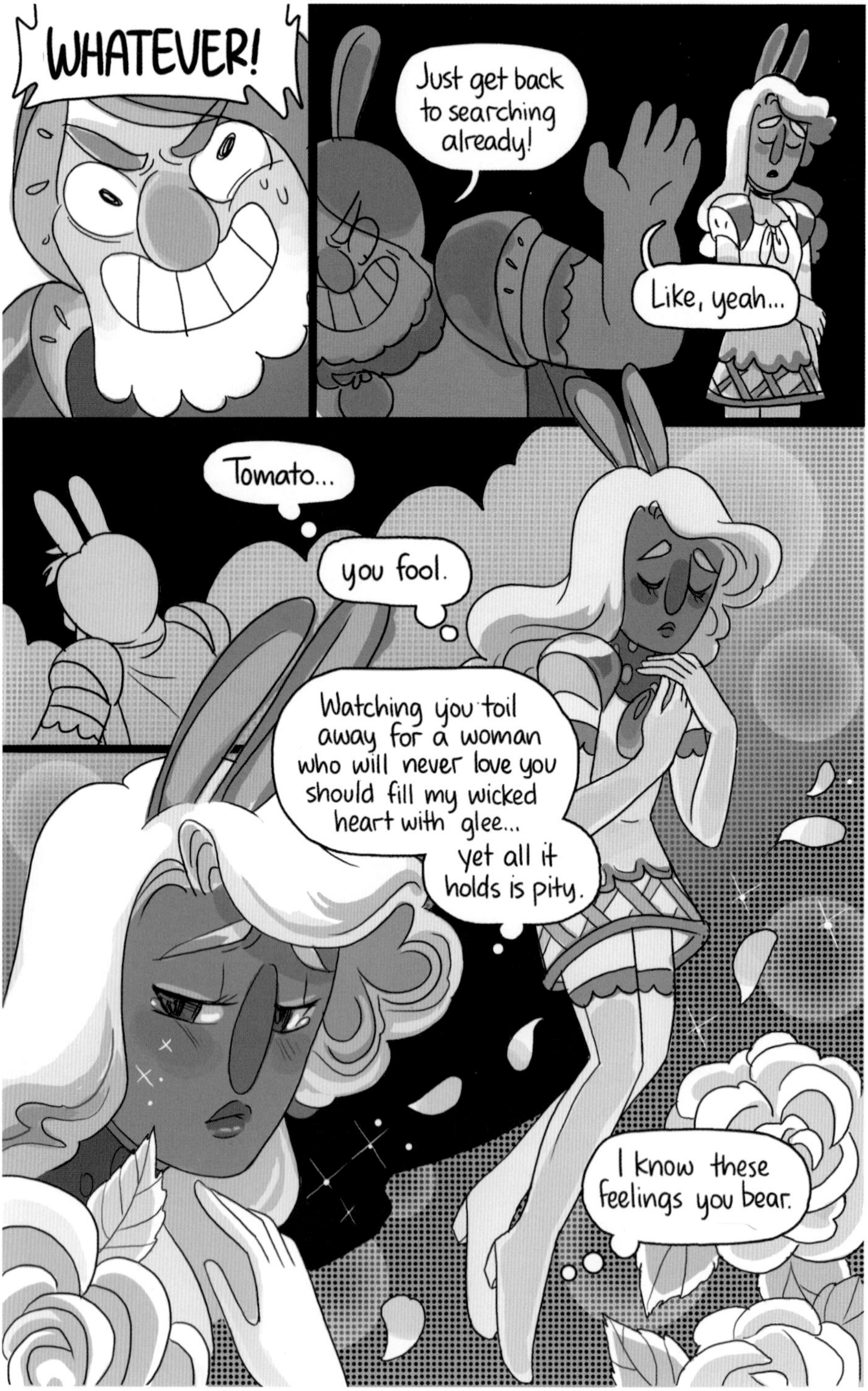
WHATEVER!
Just get back to searching already!
Like, yeah...
Tomato...
you fool.
Watching you toil away for a woman who will never love you should fill my wicked heart with glee...
yet all it holds is pity.
I know these feelings you bear.

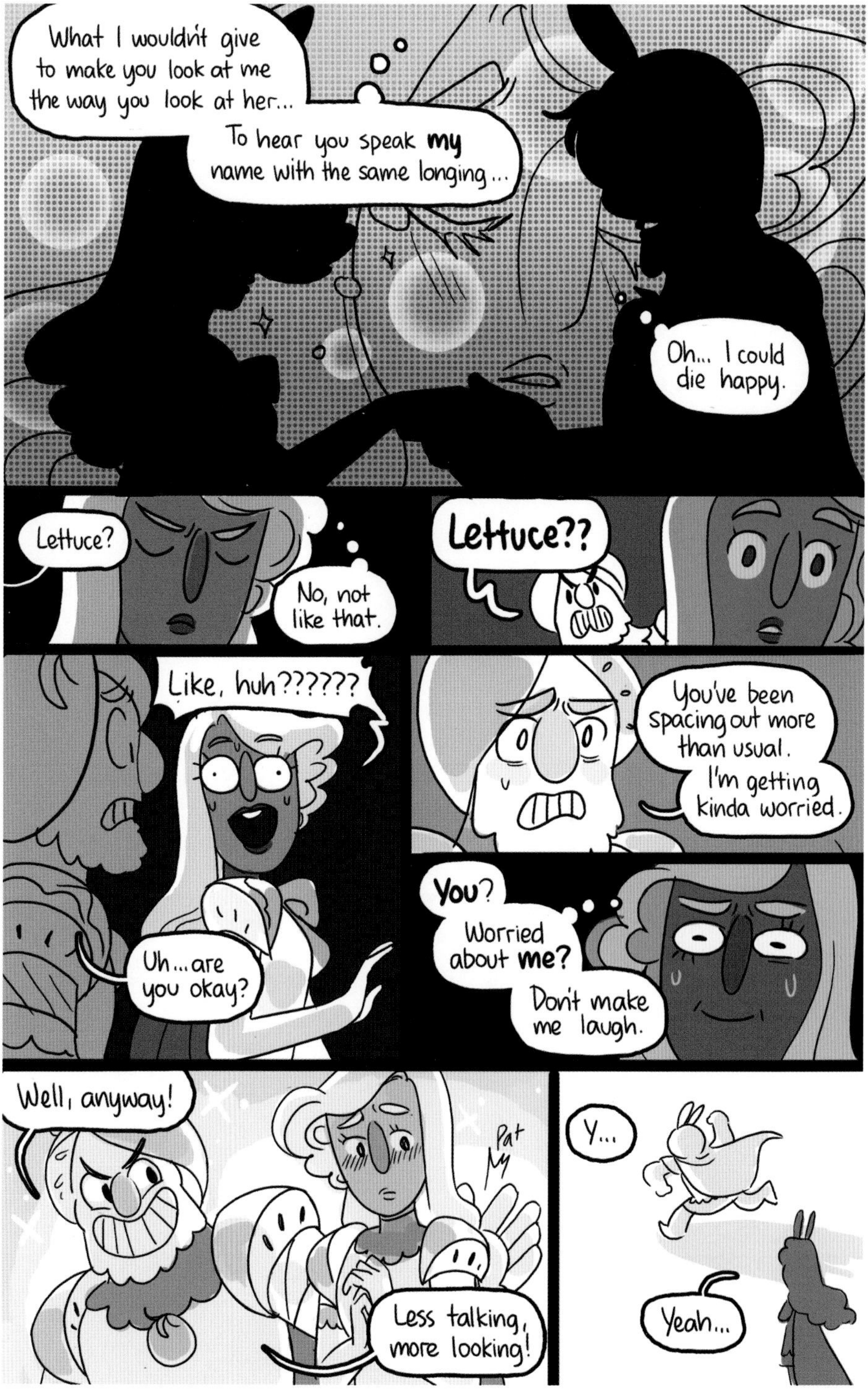

What I wouldn't give to make you look at me the way you look at her...
To hear you speak **my** name with the same longing...
Oh... I could die happy.
Lettuce?
No, not like that.
Lettuce??
Like, huh??????
Uh...are you okay?
You've been spacing out more than usual.
I'm getting kinda worried.
You?
Worried about **me**?
Don't make me laugh.
Well, anyway!
Pat
Less talking, more looking!
Y...
Yeah...

Bonus Story 2: The Sweetest Rivalry

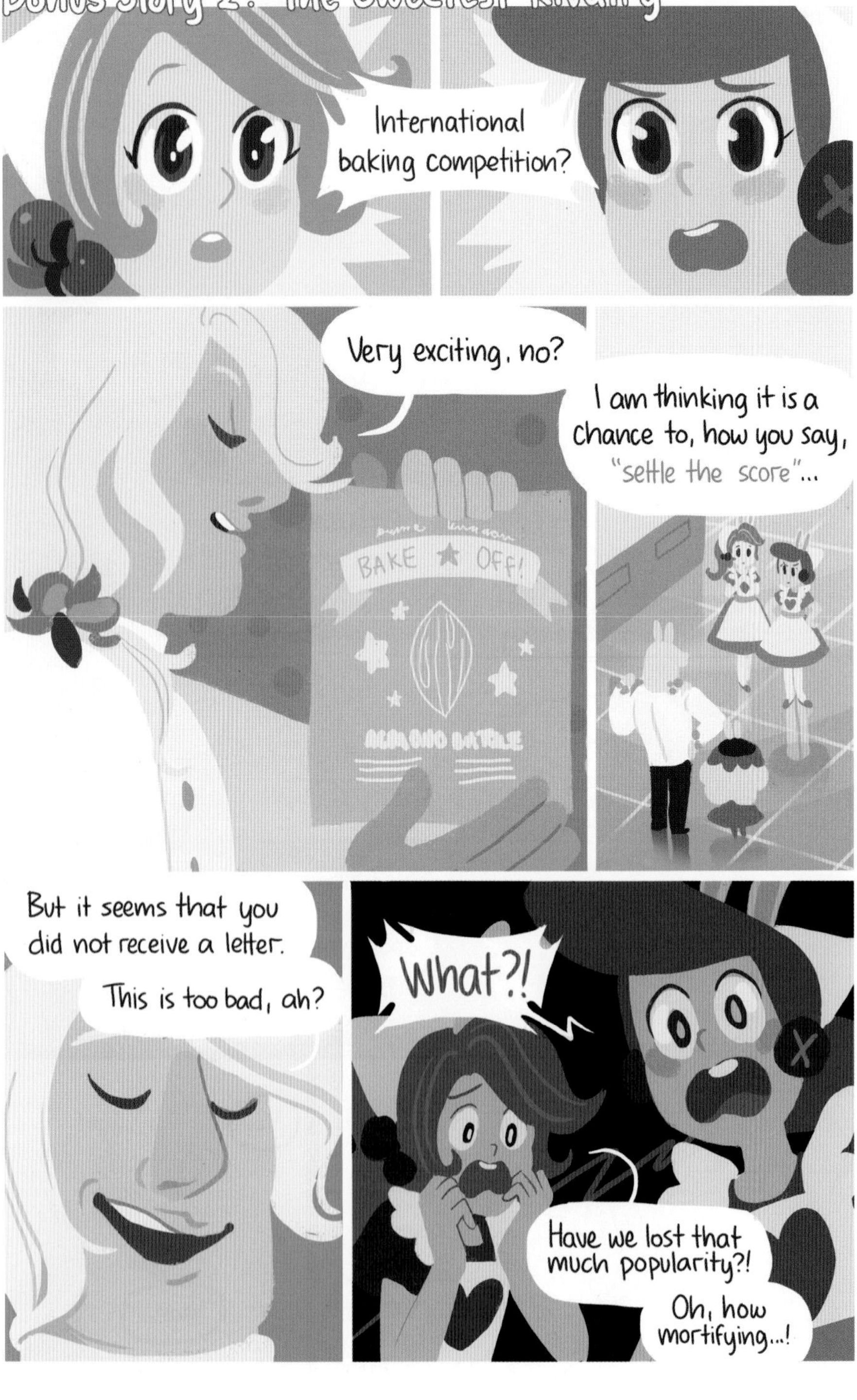
International baking competition?
Very exciting, no?
I am thinking it is a chance to, how you say, "settle the score"...
BAKE ★ OFF!
But it seems that you did not receive a letter.
This is too bad, ah?
What?!
Have we lost that much popularity?!
Oh, how mortifying...!

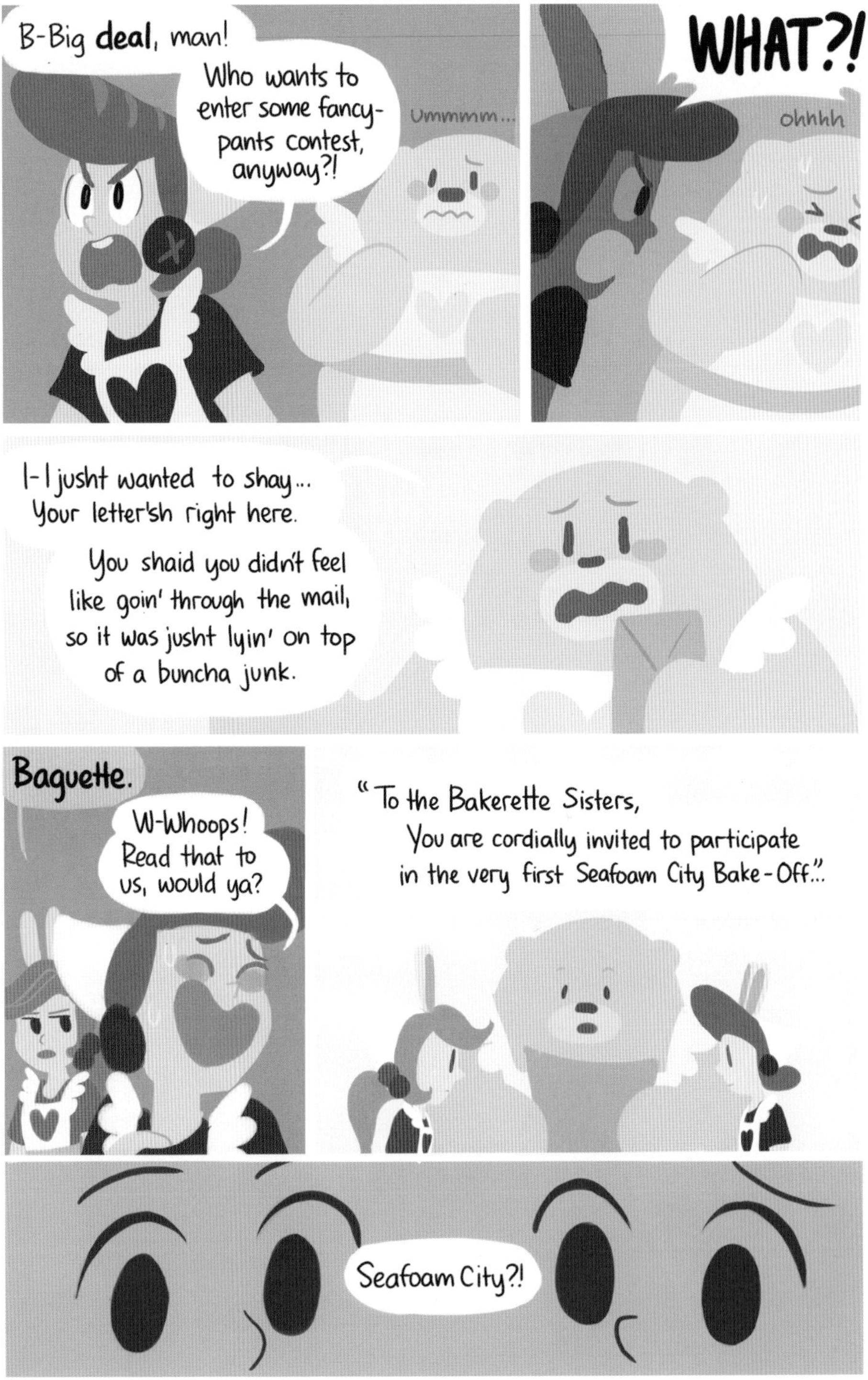
B-Big deal, man!
Who wants to enter some fancy-pants contest, anyway?!
Ummmm...
WHAT?!
ohhhh
I-I jusht wanted to shay... Your letter'sh right here.
You shaid you didn't feel like goin' through the mail, so it was jusht lyin' on top of a buncha junk.
Baguette.
W-Whoops! Read that to us, would ya?
"To the Bakerette Sisters,
You are cordially invited to participate in the very first Seafoam City Bake-Off."
Seafoam City?!

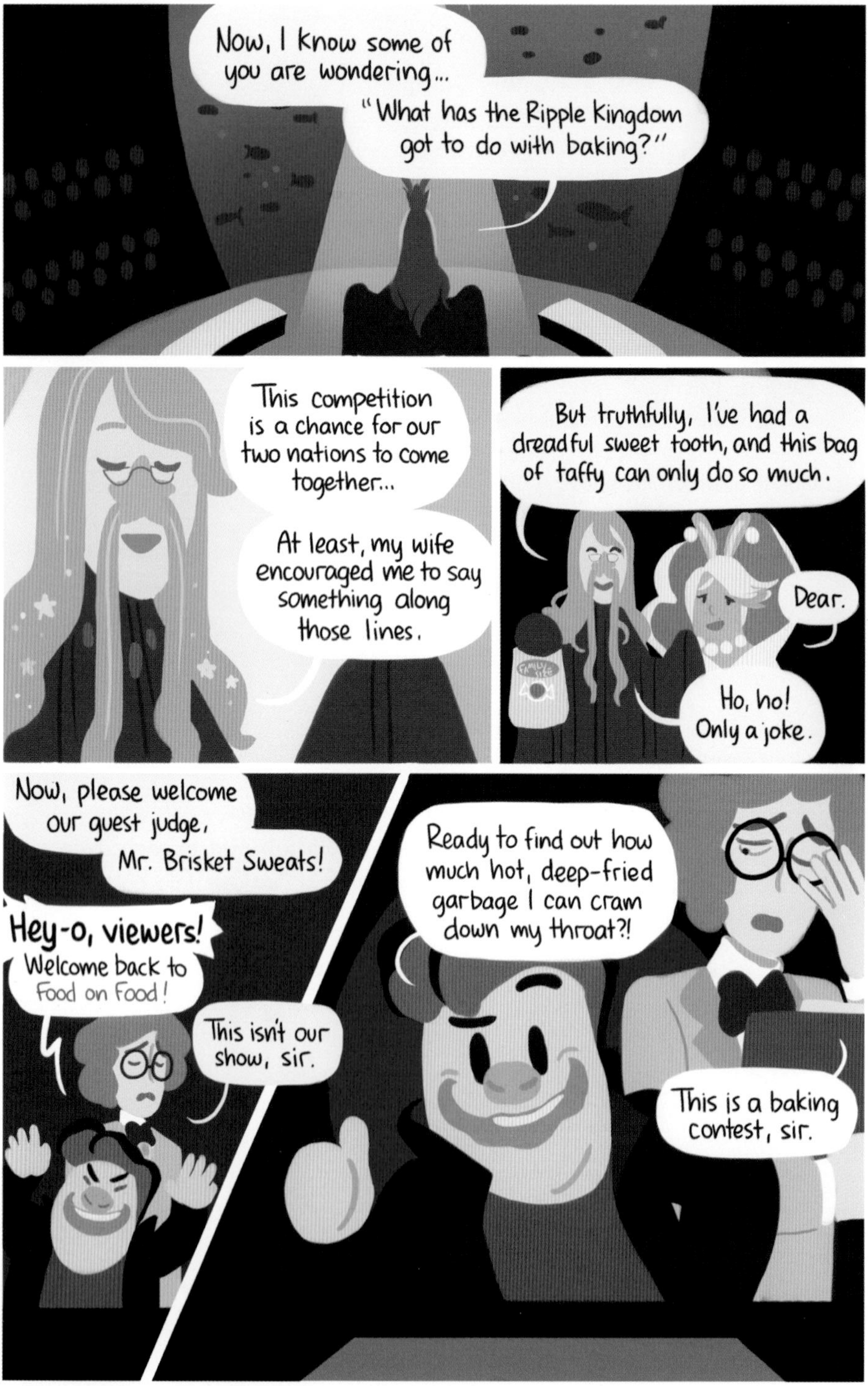
Now, I know some of you are wondering...
"What has the Ripple Kingdom got to do with baking?"
This competition is a chance for our two nations to come together...
At least, my wife encouraged me to say something along those lines.
But truthfully, I've had a dreadful sweet tooth, and this bag of taffy can only do so much.
Dear.
Ho, ho! Only a joke.
Now, please welcome our guest judge, Mr. Brisket Sweats!
Hey-o, viewers! Welcome back to Food on Food!
This isn't our show, sir.
Ready to find out how much hot, deep-fried garbage I can cram down my throat?!
This is a baking contest, sir.

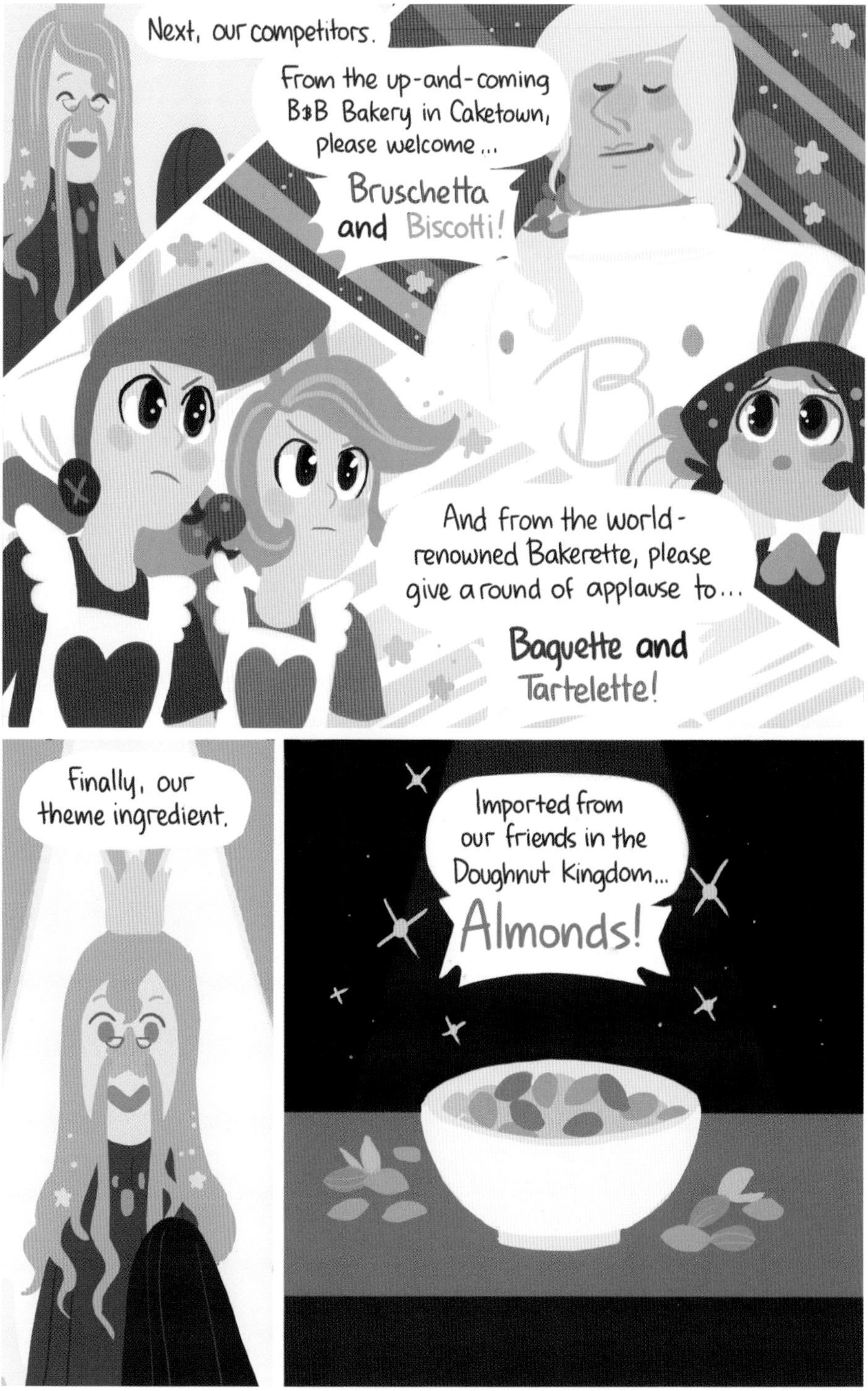
Next, our competitors.
From the up-and-coming B$B Bakery in Caketown, please welcome...
Bruschetta and Biscotti!
And from the world-renowned Bakerette, please give a round of applause to...
Baguette and Tartelette!
Finally, our theme ingredient.
Imported from our friends in the Doughnut Kingdom...
Almonds!

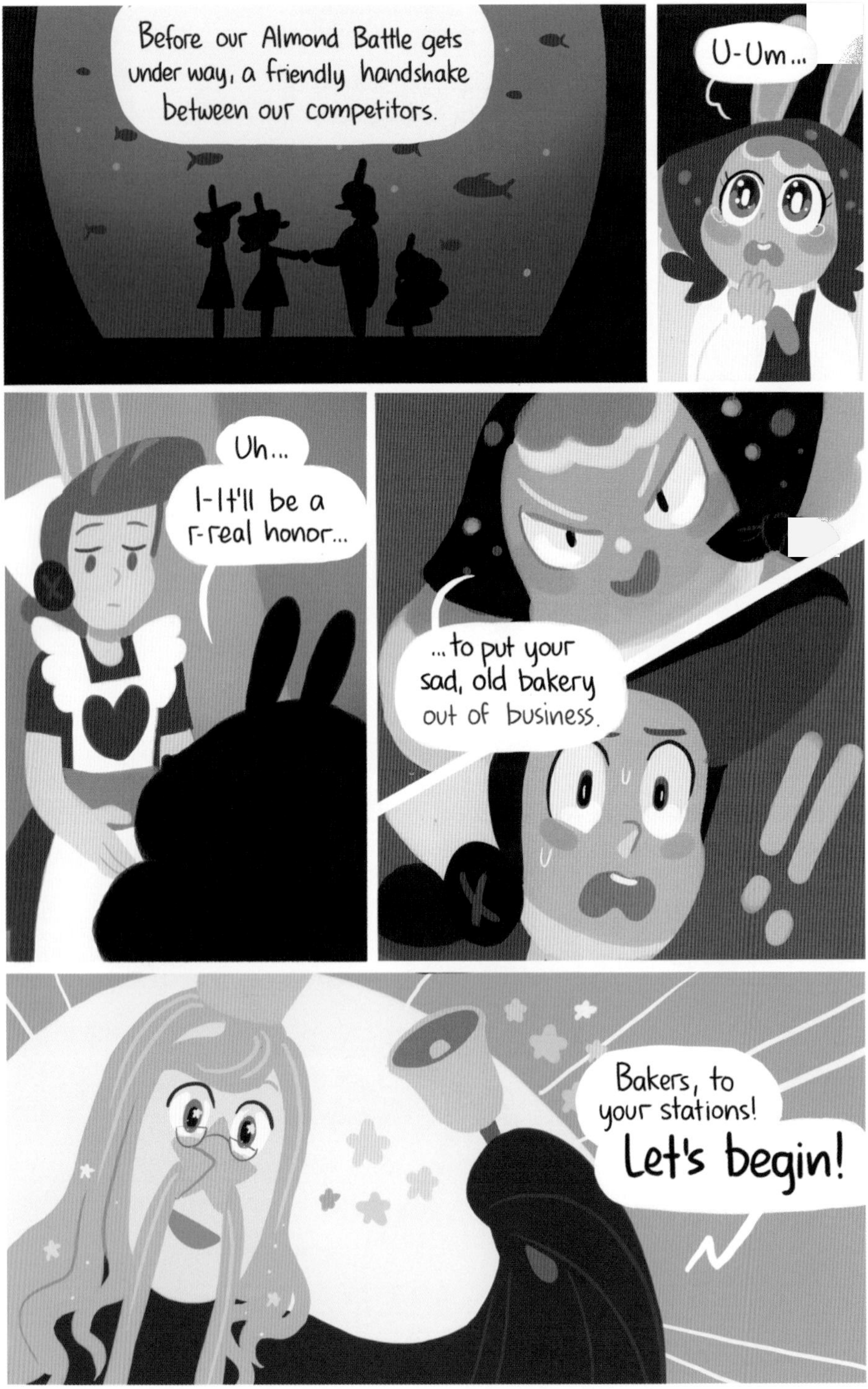
Before our Almond Battle gets under way, a friendly handshake between our competitors.
U-Um...
Uh...
I-It'll be a r-real honor...
...to put your sad, old bakery out of business.
Bakers, to your stations!
Let's begin!

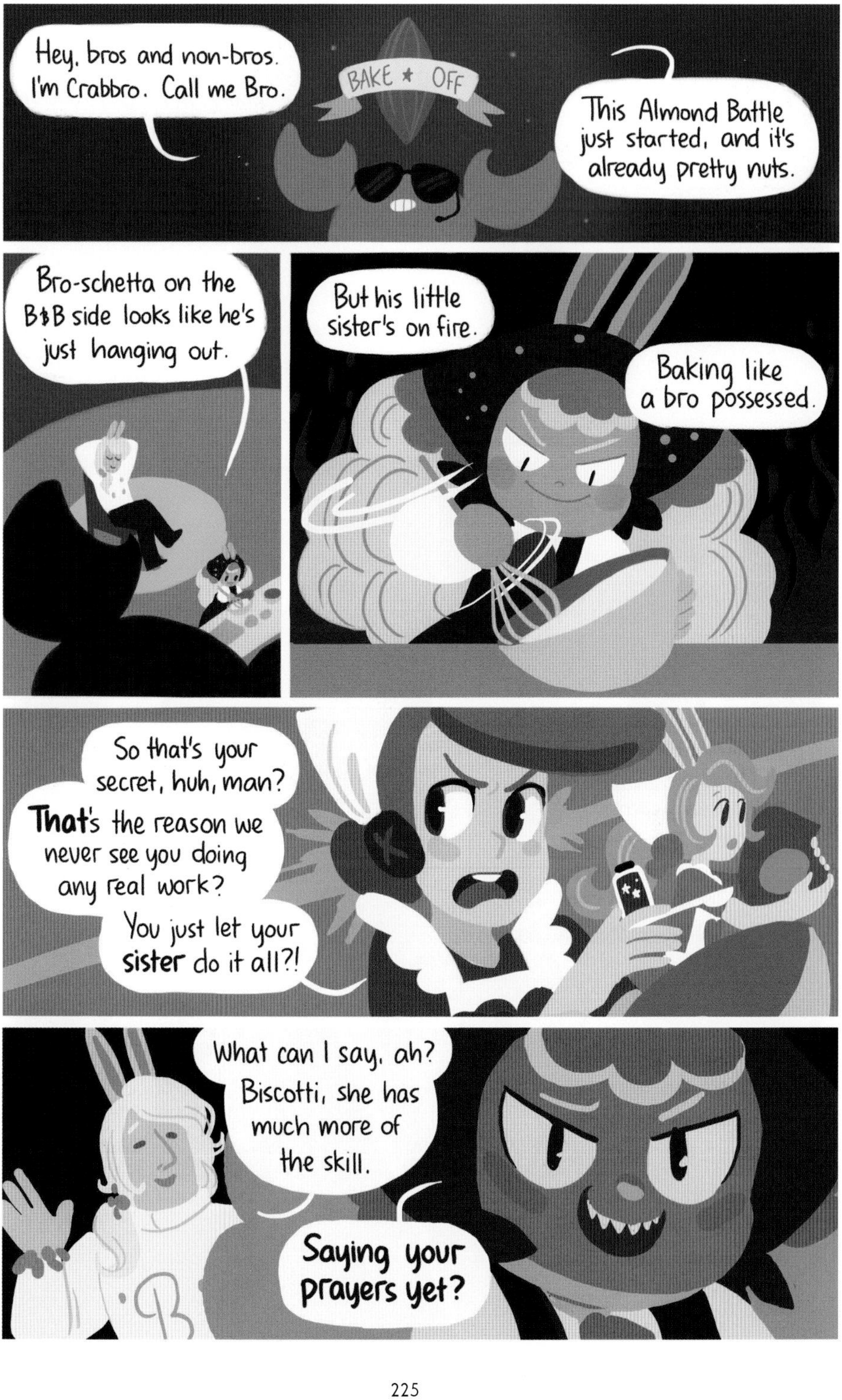
Hey, bros and non-bros. I'm Crabbro. Call me Bro.
BAKE ★ OFF
This Almond Battle just started, and it's already pretty nuts.
Bro-schetta on the B&B side looks like he's just hanging out.
But his little sister's on fire.
Baking like a bro possessed.
So that's your secret, huh, man?
That's the reason we never see you doing any real work?
You just let your **sister** do it all?!
What can I say, ah? Biscotti, she has much more of the skill.
Saying your prayers yet?

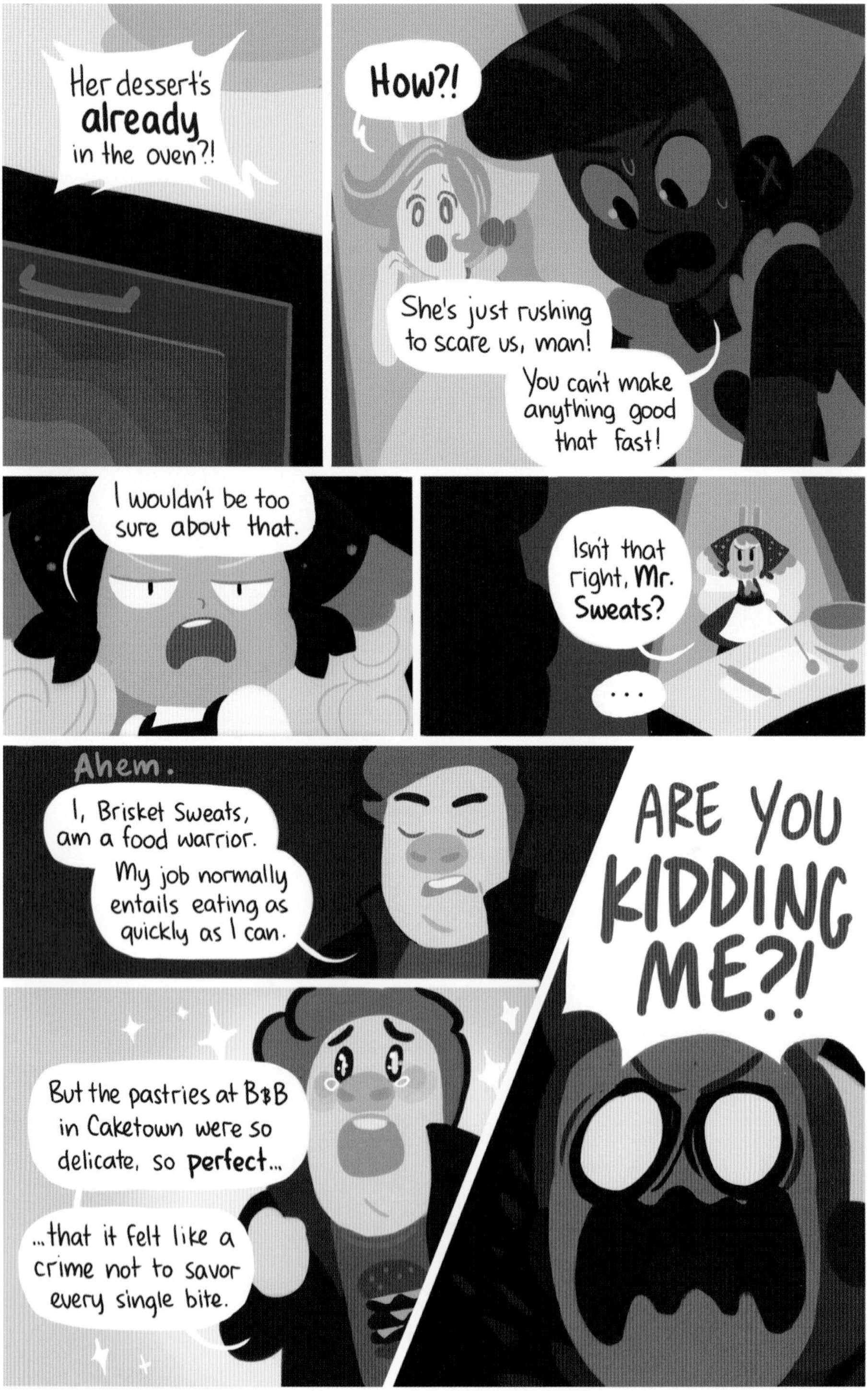
Her dessert's **already** in the oven?!
How?!
She's just rushing to scare us, man!
You can't make anything good that fast!
I wouldn't be too sure about that.
Isn't that right, Mr. Sweats?
...
Ahem.
I, Brisket Sweats, am a food warrior.
My job normally entails eating as quickly as I can.
But the pastries at B&B in Caketown were so delicate, so **perfect**...
...that it felt like a crime not to savor every single bite.
ARE YOU KIDDING ME?!

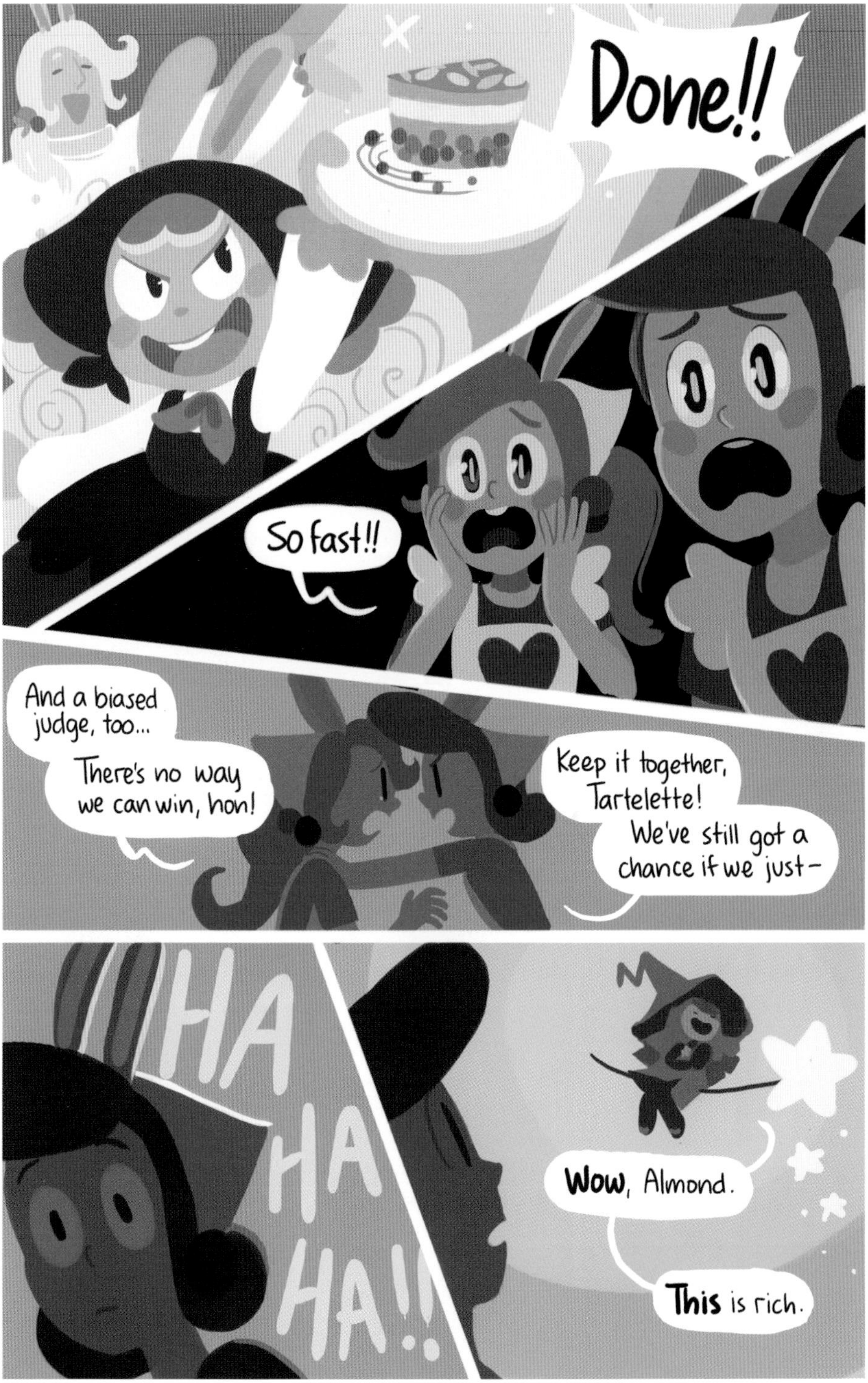
Done!!
So fast!!
And a biased judge, too...
There's no way we can win, hon!
Keep it together, Tartelette!
We've still got a chance if we just-
HA HA HA!!
Wow, Almond.
This is rich.

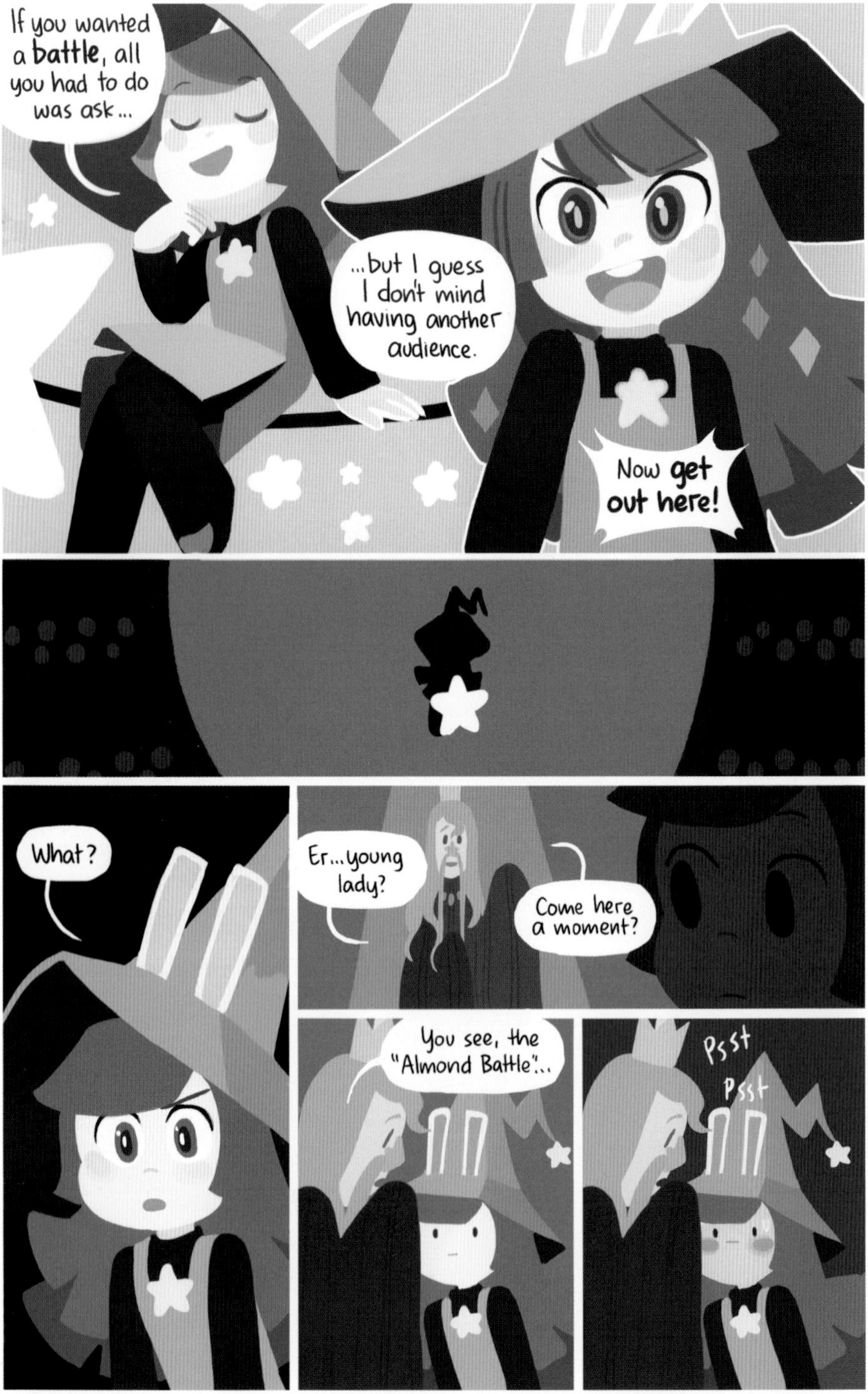
If you wanted a **battle**, all you had to do was ask...
...but I guess I don't mind having another audience.
Now **get out here!**
What?
Er...young lady?
Come here a moment?
You see, the "Almond Battle"...
Psst
Psst

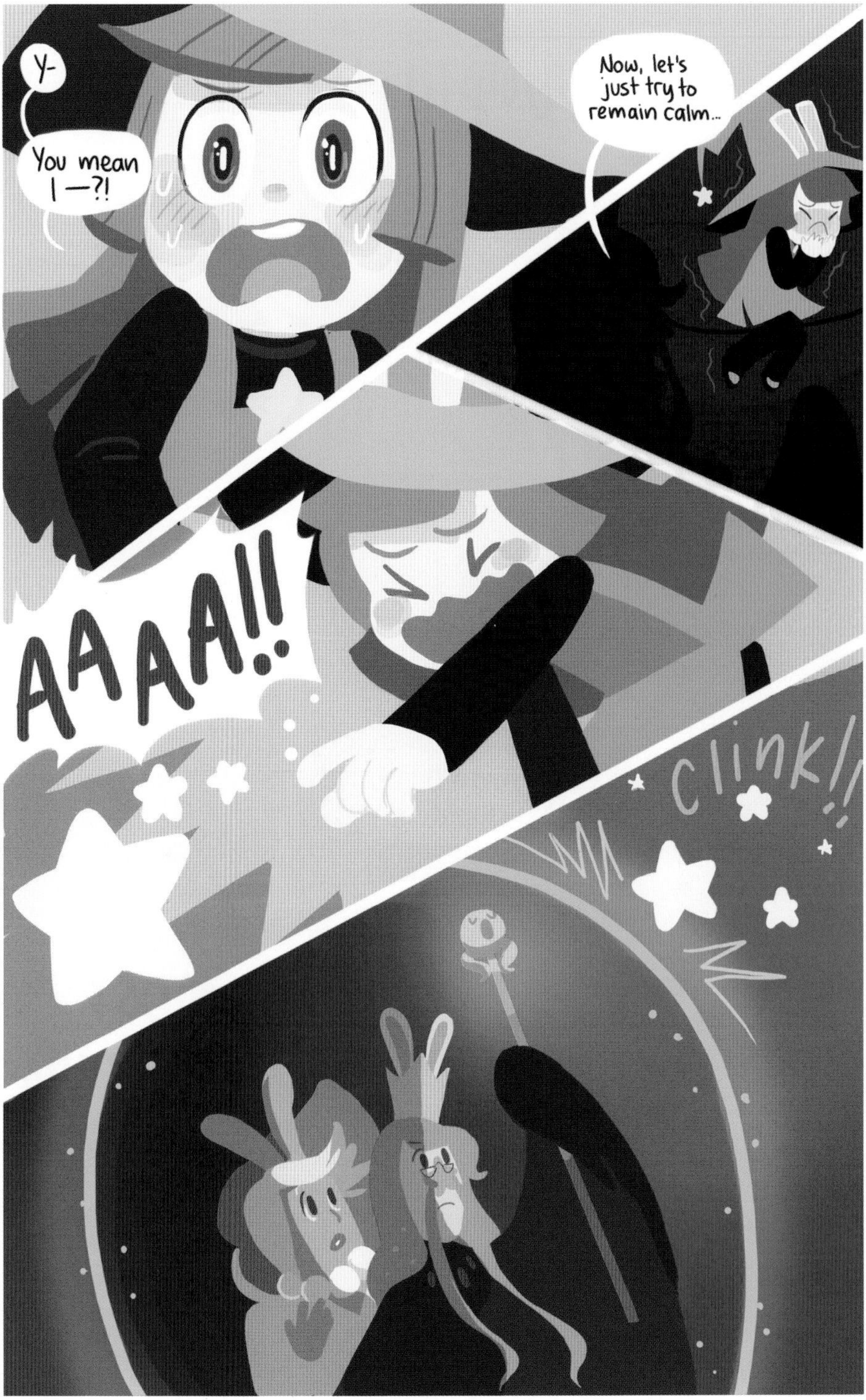
Y-
You mean I—?!
Now, let's just try to remain calm...
AAAA!!
clink!!

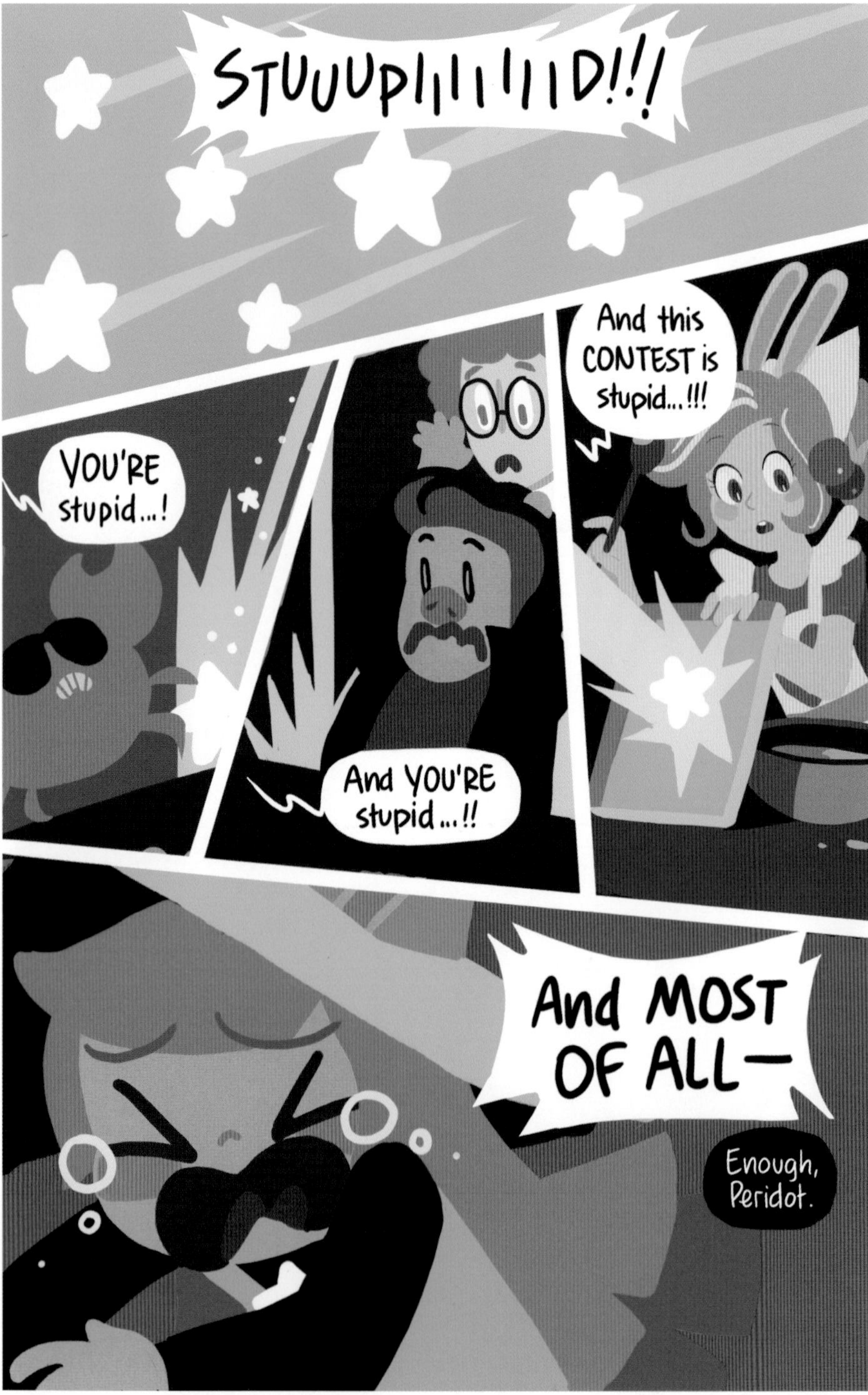
STUUUPIIIIIIIIID!!!
YOU'RE stupid...!
And YOU'RE stupid...!!
And this CONTEST is stupid...!!!
And MOST OF ALL—
Enough, Peridot.

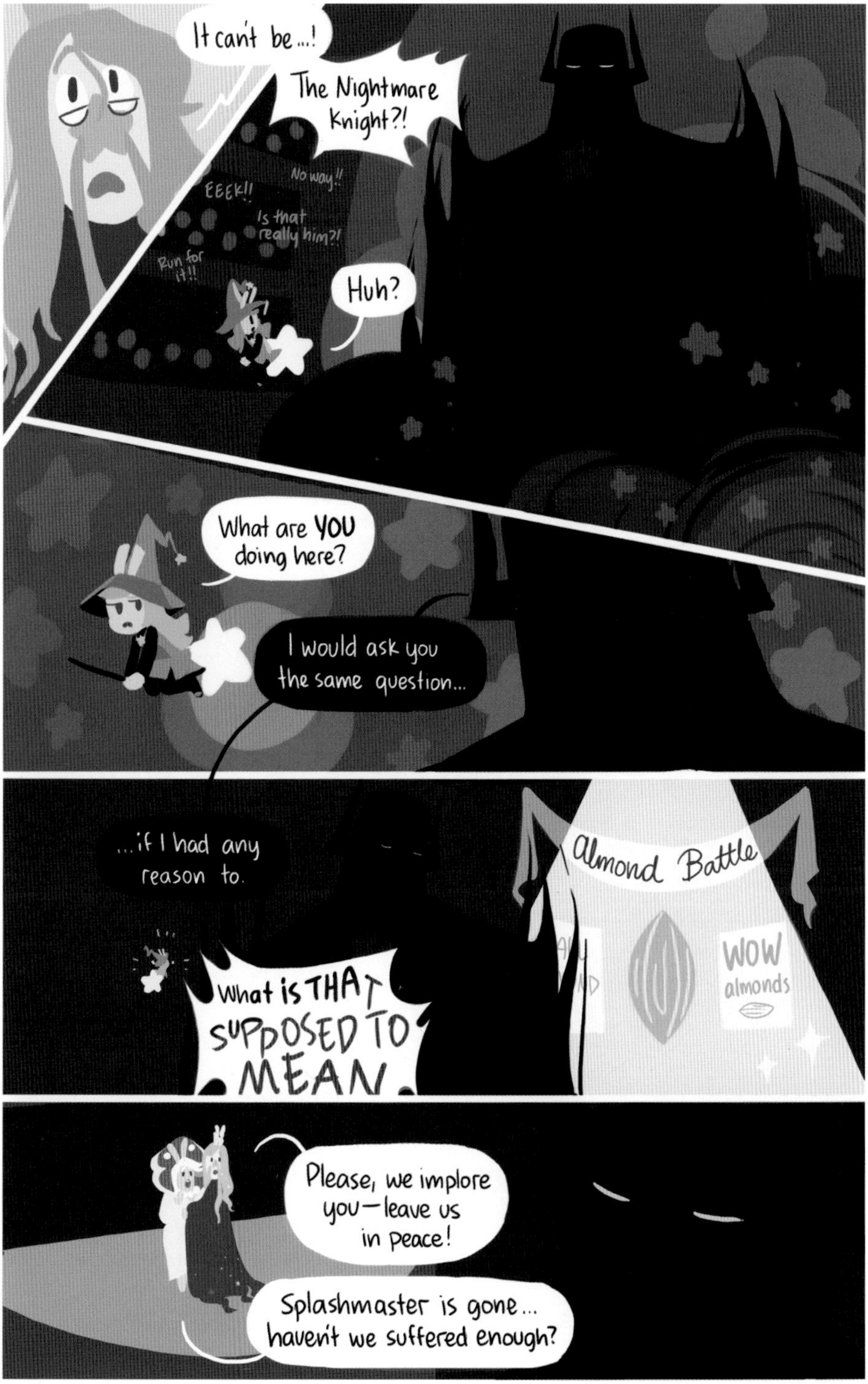
It can't be...!
The Nightmare Knight?!
EEEK!!
No way!!
Is that really him?!
Run for it!!
Huh?
What are YOU doing here?
I would ask you the same question...
...if I had any reason to.
What is THAT SUPPOSED TO MEAN
Almond Battle
WOW almonds
Please, we implore you—leave us in peace!
Splashmaster is gone... haven't we suffered enough?

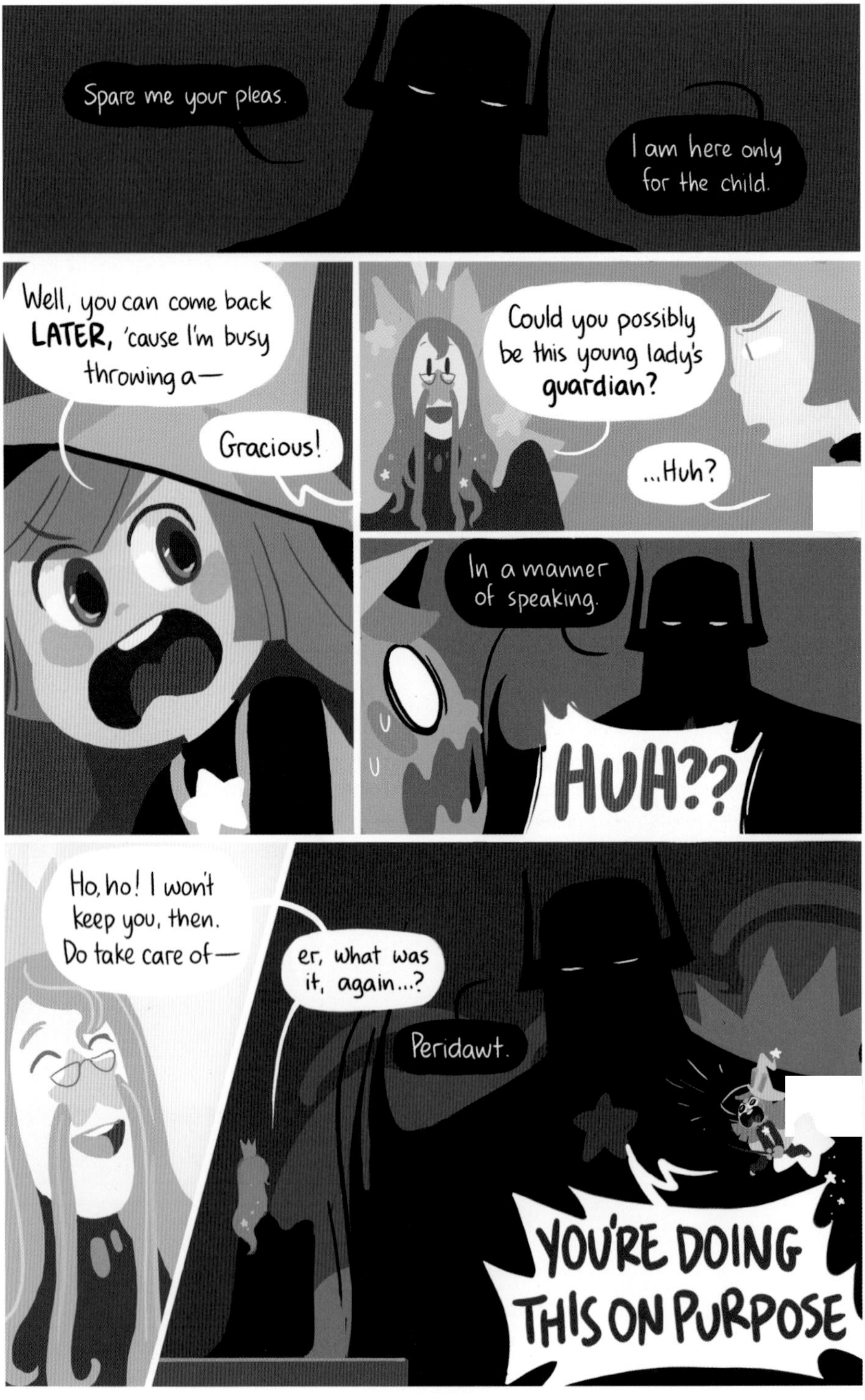
Spare me your pleas.
I am here only for the child.
Well, you can come back LATER, 'cause I'm busy throwing a—
Gracious!
Could you possibly be this young lady's guardian?
...Huh?
In a manner of speaking.
HUH??
Ho, ho! I won't keep you, then. Do take care of—
er, what was it, again...?
Peridawt.
YOU'RE DOING THIS ON PURPOSE

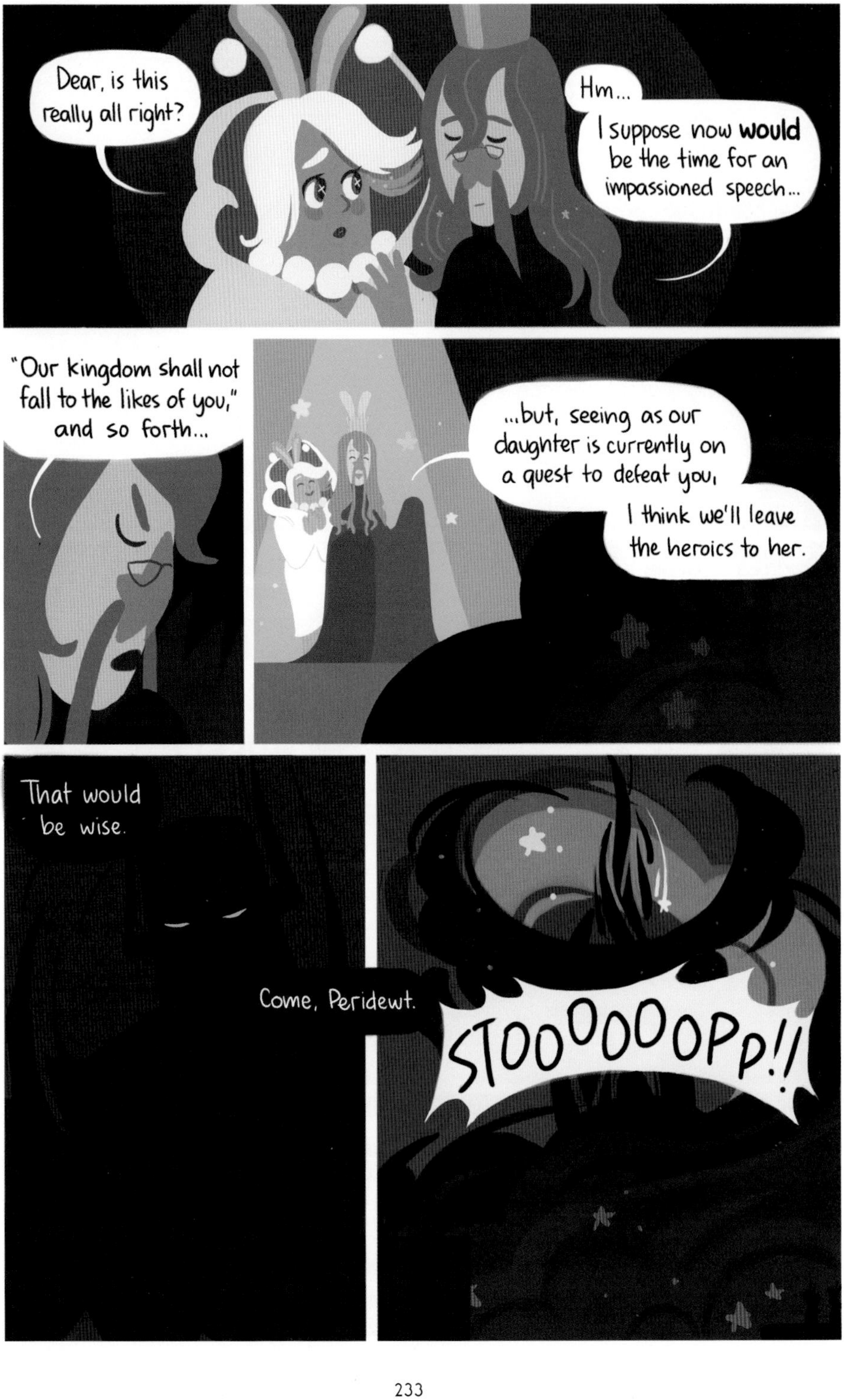
Dear, is this really all right?
Hm...
I suppose now **would** be the time for an impassioned speech...
"Our kingdom shall not fall to the likes of you," and so forth...
...but, seeing as our daughter is currently on a quest to defeat you,
I think we'll leave the heroics to her.
That would be wise.
Come, Peridewt.
STOOOOOOPP!!

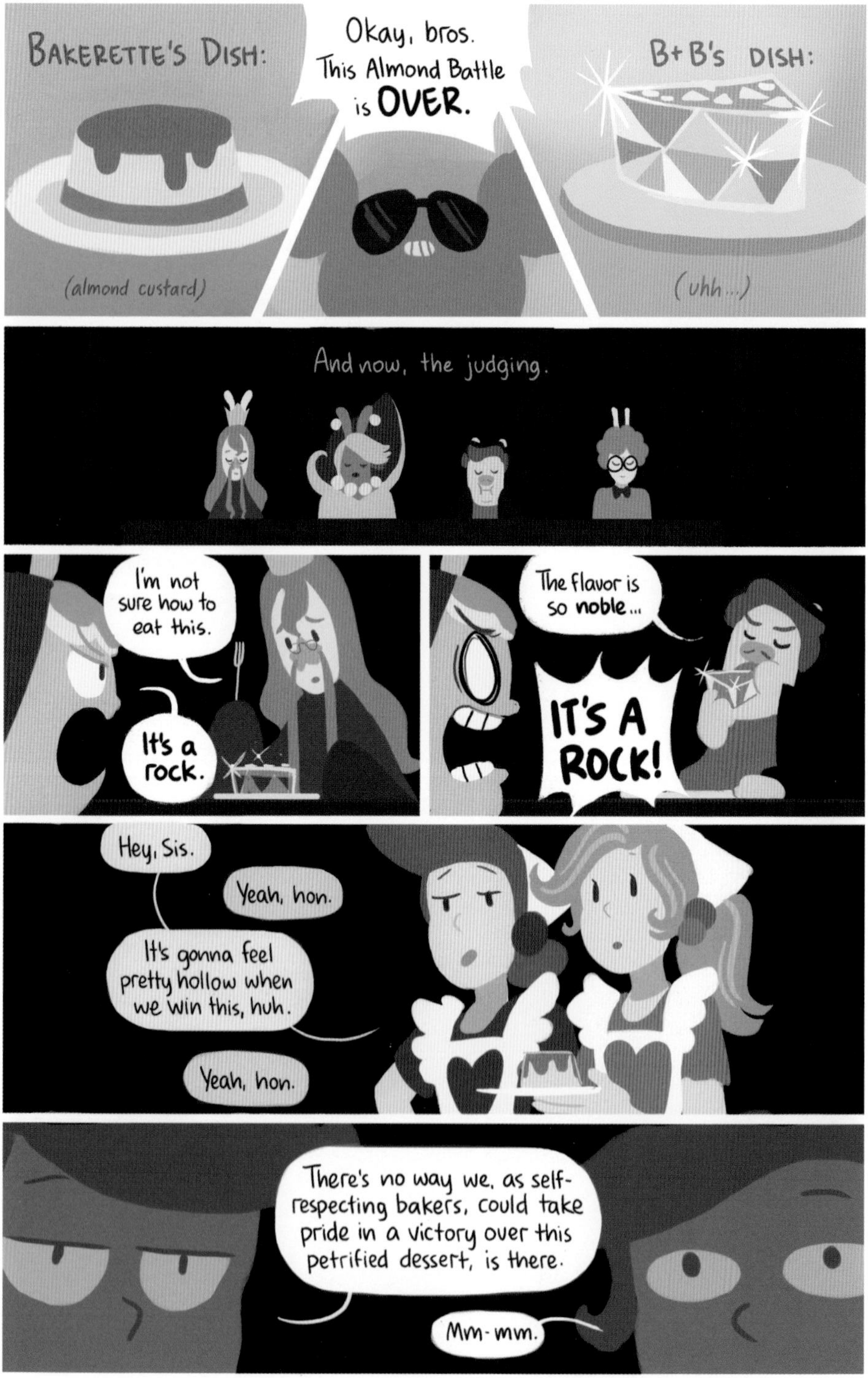
BAKERETTE'S DISH:
(almond custard)
Okay, bros. This Almond Battle is OVER.
B+B's DISH:
(uhh...)
And now, the judging.
I'm not sure how to eat this.
It's a rock.
The flavor is so noble...
IT'S A ROCK!
Hey, Sis.
Yeah, hon.
It's gonna feel pretty hollow when we win this, huh.
Yeah, hon.
There's no way we, as self-respecting bakers, could take pride in a victory over this petrified dessert, is there.
Mm-mm.

SLAM!
Yo, Grizz.
Nailed it.
#1
BEST BAKERS EVER
Wowwww!!

Thank you for reading!

The Melody Kingdom

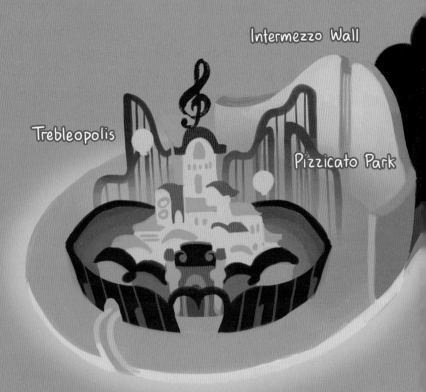

Intermezzo Wall

Trebleopolis

Pizzicato Park

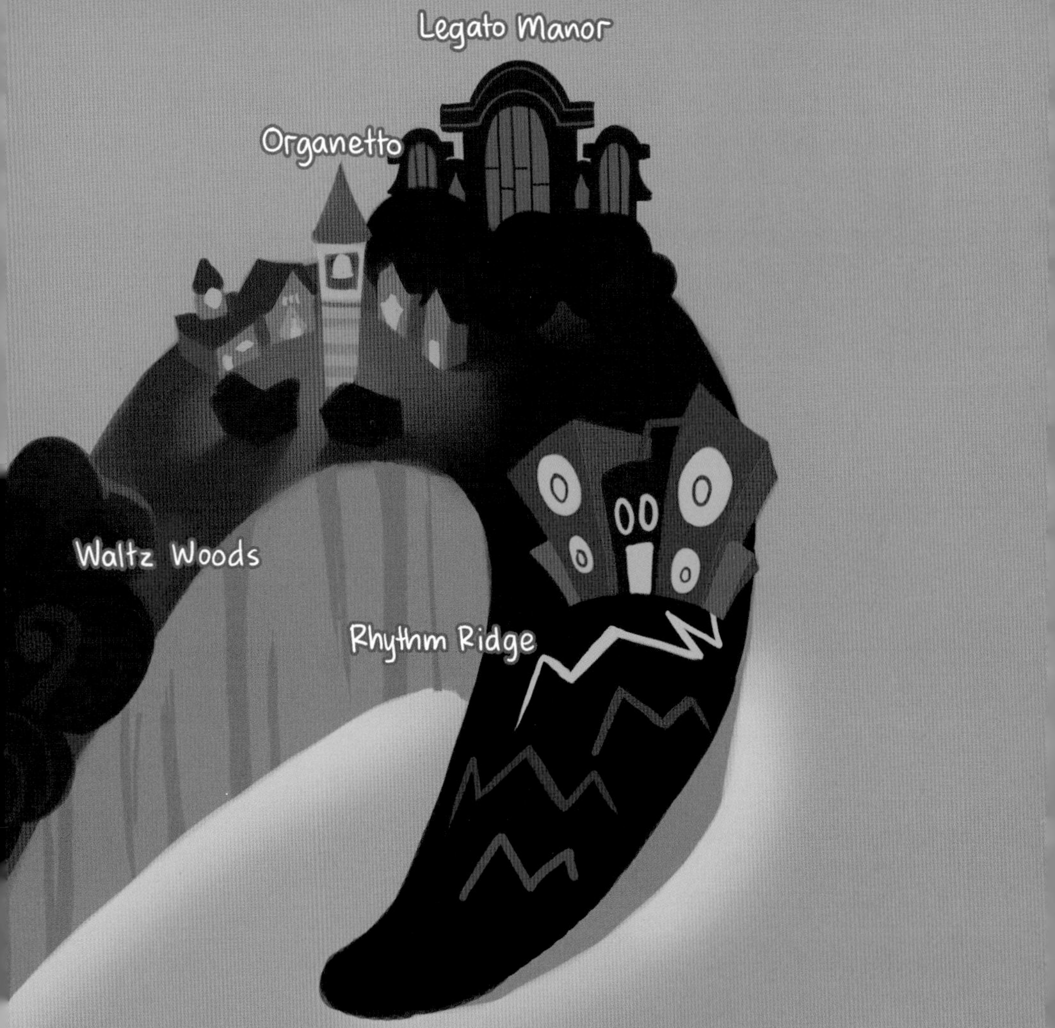
Legato Manor
Organetto
Waltz Woods
Rhythm Ridge

First Second
New York

Published by First Second
First Second is an imprint of Roaring Brook Press, a division of
Holtzbrinck Publishing Holdings Limited Partnership
120 Broadway, New York, NY 10271

Library of Congress Control Number: 2017946148

Hardcover ISBN: 978-1-250-15983-0
Paperback ISBN: 978-1-62672-834-9

Our books may be purchased in bulk for promotional, educational,
or business use. Please contact your local bookseller or the Macmillan
Corporate and Premium Sales Department at (800) 221-7945 ext. 5442
or by e-mail at MacmillanSpecialMarkets@macmillan.com.

FIRST EDITION

First edition, 2018
Book design by Rob Steen

Cucumber Quest is created entirely in Photoshop.

Printed in China by RR Donnelley Asia Printing Solutions Ltd.,
Dongguan City, Guangdong Province

Hardcover: 10 9 8 7 6 5 4 3 2
Paperback: 10 9 8 7 6 5 4 3

BY ART WE LIVE